Alfred Hitchcock Presents

MY FAVOURITES IN
SUSPENSE

PART ONE

Also Available in PAN Books

ALFRED HITCHCOCK PRESENTS:

STORIES THEY WOULDN'T LET ME DO
ON TV

Alfred Hitchcock
Presents

MY FAVOURITES
IN SUSPENSE

PAN BOOKS LTD : LONDON

First published in this form 1960 by Max Reinhardt
This edition (first part only) published 1963 by
Pan Books Ltd.,
8 Headfort Place, London, S.W.1

*Printed in Great Britain by Richard Clay and Company, Ltd.,
Bungay, Suffolk*

CONTENTS

*The editor gratefully acknowledges
the invaluable assistance of Patricia O'Connell
in preparation of this volume*

ACKNOWLEDGEMENTS

The editor gratefully acknowledges permission to reprint copyright material to the following:

Guy Cullingford and the American Literary Exchange for *My Unfair Lady*, first published in Alfred Hitchcock's *Mystery Magazine*.

Curtis Brown, Ltd. for *The Birds* by Daphne du Maurier, from 'The Apple Tree' (Victor Gollancz).

Ann Elmo Agency for *Man with a Problem* by Donald Honig, first published in Alfred Hitchcock's *Mystery Magazine*, Copyright © 1958 by Donald Honig.

C. B. Gilford and Scott Meredith Literary Agency for *Terrified*.

A. M. Heath & Co. Ltd. and Peter Davies Ltd. for *The Enemy* by Charlotte Armstrong, from 'The Albatross'.

David Higham Associate Ltd. and William Heinemann Ltd. for *New Murders for Old* by Carter Dickson, from 'The Department of Queer Complaints'.

Hilda Lawrence and Chapman and Hall Ltd. for *Composition for Four Hands*, from 'Duet For Two Hands'.

Sterling Lord Agency for *Spring Fever* by Dorothy Salisbury Davis, Copyright © 1952 by Dorothy Salisbury Davis: and *The Crate at Outpost 1* by Matthew Gant, Copyright © 1954 by Matthew Gant.

Thomas Walsh for *Sentence of Death*.

A. P. Watt & Son, executors of H. G. Wells for *The Inexperienced Ghost*, from 'Twelve Stories and a Dream'.

Willis Kingsley Wing for *They Bite* by Anthony Boucher, Copyright © 1943 by Street and Smith Publications, Inc.

PREFACE

AFTER SPENDING a weekend in the country, a friend of mine invariably sends his host a book. Recently it occurred to me that through television I have spent many Sunday evenings in your homes yet I have never thanked you properly. Ergo, this book. Of course I don't believe my friend charges for the books he sends, but no matter. It's the thought that counts.

Most prefaces soon become defensive, disintegrate into lengthy explanations of why certain stories have been chosen, and the anthologists quickly become apologists. The stories in this volume have only one reason for being here and that is explained in the title. I can only say that I like them. I very much hope that you will too.

A suspense story is not simply a Who-done-it. It might better be called a When's-he-gonna-do-it. I don't think I'm giving away any secrets when I tell you that in most of these stories somebody *does* do it. So don't say you haven't been warned.

There are those who say that the reading of a mystery or suspense story has a therapeutic value; cleansing one of his homicidal tendencies and allowing him to enjoy those crimes he has always wanted to commit but didn't because he lacked the get-up-and-go. If this is true, I think we have crimes to relieve every possible suppressed desire—or at least all the normal ones. You will find mentioned herein: a knifing, a bludgeoning, a strangling, and some shootings. Furthermore there are cases which defy classification since the characters meet their ends in highly original ways, having little or no known precedent. I am confident that several of these cheerful little stories will put an end to the loose talk about truth being stranger than fiction.

I don't wish to spend too much time introducing these tales. I believe it was Henry James who observed, when speaking of prefatory pieces such as this, that when a work of creative literature is introduced to the reader at great length, when fiction is too carefully interpreted, explained and annotated, it is like having a dinner guest brought to the house by a policeman. This is the last thing I wish to do. I much prefer that you feel that this dinner guest to whom you are opening your home is a complete stranger and that there is no police-man within screaming distance.

And now, if you are anxious to curl up with a good book, perhaps we should be getting on. (My final parenthetical re-mark: the only things I know of that actually like to curl up with a good book are the silverfish in my basement.) When you begin reading, may I suggest you choose a time when you are alone in the house. If there are people there, get rid of them. The book is full of suggestions of how this can be accomplished. Now turn out all the lights you possibly can, look over the stories and take one before retiring. If you want to sample another, help yourself, but be careful. An overdose could be fatal. After all, this is a highly toxic book.

Alfred Hitchcock

THE BIRDS

DAPHNE DU MAURIER

ON DECEMBER the third the wind changed overnight and it was winter. Until then the autumn had been mellow, soft. The earth was rich where the plough had turned it.

Nat Hocken, because of a wartime disability, had a pension and did not work full-time at the farm. He worked three days a week, and they gave him the lighter jobs. Although he was married, with children, his was a solitary disposition; he liked best to work alone.

It pleased him when he was given a bank to build up, or a gate to mend, at the far end of the peninsula, where the sea surrounded the farmland on either side. Then, at midday, he would pause and eat the meat pie his wife had baked for him and, sitting on the cliff's edge, watch the birds.

In autumn great flocks of them came to the peninsula, restless, uneasy, spending themselves in motion; now wheeling, circling in the sky; now settling to feed on the rich, new-turned soil, but even when they fed, it was as though they did so without hunger, without desire.

Restlessness drove them to the skies again. Crying, whistling, calling, they skimmed the placid sea and left the shore.

Make haste, make speed, hurry and begone; yet where, and to what purpose? The restless urge of autumn, unsatisfying, sad, had put a spell upon them, and they must spill themselves of motion before winter came.

Perhaps, thought Nat, a message comes to the birds in autumn, like a warning. Winter is coming. Many of them will perish. And like people who, apprehensive of death before their time, drive themselves to work or folly, the birds do likewise; tomorrow we shall die.

The birds had been more restless than ever this fall of the year. Their agitation more remarked because the days were still.

11

As Mr Trigg's tractor traced its path up and down the western hills, and Nat, hedging, saw it dip and turn, the whole machine and the man upon it were momentarily lost in the great cloud of wheeling, crying birds.

Nat remarked upon them to Mr Trigg when the work was finished for the day.

"Yes," said the farmer, "there are more birds about than usual. I have a notion the weather will change. It will be a hard winter. That's why the birds are restless."

The farmer was right. That night the weather turned.

The bedroom in the cottage faced east. Nat woke just after two and heard the east wind, cold and dry. It sounded hollow in the chimney, and a loose slate rattled on the roof. Nat listened, and he could hear the sea roaring in the bay. He drew the blanket round him, leaned closer to the back of his wife, deep in sleep. Then he heard the tapping on the window-pane. It continued until, irritated by the sound, Nat got out of bed and went to the window. He opened it; and as he did so something brushed his hand, jabbing at his knuckles, grazing the skin. Then he saw the flutter of wings and the thing was gone again, over the roof, behind the cottage.

It was a bird. What kind of bird he could not tell. The wind must have driven it to shelter on the sill.

He shut the window and went back to bed, but feeling his knuckles wet, put his mouth to the scratch. The bird had drawn blood.

Frightened, he supposed, bewildered, seeking shelter, the bird had stabbed at him in the darkness. Once more he settled himself to sleep.

Presently the tapping came again—this time more forceful, more insistent. And now his wife woke at the sound, and turning in the bed, said to him, "See to the window, Nat; it's rattling."

"I've already been to it," he told her. "There's some bird there, trying to get in."

"Send it away," she said. "I can't sleep with that noise."

He went to the window for the second time, and now when he opened it, there was not one bird on the sill but half a dozen; they flew straight into his face.

He shouted, striking out at them with his arms, scattering them; like the first one, they flew over the roof and disappeared.

He let the window fall and latched it.

12

Suddenly a frightened cry came from the room across the passage where the children slept.

"It's Jill," said his wife, roused at the sound.

There came a second cry, this time from both children. Stumbling into their room, Nat felt the beating of wings about him in the darkness. The window was wide open. Through it came the birds, hitting first the ceiling and the walls, then swerving in mid-flight and turning to the children in their beds.

"It's all right. I'm here," shouted Nat, and the children flung themselves, screaming, upon him, while in the darkness the birds rose, and dived, and came for him again.

"What is it, Nat? What's happened?" his wife called. Swiftly he pushed the children through the door to the passage and shut it upon them, so that he was alone in their bedroom with the birds.

He seized a blanket from the nearest bed, and using it as a weapon, flung it right and left about him.

He felt the thud of bodies, heard the fluttering of wings; but the birds were not yet defeated, for again and again they returned to the assault, jabbing his hands, his head, their little stabbing beaks sharp as pointed forks.

The blanket became a weapon of defence. He wound it about his head, and then in greater darkness, beat at the birds with his bare hands. He dared not stumble to the door and open it lest the birds follow him.

How long he fought with them in the darkness he could not tell; but at last the beating of the wings about him lessened, withdrew; and through the dense blanket he was aware of light.

He waited, listened; there was no sound except the fretful crying of one of the children from the bedroom beyond.

He took the blanket from his head and stared about him. The cold grey morning light exposed the room.

Dawn and the open window had called the living birds; the dead lay on the floor.

Sickened, Nat went to the window and stared out across his patch of garden to the fields.

It was bitter cold, and the ground had all the hard, black look of the frost that the east wind brings. The sea, fiercer now with turning tide, whitecapped and steep, broke harshly in the bay. Of the birds there was no sign.

Nat shut the window and door of the small bedroom and went back across the passage to his own room.

13

His wife sat up in bed, one child asleep beside her; the smaller one in her arms, his face bandaged.

"He's sleeping now," she whispered. "Something must have cut him; there was blood at the corners of his eyes. Jill said it was the birds. She said she woke up and the birds were in the room."

His wife looked up at Nat, searching his face for confirmation. She looked terrified, bewildered. He did not want her to know that he also was shaken, dazed almost, by the events of the past few hours.

"There are birds in there," he said. "Dead birds, nearly fifty of them."

He sat down on the bed beside his wife.

"It's the hard weather," he said. "It must be that; it's the hard weather. They aren't the birds, maybe, from around here. They've been driven down from up-country."

"But Nat," whispered his wife, "it's only this night that the weather turned. They can't be hungry yet. There's food for them out there in the fields."

"It's the weather," repeated Nat. "I tell you, it's the weather."

His face, too, was drawn and tired, like hers. They stared at one another for a while without speaking.

Nat went to the window and looked out. The sky was hard and leaden, and the brown hills that had gleamed in the sun the day before looked dark and bare. Black winter had descended in a single night.

The children were awake now. Jill was chattering, and young Johnny was crying once again. Nat heard his wife's voice, soothing, comforting them as he went downstairs.

Presently they came down. He had breakfast ready for them.

"Did you drive away the birds?" asked Jill.

"Yes, they've all gone now," Nat said. "It was the east wind brought them in."

"I hope they won't come again," said Jill.

"I'll walk with you to the bus," Nat said to her.

Jill seemed to have forgotten her experience of the night before. She danced ahead of him, chasing the leaves, her face rosy under her pixy hood.

All the while Nat searched the hedgerows for the birds, glanced over them to the fields beyond, looked to the small wood above the farm where the rooks and jackdaws gathered; he saw none. Soon the bus came ambling up the hill.

14

Nat saw Jill onto the bus, then turned and walked back toward the farm. It was not his day for work, but he wanted to satisfy himself that all was well. He went to the back door of the farmhouse; he heard Mrs Trigg singing, the wireless making a background for her song.

"Are you there, missus?" Nat called.

She came to the door, beaming, broad, a good-tempered woman.

"Hullo, Mr Hocken," she said. "Can you tell me where this cold is coming from? Is it Russia? I've never seen such a change. And it's going on, the wireless says. Something to do with the Arctic Circle."

"We didn't turn on the wireless this morning," said Nat. "Fact is, we had trouble in the night."

"Kiddies poorly?"

"No." He hardly knew how to explain. Now, in daylight, the battle of the birds would sound absurd.

He tried to tell Mrs Trigg what had happened, but he could see from her eyes that she thought his story was the result of nightmare following a heavy meal.

"Sure they were real birds?" she said, smiling.

"Mrs Trigg," he said, "there are fifty dead birds—robins, wrens, went for me; they tried to go for young Johnny's eyes."

Mrs Trigg stared at him doubtfully. "Well, now," she answered. "I suppose the weather brought them; once in the bedroom they wouldn't know where they were. Foreign birds maybe, from that Arctic Circle."

"No," said Nat. "They were the birds you see about here every day."

"Funny thing," said Mrs Trigg. "No explaining it, really. You ought to write up and ask the *Guardian*. They'd have some answer for it. Well, I must be getting on."

Nat walked back along the lane to his cottage. He found his wife in the kitchen with young Johnny.

"See anyone?" she asked.

"Mrs Trigg," he answered. "I don't think she believed me. Anyway, nothing wrong up there."

"You might take the birds away," she said. "I daren't go into the room to make the beds until you do. I'm scared."

"Nothing to scare you now," said Nat. "They're dead, aren't they?"

He went up with a sack and dropped the stiff bodies into

it, one by one. Yes, there were fifty of them all told. Just the ordinary, common birds of the hedgerow; nothing as large even as a thrush. It must have been fright that made them act the way they did.

He took the sack out into the garden and was faced with a fresh problem. The ground was frozen solid, yet no snow had fallen; nothing had happened in the past hours but the coming of the east wind. It was unnatural, queer. He could see the whitecapped seas breaking in the bay. He decided to take the birds to the shore and bury them.

When he reached the beach below the headland, he could scarcely stand, the force of the east wind was so strong. It was low tide; he crunched his way over the shingle to the softer sand and then, his back to the wind, opened up his sack.

He ground a pit in the sand with his heel, meaning to drop the birds into it; but as he did so, the force of the wind lifted them as though in flight again, and they were blown away from him along the beach, tossed like feathers, spread and scattered.

The tide will take them when it turns, he said to himself.

He looked out to sea and watched the crested breakers, combing green. They rose stiffly, curled, and broke again; and because it was ebb tide, the roar was distant, more remote, lacking the sound and thunder of the flood.

Then he saw them. The gulls. Out there, riding the seas.

What he had thought at first were the whitecaps of the waves were gulls. Hundreds, thousands, tens of thousands.

They rose and fell in the troughs of the seas, heads to the wind, like a mighty fleet at anchor, waiting on the tide.

Nat turned; leaving the beach, he climbed the steep path home.

Someone should know of this. Someone should be told. Something was happening, because of the east wind and the weather, that he did not understand.

As he drew near the cottage, his wife came to meet him at the door. She called to him, excited. "Nat," she said, "it's on the wireless. They've just read out a special news bulletin. It's not only here, it's everywhere. In London, all over the country. Something has happened to the birds. Come and listen; they're repeating it."

Together they went into the kitchen to listen to the announcement.

'Statement from the Home Office, at eleven am this morning. Reports from all over the country are coming in hourly about the vast quantity of birds flocking above towns, villages, and outlying districts, causing obstruction and damage and even attacking individuals. It is thought that the Arctic air stream at present covering the British Isles is causing birds to migrate south in immense numbers, and that intense hunger may drive these birds to attack human beings. Householders are warned to see to their windows, doors and chimneys, and to take reasonable precautions for the safety of their children. A further statement will be issued later.'

A kind of excitement seized Nat. He looked at his wife in triumph. "There you are," he said. "I've been telling myself all morning there's something wrong. And just now, down on the beach, I looked out to sea and there were gulls, thousands of them, riding on the sea, waiting."

"What are they waiting for, Nat?" she asked.

He stared at her. "I don't know," he said slowly.

He went over to the drawer where he kept his hammer and other tools.

"What are you going to do, Nat?"

"See to the windows and the chimneys, like they tell you to."

"You think they would break in with the windows shut? Those wrens and robins and such? Why, how could they?"

He did not answer. He was not thinking of the robins and the wrens. He was thinking of the gulls.

He went upstairs and worked there the rest of the morning, boarding the windows of the bedrooms, filling up the chimney bases.

"Dinner's ready." His wife called him from the kitchen.

"All right. Coming down."

When dinner was over and his wife was washing up, Nat switched on the one o'clock news. The same announcement was repeated, but the news bulletin enlarged upon it. 'The flocks of birds have caused dislocation in all areas,' said the announcer, 'and in London the mass was so dense at ten o'clock this morning that it seemed like a vast black cloud. The birds settled on rooftops, on window ledges, and on chimneys. The species included blackbird, thrush, the common house sparrow, and as might be expected in the metropolis, a vast quantity of pigeons, starlings, and that frequenter of the London river, the black-headed gull. The sight was so unusual that traffic came to a standstill in many thoroughfares, work was abandoned in shops and offices, and the streets and pavements were crowded with people standing about to watch the birds.'

The announcer's voice was smooth and suave; Nat had the impression that he treated the whole business as he would an elaborate joke. There would be others like him, hundreds of them, who did not know what it was to struggle in darkness with a flock of birds.

Nat switched off the wireless. He got up and started work on the kitchen windows. His wife watched him, young Johnny at her heels.

"What they ought to do," she said, "is to call the Army out and shoot the birds."

"Let them try," said Nat. "How'd they set about it?"

"I don't know. But something should be done. They ought to do something."

Nat thought to himself that 'they' were no doubt considering the problem at that very moment, but whatever 'they' decided to do in London and the big cities would not help them here, nearly three hundred miles away.

"How are we off for food?" he asked.

"It's shopping day tomorrow, you know that. I don't keep uncooked food about. Butcher doesn't call till the day after. But I can bring back something when I go in tomorrow."

Nat did not want to scare her. He looked in the larder for himself and in the cupboard where she kept her tins.

They could hold out for a couple of days.

He went on hammering the boards across the kitchen windows. Candles. They were low on candles. That must be another thing she meant to buy tomorrow. Well, they must go early to bed tonight. That was, if——

He got up and went out the back door and stood in the garden, looking down toward the sea.

There had been no sun all day, and now, at barely three o'clock, a kind of darkness had already come; the sky was sullen, heavy, colourless like salt. He could hear the vicious sea drumming on the rocks.

He walked down the path halfway to the beach. And then he stopped. He could see the tide had turned. The gulls had risen. They were circling, hundreds of them, thousands of them, lifting their wings against the wind.

It was the gulls that made the darkening of the sky.

And they were silent. They just went on soaring and

18

circling, rising, falling, trying their strength against the wind. Nat turned. He ran up the path back to the cottage.

"I'm going for Jill," he said to his wife.

"What's the matter?" she asked. "You've gone quite white."

"Keep Johnny inside," he said. "Keep the door shut. Light up now and draw the curtains."

"It's only gone three," she said.

"Never mind. Do what I tell you."

He looked inside the tool shed and took the hoe.

He started walking up the lane to the bus stop. Now and again he glanced back over his shoulder; and he could see the gulls had risen higher now, their circles were broader, they were spreading out in huge formation across the sky.

He hurried on. Although he knew the bus would not come before four o'clock, he had to hurry.

He waited at the top of the hill. There was half an hour still to go.

The east wind came whipping across the fields from the higher ground. In the distance he could see the clay hills, white and clean against the heavy pallor of the sky.

Something black rose from behind them, like a smudge at first, then widening, becoming deeper. The smudge became a cloud; and the cloud divided again into five other clouds, spreading north, east, south, and west; and then they were not clouds at all but birds.

He watched them travel across the sky, within two or three hundred feet of him. He knew, from their speed, that they were bound inland; they had no business with the people here on the peninsula. They were rooks, crows, jackdaws, magpies, jays, all birds that usually preyed upon the smaller species, but bound this afternoon on some other mission.

He went to the telephone call box, stepped inside, lifted the receiver. The exchange would pass the message on. "I'm speaking from the highway," he said, "by the bus stop. I want to report large formations of birds travelling up-country. The gulls are also forming in the bay."

"All right," answered the voice, laconic, weary.

"You'll be sure and pass this message on to the proper quarter?"

"Yes. Yes." Impatient now, fed up. The buzzing note resumed. She's another, thought Nat. She doesn't care.

The bus came lumbering up the hill. Jill climbed out.

"What's the hoe for, Dad?"

"I just brought it along," he said. "Come on now, let's get home. It's cold; no hanging about. See how fast you can run."

He could see the gulls now, still silent, circling the fields, coming in toward the land.

"Look, Dad; look over there. Look at all the gulls."

"Yes. Hurry now."

"Where are they flying to? Where are they going?"

"Up-country, I dare say. Where it's warmer."

He seized her hand and dragged her after him along the lane.

"Don't go so fast. I can't keep up."

The gulls were copying the rooks and crows. They were spreading out, in formation, across the sky. They headed, in bands of thousands, to the four compass points.

"Dad, what is it? What are the gulls doing?"

They were not intent upon their flight, as the crows, as the jackdaws, had been. They still circled overhead. Nor did they fly so high. It was as though they waited upon some signal; as though some decision had yet to be given.

"I wish the gulls would go away." Jill was crying. "I don't like them. They're coming closer to the lane."

He started running, swinging Jill after him. As they went past the farm turning, he saw the farmer backing his car into the garage. Nat called to him.

"Can you give us a lift?" he said.

Mr Trigg turned in the driver's seat and stared at them. Then a smile came to his cheerful, rubicund face. "It looks as though we're in for some fun," he said. "Have you seen the gulls? Jim and I are going to take a crack at them. Everyone's gone bird crazy, talking of nothing else. I hear you were troubled in the night. Want a gun?"

Nat shook his head.

The small car was packed, but there was room for Jill on the back seat.

"I don't want a gun," said Nat, "but I'd be obliged if you'd run Jill home. She's scared of the birds."

"Okay," said the farmer. "I'll take her home. Why don't you stop behind and join in the shooting-match? We'll make the feathers fly."

Jill climbed in, and turning the car, the driver sped up the lane. Nat followed after. Trigg must be crazy. What use was a gun against a sky of birds?

They were coming in now toward the farm, circling lower in the sky. The farm, then, was their target. Nat increased his pace toward his own cottage. He saw the farmer's car turn and come back along the lane. It drew up beside him with a jerk.

"The kid has run inside," said the farmer. "Your wife was watching for her. Well, what do you make of it? They're saying in town the Russians have done it. The Russians have poisoned the birds."

"How could they do that?" asked Nat.

"Don't ask me. You know how stories get around."

"Have you boarded your windows?" asked Nat.

"No. Lot of nonsense. I've had more to do today than to go round boarding up my windows."

"I'd board them now if I were you."

"Garn. You're windy. Like to come to our place to sleep?"

"No, thanks all the same."

"All right. See you in the morning. Give you a gull breakfast."

The farmer grinned and turned his car to the farm entrance. Nat hurried on. Past the little wood, past the old barn, and then across the stile to the remaining field. As he jumped the stile, he heard the whir of wings. A black-backed gull dived down at him from the sky. It missed, swerved in flight, and rose to dive again. In a moment it was joined by others—six, seven, a dozen.

Nat dropped his hoe. The hoe was useless. Covering his head with his arms, he ran toward the cottage.

They kept coming at him from the air—noiseless, silent, save for the beating wings. The terrible, fluttering wings. He could feel the blood on his hands, his wrists, upon his neck. If only he could keep them from his eyes. Nothing else mattered.

With each dive, with each attack, they became bolder. And they had no thought for themselves. When they dived low and missed, they crashed, bruised and broken on the ground.

As Nat ran he stumbled, kicking their spent bodies in front of him.

He found the door and hammered upon it with bleeding hands. "Let me in," he shouted. "It's Nat. Let me in."

Then he saw the gannet, poised for the dive, above him in the sky.

The gulls circled, retired, soared, one with another, against the wind.

Only the gannet remained. One single gannet, above him in the sky. Its wings folded suddenly to its body. It dropped like a stone.

Nat screamed; and the door opened.

He stumbled across the threshold, and his wife threw her weight against the door.

They heard the thud of the gannet as it fell.

His wife dressed his wounds. They were not deep. The backs of his hands had suffered most, and his wrists. Had he not worn a cap, the birds would have reached his head. As for the gannet—the gannet could have split his skull.

The children were crying, of course. They had seen the blood on their father's hands.

"It's all right now," he told them. "I'm not hurt."

His wife was ashen. "I saw them overhead," she whispered. "They began collecting just as Jill ran in with Mr Trigg. I shut the door fast, and it jammed. That's why I couldn't open it at once when you came."

"Thank God the birds waited for me," he said. "Jill would have fallen at once. They're flying inland, thousands of them. Rooks, crows, all the bigger birds. I saw them from the bus stop. They're making for the towns."

"But what can they do, Nat?"

"They'll attack. Go for everyone out in the streets. Then they'll try the windows, the chimneys."

"Why don't the authorities do something? Why don't they get the Army, get machine guns?"

"There's been no time. Nobody's prepared. We'll hear what they have to say on the six o'clock news."

"I can hear the birds," Jill said. "Listen, Dad."

Nat listened. Muffled sounds came from the windows, from the door. Wings brushing the surface, sliding, scraping, seeking a way of entry. The sound of many bodies pressed together, shuffling on the sills. Now and again came a thud, a crash, as some bird dived and fell.

Some of them will kill themselves that way, he thought, but not enough. Never enough.

"All right," he said aloud. "I've got boards over the windows, Jill. The birds can't get in."

He went and examined all the windows. He found wedges —pieces of old tin, strips of wood and metal—and fastened them at the sides of the windows to reinforce the boards.

His hammering helped to deafen the sound of the birds,

the shuffling, the tapping, and—more ominous— the splinter of breaking glass.

"Turn on the wireless," he said.

He went upstairs to the bedrooms and reinforced the windows there. Now he could hear the birds on the roof—the scraping of claws, a sliding, jostling sound.

He decided the whole family must sleep in the kitchen and keep up the fire. He was afraid of the bedroom chimneys. The boards he had placed at their bases might give way. In the kitchen they would be safe because of the fire.

He would have to make a joke of it. Pretend to the children they were playing camp. If the worst happened and the birds forced an entry by way of the bedroom chimneys, it would be hours, days perhaps, before they could break down the doors. The birds would be imprisoned in the bedrooms. They could do no harm there. Crowded together, they would stifle and die. He began to bring the mattresses downstairs.

At sight of them, his wife's eyes widened in apprehension.

"All right," he said cheerfully. "We'll all sleep together in the kitchen tonight. More cosy, here by the fire. Then we won't be worried by those silly old birds tapping at the windows."

He made the children help him rearrange the furniture, and he took the precaution of moving the dresser against the windows.

We're safe enough now, he thought. We're snug and tight. We can hold out. It's just the food that worries me. Food and coal for the fire. We've enough for two or three days, not more. By that time——

No use thinking ahead as far as that. And they'd be given directions on the wireless.

And now, in the midst of many problems, he realized that only dance music was coming over the air. He knew the reason. The usual programmes had been abandoned; this only happened at exceptional times.

At six o'clock the records ceased. The time signal was given. There was a pause, and then the announcer spoke. His voice was solemn, grave. Quite different from midday.

'This is London,' he said. 'A national emergency was proclaimed at four o'clock this afternoon. Measures are being taken to safeguard the lives and property of the population, but it must be understood that these are not easy to effect immediately, owing to the unforeseen and unparalleled nature of the present crisis. Every householder must take precautions about his own building. Where several people live together, as in flats and hotels, they must unite to do the utmost that they can to prevent entry. It is absolutely imperative that every individual stay indoors tonight.

'The birds, in vast numbers, are attacking anyone on sight, and have already begun an assault upon buildings; but these, with due care, should be impenetrable.

'The population is asked to remain calm.

'Owing to the exceptional nature of the emergency, there will be no further transmission from any broadcasting station until seven am tomorrow.'

They played 'God Save the Queen'. Nothing more happened.

Nat switched off the set. He looked at his wife. She stared back at him.

"We'll have supper early," suggested Nat. "Something for a treat—toasted cheese, eh? Something we all like."

He winked and nodded at his wife. He wanted the look of dread, of apprehension, to leave her face.

He helped with the supper, whistling, singing, making as much clatter as he could. It seemed to him that the shuffling and the tapping were not so intense as they had been at first, and presently he went up to the bedrooms and listened. He no longer heard the jostling for place upon the roof.

They've got reasoning powers, he thought. They know it's hard to break in here. They'll try elsewhere.

Supper passed without incident. Then, when they were clearing away, they heard a new sound, a familiar droning.

His wife looked up at him, her face alight.

"It's planes," she said. "They're sending out planes after the birds. That will get them. Isn't that gunfire? Can't you hear guns?"

It might be gunfire, out at sea. Nat could not tell. Big naval guns might have some effect upon the gulls out at sea, but the gulls were inland now. The guns couldn't shell the shore because of the population.

"It's good, isn't it," said his wife, "to hear the planes?"

Catching her enthusiasm, Jill jumped up and down with Johnny. "The planes will get the birds."

Just then they heard a crash about two miles distant. Followed by a second, then a third. The droning became more distant, passed away out to sea.

24

"What was that?" asked his wife.

"I don't know," answered Nat. He did not want to tell her that the sound they had heard was the crashing of aircraft.

It was, he had no doubt, a gamble on the part of the authorities to send out reconnaissance forces, but they might have known the gamble was suicidal. What could aircraft do against birds that flung themselves to death against propeller and fuselage but hurtle to the ground themselves?

"Where have the planes gone, Dad?" asked Jill.

"Back to base," he said. "Come on now, time to tuck down for bed."

There was no further drone of aircraft, and the naval guns had ceased. Waste of life and effort, Nat said to himself. We can't destroy enough of them that way. Cost too heavy. There's always gas. Maybe they'll try spraying with gas, mustard gas. We'll be warned first, of course, if they do. There's one thing, the best brains of the country will be on it tonight.

Upstairs in the bedrooms all was quiet. No more scraping and stabbing at the windows. A lull in battle. The wind hadn't dropped, though. Nat could still hear it roaring in the chimneys. And the sea breaking down on the shore.

Then he remembered the tide. The tide would be on the turn. Maybe the lull in battle was because of the tide. There was some law the birds obeyed, and it had to do with the east wind and the tide.

He glanced at his watch. Nearly eight o'clock. It must have gone high water an hour ago. That explained the lull. The birds attacked with the flood tide.

He reckoned the time limit in his head. They had six hours to go without attack. When the tide turned again, around 1.20 in the morning, the birds would come back.

He called softly to his wife and whispered to her that he would go out and see how they were faring at the farm, see if the telephone was still working there so that they might get news from the exchange.

"You're not to go," she said at once, "and leave me alone with the children. I can't stand it."

"All right," he said, "all right. I'll wait till morning. And we can get the wireless bulletin then, too, at seven. But when the tide ebbs again, I'll try for the farm; they may let us have bread and potatoes."

His mind was busy again, planning against emergency.

25

They would not have milked, of course, this evening. The cows would be standing by the gate, waiting; the household would be inside, battened behind boards as they were here at the cottage.

That is, if they had had time to take precautions.

Softly, stealthily, he opened the back door and looked outside.

It was pitch-dark. The wind was blowing harder than ever, coming in steady gusts, icy, from the sea.

He kicked at the step. It was heaped with birds. These were the suicides, the divers, the ones with broken necks. Wherever he looked, he saw dead birds. The living had flown seaward with the turn of the tide. The gulls would be riding the seas now, as they had done in the forenoon.

In the far distance on the hill, something was burning. One of the aircraft that had crashed; the fire, fanned by the wind, had set light to a stack.

He looked at the bodies of the birds. He had a notion that if he stacked them, one upon the other, on the window sills, they would be added protection against the next attack.

Not much, perhaps, but something. The bodies would have to be clawed at, pecked and dragged aside before the living birds gained purchase on the sills and attacked the panes.

He set to work in the darkness. It was queer. He hated touching the dead birds, but he went on with his work. He noticed grimly that every window-pane was shattered. Only the boards had kept the birds from breaking in.

He stuffed the cracked panes with the bleeding bodies of the birds and felt his stomach turn. When he had finished, he went back into the cottage and barricaded the kitchen door, making it doubly secure.

His wife had made him cocoa; he drank it thirstily. He was very tired. "All right," he said, smiling, "don't worry. We'll get through."

He lay down on his mattress and closed his eyes.

He dreamed uneasily because, through his dreams, ran the dread of something forgotten. Some piece of work that he should have done. It was connected, in some way, with the burning aircraft.

It was his wife, shaking his shoulder, who awoke him finally.

"They've begun," she sobbed. "They've started this last

hour. I can't listen to it any longer alone. There's something smells bad too, something burning."

Then he remembered. He had forgotten to make up the fire. The fire was smouldering, nearly out. He got up swiftly and lighted the lamp.

The hammering had started at the windows and the door, but it was not that he minded now. It was the smell of singed feathers.

The smell filled the kitchen. He knew what it was at once. The birds were coming down the chimney, squeezing their way down to the kitchen range.

He got sticks and paper and put them on the embers, then reached for the can of kerosene.

"Stand back," he shouted to his wife. He threw some of the kerosene on to the fire.

"The flame roared up the pipe, and down into the fire fell the scorched, blackened bodies of the birds.

The children waked, crying. "What is it?" asked Jill. "What's happened?"

Nat had no time to answer her. He was raking the bodies from the chimney, clawing them out on to the floor.

The flames would drive away the living birds from the chimney top. The lower joint was the difficulty though. It was choked with the smouldering, helpless bodies of the birds caught by fire.

He scarcely heeded the attack on the windows and the door. Let them beat their wings, break their backs, lose their lives, in the desperate attempt to force an entry into his home. They would not break in.

"Stop crying," he called to the children. "There's nothing to be afraid of. Stop crying."

He went on raking out the burning, smouldering bodies as they fell into the fire.

This'll fetch them, he said to himself. The draught and the flames together. We're all right as long as the chimney doesn't catch.

Amid the tearing at the window boards came the sudden homely striking of the kitchen clock. Three o'clock.

A little more than four hours to go. He could not be sure of the exact time of high water. He reckoned the tide would not turn much before half-past seven.

He waited by the range. The flames were dying. But no

27

more blackened bodies fell from the chimney. He thrust his poker up as far as it could go and found nothing.

The danger of the chimney's being choked up was over. It could not happen again, not if the fire was kept burning day and night.

I'll have to get more fuel from the farm tomorrow, he thought. I can do all that with the ebb tide. It can be worked; we can fetch what we need when the tide's turned. We've just got to adapt ourselves, that's all.

They drank tea and cocoa, ate slices of bread. Only half a loaf left, Nat noticed. Never mind, though; they'd get by.

If they could hang on like this until seven, when the first news bulletin came through, they would not have done too badly.

"Give us a smoke," he said to his wife. "It will clear away the smell of the scorched feathers."

"There's only two left in the packet," she said. "I was going to buy you some."

"I'll have one," he said.

He sat with one arm around his wife and one around Jill, with Johnny on his lap, the blankets heaped about them on the mattress.

"You can't help admiring the beggars," he said. "They've got persistency. You'd think they'd tire of the game, but not a bit of it."

Admiration was hard to sustain. The tapping went on and on; and a new, rasping note struck Nat's ear, as though a sharper beak than any hitherto had come to take over from its fellows.

He tried to remember the names of birds; he tried to think which species would go for this particular job.

It was not the tap of the woodpecker. That would be light and frequent. This was more serious; if it continued long, the wood would splinter as the glass had done.

Then he remembered the hawks. Could the hawks have taken over from the gulls? Were there buzzards now upon the sills, using talons as well as beaks? Hawks, buzzards, kestrels, falcons; he had forgotten the birds of prey. He had forgotten the gripping power of the birds of prey. Three hours to go; and while they waited, the sound of the splintering wood, the talons tearing at the wood.

Nat looked about him, seeing what furniture he could destroy to fortify the door.

28

The windows were safe because of the dresser. He was not certain of the door. He went upstairs; but when he reached the landing, he paused and listened.

There was a soft patter on the floor of the children's bedroom. The birds had broken through.

The other bedroom was still clear. He brought out the furniture to pile at the head of the stairs should the door of the children's bedroom go.

"Come down, Nat. What are you doing?" called his wife.

"I won't be long," he shouted. "I'm just making everything ship-shape up here."

He did not want her to come. He did not want her to hear the pattering in the children's bedroom, the brushing of those wings against the door.

After he suggested breakfast, he found himself watching the clock, gazing at the hands that went so slowly around the dial. If his theory was not correct, if the attack did not cease with the turn of the tide, he knew they were beaten. They could not continue through the long day without air, without rest, without fuel.

A crackling in his ears drove away the sudden desperate desire for sleep.

"What is it? What now?" he said sharply.

"The wireless," said his wife. "I've been watching the clock. It's nearly seven."

The comfortable crackling of the wireless brought new life.

They waited. The kitchen clock struck seven.

The crackling continued. Nothing else. No chimes. No music.

They waited until a quarter past. No news bulletin came through.

"We heard wrong," he said. "They won't be broadcasting until eight o'clock."

They left the wireless switched on. Nat thought of the battery, wondered how much power was left in the battery. If it failed, they would not hear the instructions.

"It's getting light," whispered his wife. "I can't see it but I can feel it. And listen! The birds aren't hammering so loud now."

She was right. The rasping, tearing sound grew fainter every moment. So did the shuffling, the jostling for place upon the step, upon the sills. The tide was on the turn.

By eight there was no sound at all. Only the wind. And the

29

crackling of the wireless. The children, lulled at least by the stillness, fell asleep.

At half-past eight Nat switched the wireless off.

"We'll miss the news," said his wife.

"There isn't going to be any news," said Nat. "We've got to depend upon ourselves."

He went to the door and slowly pulled away the barricades. He drew the bolts, and kicking the broken bodies from the step outside the door, breathed the cold air.

He had six working hours before him, and he knew he must reserve his strength to the utmost, not waste it in any way.

Food and light and fuel; these were the most necessary things. If he could get them, they could endure another night.

He stepped into the garden; and as he did so, he saw the living birds. The gulls had gone to ride the sea, as they had done before. They sought sea food and the buoyancy of the tide before they returned to the attack.

Not so the land birds. They waited and watched.

Nat saw them on the hedgerows, on the soil, crowded in the trees, outside in the field—line upon line of birds, still, doing nothing. He went to the end of his small garden.

The birds did not move. They merely watched him.

I've got to get food, Nat said to himself. I've got to go to the farm to get food.

He went back to the cottage. He saw to the windows and the door.

"I'm going to the farm," he said.

His wife clung to him. She had seen the living birds from the open door.

"Take us with you," she begged. "We can't stay here alone. I'd rather die than stay here alone."

"Come on, then," he said. "Bring baskets and Johnny's pram. We can load up the pram."

They dressed against the biting wind. His wife put Johnny in the pram, and Nat took Jill's hand.

"The birds," Jill whimpered. "They're all out there in the fields."

"They won't hurt us," he said. "Not in the light."

They started walking across the field toward the stile, and the birds did not move. They waited, their heads turned to the wind.

When they reached the turning to the farm, Nat stopped

30

and told his wife to wait in the shelter of the hedge with the two children. "But I want to see Mrs Trigg," she protested. "There are lots of things we can borrow if they went to market yesterday, and ———"

"Wait here," Nat interrupted. "I'll be back in a moment."

The cows were lowing, moving restlessly in the yard, and he could see a gap in the fence where the sheep had knocked their way through to roam unchecked in the front garden before the farmhouse.

No smoke came from the chimneys. Nat was filled with misgiving. He did not want his wife or the children to go down to the farm.

He went down alone, pushing his way through the herd of lowing cows, who turned this way and that, distressed, their udders full.

He saw the car standing by the gate. Not put away in the garage.

All the windows of the farmhouse were smashed. There were many dead gulls lying in the yard and around the house.

The living birds perched on the group of trees behind the farm and on the roof of the house. They were quite still. They watched him. Jim's body lay in the yard. What was left of it. His gun was beside him.

The door of the house was shut and bolted, but it was easy to push up a smashed window and climb through.

Trigg's body was close to the telephone. He must have been trying to get through to the exchange when the birds got him. The receiver was off the hook, and the instrument was torn from the wall.

No sign of Mrs Trigg. She would be upstairs. Was it any use going up? Sickened, Nat knew what he would find there.

Thank God, he said to himself, there were no children.

He forced himself to climb the stairs, but halfway up he turned and descended again. He could see Mrs Trigg's legs protruding from the open bedroom door. Beside her were the bodies of black-backed gulls and an umbrella, broken. It's no use doing anything, Nat thought. I've only got five hours; less than that. The Triggs would understand. I must load up with what I can find.

He tramped back to his wife and children.

"I'm going to fill up the car with stuff," he said. "We'll take it home and return for a fresh load."

"What about the Triggs?" asked his wife.

"They must have gone to friends," he said.

"Shall I come and help you then?"

"No, there's a mess down there. Cows and sheep all over the place. Wait; I'll get the car. You can sit in the car."

Her eyes watched his all the time he was talking. He believed she understood. Otherwise she certainly would have insisted on helping him find the bread and groceries.

They made three journeys altogether, to and from the farm, before he was satisfied they had everything they needed. It was surprising, once he started thinking, how many things were necessary. Almost the most important of all was planking for the windows. He had to go around searching for timber. He wanted to renew the boards on all the windows at the cottage.

On the final journey he drove the car to the bus stop and got out and went to the telephone box.

He waited a few minutes, jangling the hook. No good, though. The line was dead. He climbed on to a bank and looked over the countryside, but there was no sign of life at all, nothing in the fields but the waiting, watching birds.

Some of them slept; he could see their beaks tucked into their feathers.

You'd think they'd be feeding, he said to himself, not just standing that way.

Then he remembered. They were gorged with food. They had eaten their fill during the night. That was why they did not move this morning.

He lifted his face to the sky. It was colourless, grey. The bare trees looked bent and blackened by the east wind.

The cold did not affect the living birds, waiting out there in the fields.

This is the time they ought to get them, Nat said to himself. They're a sitting target now. They must be doing this all over the country. Why don't our aircraft take off now and spray them with mustard gas? What are all our chaps doing? They must know; they must see for themselves.

He went back to the car and got into the driver's seat.

"Go quickly past the second gate," whispered his wife. "The postman's lying there. I don't want Jill to see."

It was a quarter to one by the time they reached the cottage. Only an hour to go.

"Better have dinner," said Nat. "Hot up something for

yourself and the children, some of that soup. I've no time to eat now. I've got to unload all this stuff from the car."

He got everything inside the cottage. It could be sorted later. Give them all something to do during the long hours ahead.

First he must see to the windows and the door.

He went around the cottage methodically, testing every window and the door. He climbed on to the roof also, and fixed boards across every chimney except the kitchen's.

The cold was so intense he could hardly bear it, but the job had to be done. Now and again he looked up, searching the sky for aircraft. None came. As he worked, he cursed the inefficiency of the authorities.

He paused, his work on the bedroom chimney finished, and looked out to sea. Something was moving out there. Something grey and white among the breakers.

"Good old Navy," he said. "They never let us down. They're coming down channel; they're turning into the bay."

He waited, straining his eyes toward the sea. He was wrong, though. The Navy was not there. It was the gulls rising from the sea. And the massed flocks in the fields, with ruffled feathers, rose in formation from the ground and, wing to wing, soared upward to the sky.

The tide had turned again.

Nat climbed down the ladder and went inside the cottage. The family were at dinner. It was a little after two.

He bolted the door, put up the barricade, and lighted the lamp.

"It's night-time," said young Johnny.

His wife had switched on the wireless once again. The crackling sound came, but nothing else.

"I've been all round the dial," she said, "foreign stations and all. I can't get anything but the crackling."

"Maybe they have the same trouble," he said. "Maybe it's the same right through Europe."

They ate in silence.

The tapping began at the windows, at the door, the rustling, the jostling, the pushing for position on the sills. The first thud of the suicide gulls upon the step.

When he had finished dinner, Nat planned, he would put the supplies away, stack them neatly, get everything ship-shape. The boards were strong against the windows and across

B 33

the chimneys. The cottage was filled with stores, with fuel, with all they needed for the next few days.

His wife could help him, and the children too. They'd tire themselves out between now and a quarter to nine, when the tide would ebb; then he'd tuck them down on their mattresses, see that they slept good and sound until three in the morning.

He had a new scheme for the windows, which was to fix barbed wire in front of the boards. He had brought a great roll of it from the farm. The nuisance was, he'd have to work at this in the dark, when the lull came between nine and three. Pity he had not thought of it before. Still, as long as the wife and kids slept—that was the main thing.

The smaller birds were at the windows now. He recognized the light tap-tapping of their beaks and the soft brush of their wings.

The hawks ignored the windows. They concentrated their attack upon the door.

Nat listened to the tearing sound of splintering wood, and wondered how many million years of memory were stored in those little brains, behind the stabbing beaks, the piercing eyes, now giving them this instinct to destroy mankind with all the deft precision of machines.

"I'll smoke that last cigarette," he said to his wife. "Stupid of me. It was the one thing I forgot to bring back from the farm."

He reached for it, switched on the crackling wireless.

He threw the empty packet on to the fire and watched it burn.

MAN WITH A PROBLEM

DONALD HONIG

WITH DULL curiosity he watched the crowds gathering far below on the sidewalk. They had become a sea of bobbing upturned faces. It was rapidly increasing in size, swelling out into the street. The hurrying newcomers moved with insect-like briskness, drawn into the rest as if by magnetic tides. The traffic was beginning to back up with a cacophony of agitated horn sounds. It all looked very tiny and mysterious and incredible from twenty-six storeys up. The sounds that reached him were faint, but the excitement in them unmistakable.

He was paying little heed to the startled, gasping faces that kept popping in and out of the window to gape or plead. First it had been a bell-hop, staring with a disapproving look, crinkling his nose; then an elevator operator who in a hard gravelly voice had demanded to know what this was all about.

He looked at the elevator operator's face. "What do you think it is all about?" he asked calmly.

"You gonna jump?" the man asked, intrigued.

"Go away," the man on the ledge said irascibly and looked down at the streets. The traffic was still flowing quietly, undisturbed; he had not been noticed yet.

"You won't walk away from a jump like that," the elevator man growled as his head ducked in.

A moment later, the head of the assistant manager poked through the window, the curtain flying around his distinguished, clean-shaven, rather indignant face.

"I beg your pardon," the assistant manager said.

The man waved him away.

"You're contemplating a very foolish thing" the assistant manager said, smug and comfortable in what he knew was unassailable logic.

The manager finally appeared, a fat, red face that first

35

looked down and then looked over at the man standing on the ledge, contemplating him for a moment.

"What are you doing out there?" the manager asked.

"Im going to jump."

"Who are you? What's your name?"

"Carl Adams. And the reason why I'm doing this does not concern you."

"Think what you're doing, man," the manager said, his double chin trembling as he spoke, the strain of leaning forward out of the window turning his face even redder.

"I've thought about it. Now go away and leave me alone."

The ledge was narrow, about eighteen inches in width. He stood between two windows, but there was no chance of reaching him from either of the windows. His back was against the wall, the bright sun falling full upon him. He had left his jacket inside. His white shirt was open at the throat and he quite resembled a figure prepared for execution.

Successive heads kept poking through the window. They spoke quietly to him, addressing him as Mr Adams. Some spoke to him condescendingly, as though they had already convinced themselves he was a paranoid. They identified themselves as a physician, various hotel officials, a clergyman.

"Why not come in and talk it over?" the clergyman asked gently.

"There's nothing left to say," Adams said.

"Do you want me to come out and guide you back through the window?"

"If you or anyone else steps out," Adams said tersely, "so help me I'll jump."

"Can't you tell us your problem?"

"No."

"How can we help you then?"

"You can't. Go away."

For a short while no one came to the window. And then a policeman's head popped out, looking at him for a moment, rather cynically.

"Hey fella," the policeman said.

Adams looked at him, studying his face. "What do you want?" he asked.

"They called me up from downstairs. Said there's a guy up here threatening to take a dive. You're not really going to jump, are you?"

"Yes."

"What do you want to do that for?"

"It's my nature to do spectacular things."

"Hey, you got a sense of humour," the policeman said. He pushed his cap back on his head, sitting out on the window sill. "I like that. Want a cigarette?"

"No," Adams said.

The policeman shook a cigarette loose from his packet and lighted it. He inhaled deeply, expelling the smoke out into the sunshine where the wind snapped it up. "It's sure a pretty day, you know?"

"A good day to die," Adams said, looking at him.

"You're pretty morbid, fella. You got a family."

"No. Do you?"

"I've got a wife."

"Well, I have no one."

"That's too bad."

"Yes," Adams said. It wasn't so long ago that I did have a family, he thought. Only yesterday in fact. He had left the house in the morning to go to work and Karen had said good-bye to him at the door (not kissed him, like she used to do; theirs was a kiss-less marriage now, but she was still his wife, he still loved her, then and forever, would never give her the divorce, remained firm about that even though she said she would leave him eventually). And then he had come home at six o'clock and there was no wife any more, no love, nothing, only the empty bottle of sleeping pills and the note and the silent apartment . . . and Karen's body lying on the couch.

She had left the note on his pillow. It was written neatly, thoughtfully, explaining. Steve had told her he could not go away with her. Steve had deceived her. (It was that open, that blunt and brusque; she could mention Steve like that and he would know—as he had known for months now. Once he had even seen them together in a neighbourhood cabaret. There had been nothing surreptitious about it on her part. She told him that their marriage was over, spoke freely of Steve to him.)

He had gone out that night and walked the streets until after midnight, come back to the house and gone to sleep. He awoke that morning knowing immediately that his mind had been made up, that he was going to do this which he was now planning. He walked to this part of town and checked into the hotel, asking for a room near the top. He knew that what would happen after that would happen naturally, as a matter of course.

The streets were black with gaping, morbid, curious people now. The police had forced the throngs back, creating a great clearing directly below, should he decide to jump. He could see the firemen standing with their canvas life-net that looked like a round black pancake, a red circle painted in the centre, but he knew that that could do nothing for a body hurtling twenty-six floors. There was no way his would-be rescuers could get at him. The fire ladders did not reach that high. A cornice protruding directly above him from the roof precluded any rescue attempts from that quarter.

"This is useless, senseless," a man was saying to him, his head leaning out of the window.

"You might think so," Adams said.

"Look, I'm a doctor," the man said earnestly. "I can help you."

"In which ward?"

"No wards, Mr Adams. I promise you."

"It's too late now."

"If you jump then it will be too late. Now there's still time."

"You'd better go and attend to somebody who needs you, doctor. I don't need you."

The doctor disappeared. Adams stared critically down at the crowds. Already he had the strange, singular feeling of apartness, the nearness of death having established the gulf between him and other men. He was different now, apart and alone. All those people down there waiting, waiting. They'll see something all right, he thought. And those men in the room, he could hear them jabbering, plotting, scheming, figuring ways of seducing his mind, probably making frantic phone calls to experts on the subject of suicide.

He looked around, a face was out of the window, staring at him. It was the clergyman again, a round, concerned, sincere face.

"Is there anything we can do for you?" the clergyman asked.

"No," he said.

"Do you want to come in now?"

"You're wasting your time, father."

"I'm not wasting my time."

"Yes you are. I'm not coming in."

"Do you want us to leave you alone to think?"

"Do as you please."

The clergyman's head disappeared. He was alone again. He watched the crowds, a soft amusement in his eyes now. The height did not bother him any longer, as it had when he had first stepped out on to the ledge. He felt close to the buildings that soared around him.

He wondered what intricate methods of rescue they were planning. Ropes, ladders, nets, dangling chairs. They would have to be very careful, he knew, because they were never quite certain what his state of mind was.

The policeman reappeared. Adams knew he would. He had been more responsive to him than any of the others and so the policeman would try again.

"You know, Adams," the officer said, sitting out on the window sill again, casually, "in a way you're doing me a favour."

"How's that?"

"Well, normally I'd be down there directing traffic. But because of you I'm up here taking it easy."

"Is that so?"

"That's so."

"You might just as well be up here. That traffic isn't moving anyway."

The policeman laughed. "That's right," he said. "Those people down there," he said with a gesture, "are expecting you to jump. They're looking forward to it."

Adams looked at him. "Looking forward to it?"

"Sure. They've made up their minds that you're going to jump and they want to see it. You going to disappoint them?"

Adams looked down, his eyes sweeping over the blocks and blocks of clustered people.

"You can't hear them up here," the policeman said, "but they're yelling for you to jump."

"Are they?"

"Uh-huh. They feel you owe them that for making them stand around here all afternoon."

"They're like a pack of hungry wolves," Adams said.

"That's right. Why give up your life just so they can have a thrill?" The policeman watched Adams' face, thought he detected a flicker of uncertainty. "Come on in," he said in a low, cajoling voice. "The hell with all those people."

"Maybe you're right," Adams said.

"Sure."

Adams wavered, his back coming away from the wall for a moment, then he fell back, covering his eyes for a second.

"What's the matter?" the policeman asked.

"I guess I'm a bit dizzy. Maybe you'd better give me a hand."

The policeman looked across the street, there were news photographers on the roof there, their cameras poised. It would make quite a picture for the morning papers.

"All right," the policeman said. "Hold on."

The crowd sent up a roar of thrill and terror when they saw the policeman climb out of the window and stand on the ledge, a few feet from the immobile man in the white shirt. They watched him edge along, carefully extending his hand.

Adams reached his hand toward the policeman's.

"I knew you would come up eventually," Adams said. "That's why I chose this place."

"What?" the policeman said, trying to maintain his balance on the narrow ledge.

"My name isn't Adams, Steve. Karen was my wife. Do you know that last night she . . ."

The terror spread over the policeman's face as he tried to draw back, but his hand was locked in the other's and then there was a sudden lunge and sickening thrust and twist and as he began to topple softly out into space, toward the rising roar from the crowd, the last conscious thing he felt was the firm, hard hand gripping his like a vice.

THEY BITE

ANTHONY BOUCHER

THERE WAS no path, only the almost vertical ascent. Crumbled rock for a few yards, with the roots of sage finding their scanty life in the dry soil. Then jagged outcroppings of crude crags, sometimes with accidental footholds, sometimes with overhanging and untrustworthy branches of greasewood, sometimes with no aid to climbing but the leverage of your muscles and the ingenuity of your balance.

The sage was as drably green as the rock was drably brown. The only colour was the occasional rosy spikes of a barrel cactus.

Hugh Tallant swung himself up on to the last pinnacle. It had a deliberate, shaped look about it—a petrified fortress of Lilliputians, a Gibraltar of pygmies. Tallant perched on its battlements and unslung his field glasses.

The desert valley spread below him. The tiny cluster of buildings that was Oasis, the exiguous cluster of palms that gave name to the town and shelter to his own tent and to the shack he was building, the dead-ended highway leading straightforwardly to nothing, the oiled roads diagramming the vacant blocks of an optimistic sub-division.

Tallant saw none of these. His glasses were fixed beyond the oasis and the town of Oasis on the dry lake. The gliders were clear and vivid to him, and the uniformed men busy with them were as sharply and minutely visible as a nest of ants under glass. The training school was more than usually active. One glider in particular, strange to Tallant, seemed the focus of attention. Men would come and examine it and glance back at the older models in comparison.

Only the corner of Tallant's left eye was not preoccupied with the new glider. In that corner something moved, something little and thin and brown as the earth. Too large for a rabbit, much too small for a man. It darted across that corner of vision, and Tallant found gliders oddly hard to concentrate on.

41

He set down the bifocals and deliberately looked about him. His pinnacle surveyed the narrow, flat area of the crest. Nothing stirred. Nothing stood out against the sage rock but one barrel of rosy spikes. He took up the glasses again and resumed his observations. When he was done, he methodically entered the results in the little black notebook.

His hand was still white. The desert is cold and often sunless in winter. But it was a firm hand, and as well trained as his eyes, fully capable of recording faithfully the designs and dimensions which they had registered so accurately.

Once his hand slipped, and he had to erase and re-draw, leaving a smudge that displeased him. The lean, brown thing had slipped across the edge of his vision again. Going toward the east edge, he would swear, where that set of rocks jutted like the spines on the back of a stegosaur.

Only when his notes were completed did he yield to curiosity, and even then with cynical self-reproach. He was physically tired, for him an unusual state, from this daily climbing and from clearing the ground for his shack-to-be. The eye muscles play odd nervous tricks. There could be nothing behind the stegosaur's armour.

There was nothing. Nothing alive and moving. Only the torn and half-plucked carcass of a bird, which looked as though it had been gnawed by some small animal.

It was halfway down the hill—hill in Western terminology, though anywhere east of the Rockies it would have been considered a sizable mountain—that Tallant again had a glimpse of a moving figure.

But this was no trick of a nervous eye. It was not little nor thin nor brown. It was tall and broad and wore a loud red-and-black lumberjacket. It bellowed "Tallant!" in a cheerful and lusty voice.

Tallant drew near the man and said "Hello." He paused and added, "Your advantage, I think."

The man grinned broadly. "Don't know me? Well, I daresay ten years is a long time, and the California desert ain't exactly the Chinese rice fields. How's stuff? Still loaded down with Secrets for Sale?"

Tallant tried desperately not to react to that shot, but he stiffened a little. "Sorry. The prospector get-up had me fooled. Good to see you again, Morgan."

The man's eyes had narrowed. "Just having my little joke." he smiled. "Of course you wouldn't have no serious reason

42

for mountain-climbing around a glider school, now would you? And you'd kind of need field-glasses to keep an eye on the pretty birdies."

"I'm out here for my health." Tallant's voice sounded unnatural even to himself.

"Sure, sure. You were always in it for your health. And come to think of it, my own health ain't been none too good lately. I've got me a little cabin way to hell-and-gone around here, and I do me a little prospecting now and then. And somehow it just strikes me, Tallant, like maybe I hit a pretty good lode today."

"Nonsense, old man. You can see——"

"I'd sure hate to tell any of them Army men out at the field some of the stories I know about China and the kind of men I used to know out there. Wouldn't cotton to them stories a bit, the Army wouldn't. But if I was to have a drink too many and get talkative-like——"

"Tell you what," Tallant suggested brusquely. "It's getting near sunset now, and my tent's chilly for evening visits. But drop around in the morning and we'll talk over old times. Is rum still your tipple?"

"Sure is. Kind of expensive now, you understand——"

"I'll lay some in. You can find the place easily—over by the oasis. And we . . . we might be able to talk about your prospecting, too."

Tallant's thin lips were set firm as he walked away.

The bartender opened a bottle of beer and plunked it on the damp-circled counter. "That'll be twenty cents," he said, then added as an afterthought, "Want a glass? Sometimes tourists do."

Tallant looked at the others sitting at the counter—the red-eyed and unshaven old man, the flight sergeant unhappily drinking a Coke—it was after Army hours for beer—the young man with the long, dirty trench coat and the pipe and the new-looking brown beard—and saw no glasses. "I guess I won't be a tourist," he decided.

This was the first time Tallant had had a chance to visit the Desert Sport Spot. It was as well to be seen around in a community. Otherwise people begin to wonder and say, "Who is that man out by the oasis? Why don't you ever see him any place?"

The Sport Spot was quiet that night. The four of them at

43

the counter, two Army boys shooting pool, and a half-dozen of the local men gathered about a round poker table, soberly and wordlessly cleaning a construction worker whose mind seemed more on his beer than on his cards.

"You just passing through?" the bartender asked sociably.

Tallant shook his head. "I'm moving in. When the Army turned me down for my lungs I decided I better do something about it. Heard so much about your climate here I thought I might as well try it."

"Sure thing," the bartender nodded. "You take up until they started this glider school, just about every other guy you meet in the desert is here for his health. Me, I had sinus, and look at me now. It's the air."

Tallant breathed the atmosphere of smoke and beer suds, but did not smile. "I'm looking forward to miracles."

"You'll get 'em. Whereabouts you staying?"

"Over that way a bit. The agent called it 'the old Carker place'."

Tallant felt the curious listening silence and frowned. The bartender had started to speak and then thought better of it. The young man with the beard looked at him oddly. The old man fixed him with red and watery eyes that had a faded glint of pity in them. For a moment Tallant felt a chill that had nothing to do with the night air of the desert.

The old man drank his beer in quick gulps, and frowned as though trying to formulate a sentence. At last he wiped beer from his bristly lips and said, "You wasn't aiming to stay in the adobe, was you?"

"No. It's pretty much gone to pieces. Easier to rig me up a little shack than try to make the adobe livable. Meanwhile, I've got a tent."

"That's all right, then, mebbe. But mind you don't go poking around that there adobe."

"I don't think I'm apt to. But why not? Want another beer?"

The old man shook his head reluctantly and slid from his stool to the ground. "No thanks. I don't rightly know as I——"

"Yes?"

"Nothing. Thanks all the same." He turned and shuffled to the door.

Tallant smiled. "But why should I stay clear of the adobe?" he called after him.

The old man mumbled.

44

"What?"

"They bite," said the old man, and went out shivering into the night.

The bartender was back at his post. "I'm glad he didn't take that beer you offered him," he said. "Along about this time in the evening I have to stop serving him. For once he had the sense to quit."

Tallant pushed his own empty bottle forward. "I hope I didn't frighten him away?"

"Frighten? Well, mister, I think maybe that's just what you did do. He didn't want beer that sort of came, like you might say, from the old Carker place. Some of the old-timers here, they're funny that way."

Tallant grinned. "Is it haunted?"

"Not what you'd call haunted, no. No ghosts there that I ever heard of." He wiped the counter with a cloth, and seemed to wipe the subject away with it.

The flight sergeant pushed his Coke bottle away, hunted in his pocket for nickels, and went over to the pinball machine. The young man with the beard slid onto his vacant stool. "Hope old Jake didn't worry you," he said.

Tallant laughed. "I suppose every town has its deserted homestead with a grisly tradition. But this sounds a little different. No ghosts, and they bite. Do you know anything about it?"

"A little," the young man said seriously. "A little. Just enough to——"

Tallant was curious. "Have one on me and tell me about it."

The flight sergeant swore bitterly at the machine.

Beer gurgled through the beard. "You see," the young man began, "the desert's so big you can't be alone in it. Ever notice that? It's all empty and there's nothing in sight, but there's always something moving over there where you can't quite see it. It's something very dry and thin and brown, only when you look around it isn't there. Ever see it?"

"Optical fatigue——" Tallant began.

"Sure. I know. Every man to his own legend. There isn't a tribe of Indians hasn't got some way of accounting for it. You've heard of the Watchers? And the twentieth-century white man comes along, and it's optical fatigue. Only in the

45

nineteenth century things weren't quite the same, and there were the Carkers."

"You've got a special localized legend?"

"Call it that. You glimpse things out of the corner of your mind, same like you glimpse lean, dry things out of the corner of your eye. You encase 'em in solid circumstance and they're not so bad. That is known as the Growth of Legend. The Folk Mind in Action. You take the Carkers and the things you don't quite see and you put 'em together. And they bite."

Tallant wondered how long the beard had been absorbing beer. "And what were the Carkers?" he prompted politely.

"Ever hear of Sawney Bean? Scotland—reign of James First or maybe the Sixth, though I think Roughead's wrong on that for once. Or let's be more modern—ever hear of the Benders? Kansas in the 1870s? No? Ever hear of Procrustes? Or Polyphemus? Or Fee-fi-fo-fum?

"There are ogres, you know. They're not legend. They're fact, they are. The inn where nine guests left for every ten that arrived, the mountain cabin that sheltered travellers from the snow, sheltered them all winter till the melting spring uncovered their bones, the lonely stretches of road that so many passengers travelled halfway—you find 'em everywhere. All over Europe and pretty much in this country too before communications became what they are. Profitable business. And it wasn't just the profit. The Benders made money, sure; but that wasn't why they killed all their victims as carefully as a kosher butcher. Sawney Bean got so he didn't give a damn about the profit; he just needed to lay in more meat for the winter.

"And think of the chances you'd have at an oasis."

"So these Carkers of yours were, as you call them, ogres?"

"Carkers, ogres—maybe they were Benders. The Benders were never seen alive, you know, after the townspeople found those curiously butchered bodies. There's a rumour they got this far west. And the time checks pretty well. There wasn't any town here in the eighties. Just a couple of Indian families, last of a dying tribe living on at the oasis. They vanished after the Carkers moved in. That's not so surprising. The white race is a sort of super-ogre, anyway. Nobody worried about them. But they used to worry about why so many travellers never got across this stretch of desert. The travellers used to stop over at the Carkers, you see, and somehow they often never got any farther. Their wagons'd be found maybe

46

fifteen miles beyond in the desert. Sometimes they found the bones, too, parched and white. Gnawed-looking, they said sometimes."

"And nobody ever did anything about these Carkers?"

"Oh, sure. We didn't have King James Sixth—only I still think it was First—to ride up on a great white horse for a gesture, but twice Army detachments came here and wiped them all out."

"Twice? One wiping-out would do for most families," Tallant smiled.

"Uh-huh. That was no slip. They wiped out the Carkers twice because you see once didn't do any good. They wiped 'em out and still travellers vanished and still there were gnawed bones. So they wiped 'em out again. After that they gave up, and people detoured the oasis. It made a longer, harder trip, but after all——"

Tallant laughed. "You mean these Carkers were immortal?"

"I don't know about immortal. They somehow just didn't die very easy. Maybe, if they were the Benders—and I sort of like to think they were—they learned a little more about what they were doing out here on the desert. Maybe they put together what the Indians knew and what they knew, and it worked. Maybe whatever they made their sacrifices to, understood them better out here than in Kansas."

"And what's become of them—aside from seeing them out of the corner of the eye?"

"There's forty years between the last of the Carker history and this new settlement at the oasis. And people won't talk much about what they learned here in the first year or so. Only that they stay away from that old Carker adobe. They tell some stories—The priest says he was sitting in the confessional one hot Saturday afternoon and thought he heard a penitent come in. He waited a long time and finally lifted the gauze to see was anybody there. Something was there, and it bit. He's got three fingers on his right hand now, which looks funny as hell when he gives a benediction."

Tallant pushed their two bottles toward the bartender. "That yarn, my young friend, has earned another beer. How about it, bartender? Is he always cheerful like this, or is this just something he's improvised for my benefit?"

The bartender set out the fresh bottles with great solemnity. "Me, I wouldn't've told you all that myself, but then

47

he's a stranger, too, and maybe don't feel the same way we do here. For him it's just a story."

"It's more comfortable that way," said the young man with the beard, and took a firm hold on his beer bottle.

"But as long as you've heard that much," said the bartender, "you might as well—It was last winter, and we had that cold spell. You heard funny stories that winter. Wolves coming into prospectors' cabins just to warm up. Well, business wasn't so good. We don't have a licence for hard liquor and the boys don't drink much beer when it's that cold. But they used to come in anyway because we've got that big oil burner.

"So one night there's a bunch of 'em in here—old Jake was here, that you was talking to, and his dog Jigger—and I think I hear somebody else come in. The door creaks a little. But I don't see anybody and the poker game's going and we're talking just like we're talking now, and all of a sudden I hear a kind of noise like *crack!* over there in that corner behind the jukebox near the burner.

"I go over to see what goes and it gets away before I can see it very good. But it was little and thin and it didn't have no clothes on. It must've been damned cold that winter."

"And what was the cracking noise?" Tallant asked dutifully.

"That? That was a bone. It must've strangled Jigger without any noise. He was a little dog. It ate most of the flesh, and if it hadn't cracked the bone for the marrow it could've finished. You can still see the spots over there. The blood never did come out."

There had been silence all through the story. Now suddenly all hell broke loose. The flight sergeant let out a splendid yell and began pointing excitedly at the pinball machine and yelling for his pay-off. The construction worker dramatically deserted the poker game, knocking his chair over in the process, and announced lugubriously that these guys here had their own rules, see?

Any atmosphere of Carker-inspired horror was dissipated. Tallant whistled as he walked over to put a nickel in the jukebox. He glanced casually at the floor. Yes, there was a stain, for what that was worth.

He smiled cheerfully and felt rather grateful to the Carkers. They were going to solve his blackmail problem very neatly.

Tallant dreamed of power that night. It was a common

dream with him. He was ruler of the new American Corporate State that should follow the war; and he said to this man "Come!" and he came, and to that man "Go!" and he went, and to his servants "Do this!" and they did it.

Then the young man with the beard was standing before him, and the dirty trench coat was like the robes of an ancient prophet. And the young man said, "You see yourself riding high, don't you? Riding the crest of the wave—the Wave of the Future, you call it. But there's a deep, dark undertow that you don't see, and that's a part of the Past. And the Present and even the Future. There is evil in mankind that is blacker even than your evil, and infinitely more ancient."

And there was something in the shadows behind the young man, something little and lean and brown.

Tallant's dream did not disturb him the following morning. Nor did the thought of the approaching interview with Morgan. He fried his bacon and eggs and devoured them cheerfully. The wind had died down for a change, and the sun was warm enough so that he could strip to the waist while he cleared land for his shack. His machete glinted brilliantly as it swung through the air and struck at the roots of the brush.

Morgan's full face was red and sweating when he arrived.

"It's cool over there in the shade of the adobe," Tallant suggested. "We'll be more comfortable." And in the comfortable shade of the adobe he swung the machete once and clove Morgan's full red sweating face in two.

It was so simple. It took less effort than uprooting a clump of sage. And it was so safe. Morgan lived in a cabin way to hell-and-gone and was often away on prospecting trips. No one would notice his absence for months, if then. No one had any reason to connect him with Tallant. And no one in Oasis would hunt for him in the Carker-haunted adobe.

The body was heavy, and the blood dripped warm on Tallant's bare skin. With relief he dumped what had been Morgan on the floor of the adobe. There were no boards, no flooring. Just earth. Hard, but not too hard to dig a grave in. And no one was likely to come poking around in this taboo territory to notice the grave. Let a year or so go by, and the grave and the bones it contained would be attributed to the Carkers.

The corner of Tallant's eye bothered him again. Deliberately he looked about the interior of the adobe.

49

The little furniture was crude and heavy, with no attempt to smooth down the strokes of the axe. It was held together with wooden pegs or half-rotted thongs. There were age-old cinders in the fireplace, and the dusty shards of a cooking jar among them.

And there was a deeply hollowed stone, covered with stains that might have been rust, if stone rusted. Behind it was a tiny figure, clumsily fashioned of clay and sticks. It was something like a man and something like a lizard, and something like the things that flit across the corner of the eye.

Curious now, Tallant peered about further. He penetrated to the corner that the one unglassed window lighted but dimly. And there he let out a little choking gasp. For a moment he was rigid with horror. Then he smiled and all but laughed aloud.

This explained everything. Some curious individual had seen this, and from his account burgeoned the whole legend. The Carkers had indeed learned something from the Indians, but that secret was the art of embalming.

It was a perfect mummy. Either the Indian art had shrunk bodies, or this was that of a ten-year-old boy. There was no flesh. Only skin and bone and taut dry stretches of tendon between. The eyelids were closed; the sockets looked hollow under them. The nose was sunken and almost lost. The scant lips were tightly curled back from the long and very white teeth, which stood forth all the more brilliantly against the deep-brown skin.

It was a curious little trove, this mummy. Tallant was already calculating the chances for raising a decent sum of money from an interested anthropologist—murder can produce such delightfully profitable chance by-products—when he noticed the infinitesimal rise and fall of the chest.

The Carker was not dead. It was sleeping.

Tallant did not dare stop to think beyond the instant. This was not time to pause to consider if such things were possible in a well-ordered world. It was no time to reflect on the disposal of the body of Morgan. It was a time to snatch up your machete and get out of there.

But in the doorway he halted. There coming across the desert, heading for the adobe, clearly seen this time, was another—a female.

He made an involuntary gesture of indecision. The blade of the machete clanged ringingly against the adobe wall.

He heard the dry shuffling of a roused sleeper behind him.

He turned fully now, the machete raised. Dispose of this nearer one first, then face the female. There was no room even for terror in his thoughts, only for action.

The lean brown shape darted at him avidly. He moved lightly away and stood poised for its second charge. It shot forward again. He took one step back, machete-arm raised, and fell headlong over the corpse of Morgan. Before he could rise the thin thing was upon him. Its sharp teeth had met through the palm of his left hand.

The machete moved swiftly. The thin, dry body fell headless to the floor. There was no blood.

The grip of the teeth did not relax. Pain coursed up Tallant's left arm—a sharper, more bitter pain than you would expect from the bite. Almost as though venom——

He dropped the machete, and his strong white hand plucked and twisted at the dry brown lips. The teeth stayed clenched, unrelaxing. He sat bracing his back against the wall and gripped the head between his knees. He pulled. His flesh ripped, and blood formed dusty clots on the dirt floor. But the bite was firm.

His world had become reduced now to that hand and that head. Nothing outside mattered. He must free himself. He raised his aching arm to his face, and with his own teeth he tore at that unrelenting grip. The dry flesh crumbled away in the desert dust, but the teeth were locked fast. He tore his lip against their white keenness, and tasted in his mouth the sweetness of blood and something else.

He staggered to his feet again. He knew what he must do. Later he could use cautery, a tourniquet, see a doctor with a story about a Gila monster—their heads grip, too, don't they?—but he knew what he must do now.

He raised the machete and struck again.

His white hand lay on the brown floor, gripped by the white teeth in the brown face. He propped himself against the adobe wall, momentarily unable to move. His open wrist hung over the deeply hollowed stone. His blood and his strength and his life poured out before the little figure of sticks and clay.

The female stood in the doorway now, the sun bright on her thin brownness. She did not move. He knew that she was waiting for the hollow stone to fill.

THE ENEMY

CHARLOTTE ARMSTRONG

THEY SAT late at the lunch table and afterwards moved through the dim, cool, high-ceilinged rooms to the judge's library, where, in their quiet talk, the old man's past and the young man's future seemed to telescope and touch. But at twenty minutes after three, on that hot, bright, June Saturday afternoon, the present tense erupted. Out in the quiet street arose the sound of trouble.

Judge Kittinger adjusted his pince-nez, rose, and led the way to his old-fashioned veranda from which they could overlook the tree-roofed intersection of Greenwood Lane and Hannibal Street. Near the steps to the corner house, opposite, there was a surging knot of children and one man. Now, from the house on the judge's left, a woman in a blue house dress ran diagonally toward the excitement. And a police car slipped up Hannibal Street, gliding to the kerb. One tall officer plunged into the group and threw restraining arms around a screaming boy.

Mike Russell, saying to his host, "Excuse me, sir," went rapidly across the street. Trouble's centre was the boy, ten or eleven years old, a tow-headed boy with tawny-lashed blue eyes, a straight nose, a fine brow. He was beside himself, writhing in the policeman's grasp. The woman in the blue dress was yammering at him. "Freddy! Freddy! Freddy!" Her voice simply did not reach his ears.

"You ole stinker! You rotten ole stinker! You ole nut!" All the boy's heart was in the epithets.

"Now, listen. . . ." The cop shook the boy who, helpless in those powerful hands, yet blazed. His fury had stung to crimson the face of the grown man at whom it was directed.

This man, who stood with his back to the house as one besieged, was plump, half-bald, with eyes much magnified by glasses. "Attacked me!" he cried in a high whine. "Rang my bell and absolutely leaped on me!"

52

Out of the seven or eight small boys clustered around them came overlapping fragments of shrill sentences. It was clear only that they opposed the man. A small woman in a print dress, a man in shorts, whose bare chest was winter-white, stood a little apart, hesitant and distressed. Up on the veranda of the house the screen door was half open, and a woman seated in a wheel-chair peered forth anxiously.

On the green grass, in the shade perhaps thirty feet away, there lay in death a small brown-and-white dog.

The judge's luncheon guest observed all this. When the judge drew near, there was a lessening of the noise. Judge Kittinger said, "This is Freddy Titus, isn't it? Mr Matlin? What's happened?"

The man's head jerked. "I," he said, "did nothing to the dog. Why would I trouble to hurt the boy's dog? I try—you know this, Judge—I try to live in peace here. But these kids are terrors! They've made this block a perfect hell for me and my family." The man's voice shook. "My wife, who is not strong . . . My step-daughter, who is a cripple . . . These kids are no better than a slum gang. They are vicious. That boy rang my bell and *attacked* . . . ! I'll have him up for assault! I . . . "

The judge's face was old ivory and he was aloof behind it.

On the porch a girl pushed past the woman in the chair, a girl who walked with a lurching gait.

Mike Russell asked, quietly, "Why do the boys say it was you, Mr Matlin, who hurt the dog?"

The kids chorused. "He's an ole mean . . ." "He's a nut . . ." "Just because . . ." ". . . took Clive's hat and . . ." ". . . chases us . . ." ". . . tries to put everything on us." ". . . told my mother lies . . ." ". . . just because . . ."

He is our enemy, they were saying; *he is our enemy*.

"They . . ." began Matlin, his throat thick with anger.

"Hold it a minute." The second cop, the thin one, walked toward were the dog was lying.

"Somebody," said Mike Russell in a low voice, "must do something for the boy."

The judge looked down at the frantic child. He said, gently, "I am as sorry as I can be, Freddy." But in his old heart there was too much known, and too many little dogs he remembered that had already died, and even if he were as sorry as he could be, he couldn't be sorry enough. The boy's eyes turned, rejected, returned. To the enemy.

Russell moved near the woman in blue, who pertained to this boy somehow. "His mother?"

"His folks are away. I'm there to take care of him," she snapped, as if she felt herself put upon by a crisis she had not contracted to face.

"Can they be reached?"

"No," she said decisively.

The young man put his stranger's hand on the boy's rigid little shoulder. But he too was rejected. Freddy's eyes, brilliant with hatred, clung to the enemy. Hatred doesn't cry.

"Listen," said the tall cop, "if you could hang onto him for a minute——"

"Not I," said Russell.

The thin cop came back. "Looks like the dog got poison. When was he found?"

"Just now," the kids said.

"Where? There?"

"Up Hannibal Street. Right on the edge of ole Matlin's back lot."

"Edge of *my* lot!" Matlin's colour freshened again. "On the sidewalk, why don't you say? Why don't you tell the truth?"

"We are! *We* don't tell lies!"

"Quiet, you guys," the cop said. "Pipe down, now."

"Heaven's my witness, I wasn't here!" cried Matlin. "I played nine holes of golf today. I didn't get home until . . . May?" he called over his shoulder. "What time did I come in?"

The girl on the porch came slowly down, moving awkwardly on her uneven legs. She was in her twenties, no child. Nor was she a woman. She said in a blurting manner, "About three o'clock, Daddy Earl. But the dog was dead."

"What's that, miss?"

"This is my step-daughter."

"The dog was dead," the girl said, "before he came home. I saw it from upstairs before three o'clock. Lying by the sidewalk."

"You drove in from Hannibal Street, Mr Matlin? Looks like you'd have seen the dog."

Matlin said with nervous thoughtfulness, "I don't know. My mind . . . Yes, I . . ."

"He's telling a lie!"

"Freddy!"

54

"Listen to that," said May Matlin, "will you?"

"She's a liar, too!"

The cop shook Freddy. Mr Matlin made a sound of helpless exasperation. He said to the girl, "Go keep your mother inside, May." He raised his arm as if to wave. "It's all right, honey," he called to the woman in the chair, with a false cheeriness that grated on the ear. "There's nothing to worry about now."

Freddy's jaw shifted and young Russell's watching eyes winced. The girl began to lurch back to the house.

"It was my wife who put in the call," Matlin said. "After all, they were on me like a pack of wolves. Now, I—I *understand* that the boy's upset. But all the same, he cannot . . . He must learn . . . I will not have . . . I have enough to contend with, without this malice, this unwarranted antagonism, this persecution."

Freddy's eyes were unwinking.

"It has got to stop!" said Matlin almost hysterically.

"Yes," murmured Mike Russell, "I should think so." Judge Kittinger's white head, nodding, agreed.

"We've heard about quite a few dog-poisoning cases over the line in Redfern," said the thin cop with professional calm. "None here."

The man in the shorts hitched them up, looking shocked. "Who'd do a thing like that?"

A boy said, boldly, "Ole Matlin would." He had an underslung jaw and wore spectacles on his snug nose. "I'm Phil Bourchard," he said to the cop. He had courage.

"We jist know," said another. "I'm Ernie Allen." Partisanship radiated from his whole thin body. "Ole Matlin doesn't want anybody on his ole property."

"Sure." "He doesn't want anybody on his ole property." "It was ole Matlin."

"It was. It was," said Freddy Titus.

"Freddy," said the housekeeper in blue, "now, you better be still. I'll tell your dad." It was a meaningless fumble for control. The boy didn't even hear it.

Judge Kittinger tried, patiently. "You can't accuse without cause, Freddy."

"Bones didn't hurt his ole property. Bones wouldn't hurt anything. Ole Matlin did it."

"You lying little devil!"

"*He's* a liar!"

55

The cop gave Freddy another shake. "You kids found him, eh?"

"We were up at Bourchard's and were going down to the Titus house."

"And he was dead," said Freddy.

"*I* know nothing about it," said Matlin icily. "Nothing at all."

The cop, standing between, said wearily. "Any of you people see what coulda happened?"

"I was sitting in my backyard," said the man in shorts. "I'm Daugherty, next door, up Hannibal Street. Didn't see a thing."

The small woman in a print dress spoke up. "I am Mrs Page. I live across on the corner, Officer. I believe I did see a strange man go into Mr Matlin's driveway this morning."

"When was this, ma'am?"

"About eleven o'clock. He was poorly dressed. He walked up the drive and around the garage."

"Didn't go on to the house?"

"No. He was only there a minute. I believe he was carrying something. He was rather furtive. And very poorly dressed, almost like a tramp."

There was a certain relaxing among the elders. "Ah the tramp," said Mike Russell. "The good old reliable tramp. Are you sure, Mrs Page? It's very unlikely."

But she bristled. "Do you think I am lying?"

Russell's lips parted, but he felt the judge's hand on his arm. "This is my guest, Mr Russell . . . Freddy." The judge's voice was gentle. "Let him go, Officer. I'm sure he understands now. Mr Matlin was not even at home, Freddy. It's possible that this—er—stranger . . . Or it may have been an accident."

"Wasn't a tramp. Wasn't an accident."

"You can't know that, boy," said the judge, somewhat sharply. Freddy said nothing. As the officer slowly released his grasp, the boy took a free step backwards, and the other boys surged to surround him. There stood the enemy, the monster, who killed and lied, and the grown-ups with their reasonable doubts were on the monster's side. But the boys knew what Freddy knew. They stood together.

"Somebody," murmured the judge's guest, "somebody's got to help the boy." And the judge sighed.

The cops went up Hannibal Street toward Matlin's back

lot, with Mr Daugherty. Matlin lingered at the corner talking to Mrs Page. In the front window of Matlin's house the curtain fell across the glass.

Mike Russell sidled up to the housekeeper. "Any uncles or aunts here in town? A grandmother?"

"No," she said, shortly.

"Brothers or sisters, Mrs . . . ?"

"Miz Somers. No, he's the only one. Only reason they didn't take him along was it's the last week of school and he didn't want to miss."

Mike Russell's brown eyes suggested the soft texture of velvet, and they were deeply distressed. She slid away from their appeal. "He'll just have to take it, I guess, like everybody else," Mrs Somers said. "These things happen."

He was listening intently. "Don't you care for dogs?"

"I don't mind a dog," she said. She arched her neck. She was going to call to the boy.

"Wait. Tell me, does the family go to church? Is there a pastor or a priest who knows the boy?"

"They don't go, far as I ever saw." She looked at him as if he were an eccentric.

"Then school. He has a teacher. What grade?"

"Sixth grade," she said. "Miss Dana. Oh, he'll be okay." Her voice grew loud, to reach the boy and hint to him. "He's a big boy."

Russell said, desperately, "Is there no way to telephone his parents?"

"They're on the road. They'll be in some time tomorrow. That's all I know." She was annoyed. "I'll take care of him. That's why I'm here." She raised her voice and this time it was arch and seductive. "Freddy, better come wash your face. I know where there's some chocolate cookies."

The velvet left the young man's eyes. Hard as buttons, they gazed for a moment at the woman. Then he whipped around and left her. He walked over to where the kids had drifted, near the little dead creature on the grass. He said softly, "Bones had his own doctor, Freddy? Tell me his name?" The boy's eyes flickered. "We must know what it was that he took. A doctor can tell. I think his own doctor would be best, don't you?"

The boy nodded, mumbled a name, an address. That Russell mastered the name and the numbers, asking for no repetition, was a sign of his concern. Besides, it was this

57

young man's quality—that he listened. "May I take him, Freddy? I have a car. We ought to have a blanket," he added softly, "a soft, clean blanket."

"I got one, Freddy. . . ." "My mother'd let me . . ."

"I can get one," Freddy said brusquely. They wheeled, almost in formation.

Mrs Somers frowned. "You must let them take a blanket," Russell warned her, and his eyes were cold.

"I will explain to Mrs Titus," said the judge quickly.

"Quite a fuss," she said, and tossed her head and crossed the road.

Russell gave the judge a quick, nervous grin. He walked to the returning cops. "You'll want to run tests, I suppose? Can the dog's own vet do it?"

"Certainly. Humane officer will have to be in charge. But that's what the vet'll want."

"I'll take the dog, then. Any traces up there?"

"Not a thing."

"Will you explain to the boy that you are investigating?"

"Well, you know how these things go." The cop's feet shuffled. "Humane officer does what he can. Probably Monday, after we identify the poison, he'll check the drug stores. Usually, if it *is* a cranky neighbour, he has already put in a complaint about the dog. This Matlin says he never did. The humane officer will get on it Monday. He's out of town today. The devil of these cases, we can't prove a thing, usually. You get an idea who it was, maybe you can scare him. It's a misdemeanour all right. Never heard of a conviction myself."

"But will you explain to the boy . . . ?" Russell stopped, chewed his lip, and the judge sighed.

"Yeah, it's tough on a kid," the cop said.

When the judge's guest came back it was nearly five o'clock. He said, "I came to say goodbye, sir, and to thank you for the . . ." But his mind wasn't on the sentence and he lost it and looked up.

The judge's eyes were affectionate. "Worried?"

"Judge, sir," the young man said, "*must* they feed him? Where, sir, in this classy neighbourhood is there an understanding woman's heart? I herded them to that Mrs Allen. But she winced, sir, and she diverted them. She didn't want to deal with tragedy, didn't want to think about it. She offered cakes and Cokes and games."

"But my dear boy . . ."

58

"What do they teach the kids these days, judge? To turn away? Put something in your stomach. Take a drink. Play a game. Don't weep for your dead. Just skip it, think about something else."

"I'm afraid the boy's alone," the judge said gently, "but it's only for the night." His voice was melodious. "Can't be sheltered from grief when it comes. None of us can."

"Excuse me, sir, but I wish he *would* grieve. I wish he would bawl his heart out. Wash out that black hate. I ought to go home. None of my concern. It's a woman's job." He moved and his hand went toward the phone. "He has a teacher. I can't help feeling concerned, sir. May I try?"

The judge said, "Of course, Mike," and he put his brittle old bones into a chair.

Mike Russell pried the number out of the Board of Education. "Miss Lillian Dana? My name is Russell. You know a boy named Freddy Titus?"

"Oh, yes. He's in my class." The voice was pleasing.

"Miss Dana, there is trouble. You know Judge Kittinger's house? Could you come there?"

"What is the trouble?"

"Freddy's little dog is dead of poison. I'm afraid Freddy is in a bad state. There is no one to help him. His folks are away. The woman taking care of him," Mike's careful explanatory sentences burst into indignation, "has no more sympathetic imagination than a broken clothes pole." He heard a little gasp. "I'd like to help him, Miss Dana, but I'm a man and a stranger, and the judge . . ." He paused.

". . . is old," said the judge in his chair.

"I'm terribly sorry," the voice on the phone said slowly. "Freddy's a wonderful boy."

"You are his friend?"

"Yes, we are friends."

"Then could you come? You see, we've got to get a terrible idea out of his head. He thinks a man across the street poisoned his dog on purpose. Miss Dana, *he has no doubt!* And he doesn't cry." She gasped again. "Greenwood Lane," he said, "and Hannibal Street—the south-east corner."

She said, "I'll come. I have a car. I'll come as soon as I can."

Russell turned and caught the judge biting his lips. "Am I making too much of this, sir?" he inquired humbly.

"I don't like the boy's stubborn conviction." The judge's

59

voice was dry and clear. "Any more than you do. I agree that he must be brought to understand. But . . ." the old man shifted in the chair. "Of course, the man, Matlin, is a fool, Mike. There is something solemn and silly about him that makes him fair game. He's unfortunate. He married a widow with a crippled child, and no sooner were they married than *she* collapsed. And he's not well off. He's encumbered with that enormous house."

"What does he do, sir?"

"He's a photographer. Oh, he struggles, tries his best, and all that; but with such tension, Mike. That poor misshapen girl over there tries to keep the house; devoted to her mother. Matlin works hard, is devoted, too. And yet the sum comes out in petty strife, nerves, quarrels, uproar. And certainly it cannot be necessary to feud with children."

"The kids have done their share of that, I'll bet," mused Mike. "The kids are delighted—a neighbourhood ogre, to add the fine flavour of menace. A focus for mischief. An enemy."

"True enough." The judged sighed.

"So the myth is made. No rumour about ole Matlin loses anything in the telling. I can see it's been built up. You don't knock it down in a day."

"No," said the judge uneasily. He got up from the chair.

The young man rubbed his dark head. "I don't like it, sir. We don't know what's in the kids' minds, or who their heroes are. There is only the gang. What do you suppose it advises?"

"What could it advise, after all?" said the judge crisply. "This isn't the slums, whatever Matlin says." He went nervously to the window. He fiddled with the shade pull. He said, suddenly, "From my little summerhouse in the backyard you can overhear the gang. They congregate under that oak. Go and eavesdrop, Mike."

The young man snapped to attention. "Yes, sir."

"I . . . think we had better know," said the judge, a trifle sheepishly.

The kids sat under the oak, in a grassy hollow. Freddy was the core. His face was tight. His eyes never left off watching the house of the enemy. The others watched him, or hung their heads, or watched their own brown hands play with the grass.

They were not chattering. There hung about them a heavy, sullen silence, heavy with a sense of tragedy, sullen with a

60

sense of wrong, and from time to time one voice or another would fling out a pronouncement which would sink into the silence, thickening its ugliness.

The judge looked up from his paper. "Could you . . . ?"

"I could hear," said Mike in a quiet voice. "They are condemning the law, sir. They call it corrupt. They are quite certain that Matlin killed the dog. They see themselves as Robin Hoods, vigilantes defending the weak, the wronged, the dog. They think they are discussing justice. They are waiting for dark. They speak of weapons, sir—the only ones they have. BB guns, after dark."

"Great heavens!"

"Don't worry. Nothing's going to happen."

"What are you going to do?"

"I'm going to stop it."

Mrs Somers was cooking supper when he tapped on the screen. "Oh, it's you. What do you want?"

"I want your help, Mrs Somers. For Freddy."

"Freddy," she interrupted loudly, with her nose high, "is going to have his supper and go to bed his regular time, and that's all about Freddy. Now, what did you want?"

He said, "I want you to let me take the boy to my apartment for the night."

"I couldn't do that!" She was scandalized.

"The judge will vouch . . ."

"Now, see here, Mr what's your name—Russell. This isn't my house and Freddy's not my boy. I'm responsible to Mr and Mrs Titus. You're a stranger to me. As far as I can see, Freddy is no business of yours whatsoever."

"Which is his room?" asked Mike sharply.

"Why do you want to know?" She was hostile and suspicious.

"Where does he keep his BB gun?"

She was startled to an answer. "In the shed out back. Why?"

He told her.

"Kid's talk," she scoffed. "You don't know much about kids, do you, young man? Freddy will go to sleep. First thing he'll know, it's morning. That's about the size of it."

"You may be right. I hope so."

Mrs Somers slapped potatoes into the pan. Her lips quivered indignantly. She felt annoyed because she was a little shaken. The strange young man really had hoped so.

Russell scanned the street, went across to Matlin's house. The man himself answered the bell. The air in this house was stale, and bore the faint smell of old grease. There was over everything an atmosphere of struggle and despair. Many things ought to have been repaired and had not been repaired. The place was too big. There wasn't enough money, or strength. It was too much.

Mrs Matlin could not walk. Otherwise, one saw, she struggled and did the best she could. She had a lost look, as if some anxiety, ever present, took about nine-tenths of her attention. May Matlin limped in and sat down, lumpishly.

Russell began earnestly, "Mr Matlin, I don't know how this situation between you and the boys began. I can guess that the kids are much to blame. I imagine they enjoy it." He smiled. He wanted to be sympathetic toward this man.

"Of course they enjoy it." Matlin looked triumphant.

"They call me the Witch," the girl said. "Pretend they're scared of me. The devils. I'm scared of them."

Matlin flicked a nervous eye at the woman in the wheel-chair. "The truth is, Mr Russell," he said in his high whine, "they're vicious."

"It's too bad," said his wife in a low voice. "I think it's dangerous."

"Mama, you mustn't worry," said the girl in an entirely new tone. "I won't let them hurt you. Nobody will hurt you."

"Be quiet, May," said Matlin. "You'll upset her. Of course nobody will hurt her."

"Yes, it is dangerous, Mrs Matlin," said Russell quietly. "That's why I came over."

Matlin goggled. "What? What's this?"

"Could I possibly persuade you, sir, to spend the night away from this neighbourhood—and depart noisily?"

"No," said Matlin, raring up, his ego bristling, "no, you cannot! I will under no circumstance be driven away from my own home." His voice rose. "Furthermore, I certainly will not leave my wife and stepdaughter."

"We could manage, dear," said Mrs Matlin anxiously.

Russell told them about the talk under the oak, the BB gun.

"Devils," said May Matlin, "absolutely . . ."

"Oh, Earl," trembled Mrs Matlin, "maybe we had all better go away."

Matlin, red-necked, furious, said, "We own this property.

62

We pay our taxes. We have our rights. Let them! Let them try something like that! Then, I think, the law would have something to say. This is outrageous! I did not harm that animal. Therefore, I defy . . ." He looked solemn and silly, as the judge had said, with his face crimson, his weak eyes rolling.

Russell rose. "I thought I ought to make the suggestion," he said mildly, "because it would be the safest thing to do. But don't worry, Mrs Matlin, because I——"

"A BB gun can blind," she said tensely.

"Or even worse," Mike agreed. "But I am thinking of the——"

"Just a minute," Matlin roared. "You can't come in here and terrify my wife! She is not strong. You have no right." He drew himself up with his feet at a right angle, his pudgy arm extended, his plump jowls quivering. "Get out," he cried. He looked ridiculous.

Whether the young man and the bewildered woman in the chair might have understood each other was not to be known. Russell, of course, got out. May Matlin hobbled to the door and as Russell went through it she said, "Well, you warned us, anyhow."

Russell plodded across the pavement again. Long enchanting shadows from the lowering sun struck aslant through the golden air and all the old houses were gilded and softened in their green setting. He moved toward the big oak. He hunkered down. The sun struck its golden shafts deep under the boughs. "How's it going?" he asked.

Freddy Titus looked frozen and still. "Okay," said Phil Bourchard with elaborate ease. Light on his owlish glasses hid the eyes.

Mike opened his lips, hesitated. Supper-time struck on the neighbourhood clock. Calls, like chimes, were sounding.

" 'S my Mom," said Ernie Allen. "See you after."

"See you after, Freddy."

"Okay."

"Okay."

Mrs Somers' hoot had chimed with the rest and now Freddy got up, stiffly.

"Okay," said Mike Russell. The useful syllables that take any meaning at all in American mouths asked, "Are you feeling less bitter, boy? Are you any easier?"

"Okay," said Freddy. The same syllables shut the man out.

Mike opened his lips. Closed them. Freddy went across the lawn to his kitchen door. There was a brown crockery bowl on the back stoop. His sneaker, rigid on the ankle, stepped over it. Mike Russell watched, and then, with a movement of his arms, almost as if he would wring his hands, he went up the judge's steps.

"Well?" The judge opened his door. "Did you talk to the boy?"

Russell didn't answer. He sat down.

The judge stood over him. "The boy . . . The enormity of this whole idea *must* be explained to him."

"I can't explain," Mike said. "I open my mouth. Nothing comes out."

"Perhaps *I* had better . . ."

"What are you going to say, sir?"

"Why, give him the facts!"

"The facts are . . . the dog is dead."

"There are no facts that point to Matlin."

"There are no facts that point to a tramp, either. That's too sloppy, sir."

"What are you driving at?"

"Judge, the boy is more rightfully suspicious than we are."

"Nonsense," said the judge. "The girl saw the dog's body before Matlin came . . ."

"There is no alibi for poison," Mike said sadly.

"Are you saying the man is a liar?"

"Liars," sighed Mike. "Truth and lies. How are those kids going to understand, sir? To that Mrs Page, to the lot of them, truth is only a subjective intention. 'I am no liar,' sez she, sez he. 'I *intend* to be truthful. So do not insult me.' Lord, when will we begin? It's what we were talking about at lunch, sir. What you and I believe. What the race has been told and told in such agony, in a million years of bitter lesson. *Error,* we were saying. Error is the enemy."

He flung out of the chair. "We know that to tell the truth is not merely a good intention. It's a damned difficult thing to do. It's a skill, to be practised. It's a technique. It's an effort. It takes brains. It takes watching. It takes humility and self-examination. It's a science and an art. Why don't we tell the *kids* these things? Why is everyone locked up in anger, shouting liar at the other side? Why don't they automatically know how easy it is to be, not wicked, but mistaken? Why is there this notion of violence? Because Freddy doesn't think to himself, 'Wait a minute. I might be wrong.' The habit isn't there. Instead, there are the heroes—the big-muscled, noble-hearted, gun-toting heroes, blind in a righteousness totally arranged by the author. Excuse me, sir."

"All that may be," said the judge grimly, "and I agree. But the police know the lesson. They——"

"They don't care."

"What?"

"Don't care enough, sir. None of us cares enough—about the dog."

"I see," said the judge. "Yes, I see. We haven't the least idea what happened to the dog." He touched his pince-nez.

Mike rubbed his head wearily. "Don't know what to do except sit under his window the night through. Hardly seems good enough."

The judge said, simply, "Why don't you find out what happened to the dog?"

The young man's face changed. "What we need, sir," said Mike slowly, "is to teach Freddy how to ask for it. Just to ask for it. Just to want it." The old man and the young man looked at each other. Past and future telescoped. "*Now*," Mike said. "Before dark."

Supper-time, for the kids, was only twenty minutes long. When the girl in the brown dress with the bare blonde head got out of the shabby coupé, the gang was gathered again in its hollow under the oak. She went to them and sank down on the ground. "Ah, Freddy, was it Bones? Your dear little dog you wrote about in the essay?"

"Yes, Miss Dana." Freddy's voice was shrill and hostile. *I won't be touched!* it cried to her. So she said no more, but sat there on the ground, and presently she began to cry. There was contagion. The simplest thing in the world. First, one of the smaller ones whimpering Finally, Freddy Titus, bending over. Her arm guided his head, and then he lay weeping in her lap.

Russell, up in the summerhouse, closed his eyes and praised the Lord. In a little while he swung his legs over the railing and slid down the bank. "How do? I'm Mike Russell."

"I'm Lillian Dana." She was quick and intelligent, and her tears were real.

"Fellows," said Mike briskly, "you know what's got to be done, don't you. We've got to solve this case."

They turned their woeful faces.

He said, deliberately, "It's just the same as murder. It is a murder."

"Yeah," said Freddy and sat up, tears drying. "And it was ole Matlin."

"Then we have to prove it."

Miss Lillian Dana saw the boy's face lock. He didn't need to prove anything, the look proclaimed. He knew. She leaned over a little and said, "But we can't make an ugly mistake and put it on Bones's account. Bones was a fine dog. That would be a terrible monument." Freddy's eyes turned, startled.

"It's up to us," said Mike gratefully, "to go after the real facts, with real detective work. For Bones's sake."

"It's the least we can do for him," said Miss Dana, calmly and decisively.

Freddy's face lifted.

"Trouble is," Russell went on quickly, "people get things wrong. Sometimes they don't remember straight. They make mistakes."

"Ole Matlin tells lies," said Freddy.

"If he does," said Russell cheerfully, "then we've got to *prove* that he does. Now, I've figured out a plan, if Miss Dana will help us. You pick a couple of the fellows, Fred. Have to go to all the houses around and ask some questions. Better pick the smartest ones. To find out the truth is very hard," he challenged.

"And then?" said Miss Dana in a fluttery voice.

"Then they, and you, if you will . . ."

"Me?" She straightened. "I'm a school-teacher, Mr Russell. Won't the police . . . ?"

"Not before dark."

"What are *you* going to be doing?"

"Dirtier work."

She bit her lip. "It's nosy. It's . . . not done."

"No," he agreed. "You may lose your job."

She wasn't a bad-looking young woman. Her eyes were fine. Her brow was serious, but there was the ghost of a dimple in her cheek. Her hands moved. "Oh, well, I can always take up beauty culture or something. What are the questions?" She had a pad of paper and a pencil half out of her purse, and looked alert and efficient.

Now, as the gang huddled, there was a warm sense of

66

conspiracy growing. "Going to be the dickens of a job," Russell warned them. And he outlined some questions. "Now, don't let anybody fool you into taking a sloppy answer," he concluded. "Ask how they know. Get real evidence. But don't go to Matlin's—I'll go there."

"I'm not afraid of him." Freddy's nostrils flared.

"I think I stand a better chance of getting the answers," said Russell coolly. "Aren't we after the answers?"

Freddy swallowed. "And if it turns out . . . ?"

"It turns out the way it turns out," said Russell, rumpling the towhead. "Choose your henchmen. Tough, remember."

"Phil. Ernie." The kids who were left out wailed as the three small boys and their teacher, who wasn't a lot bigger, rose from the ground.

"It'll be tough Mr Russell," Miss Dana said grimly. "Whoever you are, thank you for getting me into this."

"I'm just a stranger," he said gently, looking down at her face. "But you are a friend and a teacher." Pain crossed her eyes. "You'll be teaching now, you know."

Her chin went up. "Okay, kids. I'll keep the paper and pencil. Freddy, wipe your face. Stick your shirt in, Phil. Now, let's organize. . . ."

It was nearly nine o'clock when the boys and the teacher, looking rather exhausted, came back to the judge's house. Russell, whose face was grave, reached for the papers in her hands.

"Just a minute," said Miss Dana. "Judge, we have some questions."

Ernie Allen bared all his heap of teeth and stepped forward. "Did you see Bones today?" he asked with the firm skill of repetition. The judge nodded. "How many times and when?"

"Once. Er—shortly before noon. He crossed my yard, going east."

The boys bent over the pad. Then Freddy's lips opened hard. "How do you know the time, Judge Kittinger?"

"Well," said the judge, "hm . . . let me think. I was looking out of the window for my company and just then he arrived."

"Five minutes past one, sir," Mike said.

Freddy flashed around. "What makes you sure?"

"I looked at my watch," said Russell. "I was taught to be exactly five minutes early when I'm asked to a meal." There

67

was a nodding among the boys, and Miss Dana wrote on the pad.

"Then I was mistaken," said the judge, thoughtfully. "It was shortly before one. Of course."

Phil Bourchard took over. "Did you see anyone go into Matlin's driveway or back lot?"

"I did not."

"Were you out of doors or did you look up that way?"

"Yes, I . . . When we left the table. Mike?"

"At two-thirty, sir."

"How do you know that time for sure?" asked Freddy Titus.

"Because I wondered if I could politely stay a little longer." Russell's eyes congratulated Miss Lillian Dana. She had made them a team, and on it, Freddy was the How-do-you-know-for-sure Department.

"Can you swear," continued Phil to the judge, "there was nobody at all around Matlin's back lot then?"

"As far as my view goes," answered the judge cautiously.

Freddy said promptly, "He couldn't see much. Too many trees. We can't count that."

They looked at Miss Dana and she marked on the pad. "Thank you. Now you have a cook, sir. We must question her."

"This way," said the judge, rising and bowing.

Russell looked after them and his eyes were velvet again. He met the judge's twinkle. Then he sat down and ran an eye quickly over some of the sheets of paper, passing each on to his host.

Startled, he looked up. Lillian Dana, standing in the door, was watching his face.

"Do you think, Mike . . . ?"

A paper drooped in the judge's hand.

"We can't stop," she challenged.

Russell nodded, and turned to the judge. "May need some high brass, sir." The judge rose. "And tell me, sir, where Matlin plays golf. And the telephone number of the Salvage League. No, Miss Dana, we can't stop. We'll take it where it turns."

"We must," she said.

It was nearly ten when the neighbours began to come in. The judge greeted them soberly. The Chief of Police arrived. Mrs Somers, looking grim and uprooted in a crêpe dress,

68

came. Mr Matlin, Mrs Page, Mr and Mrs Daugherty, a Mr and Mrs Baker, and Diane Bourchard, who was sixteen. They looked curiously at the tight little group, the boys and their blonde teacher.

Last of all to arrive was young Mr Russell, who slipped in from the dark veranda, accepted the judge's nod, and called the meeting to order.

"We have been investigating the strange death of a dog," he began. "Chief Anderson, while we know your department would have done so in good time, we also know you are busy, and some of us"—he glanced at the dark window-pane—"couldn't wait. Will you help us now?"

The chief said, genially, "That's why I'm here, I guess." It was the judge and his stature that gave this meeting any standing. Naïve, young, a little absurd it might have seemed had not the old man sat so quietly attentive among them.

"Thank you, sir. Now, all we want to know is what happened to the dog." Russell looked about him. "First, let us demolish the tramp." Mrs Page's feathers ruffled. Russell smiled at her. "Mrs Page saw a man go down Matlin's drive this morning. The Salvage League sent a truck, to pick up rags and papers, which at ten-forty-two was parked in front of the Daughertys. The man, who seemed poorly dressed in his working clothes, went to the tool-room behind Matlin's garage, as he had been instructed to. He picked up a bundle and returned to his truck. Mrs Page," purred Mike to her scarlet face, "the man was there. It was only your opinion about him that proves to have been, not a lie, but an error."

He turned his head. "Now, we have tried to trace the dog's day and we have done remarkably well, too." As he traced it for them, some faces began to wear at least the ghost of a smile, seeing the little dog frisking through the neighbourhood. "Just before one," Mike went on, "Bones ran across the judge's yard to the Allens' where the kids were playing ball. Up to this time no one saw Bones *above* Greenwood Lane or *up* Hannibal Street. But Miss Diane Bourchard, recovering from a sore throat, was not in school today. After lunch, she sat on her porch directly across from Mr Matlin's back lot. She was waiting for school to be out, when she expected her friends to come by.

"She saw, not Bones, but Corky, an animal belonging to Mr Daugherty, playing in Matlin's lot at about two o'clock.

I want your opinion. If poisoned bait had been lying there at two, would Corky have found it?"

"Seems so," said Daugherty. "Thank God Corky didn't." He bit his tongue. "Corky's a show dog," he blundered.

"But Bones," said Russell gently, "was more like a friend. That's why we care, of course."

"It's a damned shame!" Daugherty looked around angrily.

"It is," said Mrs Baker. "He was a friend of mine, Bones was."

"Go on," growled Daugherty. "What else did you dig up?"

"Mr Matlin left for his golf at eleven-thirty. Now, you see, it looks as if Matlin couldn't have left poison behind him."

"I most certainly did not," snapped Matlin. "I have said so. I will not stand for this sort of innuendo, I am not a liar. You said it was a conference."

Mike held the man's eye. "We are simply trying to find out what happened to the dog," he said. Matlin fell silent.

"Surely you realize," purred Mike, "that, human frailty being what it is, there may have been other errors in what we were told this afternoon. There was at least one more.

"Mr and Mrs Baker," he continued, "worked in their garden this afternoon. Bones abandoned the ball game to visit the Bakers' dog, Smitty. At three o'clock the Bakers, after discussing the time carefully lest it be too late in the day, decided to bathe Smitty. When they caught him for his ordeal, Bones was still there. So, you see, Miss May Matlin, who says she saw Bones lying by the sidewalk *before three o'clock*, was mistaken."

Matlin twitched. Russell said sharply, "The testimony of the Bakers is extremely clear." The Bakers, who looked alike, both brown outdoor people, nodded vigorously.

"The time at which Mr Matlin returned is quite well established. Diane saw him. Mrs Daugherty, next door, decided to take a nap at five after three. She had a roast to put in at four-thirty. Therefore she is sure of the time. She went upstairs and from an upper window she, too, saw Mr Matlin come home. Both witnesses say he drove his car into the garage at three-ten, got out, and went around the building to the right of it—*on the weedy side.*"

Mr Matlin was sweating. His forehead was beaded. He did not speak.

Mike shifted papers. "Now, we know that the kids trooped up to Phil Bourchard's kitchen at about a quarter of three.

70

Whereas Bones, realizing that Smitty was in for it, and shying away from soap and water like any sane dog, went up Hannibal Street at three o'clock sharp. He may have known in some doggy way where Freddy was. Can we see Bones loping up Hannibal Street, going *above* Greenwood Lane?"

"We can," said Daugherty. He was watching Matlin. "Besides, he was found above Greenwood Lane soon after."

"No one," said Mike slowly, "was seen in Matlin's back lot, except Matlin. Yet almost immediately after Matlin was there, the little dog died."

"Didn't Diane . . .?"

"Diane's friends came at three-twelve. Their evidence is not reliable." Diane blushed.

"This—this is intolerable!" croaked Matlin. "Why *my* back lot?"

Daugherty said, "There was no poison lying around my place, I'll tell you that."

"How do you know?" begged Matlin. And Freddy's eyes, with the smudges under them, followed to Russell's face. "Why not in the street? From some passing car?"

Mike said, "I'm afraid it's not likely. You see, Mr Otis Carnavon was stalled at the corner of Hannibal and Lee. Trying to flag a push. Anything thrown from a car on that block he ought to have seen."

"Was the poison quick?" demanded Daugherty. "What did he get?"

"It was quick. The dog could not go far after he got it. He got cyanide."

Matlin's shaking hand removed his glasses. They were wet.

"Some of you may be amateur photographers," Mike said. "Mr Matlin, is there cyanide in your cellar darkroom?"

"Yes, but I keep it . . . most meticulously . . ." Matlin began to cough.

When the noise of his spasm died, Mike said, "The poison was embedded in ground meat which analysed, roughly, half-beef and the rest pork and veal, half and half." Matlin encircled his throat with his fingers. "I've checked with four neighbourhood butchers and the dickens of a time I had," said Mike. No one smiled. Only Freddy looked up at him with solemn sympathy. "Ground meat was delivered to at least five houses in the vicinity. Meat that *was* one-half beef, one-quarter pork, one-quarter veal, was delivered at ten this morning to Matlin's house."

A stir like an angry wind blew over the room. The Chief of Police made some shift of his weight so that his chair creaked.

"It begins to look . . ." growled Daugherty.

"Now," said Russell sharply, "we must be very careful. One more thing. The meat had been seasoned."

"Seasoned!"

"With salt. And with . . . thyme."

"Thyme," groaned Matlin.

Freddy looked up at Miss Dana with bewildered eyes. She put her arm around him.

"As far as motives are concerned," said Mike quietly, "I can't discuss them. It is inconceivable to me that any man would poison a dog." Nobody spoke. "However, where are we?" Mike's voice seemed to catch Matlin just in time to keep him from falling off the chair. "We don't know yet what happened to the dog." Mike's voice rang. "Mr Matlin, will you help us to the answer?"

Miss Dana moved, but Russell said, "No. They have worked hard for the truth. They have earned it. And if it is to be had, they shall have it."

"You know?" whimpered Matlin.

Mike said, "I called your golf club. I've looked into your trash incinerator. Yes, I know. But I want you to tell us."

Daugherty said, "Well? Well?" And Matlin covered his face.

Mike said, gently, "I think there was an error. Mr Matlin, I'm afraid, did poison the dog. But he never meant to, and he didn't know he had done it."

Matlin went on, his voice cracking. "I never . . . You see, I didn't even know it was meat the dog got. She said—she told me the dog was already dead."

"And of course," said Mike, "in your righteous wrath, you never paused to say to yourself, 'Wait, what *did* happen to the dog?' "

"Mr Russell, I didn't lie. How could I know there was thyme in it? When I got home, I had to get rid of the hamburger she'd fixed for me—I didn't want to hurt her feelings. She tries . . . tries so hard . . ." He sat up suddenly. "*But what she tried to do today*," he said, with his eyes almost out of his head, "*was to poison me!*" His bulging eyes roved. They came to Freddy. He gasped. He said, "Your dog saved my life!"

72

"Yes," said Mike quickly, "Freddy's dog saved your life. You see, your stepdaughter would have kept trying."

People drew in their breaths. "The buns are in your incinerator," Mike said. "She guessed what happened to the dog, went for the buns, and hid them. She was late, you remember, getting to the disturbance. And she did lie."

Chief Anderson rose.

"Her mother . . ." said Matlin frantically, "her mother . . ."

Mike Russell put his hand on the plump shoulder. "Her mother's been in torment, tortured by the rivalry between you. Don't you think her mother senses something wrong?"

Miss Lillian Dana wrapped Freddy in her arms. "Oh, what a wonderful dog Bones was!" she covered the sound of the other voices. "Even when he died, he saved a man's life. Oh, Freddy, he was a wonderful dog."

And Freddy, not quite taking everything in yet, was released to simple sorrow and wept quietly against his friend. . . .

When they went to fetch May Matlin, she was not in the house. They found her in the Titus' back shed. She seemed to be looking for something.

Next day, when Mr and Mrs Titus came home, they found that although the little dog had died, their Freddy was all right. The judge, Russell, and Miss Dana told them all about it.

Mrs Titus wept. Mr Titus swore. He wrung Russell's hand. ". . . for stealing the gun . . ." he babbled.

But the mother cried, ". . . for showing him, for teaching him. . . . Oh, Miss Dana, oh, my dear!"

The judge waved from his veranda as the dark head and the blonde drove away.

"I think Miss Dana likes him," said Ernie Allen.

"How do you know for sure?" said Freddy Titus.

THE INEXPERIENCED GHOST

H. G. WELLS

THE SCENE amidst which Clayton told his last story comes back very vividly to my mind. There he sat, for the greater part of the time, in the corner of the authentic settle by the spacious open fire, and Sanderson sat beside him smoking the Broseley clay that bore his name. There was Evans, and that marvel among actors, Wish, who is also a modest man. We had all come down to the Mermaid Club that Saturday morning, except Clayton, who had slept there overnight—which indeed gave him the opening of his story. We had golf until golfing was invisible; we had dined, and we were in that mood of tranquil kindliness when men will suffer a story. When Clayton began to tell one, we naturally supposed he was lying. It may be that indeed he was lying—of that the reader will speedily be able to judge as well as I. He began, it is true, with an air of matter-of-fact anecdote, but that we thought was only the incurable artifice of the man.

"I say!" he remarked, after a long consideration of the upward rain of sparks from the log that Sanderson had thumped, "you know I was alone here last night?"

"Except for the domestics," said Wish.

"Who sleep in the other wing," said Clayton. "Yes. Well ——" He pulled at his cigar for some little time as though he still hesitated about his confidence. Then he said, quite quietly, "I caught a ghost!"

"Caught a ghost, did you?" said Sanderson. "Where is it?"

And Evans, who admires Clayton immensely and has been four weeks in America, shouted, "*Caught* a ghost, did you, Clayton? I'm glad of it! Tell us all about it right now."

Clayton said he would in a minute, and asked him to shut the door.

He looked apologetically at me. "There's no eavesdropping of course, but we don't want to upset our very excellent ser-

74

vice with any rumours of ghosts in the place. There's too much shadow and oak panelling to trifle with that. And this, you know, wasn't a regular ghost. I don't think it will come again—ever."

"You mean to say you didn't keep it?" said Sanderson.

"I hadn't the heart to," said Clayton.

And Sanderson said he was surprised.

We laughed, and Clayton looked aggrieved. "I know," he said, with the flicker of a smile, "but the fact is it really *was* a ghost, and I'm as sure of it as I am that I am talking to you now. I'm not joking. I mean what I say."

Sanderson drew deeply at his pipe, with one reddish eye on Clayton, and then emitted a thin jet of smoke more eloquent than many words.

Clayton ignored the comment. "It is the strangest thing that has ever happened in my life. You know I never believed in ghosts or anything of the sort, before, ever; and then, you know, I bag one in a corner: and the whole business is in my hands."

He meditated still more profoundly and produced and began to pierce a second cigar with a curious little stabber he affected.

"You talked to it?" asked Wish.

"For the space, probably, of an hour."

"Chatty?" I said, joining the party of sceptics.

"The poor devil was in trouble," said Clayton, bowed over his cigar-end and with the very faintest note of reproof.

"Sobbing?" someone asked.

Clayton heaved a realistic sigh at the memory. "Good Lord!" he said; "yes." And then, "Poor fellow! yes."

"Where did you strike it?" asked Evans, in his best American accent.

"I never realized," said Clayton, ignoring him, "the poor sort of thing a ghost might be," and he hung us up again for a time, while he sought for matches in his pocket and lit and warmed to his cigar.

"I took an advantage," he reflected at last.

We were none of us in a hurry. "A character," he said, "remains just the same character for all that it's been disembodied. That's a thing we too often forget. People with a certain strength or fixity of purpose may have ghosts of a certain strength and fixity of purpose—most haunting ghosts, you know, must be as one-idea'd as monomaniacs and as obstinate as mules to come back again and again. This poor creature wasn't." He suddenly looked up rather queerly, and his eye went round the room. "I say it," he said, "in all kindliness, but this is the plain truth of the case. Even at the first glance he struck me as weak."

He punctuated with the help of his cigar.

"I came upon him, you know, in the long passage. His back was toward me and I saw him first. Right off I knew him for a ghost. He was transparent and whitish; clean through his chest I could see the glimmer of the little window at the end. And not only his physique but his attitude struck me as being weak. He looked, you know, as though he didn't know in the slightest whatever he meant to do. One hand was on the panelling and the other fluttered to his mouth. Like— *so!*"

"What sort of physique?" said Sanderson.

"Lean. You know that sort of young man's neck that has two great flutings down the back, here and here—so! And a little meanish head with scrubby hair and rather bad ears. Shoulders bad, narrower than the hips; turn-down collar, ready-made short jacket, trousers baggy and a little frayed at the heels. That's how he took me. I came very quietly up the staircase. I did not carry a light, you know—the candles are on the landing table and there is that lamp—and I was in my list slippers, and I saw him as I came up. I stopped dead at that—taking him in. I wasn't a bit afraid. I think that in most of these affairs one is never nearly so afraid or excited as one imagines one would be. I was surprised and interested. I thought, 'Good Lord! Here's a ghost at last! And I haven't believed for a moment in ghosts during the last five-and-twenty years'."

"Um," said Wish.

"I suppose I wasn't on the landing a moment before he found out I was there. He turned on me sharply, and I saw the face of an immature young man, a weak nose, a scrubby little moustache, a feeble chin. So for an instant we stood— he looking over his shoulder at me—and regarded one another. Then he seemed to remember his high calling. He turned round, drew himself up, projected his face, raised his arms, spread his hands in approved ghost fashion—came toward me. As he did so his little jaw dropped, and he emitted a faint drawn-out 'Boo'. No, it wasn't—not a bit dreadful. I'd dined. I'd had a bottle of champagne, and being all alone,

76

perhaps two or three—perhaps even four or five—whiskies, so I was as solid as rocks and no more frightened than if I'd been assailed by a frog. 'Boo!' I said. 'Nonsense. You don't belong to *this* place. What are you doing here?'

"I could see him wince. 'Boo—oo,' he said.

" 'Boo—be hanged! Are you a member?' I said; and just to show I didn't care a pin for him I stepped through a corner of him and made to light my candle. 'Are you a member?' I repeated, looking at him sideways.

"He moved a little so as to stand clear of me, and his bearing became crestfallen. 'No,' he said, in answer to the persistent interrogation of my eye; 'I'm not a member—I'm a ghost.'

" 'Well, that doesn't give you the run of the Mermaid Club. Is there anyone you want to see, or anything of that sort?' And doing it as steadily as possible for fear that he should mistake the carelessness of whisky for the distraction of fear, I got my candle alight. I turned on him, holding it. 'What are you doing here?' I said.

"He had dropped his hands and stopped his booing, and there he stood, abashed and awkward, the ghost of a weak, silly, aimless young man. 'I'm haunting,' he said.

" 'You haven't any business to,' I said in a quiet voice.

" 'I'm a ghost,' he said, as if in defence.

" 'That may be, but you haven't any business to haunt here. This is a respectable private club; people often stop here with nursemaids and children, and, going about in the careless way you do, some poor little mite could easily come upon you and be scared out of her wits. I suppose you didn't think of that?'

" 'No, sir,' he said, 'I didn't.'

" 'You should have done. You haven't any claim on the place, have you? Weren't murdered here, or anything of that sort?'

" 'None, sir; but I thought as it was old and oak-panelled——'

" 'That's *no* excuse.' I regarded him firmly. 'Your coming here is a mistake,' I said, in a tone of friendly superiority. I feigned to see if I had my matches, and then looked up at him frankly. 'If I were you I wouldn't wait for cock-crow—I'd vanish right away.'

"He looked embarrassed. 'The fact *is* sir——' he began.

" 'I'd vanish,' I said, driving it home.

77

" 'The fact is, sir, that—somehow—I can't.'

" 'You *can't*?'

" 'No, sir. There's something I've forgotten. I've been hanging about here since midnight last night, hiding in the cupboards of the empty bedrooms and things like that. I'm flurried. I've never come haunting before, and it seems to put me out.'

" 'Put you out?'

" 'Yes, sir. I've tried to do it several times, and it doesn't come off. There's some little thing has slipped me, and I can't get back.'

"That, you know, rather bowled me over. He looked at me in such an abject way that for the life of me I couldn't keep up quite the high hectoring vein I had adopted. 'That's queer,' I said, and as I spoke I fancied I heard someone moving about down below. 'Come into my room and tell me more about it,' I said. I didn't, of course, understand this, and I tried to take him by the arm. But, of course, you might as well have tried to take hold of a puff of smoke! I had forgotten my number, I think; anyhow, I remember going into several bedrooms—it was lucky I was the only soul in that wing—until I saw my traps. 'Here we are,' I said, and sat down in the armchair; 'sit down and tell me all about it. It seems to me you have got yourself into a jolly awkward position, old chap.'

"Well, he said he wouldn't sit down; he'd prefer to flit up and down the room if it was all the same to me. And so he did, and in a little while we were deep in a long and serious talk. And presently, you know, something of those whiskies and sodas evaporated out of me, and I began to realize just a little what a thundering rum and weird business it was that I was in. There he was, semi-transparent—the proper conventional phantom and noiseless except for his ghost of a voice—flitting to and fro in that nice, clean, chintz-hung old bedroom. You could see the gleam of the copper candlesticks through him, and the lights on the brass fender, and the corners of the framed engravings on the wall, and there he was telling me all about this wretched little life of his that had recently ended on earth. He hadn't a particularly honest face, you know, but being transparent, of course, he couldn't avoid telling the truth."

"Eh?" said Wish, suddenly sitting up his chair.

"What?" said Clayton.

"Being transparent—couldn't avoid telling the truth—I don't see it," said Wish.

"*I* don't see it," said Clayton with inimitable assurance. "But it *is* so, I can assure you nevertheless. I don't believe he got once a nail's breadth off the Bible truth. He told me how he had been killed—he went down into a London basement with a candle to look for a leakage of gas—and described himself as a senior English master in a London private school when that release occurred."

"Poor wretch!" said I

"That's what I thought, and the more he talked the more I thought it. There he was, purposeless in life and purposeless out of it. He talked of his father and mother and his schoolmaster, and all who had ever been anything to him in the world, meanly. He had been too sensitive, too nervous; none of them had ever valued him properly or understood him, he said. He had never had a real friend in the world, I think; he had never had a success. He had shirked games and failed examinations. 'It's like that with some people,' he said; 'whenever I got into the examination-room or anywhere everything seemed to go.' Engaged to be married of course—to another over-sensitive person, I suppose—when the indiscretion with the gas escape ended his affairs. 'And where are you now?' I asked. 'Not in——?'

"He wasn't clear on that point at all. The impression he gave me was of a sort of vague, intermediate state, a special reserve for souls too non-existent for anything so positive as either sin or virtue. *I* don't know. He was much too egotistical and unobservant to give me any clear idea of the kind of place, kind of country, there is on the Other Side of Things. Wherever he was, he seems to have fallen in with a set of kindred spirits: ghosts of weak Cockney young men, who were on a footing of Christian names, and among these there was certainly a lot of talk about 'going haunting' and things like that. Yes—going haunting! They seemed to think 'haunting' a tremendous adventure, and most of them funked it all the time. And so primed, you know, he had come."

"But really!" said Wish to the fire.

"These are the impressions he gave me, anyhow," said Clayton modestly. "I may, of course, have been in a rather uncritical state, but that was the sort of background he gave to himself. He kept flitting up and down, with his thin voice going—talking, talking about his wretched self, and never a word of clear, firm statement from first to last. He was thinner and sillier and more pointless than if he had been real and alive. Only then, you know, he would not have been in my bedroom here—if he *had* been alive. I should have kicked him out."

"Of course," said Evans, "there *are* poor mortals like that."

"And there's just as much chance of their having ghosts as the rest of us," I admitted.

"What gave a sort of point to him, you know, was the fact that he did seem within limits to have found himself out. The mess he had made of haunting had depressed him terribly. He had been told it would be a 'lark'; he had come expecting it to be a 'lark', and here it was, nothing but another failure added to his record! He proclaimed himself an utter out-and-out failure. He said, and I can quite believe it, that he had never tried to do anything all his life that he hadn't made a perfect mess of—and through all the wastes of eternity he never would. If he had had sympathy, perhaps—— He paused at that, and stood regarding me. He remarked that, strange as it might seem to be, nobody, not anyone, ever, had given him the amount of sympathy I was doing now. I could see what he wanted straight away, and I determined to head him off at once. I may be a brute, you know, but being the Only Real Friend, the recipient of the confidences of one of these egotistical weaklings, ghost or body, is beyond my physical endurance. I got up briskly. 'Don't you brood on these things too much,' I said. 'The thing you've got to do is to get out of this—get out of this sharp. You pull yourself together and *try*.' 'I can't,' he said. 'You try,' I said, and try he did."

"Try!" said Sanderson. "*How?*"

"Passes," said Clayton.

"Passes?"

"Complicated series of gestures and passes with the hands. That's how he had come in and that's how he had to get out again. Lord! what a business I had!"

"But how could *any* series of passes——" I began.

"My dear man," said Clayton, turning on me and putting a great emphasis on certain words, "you want *everything* clear. I don't know *how*. All I know is that you *do*—that *he* did, anyhow, at least. After a fearful time, you know, he got his passes right and suddenly disappeared."

"Did you," said Sanderson slowly, "observe the passes?"

"Yes," said Clayton, and seemed to think. "It was tremendously queer," he said. "There we were, I and this thin vague ghost, in that silent room, in this silent, empty inn, in this silent little Friday-night town. Not a sound except our voices and a faint panting he made when he swung. There was the bedroom candle, and one candle on the dressing-table alight, that was all—sometimes one or other would flare up into a tall, lean, astonished flame for a space. And queer things happened. 'I can't,' he said; 'I shall never——!' And suddenly he sat down on a little chair at the foot of the bed and began to sob and sob. Lord! what a harrowing whimpering thing he seemed!

"'You pull yourself together,' I said, and tried to pat him on the back, and . . . my confounded hand went through him! By that time, you know, I wasn't nearly so—massive as I had been on the landing. I got the queerness of it full. I remember snatching back my hand out of him as it were, with a little thrill, and walking over to the dressing-table. 'You pull yourself together,' I said to him, 'and try.' And in order to encourage and help him I began to try as well."

"What!" said Sanderson, "the passes?"

"Yes, the passes."

"But——" I said, moved by an idea that eluded me for a space.

"This is interesting" said Sanderson, with his finger in his pipe-bowl. "You mean to say this ghost of yours gave away——"

"Did his level best to give away the whole confounded barrier? *Yes*."

"He didn't," said Wish; "he couldn't. Or you'd have gone there too."

"That's precisely it," I said, finding my elusive idea put into words for me.

"That *is* precisely it," said Clayton, with thoughtful eyes upon the fire.

For just a little while there was silence.

"And at last he did it?" said Sanderson.

"At last he did it. I had to keep him up to it hard, but he did it at last—rather suddenly. He despaired, we had a scene, and then he got up abruptly and asked me to go through the whole performance slowly so that he might see. 'I believe,' he said, 'if I could *see* I should spot what was wrong at once.' And he did. '*I* know,' he said. 'What do you know?' said I.

'*I* know,' he repeated. Then he said peevishly, 'I *can't* do it, if you look at me—I really *can't*; it's been that, partly, all along. I'm such a nervous fellow that you put me out.' Well, we had a bit of an argument. Naturally I wanted to see; but he was as obstinate as a mule, and suddenly I had come over as tired as a dog—he tired me out. 'All right,' I said, '*I* won't look at you,' and turned toward the mirror, on the wardrobe, by the bed.

"He started off very fast. I tried to follow him by looking in the looking-glass, to see just what it was had hung. Round went his arms and his hands, so, and so, and so, and then with a rush came to the last gesture of all—you stand erect and open out your arms—and so, don't you know, he stood. And then he didn't! He didn't! He wasn't! I wheeled round from the looking-glass to him. There was nothing! I was alone, with the flaring candles and a staggering mind. What had happened? Had anything happened? Had I been dreaming? . . . And then, with an absurd note of finality about it, the clock upon the landing discovered the moment was ripe for striking *one*. So!—Ping! And I was as grave and sober as a judge, with all my champagne and whisky gone into the vast serene. Feeling queer, you know—confoundedly *queer!* Queer! Good Lord!"

He regarded his cigar-ash for a moment. "That's all that happened," he said.

"And then you went to bed?" asked Evans.

"What else was there to do?"

I looked Wish in the eye. We wanted to scoff, and there was something, something perhaps in Clayton's voice and manner, that hampered our desire.

"And about these passes?" said Sanderson.

"I believe I could do them now."

"Oh!" said Sanderson, and produced a pen-knife and set himself to grub the dottel out of the bowl of his clay.

"Why don't you do them now?" said Sanderson, shutting his penknife with a click.

"That's what I'm going to do," said Clayton.

"They won't work," said Evans.

"If they do——" I suggested.

"You know, I'd rather you didn't," said Wish, stretching out his legs.

"Why?" asked Evans.

"I'd rather he didn't," said Wish.

82

"But he hasn't got 'em right," said Sanderson, plugging too much tobacco into his pipe.

"All the same, I'd rather he didn't," said Wish.

We argued with Wish. He said that for Clayton to go through those gestures was like mocking a serious matter. "But you don't believe——?" I said. Wish glanced at Clayton, who was staring into the fire, weighing something in his mind. "I do—more than half, anyhow, I do," said Wish.

"Clayton," said I, "you're too good a liar for us. Most of it was all right. But that disappearance . . . happened to be convincing. Tell us, it's a tale of cock and bull."

He stood up without heeding me, took the middle of the hearthrug, and faced me. For a moment he regarded his feet thoughtfully, and then for all the rest of the time his eyes were on the opposite wall, with an intent expression. He raised his two hands slowly to the level of his eyes and so began. . . .

Now, Sanderson is a Freemason, a member of the lodge of the Four Kings, which devotes itself so ably to the study and elucidation of all the mysteries of Masonry past and present, and among the students of this lodge Sanderson is by no means the least. He followed Clayton's motions with a singular interest in his reddish eye. "That's not bad," he said, when it was done. "You really do, you know, put things together, Clayton, in a most amazing fashion. But there's one little detail out."

"I know," said Clayton. "I believe I could tell you which."

"Well?"

"This," said Clayton, and did a queer little twist and writhing and thrust of the hands.

"Yes."

"That, you know, was what *he* couldn't get right," said Clayton. "But how do *you*——?"

"Most of this business, and particularly how you invented it, I don't understand at all," said Sanderson, "but just that phase—I do." He reflected. "These happen to be a series of gestures—connected with a certain branch of esoteric Masonry—— Probably you know. Or else—— *How*?" He reflected still further. "I do not see I can do any harm in telling you just the proper twist. After all, if you know, you know; if you don't, you don't."

"I know nothing," said Clayton, "except what the poor devil let out last night."

"Well, anyhow," said Sanderson, and placed his church-warden very carefully upon the shelf over the fireplace. Then very rapidly he gesticulated with his hands.

"So?" said Clayton, repeating.

"So," said Sanderson, and took his pipe in hand again.

"Ah, *now*," said Clayton, "I can do the whole thing—right."

He stood up before the waning fire and smiled at us all. But I think there was just a little hesitation in his smile. "If I begin——" he said.

"I wouldn't begin," said Wish.

"It's all right!" said Evans. "Matter is indestructible. You don't think any jiggery-pokery of this sort is going to snatch Clayton into the world of shades. Not it! You may try, Clayton, so far as I'm concerned, until your arms drop off at the wrists."

"I don't believe that," said Wish, and stood up and put his arm on Clayton's shoulder. "You've made me half believe in that story somehow, and I don't want to see the thing done."

"Goodness!" said I, "here's Wish frightened!"

"I am," said Wish, with real or admirably feigned intensity. "I believe that if he goes through these motions right he'll *go*."

"He'll not do anything of the sort," I cried. "There's only one way out of this world for men, and Clayton is thirty years from that. Besides . . . And such a ghost! Do you think——?"

Wish interrupted me by moving. He walked out from among the chairs and stopped beside the table and stood there. "Clayton," he said, "you're a fool."

Clayton, with a humorous light in his eyes, smiled back at him. "Wish," he said, "is right and all you others are wrong. I shall go. I shall get to the end of these passes, and as the last swish whistles through the air, Presto!—this hearthrug will be vacant, the room will be blank amazement, and a respectably dressed gentleman of fifteen stone will plump into the world of shades. I'm certain. So will you be. I decline to argue further. Let the thing be tried."

"*No*," said Wish, and made a step and ceased, and Clayton raised his hands once more to repeat the spirit's passing.

By that time, you know, we were all in a state of tension—largely because of the behaviour of Wish. We sat all of us

84

with our eyes on Clayton—I, at least, with a sort of tight, stiff feeling about me as though from the back of my skull to the middle of my thighs my body had been changed to steel. And there, with a gravity that was imperturbably serene, Clayton bowed and swayed and waved his hands and arms before us. As he drew toward the end one piled up, one tingled in one's teeth. The last gesture, I have said, was to swing the arms out wide open, with the face held up. And when at last he swung out to this closing gesture I ceased even to breathe. It was ridiculous, of course, but you know that ghost-story feeling. It was after dinner, in a queer, old shadowy house. Would he, after all——?

There he stood for one stupendous moment, with his arms open and his upturned face, assured and bright, in the glare of the hanging lamp. We hung through that moment as if it were an age, and then came from all of us something that was half a sigh of infinite relief and half a reassuring *"No!"* For visibly—he wasn't going. It was all nonsense. He had told an idle story, and carried it almost to conviction, that was all! . . . And then in that moment the face of Clayton changed.

It changed. It changed as a lit house changes when its lights are suddenly extinguished. His eyes were suddenly eyes that were fixed, his smile was frozen on his lips, and he stood there still. He stood there, very gently swaying.

That moment, too, was an age. And then, you know, chairs were scraping, things were falling, and we were all moving. His knees seemed to give, and he fell forward, and Evans rose and caught him in his arms. . . .

It stunned us all. For a minute, I suppose, no one said a coherent thing. We believed it, yet could not believe it. . . . I came out of a muddled stupefaction to find myself kneeling beside him, and his vest and shirt were torn open, and Sanderson's hand lay on his heart. . . .

Well—the simple fact before us could very well wait our convenience; there was no hurry for us to comprehend. It lay there for an hour; it lies athwart my memory, black and amazing still, to this day. Clayton had, indeed, passed into the world that lies so near to and so far from our own. And he had gone thither by the only road that mortal man may take. But whether he did indeed pass there by the poor ghost's incantation, or whether he was stricken suddenly by apoplexy in the midst of an idle tale—as the coroner's jury would have us believe—is no matter for my judging; it is just one of those inexplicable riddles that must remain unsolved until the final solution of all things shall come. All I certainly know is that, in the very moment, in the very instant, of concluding those passes, he changed and staggered, and fell down before us—dead!

SENTENCE OF DEATH

THOMAS WALSH

ITEM ONE, the grimmest and most important item, was the body of a respectable middle-aged pharmacist named Carl Sawyer. Item Two, the usual emotional item, was an attractive blonde woman, apparently his widow, who was sobbing hysterically over him when Cochran and McReynolds arrived from the precinct house. Item Three—which, to Cochran and McReynolds, explained everything at first glance and completely—was a rifled cash register. Item Four, the familiar professional headache, was a store crowded with excited and talkative neighbours.

It appeared at first that every one of these people was quite willing to furnish Cochran with detailed and significant information; it developed later, when he had attended to the necessary elimination, that just four of them had actually seen anything. Mrs Sawyer and a chance customer named Ellen Morison had witnessed the shooting; two others—a husband and wife—glimpsed a man who sprinted out of the drugstore immediately afterward, and raced away in a car which he had parked thirty or forty feet distant, in heavy shadow. This couple agreed, however, on one or two distinguishing facts about the car; and Ellen Morison, a slim and alert young girl with brown hair, intelligent dark eyes and a sensible if excited voice, described the man.

She informed Cochran that fifteen or twenty minutes ago, when she had entered the drugstore, the man had been standing in front of Mr Sawyer. They were so close together, just a bit left of the cash register, that at first she had taken him for a friend of Mr Sawyer, and had assumed that Mr Sawyer was chatting with him; then the man had turned quickly, apparently in panic, looked at her quickly, fired twice at Mr Sawyer and slapped his left hand out and down at the cash register. It was her opinion that the man was about twenty-eight years old, perhaps older; that he had blond hair, a slim

87

build and a very sharp, narrow jaw. She seemed to be breathless and considerably upset at this time, which was quite natural, but because she remembered the right things about the man—not too many of these, just the striking and obvious details—Cochran was inclined to accept her as perhaps the most dependable witness.

The married couple, who had observed the man from the side and in motion, were the only people who had seen the car. They described it to Cochran as either a black or a dark blue sedan with a dented fender—the right rear fender. One of them thought that the man had been wearing a brown suit and brown shoes; the other, that he had on slacks and a grey sports jacket. They both declared, like Ellen Morison, that the man had been hatless. They both remembered the blond hair.

McReynolds, in the meantime, had attempted first to compose Mrs Sawyer and then to question her. Both attempts failed. She did not appear to understand who McReynolds was or what he wanted; she would just shake her head dumbly and blindly at him, as if she were still in a condition of severe shock. Cochran left her alone. He was sure then that they wanted a man of a certain age, build and complexion; one who owned or who had access to a cheap sedan with a dented fender; who had a gun; and who, in all likelihood, had also a police record.

He and McReynolds set out to locate this man. They checked pictures and records downtown; they settled on a few possible suspects; they rounded up and detained four of these; and then, two days later, Mrs Sawyer picked one of the four immediately and hysterically from a line-up.

The married couple supported Mrs Sawyer's identification, even though, in Cochran's opinion, they could not be half so sure of it as they insisted they were. Ellen Morison would not corroborate. She was the only witness who had impressed Cochran to any extent, and she admitted now that the man they showed her looked something, not too much, like the man who had shot the druggist. She was not prepared to swear that he was the man . . . or that he was not. She told Cochran uncomfortably that she remembered the other man as being older and taller. This one——

She shook her head. McReynolds became impatient with her; Cochran, who suspected that bereaved women like Mrs Sawyer, after and because of their bereavement, often hit out at the first convenient and likely target, reserved judgment on the identification and went out to do some routine checking.

He discovered these facts: The man Mrs Sawyer had identified—a tough and surly young truck helper named Johnny Palica, who had a couple of minor arrests to his discredit—lived with a brother-in-law who owned a cheap black sedan. On the night in question, last Thursday, Johnny Palica had been permitted to use the sedan, which had a couple of deep scrapes on the back fender, and had kept it out from early evening until after midnight. Just driving around, he admitted uneasily to Cochran; he had his girl with him. What did anyone do when he had his girl with him? He kept to himself, didn't he? Well then——

The girl corroborated his story—only the girl. She was not an impressive or disinterested witness. There were still three people who identified Johnny Palica—who, indeed, were more certain of him now than they had been previously—and two of these people also identified the brother-in-law's car. There was another witness, Ellen Morison, who could not seem to make up her mind definitely about him. It was a shaky defence, very badly handled, and the jury convicted. After the conviction, which made the death sentence mandatory, Cochran began to avoid McReynolds for some reason; and then one afternoon he discovered suddenly, with a shock of acute physical discomfort, that McReynolds was beginning also to avoid him.

Each of them knew that an identification made under circumstances of great excitement and tension was not always trustworthy. And apparently each of them, because of a highly developed instinct in such matters, disliked this one. They did not discuss it with each other—it was not their province—but they did not forget about it either. Then March came, and on March fifth, at half past two in the afternoon, Cochran received a phone call which for some time, and in an uneasy and illogical manner, he had been anticipating.

"You remember that Morison girl?" McReynolds asked, quiet enough about it—perhaps too quiet. "The one who couldn't make up her mind about this Johnny Palica?"

"Who?" Cochran said. But, of course, he remembered her immediately; he pretended not to because he did not want McReynolds to get any ideas about him. "No. I don't seem to—— Wait a minute. That one?" He rubbed his mouth carefully. "What's the matter now? What's up."

McReynolds said stolidly, "Big news. She just told me that Palica isn't the guy. She claims she's positive. You better hustle around here, Ray. I think we're in trouble."

So Cochran got a cab for himself. He found McReynolds and Ellen Morison in an upstairs room at the precinct house, with a busy and impatient young man named Wilson who was somebody unimportant on the district attorney's staff; and he was informed by Wilson that last night, outside a tavern on Third Avenue, Miss Morison saw—or thought she saw—the man who had actually murdered Carl Sawyer. She was positive about him, Wilson added dryly, because he had turned his head and glanced at her exactly the way he had glanced at her that night in the drugstore. She did not think that he had recognized her. When she came back five or ten minutes afterwards with a policeman, he was gone. A bartender in the tavern was unable to furnish any useful information about him. That seemed to be it, Wilson said. A long silence followed.

Cochran was waiting for McReynolds to break it; McReynolds, who looked a bit pale and haggard that afternoon, appeared to be waiting for Cochran.

At last Cochran said, "Well," uncertainly, and sat down on a corner of the desk with his hat pushed back, his lips pursed and his palms on his knees.

"Exactly," said the district attorney's man, as if Cochran had made a very shrewd and penetrating remark. "The whole thing is almost childishly simple. Last night Miss Morison happened to see someone who bore a superficial resemblance to our friend Palica. So immediately——"

Cochran said, "We never found the gun."

"Granted. I wish we had too. But when we've been able to convince a jury without it, I don't see——"

McReynolds said suddenly, angrily and pugnaciously, as if the words burst out of him, "Wait a minute now. Me and Cochran are responsible for him; not you, mister. And I've kind of been sweating a little blood over it lately, if that means anything. I don't like this thing. I never did."

He went that far. Cochran—they were boosting each other along now—took his right palm from his knee, turned it over, examined it and decided to go a bit further.

Cochran said, "I've seen nervous and hysterical women like Mrs Sawyer identify cops who were just put into a line-up to fill it out. Sure, that married couple agreed with her; witnesses like them always go along with the first person who makes up her mind. I kind of agree with Mac here. Let's talk this over."

Ellen Morison, who appeared nervous but determined, glanced at him and said quietly, "Thank you. I'm beginning to feel better. I testified at the trial that the man who shot Mr Sawyer—the man I'm telling you I saw outside that tavern last night—seemed to be older and thinner, and a lot taller, than the man you arrested. I was treated then as if I didn't know what I was talking about. I wasn't sure, or I told myself I wasn't sure. But now I am. And now I want something done about it."

The man from the district attorney's office stopped looking annoyed and angry, and started looking concerned and worried. More discussion ensued; then it was decided that the first thing to do, if they wanted a reasonable standard of comparison, was to give Ellen Morison another and longer look at Johnny Palica. The lieutenant, who had been careful enough to disassociate himself entirely from this interview, was called in. The lieutenant phoned downtown, and then downtown made arrangements with a Captain Mooney.

At half-past eight the next morning, Cochran and the girl drove up to—to that place, as Cochran had begun to think of it, very uneasily—and found Mooney waiting for them. They shook hands and conferred briefly; then Mooney glanced sidewise, without much facial expression, at Ellen Morison, and conducted them out of the visitors' room and into a corridor which had high barred windows.

They went by two men who were dressed in the uniform of prison guards; they stopped in front of a steel door which was unlocked from within, and they waited for several moments, even though they had Mooney with them, in front of another door just beyond the first, and quite as massive and powerful looking, until the one through which they had been admitted was closed and locked.

Afterward there were more doors, and more prison guards, more corridors, and finally a courtyard and another and rather isolated building. When they entered that building, Cochran, who did not have to be told what it was, touched his lips in a nervous and delicate manner with his tongue. He did not look at Ellen Morison. He did not make any attempt to speak to her.

They stopped presently outside a room. It was this kind of

room. It had yellow composition walls and a brown base-board. It had a cheap oak table with a soiled blotter on it and a clean ash tray; it had two chairs, one window and one powerful ceiling lighting fixture. In this room there was a peculiar but unmistakable sort of presence waiting for Cochran. He knew why; he and McReynolds were chiefly responsible for it. He entered.

Ellen Morison, who was not to talk to Johnny Palica, but only to observe him through a grille concealed in the outside door at normal eye level, remained in the hall; but Captain Mooney entered behind Cochran, glanced at him and went out through another exit. Almost as soon as Cochran was left alone, the harsh light in the room and the intense stillness made him restless and uncomfortable. Several minutes passed; to Cochran they seemed to pass with extreme slowness Then there were steps in the inside corridor, and Cochran jabbed his hands into his hip pockets, turned and braced himself, at least physically, for this.

Mooney came in. "All right now," Mooney said, in the simplest and most matter-of-fact tone. "In here, Johnny. You remember Ray Cochran, don't you?"

Cochran spoke the first words that came into his head. "Sure," Cochran said, his lips feeling like wet flour. "Sure, he does . . . Come on in and sit down, fella. How've you been?"

He had intended to shake hands here, but he stopped awkwardly after starting the gesture, because Johnny Palica did not appear to recognize him. Because of that, and of what it meant, the tone which Cochran had decided to employ—official, authoritative, but not unfriendly—became, after the first moment or two, a shabby and ridiculous pretense. There was no necessity for it. Johnny Palica was whiter, quieter and much more nervous than Cochran remembered; and as soon as he recognized Cochran, he made a desperate and pathetic attempt to ingratiate himself.

There was no more toughness or defiance in him. He was well broken. Not by Mooney, not by a couple of months' imprisonment, but by a certain idea and a certain date which Cochran and McReynolds had arranged for him. He grinned anxiously, and when it seemed that Cochran was not going to respond to the grin, he widened it in a slow, clumsy manner, with much effort.

"Fine," he said. "I'm okay, Mr Cochran. I'm—— You got some news?"

92

It was the first time he had ever addressed Cochran by that title; it was a small thing, and it was intolerable. Cochran began to sweat at the same time, because he had been warned by Mooney not to excite Johnny Palica and not to tell him anything about the girl until they had one or two definite facts to go on; he muttered that there didn't seem to be anything new in this thing, not yet. Headquarters, he added, just thought Johnny Palica might want to go over his story about that night again. If he did——

He did. He nodded violently. So Cochran put a couple of questions to him, the answers to which he and McReynolds had already checked, in so far as was humanly possible, months ago; and then Cochran pretended to listen intently to what Johnny Palica said to him, and even checked everything off, detail by detail, in a pocket notebook. "Sure, sure," Cochran muttered, even when the words had no particular application to what had preceded them. That was another thing, he'd add huskily, which he and McReynolds would check right away. They'd talk to Johnny Palica's girl, of course. And they'd go back carefully over the whole affair. They'd——

He would have done anything, said anything, promised anything, to get out of that room quickly, to remove himself from the way in which Johnny Palica kept watching him. As if he wanted help and reassurance from somewhere, Cochran thought savagely; not as if he expected it; as if he just wanted it. And then, when Mooney concluded the interview, when Cochran picked up his coat and mumbled something hearty and cheerful and got out of there, it was worse than before. In the outside hall, Ellen Morison was waiting for him.

She was quite pale, her eyes looked extremely odd, and apparently she did not want to talk to Cochran any more than Cochran wanted to talk to her. All she did was to shake her head at him. Of course, Cochran thought, she meant that he and McReynolds had the wrong man in here. That—— He turned away from her. He did not ask himself whether she was right about Johnny Palica; before he had half completed his turn something much worse had happened to him. He felt it.

Later that afternoon, McReynolds also appeared to feel it. He did not discuss the thing logically with Cochran; he just nodded a couple of times, swallowed once, got his hat and drove over with Cochran to interview Mrs Sawyer.

They discovered that something had happened to her, too,

because she was no longer a pink and cunning little woman with demure blue eyes and fluffy gold hair. She had aged noticeably; and by gradual degrees, as Cochran talked to her, she became withdrawn, bitter, nervous and finally hysterical again.

She was still sure that it was Johnny Palica who had murdered her husband; now, Cochran reflected hopelessly, hatred and loneliness had done their usual sort of job on her. So he and McReynolds did not tackle the two supporting witnesses; that was useless unless and until they had first shaken Mrs Sawyer. That evening McReynolds went downtown and started rechecking the files for another picture and description that might approximate Johnny Palica's; and at almost the same hour Cochran and Ellen Morison established a vigil over on Third Avenue, outside the Shamrock tavern.

They would park there, in Cochran's coupé, for five or six hours a night—the late hours—and for seven nights a week. They would stay there until half past one in the morning, with elevated trains rumbling overhead monotonously, with March wind lashing at them, and then Cochran would drive the girl home and go home himself after a cup of coffee somewhere. But he would not sleep any too well—the coffee, perhaps, or perhaps the other things. He would remain restless for a while, doze again, and then rouse suddenly with the conviction in him that someone had been shouting his name just now, at an infinite distance, but quite clearly. He never managed to hear the voice—not as sound—but at the same time he recognized it, and in the end it came to have its own sort of existence for him.

He knew what it wanted from Mr Cochran. He knew that much the first time it happened to him, and every time afterward, but he could not do anything helpful because, if there was going to be any appeal made on the basis of new evidence, he and McReynolds needed this other man. They could not find him. They could not imagine how to find him. They had twelve weeks at first, and then ten, and then eight, and then six. But nothing came up, either at headquarters or outside the Shamrock tavern.

Occasionally, after his end had dried up on him, McReynolds spent a couple of uncomfortable hours with them, but for the rest of the time Cochran and the girl had no company but themselves. At that period Cochran could have described the girl well, at least partially, although he himself did not seem to retain any personal or individual impression of her. She had dark hair, of which at times he had a vague sort of recollection, and the softness and delicacy around the mouth which had never been particularly attractive to him in other girls. He liked her all right, but he did not think about her as he had thought about one or two other girls. There was no opportunity. On those endless and monotonous evenings they rarely conversed at length because the appalling significance of their watch made ordinary conversation nearly impossible; and yet, despite that, they achieved a kind of intimacy which would have seemed very new and unusual to Cochran if he had been in any position to consider it.

Every so often, instead of just sitting there and waiting for the right man to show up, she worried him by attempting to force a resemblance between the person they wanted and some unimportant client of the Shamrock tavern. And so once, in their sixth week, he explained impersonally to her that it was rather silly to get excited about this, because the only thing they could use here was patience and more patience and again patience. You couldn't rush these things, Cochran said. You waited them out. They generally came to some sort of conclusion in the long run.

But she noticed at once that Cochran did not commit himself, here and now, as to the sort of conclusion they were going to reach outside the Shamrock tavern. She sat back in her corner of the seat and then glanced at him.

She said, "I suppose they do. Only this time"—she put her lips together for a moment—"they simply have to work out in the right way. Not that I'm discouraged about anything; I can't make myself believe for one minute that a mistake like this, a cruel and vicious mistake, is going to be—well, permitted. We'll find him. You wait and see."

"I hope we do," Cochran said. But when he looked out at Third Avenue—shabby, rain-swept, deserted, watery yellow light spilling across the black pavement in front of the tavern —he felt heavily depressed. "We've got a chance, anyway."

She said, with a confidence that surprised Cochran, "Oh, we've got more than that . . . much more. Things don't happen that way. If they did, there wouldn't be much point to the whole mess."

"Maybe there isn't," Cochran said.

"Of course that's silly," Ellen Morison said. She was very

calm about it. "Or out-and-out horrible. We've just got to believe that things are true and important. If we don't——"

"What things?" Cochran asked; it was the first discussion that had interested him even slightly. "You name a couple. I'd like to find out about them."

So it was that, of all subjects, they began arguing the most profound and imponderable one. They would argue it from exactly opposed viewpoints—not with the technical skill and finish of philosophers, but from each of their individual accumulations of judgment, experience and intuition. If she knew half the things he knew, Cochran would say darkly, or if she understood half the facts about the uglier side of human nature, she wouldn't talk so much about this or that being permitted or else not permitted. Things happened; that was all you could say about them.

She was earnest at first, and then irritated, and then scornful, but, of course, she never convinced Cochran. What he did admit—reluctantly and not to her—was that it might be pretty comforting to see this as Ellen Morison saw it, to believe in reasons for things, to be sure that someone, somewhere, was keeping an eye peeled in Ray Cochran's direction or Johnny Palica's.

An idea of that kind would have provided him with some useful insulation. He admitted so much, again privately; and then, little by little, and very stubbornly, he became a bit weaker in regard to his own arguments, and a bit more responsive in regard to hers. Friday night at about half past ten, he had just declared that perhaps people did achieve happier and more useful lives when they shared Ellen Morison's belief, and not his, but that didn't prove anything at all, as Cochran saw it. True was true. And if——

A man who did not resemble Johnny Palica at all parked in front of them and went into the Shamrock tavern. Cochran glanced at him and dismissed him, but Ellen Morison froze up, made some sort of breathlessly inarticulate sound and grabbed at Cochran.

He got out of the car slowly, his heart thumping. He said, "All right. You stick here. We don't want him to know anything about you yet. I'll be back as soon as I get a better look at him." Then he walked around the front of the coupé and into the tavern . . . and went numb.

The man whom Ellen Morison had just identified for him was at least four inches taller than Johnny Palica, noticeably older, noticeably stouter; there was, apart from his blond hair, not even the slightest physical similarity between them. *What is this?* Cochran asked himself very quietly. Something broke in him. He strode back to the coupé to that girl, but what he felt for her at this moment was a mixture of cold rage and ferocious contempt.

Did she understand, Cochran demanded thickly, what she had been doing for the last six weeks to him and McReynolds? Did she have any idea of how she had put them up on the rack, and kept them there, and twisted the wheel night after night until each of them was just about out of his head?

She looked very pale and excited, but not as if she understood what he was talking about.

"What's the matter?" she said. She was still breathless. "Why don't you—— He's the man, Cochran! I know he is! Do you think I could ever——"

"Then where's the mistake?" Cochran almost shouted at her. He began pounding his fist, with an impression of infinite restrained force, against the roof of the car. "How did anybody ever take this guy for Palica? You kept telling us all along that they looked like each other. That's the thing we were going to spring on everybody. That's all we had."

"But he does!" She pushed her head out anxiously at him. "Of course, he's grown that moustache. That's what you——"

Cochran spun away from her, maddened; then he got into the car blindly, closed the door, cradled his arms in front of him on the steering wheel and laid the right side of his face against them. That way he did not have to so much as look at her.

"He grew too," Cochran said. His voice hated her. "He grew four inches. Me and McReynolds were dumbheads; all along the district attorney's office had you down for just what you were. We figured you knew what you were talking about. We were stupid enough to go through hell because somebody like you——"

She faltered out several jerky sentences. Why was he talking like this? Hadn't they waited together for the man all these weeks? And now wasn't he in their hands?

Cochran would not answer her. The only clear idea in his mind was that if this man looked like Johnny Palica, they might have got the witnesses to admit confusion and perhaps error. This way no one—not Mrs Sawyer, not the married couple, not the district attorney's office—would even consider him. So——

The girl shook him again. Then she whispered painfully, "Listen, Cochran. Will you please, please listen to me? I tell you——"

The man came out of the Shamrock tavern, had a bit of trouble in starting his car—Cochran would scarcely have noticed him otherwise—and pulled out into Third Avenue. After a few moments, Cochran—a good, careful cop—turned on his ignition and pulled into Third Avenue after him. They drove north. By now, of course, Cochran was following him more by training and dogged instinct than because of any remaining hope in this angle. He still hated the girl; he still felt that she had first argued with him, and then convinced him, and then—most shameful of all—got him almost ready to believe Ray Cochran was something a lot more significant than an ordinary precinct detective who had been instructed to straighten something out, and who had torn himself into little pieces because he was unable to manage it. Always merry and bright, Cochran thought savagely, that was the ticket. There were reasons for everything—oh, sure! Good and logical reasons, if you were stupid enough to understand what they were. If——

Twice she attempted to speak to him; twice Cochran would not listen to her. Then the sedan in front of him turned into a side street that seemed hazily familiar. He followed. He saw, halfway along this street, an apartment house which was also vaguely familiar to him, and then, when the sedan parked in front of it, he recognized that building with a complete and paralysing shock.

He whispered something. He drove past the sedan, past the man who was ringing a bell in the apartment vestibule, and parked several houses away. He noticed without hate, with a complete detachment that Ellen Morison was looking white, scared and miserable. What was the matter with her now? Cochran asked himself. What was she——

He got her out of the car. He told her where to phone McReynolds, and what to tell him; then he moved back carefull to the sedan which he had followed up here from the Shamrock tavern. All his thoughts had become quick, sharp and decisive. His heart had begun to thump heavily again. An old car with a new paint job, Cochran saw now; no marks on it. Of course. Not so much as a scratch on the rear fender.

But he and McReynolds would find the shop where that paint job had been put on, and where the right rear fender had been hammered out; and then, Cochran told himself grimly, he'd get that married couple to identify this sedan if he had to knock their heads together.

He left the sedan and secluded himself in a dim hallway just down the street from it. The girl came back, and Cochran waved her over imperatively to him, but he did not bother with explanations because he had very little time or attention for her at that moment. He got out two cigarettes and smoked them in extraordinarily long draughts; then McReynolds and a couple of precinct men cruised past him in a department car. Cochran whistled twice. McReynolds stopped.

They discussed matters for a moment or two, Cochran explaining why he was up here, McReynolds grasping the explanation almost immediately. After that the precinct men went around the rear entrance and to the fire escapes, and Cochran and McReynolds entered the apartment house after ringing a bell on the top floor—which was not the floor they wanted. They went up two flights rapidly. They each took deep breaths. Then Cochran rang a bell on that landing, and after some delay the door was opened about three inches and Cochran put a palm against it, shoved and walked in.

The blond man with the dinky little moustache was in there. Cochran walked up to him, gave him a very tight, ugly smile, and hit him. Cochran hit him very hard, and for no apparent reason at all. He just felt that way. He felt fine. At the same moment, McReynolds did what he was supposed to do. McReynolds took care of Mrs Sawyer.

Of course, after the event it was all obvious. Then Cochran told himself that he and McReynolds should have paid more attention to the story Ellen Morison had told them. Hadn't she said that when she entered the drugstore, Mr Sawyer and the hold-up man were standing and talking together like old friends? And hadn't Mrs Sawyer got all excited and hysterical when he and McReynolds had gone back to question her as to how sure she was about Johnny Palica? What should have been at least indicated then was that she could be making some attempt to cover up the real killer, and that, consequently, she herself might be involved in the murder.

It was also clear that Ellen Morison had walked in at just the wrong moment. Mrs Sawyer and her masculine friend had thought up a perfectly simple and effective method through which to rid themselves of a husband who was getting along in years, and who owned a profitable business. They had attempted to arrange everything so that Mrs Sawyer, who was supposed to be the only close witness, would describe a man to the police who did not resemble the gentleman friend in any respect; and then Ellen Morison had appeared just when the gentleman friend had nerved himself up to it, and had got himself into so much of a panic that he was unable to postpone it.

And so, on that first night, Mrs Sawyer had pretended grief and horror, and had refused to understand McReynolds' questions, because it was necessary for her to learn as quickly as possible what Ellen Morison remembered about the man. If she had differed too much with the girl's description, which was fairly accurate, she might have started Cochran and McReynolds nosing around; and so she agreed with it, and identified Johnny Palica.

She did that to cover herself, obviously, and to keep the police busy on another angle. And then the married couple supported her identification, and Johnny Palica was unable to prove his whereabouts, and everything had begun to work out very nicely for Mrs Sawyer and her friend. Until he had done the one thing he should never have done—until he had visited Mrs Sawyer at home, very late at night, in the same apartment house where Cochran and McReynolds had questioned her weeks ago.

As soon as Cochran had recognized the apartment house he had asked himself the natural question: what connection was there between this man and an attractive little woman like Mrs Sawyer? Only one answer had seemed at all feasible. It explained immediately why Mrs Sawyer had identified Johnny Palica, and why Ellen Morison had refused to identify him. Now Cochran was unable to understand why he had never considered that particular aspect before; and even after McReynolds and the other two had got Mrs Sawyer and her masculine friend—screaming at each other, blaming each other—into the department car and had started downtown with them, the whole thing continued to exasperate Cochran as the evidence of a colossal personal stupidity.

"Because in something like this we always check on the wife or husband," he insisted to Ellen Morison, who was still waiting downstairs for him. "Always! We'd have done it this time if you hadn't been there to back up her story. But when

100

you saw the whole thing happen just in front of you——
Well, how were we going to question it? What for? It wasn't
reasonable."

"But I suppose this is," Ellen Morison said. She looked
very tired and miserable. "Now everything's fine. If those
two make you ashamed of the whole human race, that doesn't
matter at all. It's just——" Her mouth twisted. "Get me
away from here, Cochran, please I'm scared. I don't want to
hear anything else about this. All I——"

She began shivering. Cochran soothed her. There was a
perspective you attained in such matters, Cochran said; the
one important thing was that you did not permit an event of
this nature to throw you off balance, to make you cynical,
to—— He stopped there; he remembered suddenly that not
too long ago he had been arguing a similar question from
another position. Ah, forget it, he thought angrily. Who
understood why things like this happened the way they did?
Who wanted to? He could go this far with Ellen Morison—
they worked out pretty well frequently. They had worked
out now, hadn't they?

It did not strike him at once that he had gone much further
with her than he had ever gone with anyone else. When it did
strike him, he decided that perhaps there was some sort of
significance there. He got her into the car and patted her
hand tentatively and murmured to her. On other nights,
Cochran decided, and under different conditions, they could
argue the verities, but just now he would have to be very
firm and sensible about this.

He was. He started the car and got her away from there.
They drove aimlessly at first, with Cochran very quiet and
reassuring with her, and then he took her home and went
home himself. He slept fourteen hours with nothing disturbing him, not even the garbage trucks or the morning traffic,
and when he woke up at last, he discovered that he felt fine
and comfortable, and that he was thinking about Ellen
Morison. *Say*, Cochran thought slowly, *what is this*? But he
knew. He knew almost as soon as the question completed
itself.

SPRING FEVER

DOROTHY SALISBURY DAVIS

SARAH SHEPHERD watched her husband come down the stairs. He set his suitcase at the front door, checked his watch with the hall clock, and examined beneath his chin in the mirror. There was one spot he sometimes missed in shaving. He stepped back and examined himself full length, frowning a little. He was getting paunchy and not liking it. That critical of himself, how much more critical of her he might be. But he said nothing either in criticism or compliment, and she remembered, uncomfortably, doing all sorts of stunts to attract his eye: coy things—more becoming a girl than a woman of fifty-five. She did not feel her twelve years over Gerald . . . most of the time. Scarcely aware of the movement, she traced the shape of her stomach with her fingertips.

Gerald brought his sample spice kit into the living-room and opened it. The aroma would linger for some time after he was gone. "There's enough wood, dear, if it gets cold to-night," he said. "And I wish you wouldn't haul things from the village. That's what delivery trucks are for . . ." He numbered his solicitudes as he did the bottles in the sample case, and with the same non-committal attention.

As he took the case from the table, she got up and went to the door with him. On the porch he hesitated a moment, flexing his shoulders and breathing deeply. "On a morning like this I almost wish I drove a car."

"You could learn, Gerald. You could reach your accounts in half the time, and . . ."

"No, dear. I'm quite content with my paper in the bus, and in a town a car's a nuisance." He stooped and brushed her cheek with his lips. "Hello there!" he called as he straightened up.

Her eyes followed the direction in which he had called. Their only close neighbour, a vegetable and flower grower, was following a plough behind his horse, his head as high as

102

the horse's was low, the morning wind catching his thatch of grey hair and pointing it like a shock of wheat.

"That old boy has the life," Gerald said. "When I'm his age that's for me."

"He's not so old," she said.

"No. I guess he's not at that," he said. "Well, dear, I must be off. Till tomorrow night, take care of yourself."

His step down the road was almost jaunty. It was strange that he could not abide an automobile. But not having one was rather in the pattern. A car would be a tangible link between his life away and theirs at home. Climbing into it of an evening, she would have a feeling of his travels. The dust would rub off on her. As it was, the most she had of him away was the lingering pungency of a sample spice kit.

When he was out of sight she began her household chores —the breakfast dishes, beds, dusting. She had brought altogether too many things from the city. Her mother had left seventy years' accumulation in the old house, and now it was impossible to lay a book on the table without first moving a figurine, a vase, a piece of delft. Really the place was a clutter of bric-à-brac. Small wonder Gerald had changed toward her. It was not marriage that had changed him—it was this house, and herself settling in it like an old Buddha with a bowl of incense in his lap.

A queer thing that this should occur to her only now, she thought. But it was not the first time. She was only now finding a word for it. Nor had Gerald always been this remote. Separating a memory of a particular moment in their early days, she caught his eyes searching her—not numbering her years, as she might think were he to do it now, but measuring his own worth in her esteem.

She lined up several ornaments that might be put away, or better, sold to a junkman. But from the line-up she drew out pieces of which she had grown especially fond. They had become like children to her, as Gerald made children of the books with which he spent his evenings home. Making a basket of her apron she swept the whole tableful of trinkets into it.

Without a downward glance, she hurried them to the ash-box in the backyard. Shed of them, she felt a good deal lighter, and with the May wind in her face and the sun gentle, like an arm across her shoulders, she felt very nearly capersome. Across the fence the jonquils were in bloom, and the

103

tulips, nodding like fat little boys. Mr Joyce had unhitched the horse. He saw her then.

"Fine day this morning," he called. He gave the horse a slap on the rump that sent him into the pasture, and came to the fence.

"I'm admiring the flowers," she said.

"Lazy year for them. Two weeks late they are."

"Is that a fact?" Of course it's a fact, she thought. A silly remark, and another after it: "I've never seen them lovelier, though. What comes out next?"

"Snaps, I guess, this year. Late roses, too. The iris don't sell much, so I'm letting 'em come or stay as they like."

"That should bring them out."

"Now isn't that the truth? You can coax and tickle all year and not get a bloom for thanks. Turn your back on 'em and they run you down."

Like love, she thought, and caught her tongue. But a splash of colour took to her cheeks.

"Say, you're looking nice, Mrs Shepherd, if you don't mind my saying it."

"Thank you. A touch of spring, I suppose."

"Don't it just send your blood racing? How would you like an armful of these?"

"I'd be very pleased, Mr Joyce. But I'd like to pay you for them."

"Indeed not. I won't sell half of them—they come in a heap."

She watched his expert hand nip the blooms. He was already tanned, and he stooped and rose with a fine grace. In all the years he had lived next to them he had never been in the house, nor they in his except the day of his wife's funeral. He hadn't grieved much, she commented to Gerald at the time. And little wonder. The woman was pinched and whining, and there wasn't a sunny day she didn't expect a drizzle before nightfall. Now that Sarah thought of it, Joyce looked younger than he did when Mrs Joyce was still alive.

"There. For goodness' sakes, Mr Joyce. That's plenty."

"I'd give you the field of them this morning," he said, piling her arms with the flowers.

"I've got half of it now."

"And what a picture you are with them."

"Well, I must hurry them into water," she said "Thank you."

She hastened toward the house, flying like a young flirt from her first conquest, and aware of the pleased eye following her. The whole morning glowed in the company she kept with the flowers. She snapped off the radio: no tears for Miss Julia today. At noon she heard Mr Joyce's wagon roll out of the yard as he started to his highway stand. She watched at the window. He looked up and lifted his hat.

At odd moments during the day, she thought of him. He had given her a fine sense of herself and she was grateful. She began to wish that Gerald was returning that night. Take your time, Sarah, she told herself. You don't put away old habits and the years like bric-à-brac. She had softened up, no doubt of it. Not a fat woman, maybe, but plump. Plump. She repeated the word aloud. It had the sound of a potato falling into a tub of water.

But the afternoon sun was warm and the old laziness came over her. Only when Mr Joyce came home, his voice in a song ahead of him, did she pull herself up. She hurried a chicken out of the refrigerator and then called to him from the porch.

"Mr Joyce, would you like to have supper with me? Gerald won't be home, and I do hate cooking just for myself."

"Oh, that'd be grand. I've nothing in the house but a shank of ham that a dog wouldn't bark for. What can I bring?"

"Just come along when you're ready."

Sarah, she told herself, setting the table, you're an old bat trying your wings in daylight. A half-hour later she glanced out of the window in time to see Mr Joyce skipping over the fence like a stiff-legged colt. He was dressed in his Sunday suit and brandishing a bottle as he cleared the barbed wire. Sarah choked down a lump of apprehension. For all that she planned a little fun for herself, she was not up to galloping through the house with an old Don Juan on her heels. Mr Joyce, however, was a well-mannered guest. The bottle was May wine. He drank sparingly and was lavish in his praise of the dinner.

"You've no idea the way I envy you folks, Mrs Shepherd. Your husband especially. How can he bear the times he spends away?"

He bears it all too well, she thought. "It's his work. He's a salesman. He sells spices."

Mr Joyce showed a fine set of teeth in his smile—his own teeth, she marvelled, tracing her bridgework with the tip of her tongue while he spoke. "Then he's got sugar and spice and everything nice, as they say."

What a one he must have been with the girls, she thought, and to marry a quince as he had. It was done in a hurry no doubt, and maybe at the end of a big stick.

"It must be very lonesome for you since Mrs Joyce passed away," she said more lugubriously than she intended. After all the woman was gone three years.

"No more than when she was with me." His voice matched hers in seriousness. "It's a hard thing to say of the dead, but if she hasn't improved her disposition since, we're all in for a damp eternity." He stuffed the bowl of his pipe. "Do you mind?"

"No, I like the smell of tobacco around the house."

"Does your husband smoke?"

"Yes," she said in some surprise at the question.

"He didn't look the kind to follow a pipe," he said, pulling noisily at his. "No, dear lady," he added when the smoke was shooting from it, "you're blessed in not knowing the plague of a silent house."

It occurred to her then that he was exploring the situation. She would give him small satisfaction. "Yes. I count that among my blessings."

There was a kind of amusement in his eyes. You're as lonesome as me, old girl, they seemed to say, and their frankness bade her to add: "But I do wish Gerald was home more of the time."

"Ah, well, he's at the age when most men look to a last trot around the paddock," he said, squinting at her through the smoke.

"Gerald is only forty-three," she said, losing the words before she knew it.

"There's some take it at forty, and others among us leaping after it from the rocking chair."

The conversation had taken a turn she certainly had not intended, and she found herself threshing around in it. Beating a fire with a feather duster. "There's the moon," she said, charging to the window as though to wave to an old friend.

"Aye," he said, "there's the moon. Are you up to a trot in it?"

"What did you say, Mr Joyce?"

"I'd better say what I was thinking first. If I hitch Micky

to the old rig, would you take a turn with me on the Mill Pond Road?"

She saw his reflection in the window, a smug, daring little grin on his face. In sixteen years of settling she had forgotten her way with men. But it was something you never really forgot. Like riding a bicycle, you picked it up again after a few turns. "I would," she said.

The horse ahead of the rig was a different animal from the one on the plough that morning. Mr Joyce had not more than thrown the reins over his rump than he took a turn that almost tumbled Sarah into the sun frames. But Mr Joyce leaped to the seat and pulled Micky up on his hind legs with one hand and Sarah down to her cushion with the other, and they were off in the wake of the moon. . . .

The sun was full in her face when Sarah awoke the next morning. As usual, she looked to see if Gerald were in his bed by way of acclimating her on the day and its routine. With the first turn of her body she decided that a gallop in a rusty-springed rig was not the way to assert a stay of youth. She lay a few moments thinking about it and then got up to an aching sense of folly. It remained with her through the day, giving way at times to a nostalgia for her bric-à-brac. She had never realized how much of her life was spent in the care of it.

By the time Gerald came home she was almost the person he had left the day before. She had held out against the ornaments however. Only the flowers decorated the living-room. It was not until supper was over and Gerald had settled with his book that he commented.

"Sarah, what happened to the old Chinese philosopher?"

"I put him away. Didn't you notice? I took all the clutter out of here."

He looked about him vacantly as though trying to recall some of it. "So you did. I'll miss that old boy. He gave me something to think about."

"What?"

"Oh, I don't know. Confucius says . . . that sort of thing."

"He wasn't a philosopher at all," she said, having no notion what he was. "He was a farmer."

"Was he? Well, there's small difference." He opened the book.

"Aren't the flowers nice, Gerald?"

"Beautiful."

"Mr Joyce gave them to me, fresh out of his garden."

"That's nice."

"Must you read every night, Gerald? I'm here all day with no one to talk to, and when you get home you stick your nose into a book . . ." When the words were half out she regretted them. "I didn't tell you, Gerald. I had Mr Joyce to dinner last night."

"That was very decent of you, dear. The old gentleman must find it lonesome."

"I don't think so. It was a relief to him when his wife died."

Gerald looked up. "Did he say that?"

"Not in so many words, but practically."

"He must be a strange sort. What did she die of?"

"I don't remember. A heart condition, I think."

"Interesting." He returned to his book.

"After dinner he took me for a ride in the horse and buggy. All the way to Cos Corner and back."

"Ha!" was his only comment.

"Gerald, you're getting fat."

He looked up. "I don't think so. I'm about my usual weight. A couple of pounds maybe."

"Then you're carrying it in your stomach. I noticed you've cut the elastic out of your shorts."

"These new fabrics," he said testily.

"They're preshrunken," she said. "It's your stomach. And haven't you noticed how you pull at your collar all the time?"

"I meant to mention that, Sarah. You put too much starch in them."

"I ran out of starch last week and forgot to order it. You can take a size fifteen-and-a-half now."

"Good Lord, Sarah, you're going to tell me next I should wear a horse collar." He let the book slide closed between his thighs. "I get home only three or four nights a week. I'm tired. I wish you wouldn't aggravate me, dear."

She went to his chair and sat on the arm of it. "Did you know that I was beginning to wonder if you'd respond to the poke of a hat-pin?"

He looked directly up at her for the first time in what had seemed like years. His eyes fell away. "I've been working very hard, dear."

"I don't care what you've been doing, Gerald. I'm just glad to find out that you're still human."

He slid his arm around her and tightened it.

"Aren't spring flowers lovely?" she said.

"Yes," he said, "and so is spring."

She leaned across him and took a flower from the vase. She lingered there a moment. He touched his hand to her. "And you're lovely, too."

This is simple, she thought, getting upright again. If the rabbit had sat on a thistle, he'd have won the race.

"The three most beautiful things in the world," Gerald said thoughtfully, "a white bird flying, a field of wheat, and a woman's body."

"Is that your own, Gerald?"

"I don't know. I think it is."

"It's been a long time since you wrote any poetry. You did nice things once."

"That's how I got you," he said quietly.

"And I got you with an old house. I remember the day my mother's will was probated. The truth, Gerald—wasn't it then you made up your mind?"

He didn't speak for a moment, and then it was a continuance of some thought of his own, a subtle twist of association. "Do you remember the piece I wrote on the house?"

"I read it the other day. I often read them again."

"Do you, Sarah? And never a mention of it."

It was almost all the reading she did any more. His devotion to books had turned her from them. "Remember how you used to let me read them to you, Gerald? You thought that I was the only one besides yourself who could do them justice."

"I remember."

"Or was that flattery?"

He smiled. "It was courtship, I'm afraid. No one ever thinks anybody else can do his poetry justice. But Sarah, do you know—I'd listen tonight if you'd read some of them. Just for old times' sake."

For old times' sake, she thought, getting the folder from the cabinet and settling opposite him. He was slouched in his chair, pulling at his pipe, his eyes half-closed. Long ago this same contemplativeness in him had softened the first shock of the difference in their ages.

"I've always liked this one best—*The Morning of My Days*."

"Well you might," he murmured. "It was written for you."

She read one piece after another, wondering now and then what pictures he was conjuring up of the moment he had written them. He would suck on his pipe at times. The sound was like a baby pulling at an empty bottle. She was reading them well, she thought, giving them a mellow vibrance, an old love's tenderness. Surely there was a moment coming when he would rise from the chair and come to her. Still he sat, his eyes almost closed, the pipe now in hand on the chair's arm. A huskiness crept into her voice, so rarely used to this length any more, and she thought of the nightingale's singing, the thorn against its breast. A slit of pain in her own throat pressed her to greater effort, for the poems were almost done.

She stopped abruptly, a phrase unfinished, at a noise in the room. The pipe had clattered to the floor, Gerald's hand still cupped in its shape, but his chin now on his breast. Laying the folder aside, she went over and picked up the pipe with a rather empty regret, as she would pick up a bird that had fallen dead at her feet.

Gerald's departure in the morning was in the tradition of all their days, even to the kiss upon her cheek and the words, "Till tomorrow evening, dear, take care."

Take care, she thought, going indoors. Take care of what? For what? Heat a boiler of water to cook an egg? She hurried her chores and dressed. When she saw Mr Joyce hitch the wagon of flowers, she locked the door and waited boldly at the road for him.

"May I have a lift to the highway?" she called out, as he reined up beside her.

"You may have a lift to the world's end, Mrs Shepherd. Give me your hand." He gave the horse its rein when she was beside him. "I see your old fella's taken himself off again. I daresay it gave him a laugh, our ride in the moonlight."

"It was a giddy business," she said.

"Did you enjoy yourself?"

"I did. But I paid for it afterwards." Her hand went to her back.

"I let out a squeal now and then bending over, myself. But I counted it cheap for the pleasure we had. I'll take you into the village. I've to buy a length of hose, anyway. Or do you think you'll be taken for a fool riding in on a wagon?"

"It won't be the first time," she said. "My life's full of foolishness."

110

"It's a wise fool who laughs at his own folly. We've that in common, you and me. Where'll we take our supper tonight?"

He was sharp as mustard.

"You're welcome to come over," she said.

He nodded. "I'll fetch us a steak, and we'll give Micky his heels again after."

Sarah got off at the post office and stayed in the building until Joyce was out of sight—Joyce and the gapers who had stopped to see her get out of the wagon. Getting in was one thing, getting out another. A bumblebee after a violet. It was time for this trip. She walked to the doctor's office and waited her turn among the villagers.

"I thought I'd come in for a check-up, Dr Philips," she said at his desk. "And maybe you'd give me a diet."

"A diet?" He took off his glasses and measured her with the naked eye.

"I'm getting a little fat," she said. "They say it's a strain on the heart at my age."

"Your heart could do for a woman of twenty," he said, "but we'll have a listen."

"I'm not worried about my heart, Doctor, you understand. I just feel that I'd like to lose a few pounds."

"Uh-huh," he said. "Open your dress." He got his stethoscope.

Diet, apparently, was the rarest of his prescriptions. Given as a last resort. She should have gone into town for this, not to a country physician who measured a woman by the children she bore. "The woman next door to us died of a heart condition," she said, as though that should explain her visit.

"Who's that?" he asked, putting away the instrument.

"Mrs Joyce. Some years ago."

"She had a heart to worry about. Living on stimulants. Yours is as sound as a bullet. Let's have your arm."

She pushed up her sleeve as he prepared the apparatus for measuring her blood pressure. That, she felt, was rising out of all proportion. She was ashamed of herself before this man, and angry at herself for it, and at him for no reason more than that he was being patient with her. "We're planning insurance," she lied. "I wanted our own doctor's opinion first."

"You'll have no trouble getting it, Mrs Shepherd. And no need of a diet." He grinned and removed the apparatus. "Go easy on potatoes and bread, and on the sweets. You'll outlive your husband by twenty years. How is he, by the way?"

"Fine. Just fine, Doctor, thank you."

What a nice show you're making of yourself these days, Sarah, she thought, outdoors again. Well, come in or go out, old girl, and slam the door behind you. . . .

Micky took to his heels that night. He had had a day of ease, and new shoes were stinging his hooves by nightfall. The skipping of Joyce with each snap of the harness teased him, the giggling from the rig adding a prickle. After the wagon, the rig was no more than a fly on his tail. He took the full reins when they slapped on his flanks and charged out from the laughter behind him. It rose to a shriek the faster he galloped and tickled his ears like something alive that slithered from them down his neck and his belly and into his loins. Faster and faster he plunged, the sparks from his shoes like ocean spray. He fought a jerk of the reins, the saw of the bit in his mouth a fierce pleasure. He took turns at his own fancy and only in sight of his yard again did he yield in the fight, choking on the spume that lathered his tongue.

"By the holy, the night a horse beats me, I'll lie down in my grave," Joyce cried. "Get up now, you buzzard. You're not turning in till you go to the highway and back. Are you all right, Sarah?"

Am I all right, she thought. When in years had she known a wild ecstasy like this? From the first leap of the horse she had burst the girdle of fear and shame. If the wheels had spun out from beneath them, she would have rolled into the ditch contented.

"I've never been better," she said.

He leaned close to her to see her, for the moon had just risen. The wind had stung the tears to her eyes, but they were laughing. "By the Horn Spoon," he said, "you liked it!" He let the horse have his own way into the drive after all. He jumped down from the rig and held his hand up to her. "What a beautiful thing to be hanging in the back of the closet all these years."

"If that's a compliment," she said, "it's got a nasty bite."

"Aye. But it's my way of saying you're a beautiful woman."

"Will you come over for a cup of coffee?"

"I will. I'll put up the horse and be over."

The kettle had just come to the boil when he arrived.

"Maybe you'd rather have tea, Mr Joyce."

"Coffee or tea, so long as it's not water. And I'd like you to call me Frank. They christened me Francis but I got free of it early."

"And you know mine, I noticed," she said.

"It slipped out in the excitement. There isn't a woman I know who wouldn't of collapsed in a ride like that."

"It was wonderful." She poured the water into the coffee pot.

"There's nothing like getting behind a horse," he said, "unless it's getting astride him. I wouldn't trade Micky for a Mack truck."

"I used to ride when I was younger," she said.

"How did you pick up the man you got, if you don't mind my asking?"

And you the old woman, she thought; where did you get her? "I worked for a publishing house and he brought in some poetry."

"Ah, that's it." He nodded. "And he thought with a place like this he could pour it out like water from a spout."

"Gerald and I were in love," she said, irked that he should define so bluntly her own thoughts on the matter.

"Don't I remember it? In them days you didn't pull the blinds. It used to put me in a fine state."

"Do you take cream in your coffee? I've forgotten."

"Aye, thank you, and plenty of sugar."

"You haven't missed much," she said.

"There's things you see through a window you'd miss sitting down in the living-room. I'll wager you've wondered about the old lady and me?"

"A little. She wasn't so old, was she, Mr Joyce?" Frank, she thought. Too frank.

"That one was old in her crib. But she came with a greenhouse. I worked for her father."

Sarah poured the coffee. "You're a cold-blooded old rogue," she said.

He grinned. "No. Cool-headed I am, and warm-blooded. When I was young, I made out it was the likes of poetry. She sang like a bird on a convent wall. But when I caged her she turned into an old crow."

"That's a terrible thing to say, Mr Joyce."

The humour left his face for an instant. "It's a terribler thing to live with. It'd put a man off his nut. You don't have a bit of cake in the house, Sarah, to go with this?"

113

"How about muffins and jam?"

"That'll go fine." He smiled again. "Where does your old fella spend the night in his travels?"

"In the hotel in whatever town he happens to be in."

"That's a lonesome sort of life for a married man," he said.

She pulled a chair to the cupboard and climbed up to get a jar of preserves. He made no move to help her although she still could not reach the jar. She looked down at him. "You could give me a hand."

"Try again. You almost had it that time." He grinned, almost gleeful at her discomfort.

She bounced down in one step. "Get it yourself if you want it. I'm satisfied with a cup of coffee."

He pounded his fist on the table, getting up. "You're right, Sarah. Never fetch a man anything he can fetch himself. Which bottle is it?"

"The strawberry."

He hopped up and down, nimble as a goat. "But then maybe he doesn't travel alone?"

"What?"

"I was suggesting your man might have an outside interest. Salesmen have the great temptation, you know."

"That's rather impertinent, Mr Joyce."

"You're right, Sarah, it is. My tongue's been home so long it doesn't know how to behave in company. This is a fine cup of coffee."

She sipped hers without speaking. It was time she faced that question, she thought. She had been hedging around it for a long time, and last night with Gerald should have forced it upon her. "And if he does have an outside interest," she said, lifting her chin, "what of it?"

"Ah, Sarah, you're a wise woman, and worth waiting the acquaintance of. You like me a little now, don't you?"

"A little."

"Well," he said, getting up, "I'll take that to keep me warm for the night."

And what have I got to keep me warm, she thought. "Thank you for the ride, Frank. It was thrilling."

"Was it?" he said, coming near her. He lifted her chin with his forefinger. "We've many a night like this ahead, Sarah, if you say the word." And then when she left her chin on his finger, he bent down and kissed her, taking himself to the door after it with a skip and a jump. He paused there and looked back at her. "Will I stay or go?"

"You'd better go," she choked out, wanting to be angry but finding no anger in herself at all.

All the next day Sarah tried to anchor herself from her peculiar flights of fancy. She had no feeling for the man, she told herself. It was a fine state a woman reached when a kiss from a stranger could do that to her. It was the ride made you giddy, she said aloud. You were thinking of Gerald. You were thinking of . . . the Lord knows what. She worked upstairs until she heard the wagon go by. She would get some perspective when Gerald came home. It seemed as though he'd been gone a long time.

The day was close and damp, and the flies clung to the screens. There was a dull stillness in the atmosphere. By late afternoon the clouds rolled heavier, mulling about one another like dough in a pan. While she was peeling potatoes for supper, Frank drove in. He unhitched the horse but left him in the harness, and set about immediately building frames along the rows of flowers. He was expecting a storm. She looked at the clock. It was almost time for Gerald.

She went out on the front porch and watched for the bus. There was a haze in the sweep of land between her and the highway, and the traffic through it seemed to float thickly, slowly. The bus glided toward the intersection and passed it without stopping. She felt a sudden anger. Her whole day had been strung up to this peak. Since he had not called, it meant merely that he had missed the bus. The next one was in two hours. She crossed the yard to the fence. You're starting up again, Sarah, she warned herself, and took no heed of the warning.

Frank looked up from his work. "You'd better fasten the house," he said. "There's a fine blow coming."

"Frank, if you're in a hurry, I'll give you something to eat."

"That'd be a great kindness. I may have to go back to the stand at a gallop."

He was at the kitchen table, shovelling in the food without a word, when the heavy sky lightened. He went to the window. "By the glory, it may blow over." He looked around at her. "Your old boy missed the bus, did he?"

"He must have."

Frank looked out again. "I do like a good blow. Even if

115

it impoverished me, there's nothing in the world like a storm."

An automobile horn sounded on the road. It occurred to Sarah that on a couple of occasions Gerald had received a ride from the city. The car passed, but watching its dust she was left with a feeling of suspended urgency. Joyce was chatting now. He had tilted back in the chair and for the first time since she had known him, he was rambling on about weather, vegetables, and the price of eggs. She found it more disconcerting than his bursts of intimate comment, and she hung from one sentence to the next waiting for the end of it. Finally she passed in back of his chair and touched her fingers briefly to his neck.

"You need a haircut, Frank."

He sat bolt upright. "I never notice it till I have to scratch. Could I have a drop more coffee?"

She filled his cup, aware of his eyes on her. "Last night was something I'll never forget—that ride," she said.

"And something else last night, do you remember that?"

"Yes."

"Would you give me another now to match it if I was to ask?"

"No."

"What if I took it without asking?"

"I don't think I'd like it, Frank."

He pushed away from the table, slopping the coffee into the saucer. "Then what are you tempting me for?"

"You've a funny notion of temptation," she flared up, knowing the anger was against herself.

Joyce spread his dirt-grimed fingers on the table. "Sarah, do you know what you want?"

The tears were gathering. She fought them back. "Yes, I know what I want," she cried.

Joyce shook his head. "He's got you by the heart, hasn't he, Sarah?"

"My heart's my own!" She flung her head up.

Joyce slapped his hand on the table. "Ho! Look at the spark of the woman! That'd scorch a man if there was a stick in him for kindling." He moistened his lips and in spite of herself Sarah took a step backwards. "I'll not chase you, Sarah. Never fear that. My chasing days are over. I'll neither chase nor run, but I'll stand my ground for what's coming to me." He jerked his head toward the window. "That was

116

only a lull in the wind. There's a big blow coming now for certain."

She watched the first drops of rain splash on the glass. "Gerald's going to get drenched in it."

"Maybe it'll drown him," Joyce said, grinning from the door. "Thanks for the supper."

Let it come on hail, thunder, and lightning. Blow the roof from the house and tumble the chimney. I'd go out from it then and never turn back. When an old man can laugh at your trying to cuckold a husband, and the husband asking it, begging it, shame on you. She went through the house clamping the locks on the windows. More pleasure putting the broom through them.

An early darkness folded into the storm, and the walls of rain bleared the highway lights. There was an ugly yellow tinge to the water from the dust swirled into it. The wind sluiced down the chimney, spitting bits of soot on the living-room floor. She spread newspapers to catch it. A sudden blow, it would soon be spent. She went to the hall clock. The bus was due in ten minutes. What matter? A quick supper, a good book, and a long sleep. The wily old imp was right. A prophet needing a haircut.

The lights flickered off for a moment, then on again. Let them go out, Sarah. What's left for you, you can see by candlelight. She went to the basement and brought up the kerosene lamp and then got a flashlight from the pantry. As she returned to the living-room, a fresh gust of wind sent the newspapers out of the grate like scud. The lights flickered again. A sound drew her to the hall. She thought the wind might be muffling the ring of the telephone. When she got there, the clock was striking. The bus was now twenty minutes late. There was something about the look of the phone that convinced her the line was dead. It was unnerving to find it in order. Imagination, she murmured. Everything was going perverse to her expectations. And then, annoyed with herself, she grew angry with Gerald again. This was insult. Insult on top of indifference.

She followed a thumping noise upstairs. It was on the outside of the house. She turned off the light and pressed her face against the window. A giant maple tree was rocking and churning, one branch thudding against the house. There was not even a blur of light from the highway now. Blacked out. While she watched, a pinpoint of light shaped before her.

117

It grew larger, weaving a little. A flashlight, she thought, and wondered if Gerald had one. Then she recognized the motion: a lantern on a wagon. Frank was returning.

When she touched the light switch there was no response. Groping her way to the hall she saw that all the lights were out now. Step by step she made her way downstairs. A darkness had washed in through the chimney, stale and sickening. She lit the lamp and carried it to the kitchen. From the window there, she saw Frank's lantern bobbing as he led the horse into the barn. She could not see man or horse, only the fading light until it disappeared inside. When it reappeared she lifted her kerosene lamp, a greeting to him. This time he came around the fence. She held the door against the wind.

"I've no time now, Sarah. I've work to do," he shouted. "He didn't come, did he?"

"No!"

"Is the phone working?"

She nodded that it was and waved him close to her. "Did the bus come through?"

"It's come and gone. Close the door or you'll have the house in a shambles." He waved his lantern and was gone.

She put the pot roast she had prepared for Gerald in the refrigerator and set the perishables close to the freezing unit. She wound the clock and put away the dishes. Anything to keep her busy. She washed the kitchen floor that had been washed only the day before. The lantern across the way swung on a hook at the barn, sometimes moving toward the ground and back as Joyce examined the frame he was reinforcing.

Finally she returned to the living-room. She sat for a long time in Gerald's chair, watching the pattern of smoke in the lamp-chimney. Not even a dog or cat to keep her company. Not even a laughing piece of delft to look out at her from the mantelpiece; only the cold-eyed forebears, whom she could not remember, staring down at her from the gilt frames, their eyes fixed upon her, the last and the least of them who would leave after her—nothing.

It was not to be endured. She lunged out of the chair. In the hall she climbed to the first landing where she could see Joyce's yard. He was through work now, the lantern hanging from the porch although the house was darkened. It was the only light anywhere, and swayed in the wind like a will-o'-the-wisp.

She bounded down the stairs and caught up her raincoat.

118

Taking the flashlight she went out into the storm. She made her way around the fence, sometimes leaning into the wind, sometimes resting against it. Joyce met her in his driveway. He had been waiting, she thought, testing his nerves against her own, expecting her. Without a word, he caught her hand and led her to his back steps and into the house. "I've an oil lamp," he said then. "Hold your light there till I fix it."

She watched his wet face in the half-light. His mouth was lined with malicious humour, and his eyes as he squinted at the first flame of the wick were fierce, as fierce as the storm, and as strange to her. When the light flared up, she followed its reaches over the dirty wall, the faded calender, the gaping cupboards, the electric cord hanging from a naked bulb over the sink to the back door. There were dishes stacked on the table where they no doubt stood from one meal to the next. The curtains were stiff with dirt, three years of it. Only then did she take a full glimpse of the folly that had brought her here.

"I just ran over for a minute, Frank. . . ."

"A minute or the night, sit there, Sarah, and let me get out of these clothes."

She took the chair he motioned her into, and watched him fling his coat into the corner. Nor could she take her eyes from him as he sat down and removed his boots and socks. Each motion fascinated her separately, fascinated and revolted her. He wiped between his toes with the socks. He went barefoot toward the front of the house. In the doorway he paused, becoming a giant in the weird light.

"Put us up a pot of coffee, dear woman. The makings are there on the stove."

"I must go home. Gerald . . ."

"To hell with Gerald," he interrupted. "He's snug for the night, wherever he is. Maybe he won't come back to you at all. It's happened before, you know, men vanishing from women they don't know the worth of."

Alone, she sat stiff and erect at the table. He was just talking, poisoning her mind against Gerald. How should she get out of here? Run like a frightened doe and never face him again? No, Sarah. Stay for the bitter coffee. Scald the giddiness out of you once and for all. But on top of the resolve came the wish that Gerald might somehow appear at the door and take her home. Dear, gentle Gerald.

She got up and went to the sink to draw the water for

119

coffee. A row of medicine bottles stood on the window-sill, crusted with dust. Household remedies. She leaned close and examined a faded label: 'Mrs Joyce—— Take immediately upon need.'

She turned from the window. A rocker stood in the corner of the room. In the old days the sick woman had sat in it on the back porch, rocking, and speaking to no one. The stale sickness of her was still about the house, Sarah thought. What did she know of people like this?

He was threshing around upstairs like a penned bull. His muddy boots lay where he had taken them off, a pool of water gathering about them. Again she looked at the window-sill. No May wine there. Suddenly she remembered Dr Phillips's words: "Lived on stimulants for years." She could almost see the sour woman, even to her gasping for breath. . . .'Take immediately.'

Fix the coffee, Sarah. What kind of teasing is this? Teasing the dead from her grave before you. Teasing. Something in the thought disturbed her further . . . an association: Joyce watching her reach for the preserves last night, grinning at her. 'Try it again, Sarah. You almost had it that time.' And she could still hear him asking, 'Which bottle?' Not which jar, but which bottle.

She grabbed the kettle and filled it. Stop it, Sarah. It's the storm, the waiting, too much waiting . . . your time of life. She drew herself up against his coming, hearing his quick steps on the stairs.

"Will you give us a bit of iodine there from the window, Sarah? I've scratched myself on those blamed frames."

She selected the bottle carefully with her eyes, so that her trembling hand might not betray her.

"Dab it on here," he said, holding a white cuff away from his wrist.

The palm of his hand was moist as she bent over it and she could smell the earth and the horse from it. Familiar. Everything about him had become familiar, too familiar. She felt his breath on her neck, and the hissing sound of it was the only sound in the room. She smeared the iodine on the cut and pulled away. His lips tightened across his teeth in a grin.

"A kiss would make a tickle of the pain," he said.

Sarah thrust the iodine bottle from her and grabbed the flashlight. "I'm going home."

His jaw sagged as he stared at her. "Then what did you come for?"

"Because I was lonesome. I was foolish . . ." Fear choked off her voice. A little trickle of saliva dribbled from the corner of his mouth.

"No! You came to torture me!"

She forced one foot toward the door and the other after it. His voice rose in laughter as she lumbered away from him. "Good Lord, Sarah. Where's the magnificent woman who rode to the winds with me last night?"

She lunged into the electric cord in her retreat, searing her cheek on it. Joyce caught it and wrenched it from the wall, its splayed end springing along the floor like a whip. "And me thinking the greatest kindness would be if he never came home!"

The doorknob slipped in her sweaty hand. She dried it frantically. He's crazy, she thought. Mad-crazy.

"You're a lump, Sarah," he shouted. "And Mr Joyce is a joker. A joker and dunce. He always was and he will be till the day they hang him!"

The door yielded and she plunged down the steps and into the yard. In her wild haste she hurled herself against the rig and spun away from it as though it were something alive. She sucked in her breath to keep from screaming. She tore her coat on the fence hurtling past it, leaving a swatch of it on the wire. Take a deep breath, she told herself as she stumbled up the steps. Don't faint. Don't fall. The door swung from her grasp, the wind clamouring through the house. She forced it closed, the glass plate tingling, and bolted it. She thrust the flashlight on the table and caught up the phone. She clicked it wildly.

Finally it was the operator who broke through. "I have a call for you from Mr Gerald Shepherd. Will you hold on, please?"

Sarah could hear only her own sobbing breath in the hollow of the mouthpiece. She tried to settle her mind by pinning her eyes on the stairway. But the spokes of the staircase seemed to be shivering dizzily in the circle of light, like the plucked strings of a harp. Even the sound of them was vibrant in her head, whirring over the rasp of her breath. Then came the pounding footfalls and Joyce's fists on the door. Vainly she signalled the operator. And somewhere in the tumult of her mind she grasped at the thought that if she unlocked the

121

door, Joyce would come in and sit down. They might even light the fire. There was plenty of wood in the basement. But she could not speak. And it was too late.

Joyce's fist crashed through the glass and drew the bolt. With the door's opening the wind whipped her coat over her head; with its closing, her coat fell limp, its little pressure about her knees seeming to buckle them.

"I'm sorry," came the operator's voice, "the call was cancelled ten minutes ago."

She let the phone clatter onto the table and waited, her back still to the door. Ten minutes was not very long ago, she reasoned in sudden desolate calmness. She measured each of Joyce's footfalls toward her, knowing they marked all of time that was left to her. And somehow, she felt, she wanted very little more of it.

For only an instant she saw the loop he had made of the electric cord, and the white cuffs over the strong, gnarled hands. She closed her eyes and lifted her head high, expecting that in that way the end would come more quickly . . .

THE CRATE AT OUTPOST 1

MATTHEW GANT

THE WIND whistled through the valley, and the pyramidal
tent that signified Outpost 1 quivered before the blast. As
always, sentry Rudd placed his hand before the oil burner
that feebly lit the interior of the tent, shielding the yellow
flame from the stray gusts that whipped through the torn
canvas. And, as always, he cast a quick, nearly guilty look at
sentry Dennison, who lay fully dressed on a narrow cot in the
rear of the tent.

"It won't fizz out," Dennison said. He lay on his back, his
hands resting behind his head, and his eyes stared at the
sloping ceiling. Occasionally he wiggled his fingers and
watched with amusement the play of shadows on the canvas
overhead.

"I know," Rudd said, biting his lip and looking away.

"Then why do you do it?" Dennison said.

"I don't know," Rudd said. He spread his hands.

Outside, the wind sank for a moment and from far off
came the barking of dogs. Rudd shivered and drew the frayed
collar of his parka close about him. He stole another quick
look at Dennison, and then his eyes shifted to the corner of
the tent just to the left of the doorway flap.

The crate was still there.

"What are you afraid of?" Dennison asked. "It won't
move."

"I don't know," Rudd said, and then he flared for a
moment. "It's our job. We must see the crate."

He stood up defiantly and strode to the crate. It squatted
on the corner, four feet high, four feet long, four feet wide.
It was of wood, nailed securely across the top.

Rudd remembered the last nailing detail. They had come
in during the warm weather and ripped out the rusting nails
with their hands. One of them had howled when a nail slipped and gashed his palm. The naildriver was the biggest man

123

Rudd had ever seen. He pounded the new, shiny nails with the heel of his rifle, and soon the crate was nearly as good as new.

And while they had changed the nails, a two-striper had stood over the detail, with a rifle that shone dully in the flickering gloom of the tent.

Rudd had seen many nailing details come and go. The thought filled him with pride. Ever since they had landed on the island outpost, he and Dennison had been assigned to see the crate.

"You can see it from your bed," Dennison said, breaking the thoughts. "There's no rule about seeing it from your bed."

"I don't care," Rudd said. "It's easier to see from here."

Dennison said, "Ah-h-h," and the sound turned into a yawn. "Wake me when the two-striper comes," he said.

Rudd flinched. He wanted to tell Dennison that he was not to sleep on duty. Rudd was not supposed to see the crate alone. When the two-striper had told them the order, this had been emphasized:

"Never see the crate alone. Always make sure you're both seeing it at the same time. One man alone can't be trusted."

And both Dennison and Rudd had nodded, gravely.

But it was always the same. Dennison would sleep until the two-striper reached the flap and, cursing, tried to find the tent buttons. And Dennison would be on his feet, gripping his rifle, when the two-striper finally strode to the tent's centre and reviewed his sentries.

Once Dennison hadn't been lucky. The two-striper had found the buttons quickly and the soft mud outside had cushioned his steps, and he was inside before Dennison woke. Dennison had to stand on his feet for a very long time after that.

And the two-striper had lectured him about the crate.

"Do you know why you're here, soldier?" the two-striper had asked Dennison.

"Yes," Dennison said. "To see the crate."

"And why see the crate?" the two-striper persisted.

"So nobody gets it," Dennison answered, his face reddening under the softly-spoken questions.

"And why should nobody get it?" the two-striper probed.

Dennison had stammered then and Rudd wanted to help

him out, but he didn't want to have to stand for a very long time also. Besides, he did not know the answer.

"Because," the two-striper snapped. "That's why, you fool."

And Dennison repeated, "Because." And the two-striper imposed the sentence and left.

Later that night Rudd had whispered to Dennison, who stood there, his rifle clutched tight in his hands. "Are you awake?"

"Yes," Dennison had said.

"I was wondering," Rudd said. "I was wondering about something."

"You're always wondering about something," Dennison said. "What's it this time?"

"I was wondering because why," he said, his voice still a whisper in the pitch-black tent.

"Because why what?" Dennison asked harshly. "Because why what, you fool?"

"Nothing," Rudd said, and he turned to see the crate though it was too dark to make it out.

But gradually he found the nerve to ask, and Dennison, who had been in the service far longer than he, and who was once a two-striper himself, told him.

"Because the crate was once owned by the enemy, long, long ago," he had said, and even Dennison, who slept when he should have been seeing the crate, let his eyes creep to the flap in case the two-striper, or, even worse, the yellow-bar were near.

"The enemy," Rudd had said, involuntarily, his eyes bulging.

"Shut up, you fool," Dennison hissed.

And many, many seasons of warm to cold had gone by before Rudd had asked more questions and learned more about why the crate had to be seen.

Dennison did not know the whole story, for no man did, he said.

But the facts were these: the crate contained an enemy weapon, an old and very powerful weapon, which must never be allowed to fall into his hands again. And during bad times, such as now when the dogs were out barking in pursuit of enemy smell, the crate had to be seen all the time so that nobody got it away.

It was as simple as that.

And from that time on, Rudd had felt the pride of his job, and he wondered even more strongly how Dennison could sleep when he ought to be seeing.

Especially during bad times, when the dogs were barking.

Rudd had never heard so much barking as these past nights. He wished, sometimes, he were back with the others, not at Outpost 1. Once, last warmth, he had become ill and a doctor had visited him, a one-striper. Before he had left, the doctor had told him of the others.

"They are sick-afraid," he had said. "They say the enemy is nearer."

But though for a moment Rudd, too, was sick-afraid, he laughed at the doctor. Doctors knew so little, especially about the movement of soldiers.

But when he told Dennison of it, Dennison didn't laugh. He sat and stared through the open flap at the sun sinking behind the peaks.

And now, the dogs were barking as never before. And the two-striper had come in twice this night, instead of once, and even though their share of oil had been burned up, he had brought more. "See the crate," he said, shortly, as he left.

And Rudd saw the crate, and even Dennison lay there on his bed, his eyes wide open.

They were not relieved until the sun was high the next day.

And that night when they returned to the tent, the two-striper handed them each a bullet for their rifles. It was the first time either man had ever held a loaded rifle.

"See the crate," the two-striper had said fiercely before he left, "see the crate." And Rudd noticed the dark circles under the two-striper's eyes.

"These are bad times," Rudd said to Dennison, staring at him anxiously.

"Bad," Dennison repeated.

"Do you think——?" Rudd started.

"Do I think what, you fool?" Dennison said. But his voice was not sharp at all.

"Do you think the enemy is coming?"

Outside the wind howled again, howled loud, but even over the howl came the sound of the dogs.

"I don't know," Dennison said, at last.

Rudd quickly put his hand over the oil burner to shield it from the wind, but this time Dennison didn't say anything. Things were bad, Rudd knew.

126

He stood straight and he thought: I will do my job. He walked to the crate and leaned on it.

"Don't touch it, you fool," Dennison said.

"But why?" Rudd asked, puzzled. He had touched it many times before, feeling the creaking wood, and sometimes he had peeled splinters of wood from the crate and used them to make pictures in the mud outside.

"Ah-h-h," Dennison said. "Just don't."

And Rudd walked away, ashamed.

Suddenly the outside quivered with noise. The dogs were nearby now, and there must have been dozens of them, yapping and howling, and Dennison said, "Listen."

"The barking is loud," Rudd said.

"No, not the barking. I can hear them gnashing their teeth."

Rudd listened and he heard, too, and he thrilled to the sound. "The enemy will never get to us, not with those dogs of ours," he boasted.

And through the sound came the clomping of a man's heavy boots, running in thick mud.

"The enemy!" Rudd said, his hands tightening over the stock of his rifle, his hand reaching for the bolt.

But it wasn't the enemy. It was a one-striper, the runner from the others.

He stood swaying in the centre of the tent, a huge man with a black beard, his eyes red-rimmed and circled with the same sort of black lines, though even deeper, as those about the two-striper's.

"Is this it?" he panted, pointing to the crate. It had been many seasons since Rudd had seen the runner, and he looked much older, and Rudd felt sorry that the runner didn't even remember the crate.

"Yes," he said. "That's it."

The runner stood there and the tent was still. He bent once and lightly moved his hand toward the crate, and then drew it back quickly. He spun on his heavy boots and faced the sentries.

"You must run," he said. "We are beaten."

"Beaten?" Rudd said. "I don't believe it."

Dennison stared at the runner and then he sat on his cot and started to pull on his boots. "Come on," he said to Rudd, "we don't have all night."

"But——"

127

"Beaten," the runner insisted.

"And the crate?" Rudd said. "The crate?"

"Destroy it," the runner said. "Quickly. You have no time. You must go to the hills when you have finished. Do you have enough oil?"

Rudd stared at the lamp which flared full and strong.

"No, you fool," Dennison said, "not for the lamp. For the crate. The enemy must not get the crate."

The runner handed Rudd a can of oil, and with his bayonet, ripped it open. He stood at the flap for a long moment, and then he raised his hand to his eyes. "Goodbye," he said, "and hurry."

Rudd stared at the open can of oil, and then he started to pour it on the wooden slats across the top of the crate. The barking was frantic now, yards away it seemed.

Dennison tore the can from his hand. "No," he panted, "there must be something inside the wood that can't be destroyed this way, wet packing or metal or something. We'll have to remove the top." He reached for the wood and started to pull at the slats.

"No," Rudd said. "We're not allowed to. We must see the crate, not the inside."

But Dennison would not be stopped, and Rudd watched as the slats groaned and pulled up sharply. Some cracked in Dennison's hands as he clawed at them, and suddenly, the last two slats came up together and the top was off.

They moved back a pace and looked down. There was a sheet of yellowed paper, with five black marks on it, over the inside of the crate, and Dennison reached out and grabbed it away and they both leaned forward to see.

They looked up at each other, and there was a frown on each forehead. Inside the crate were box-like things, most of them the length of a man's hand span, maybe a little longer, not quite as wide, and two, three fingers deep. Each one was covered with cloth.

There were steps outside now, and the dogs were no longer near, their barking off down the valley.

Dennison screamed once, in rage and fear, and he sprinkled oil frantically on the top of the box-like things and he sprinkled oil on the yellowed paper with the five black marks, and he thrust the paper into the oil lamp until a corner caught fire.

128

Then he threw the burning paper on top of the crate, and they both raced from the tent for the hills.

And as Rudd ran, he was sick-afraid, and even many seasons later while he hid in the woods, he still remembered with cringing fear the crate, and sometimes when he found himself drawing in the mud, the thing he drew was the five black marks that had been on the yellowed paper covering the things inside——

BOOKS

MY UNFAIR LADY

GUY CULLINGFORD

I was sitting in a nook in the woods reading a paperback, when this little girl parted the leaves and looked in at me. At first sight she seemed no better or worse than the usual run of small females, a set of indeterminate features framed in towy pigtails which had a long way to go to reach her shoulders. She was wearing a fairly clean dress, bare legs and sandals.

"Excuse me, mister," she said, staring at me good and hard.

"Certainly," I said amiably. "But the wood's big enough for both of us, and I daresay we'll get on better at a distance."

I went on with my reading. And though I kept my eyes on the printed word, I could feel hers like a pair of gimlets boring into me.

"How about leaving me in peace?" I said. "Be a good girl."

She made no attempt to move. She was following her own line of thought, not mine. After a minute, she said, "There's a gentleman being unkind to a lady under that tree." And she turned a bit and pointed.

I felt myself getting hot under the collar, and I said, "That's none of my business or yours either. Run away home, you nasty prying little girl. I don't want to know you."

She stayed put, not budging an inch. For a full minute she remained silent, twisting one ankle round the other.

Then she said, "How'd you like it if someone stuck a knife into you?"

"What!" I leapt to my feet, slamming the book shut. "Why didn't you say that in the beginning? Where's this? What—what tree'd you say?"

She was off like a shot with me right after her. We went about twenty feet down the slope, and then the tail of the girl's little dress vanished into a tangle of undergrowth. I scrambled after her. But when we got to the foot of the tree, I stopped short, silently staring.

There the woman lay, on last year's leaves with her head

supported by a beech trunk. The knife must have found the heart, for she was just as dead as the leaves, although she hadn't been there as long. There's always something pretty shocking in sudden death, and she couldn't have been more than twenty. She must have been a good-looker, too. The haft of the knife was still in place, and suddenly I felt sick at my stomach. I turned away to throw up and realized with a start that the kid who'd brought me there had vanished; she must have melted away while I was busy taking in the situation. I hadn't time to be sick. It suddenly dawned on me that I was in a serious position. That wretched little girl was as valuable to me as her weight in diamonds; she was my one and only alibi that I'd visited the scene of the crime and nothing more. So I had to find her again as soon as possible.

I bolted down the slope, right to the bottom where there was a kind of paddling pond crammed full of children. But though I darted here and there, and there were dozens of little girls, there wasn't a trace of the one I wanted. I tell you, I stood still, and the sweat trickled down my face. I suppose ten minutes elapsed before I gave up the search. Then I had to ask myself a question. What do I do now? I was all for racing away as fast as my legs would take me. If I'd had a hat I could have pulled down over my eyes, I don't think I should have hesitated to do that. But I was bare-headed, and I'd been behaving, in the light of later events, in what might well have been described as oddly by any interested onlooker. There were several mothers who must have spared a moment from watching Bobbie get his pants splashed on to make a mental note of my interest in little girls, perhaps were even ready to have a word with a policeman. And, by heaven, there was a policeman ready made for them, standing in the shade of the trees, no doubt presiding benignly over the frolics of the young, and all set to prevent any casualty among the waders.

I had a horrid vision of myself on the run—the man the police wanted to interview in connection with the murdered girl. Well, in a choice of evils it's my motto to choose the lesser. I headed for the policeman, as if in his stalwart frame lay my only hope of salvation.

"Officer," I said in a voice that broke with uncertainty, "Officer, I want to report a crime."

That shook him. He was a youngish man, and he looked as if all his blood had suddenly drained into his boots. But he pulled himself together and asked me a few questions, and soon we were making it up the slope together, my heart pumping a great deal harder than was called for by the incline.

Of course, later on I got passed on to higher authority for questioning, first a detective sergeant and then an inspector, then both together. I stuck to my story, and they seemed to me to be decent fellows. They almost believed me.

What really rattled them was one of those fantastic coincidences which would be quite inadmissible in fiction. When the constable first bore me off to the police station, I was still clutching that confounded paperback, and when they took it off me, there on the cover, for them to see, was a blonde with a dagger in her heart. I hadn't even noticed the subject of the luridly painted cover until I had it pointed out to me. In the absence of any more substantial clue, blood or strands of hair or incriminating fingerprints, they had to make the most of that. In defence, I stuck to the little girl who had drawn me into my predicament; she was all I had.

"Pity you don't know her name," commented the inspector, a shade dryly I thought.

"I don't go round asking the names of strange little girls," I said. "I'm not fond enough of them for that."

The inspector nodded. "Mind you," he said, "if what you're telling us is the truth, there's no need to be alarmed. If the kid's above ground we'll find her, don't you worry."

"Then I'll not worry," I said.

"Lucky the schools haven't broken up," said the sergeant. "We'll go through them with a fine-tooth comb till we find her, that is . . ." He paused significantly and scratched his nose. I could see he wasn't convinced.

I got to know the sergeant quite well during the next twenty-four hours—and the local schools. As far as the children were concerned, our arrival was a welcome interruption, but the teachers were less approving. Finally, at Omega Road Girls' School we struck oil.

After a short talk with the head-mistress, we were shown into a classroom of the correct age group. There were about four and twenty little darlings present, with the one we were after practically indistinguishable from the rest—except to me. She was seated at a desk, second row from the front. We had been warned not to upset the little dears, so the sergeant in a voice flowing with milk and honey asked them if they'd any of them ever seen this gentleman (pointing to me) before any-where. Up shot a forest of hands. Only one in the second row remained at desk level. You can guess whose.

"Where?" asked the sergeant.

"Pleasir, pleasir," they chanted in unison, and one being singled out by the head-mistress for a solo speech said, "Please, Ma'am, we all saw him at the paddling pool in Hammer Wood on the afternoon the young woman got done in."

The head-mistress shot me a frosty look, as if I should be held responsible for any psychic damage done to these innocents. At once I asked the sergeant for the privilege of half a minute's private conversation. We cowered behind the black-board, and I whispered into his ear that the one who hadn't put up her hand was the one we were after. He emerged brushing his moustache, first one side, then the other, and said, "I want to ask the little girl in the second row who didn't put up her hand if she has ever seen this gentleman before?"

"Speak up, Ruby Gant," said the head-mistress, cooing at the little wretch. "No one's going to hurt you, dear."

The child's indeterminate features registered no expression whatever. She took her time about it, studying me with a sort of vacant earnestness.

"I never seen him in me life, Miss Birch," she finally said. "I don't know that gentleman at all, and . . ." here the lips parted in a grin to disclose a set of tiny, regular teeth . . . "I don't know as I want to."

A giggle ran round the class, and Miss Birch did nothing to suppress it. Instead, she asked mildly, "You weren't at the pool with the others, then?"

"No, Miss Birch, Ruby wasn't at the pool with us," said a child who was seated behind Ruby Gant. "She said she had to go straight home."

"Is that right, Ruby?"

"Yes, Miss Birch. I wanted to look after me baby brother, so our mum could get a rest."

You could practically see the halo above that flaxen crown.

"I have always found Ruby a very truthful little girl," re-marked Miss Birch, *sotto voce* to the sergeant.

That was that. I ask you, what could I do about it?

They had to let me go in the end, for there wasn't a shred of real evidence. They couldn't trace any connection between me and the murdered girl, and it wasn't any good bringing a prosecution on the strength of a lurid book jacket. Although I was told dozens of women volunteered to give information on my personal appearance down at the pool that afternoon. You know, the usual thing, the wild and glaring eyes, the maniacal frenzy, etcetera, etcetera. I never varied my story, however much opportunity I was given, and there was nothing known against me, and I was in steady employment.

As far as I could see, they would never nail anyone else for the wood-killing either. Like most of those girls who are found murdered, she was not known to have had any men friends. Apparently, she ran to type, quiet and reserved and self-respecting. Well, she was now, anyway, poor thing. The knife was of a common sort which might be found in the possession of any boy scout. Although it had been sharpened to a fine edge, there were no fingerprints on it. As for fallen leaves, they don't measure up to flower beds when it comes to holding the impression of a distinctive shoe heel. If I'd done the murder myself, I couldn't have made a neater job of it.

Finally, the CID had to admit themselves beaten, and I left the police station for the last time without a stain on my character. Huh! I lost my job, I lost my place of residence, I lost my friends. And, in addition to all this, no girl in that district would be seen dead with me. Though for weeks afterwards, had girls permitted me to escort them, they would have been the safest girls in the world. I never took a step without police protection, very, very unobtrusive. The smallest squeak would have brought the man on my tail to my side.

All the same, I wasn't moving from the neighbourhood, not yet awhile. I found a fresh dwelling with a deaf mute for a landlady, a fresh job at half the pay, and there I stuck, waiting for time to pass which is reputedly a great healer.

But I was waiting with a purpose. When three months were up, I found myself alone again—without police protection, that is. Then I thought it was safe to get busy. They say a child's memory is short, and I didn't want to leave it too long. I started to hang about the Omega Road Girls' School, at four o'clock when the kids were coming out. I marked my prey; three months had made very little difference to her, and I herded her off from the rest of the flock. As a matter of fact, it was easy as pie because she left the others at a road junction and trailed off on her own. I guess it was like that the day at the pool; she was strictly an individualist. I had decided to use guile, and had been toting round with me for days a big bag of toffees.

"Hey, Ruby," I said, catching up with her and offering the bag. "Have a sweetie."

She recognized me at once. She didn't look scared at all, but she shook her head and said, "My mum says I'm never to take sweets from strangers."

"I'm not a stranger. I'm the man you nearly put behind bars for life, don't you remember?"

"Serves yer right. You shouldn't have spoken nasty to me."

Then she showed her teeth in the famous grin. You could see she didn't bear me an ounce of spite.

"Besides . . ." she said.

"Besides what?"

"I didn't want to get meself in trouble. I didn't want to draw attention to meself, see."

My God, she'd got it all there in her little brain-pan at the age of eight or thereabouts. She didn't care a fig what became of me; it was her own skin she was intent on preserving.

She undoubtedly knew who had killed the girl . . .

I tried not to show any excitement, and I said as casually as I could, matching my step to hers: "Then you saw the chap who did it. I thought it was one of your lies!"

"Don't be saucy. Of course I saw 'im. Leastways, I saw his back. He was bending over."

"You mean you never saw his face at all. Well, that's no good, you couldn't pick him out."

"I could and all, if I wanted to. Wears a blue suit."

"So does my Uncle Bert. What the hell! Why every——"

"You shouldn't swear. My mum says it's not nice."

"You and your mum! I'll tell you what your mum is, she's as big a liar as you are if she says you were at home minding the baby when you were busy snooping at people in the wood."

"She can't keep her eye on the clock all the time, can she? Not with my young brother she can't. And I wasn't snooping, Mister Clever. I was playing 'ouses under the trees."

"And you say you know this chap?"

"I didden say I knew 'im. I said I could put my finger on 'im if I liked."

"Then why don't you?"

"It's none of my business." She brought it out with an air of secret triumph.

135

But it was my business all right, and my particular business to keep on baiting her until I got the response I wanted. I've often heard little girls doing it to each other, and nine times out of ten it works.

So I gathered my resources together, and packing all the scorn I could into my voice, said: "Huh! Ruby Gant, you don't know a thing!"

"I do."

"You're just making it up."

"I'm not."

"Yes you are. You never saw the chap at all, or if you did, you wouldn't know him from Adam."

"I told you 'e'd got blue clothes on."

"Well, where does he live?"

"I dunno where 'e lives, but I know where 'e is this minnit."

"You're a nasty story teller!"

"No I'm not."

"Yes you are."

I was thoroughly into the spirit of the thing, when she suddenly capitulated.

"If I take you to where he is, then will you believe me?"

"Now you're talking," I said. "You take me to him and I'll believe you."

She looked at me hard with that intent yet somehow vacant stare which was part of her make-up.

"If I do, will yer swear not to tell anyone?"

"Of course I will."

"Then say it after me."

"What is it? What have I got to say?"

She licked her grubby first finger and held it up in the air.

"See my finger's wet . . . go on and say it."

I licked my own finger and followed her instructions.

"See my finger's dry."

"See my finger's dry."

"Slit my throat if I tell a lie." Here she drew her finger ominously across her scraggy little throat.

I repeated the childish oath. I hadn't the faintest intention of sticking to it. I'd have been an outright fool if I considered I owed any allegiance to that child.

But my having taken the oath seemed to satisfy her. She said, "Come on, then."

She pranced off and I followed her as I'd done once before. The only difference was that now she wore a skimpy cloth coat and we were on the pavements and not in the path in the wood.

She led me from this by-road into another and yet another until at last we came out on the High Street. There were lots of people about shopping, but she didn't moderate her pace, but slipped between them like an eel, while I blundered after. I must have looked odd chasing after that scrap of a kid, as if life depended on it. But I wasn't conscious of making a fool of myself; my heart was thumping wildly, because I felt sure I was on to something important.

Finally, we came to the crossroads where the High Street joins the main arterial road coming from the city.

Ruby Gant came to a sudden standstill, which brought me right up on her heels.

She dropped back to my side, and looking up at me, gave the faintest flick to her thumb.

"There 'e is, then. What did I tell yer?"

There he was, with his back to us, blue suit, white gloves and all, directing the home-going traffic, the young cop I'd given myself up to that day in the wood, by the paddling pool.

I stood gazing stupidly at him, my mind in a whirl, for perhaps ten seconds. Then I turned to Ruby. You know what? The little devil wasn't there. She'd played the same trick on me as before. She must have moved like greased lightning.

It was hopeless to look for her among the crowd. A child as small as that could take cover anywhere. She might have darted into the nearest chain store for temporary refuge, or be halfway home already.

So there I was, up a tree. I turned about and began to walk slowly back along the High Street, mechanically dodging the busy shoppers while I mulled what had happened over in my mind. Was Miss Ruby Gant stringing me along in her own inimitable fashion? And was this last audacity—pure invention on the spur of the moment—a final thumb at the nose at me, for venturing to criticize her past conduct?

Did her fiendish ingenuity prompt her to select a policeman as the supreme example of improbability? Was she even now giggling away at the idea of it?

Did she really know who had murdered the girl in the wood? Was the blue suit merely a product of her fertile fancy, or had it some basis in fact?

It was a matter beyond dispute that the cop had been right on the spot, or as near as makes no difference. It would have

137

taken him less than no time to have slipped down the slope from the fatal tree into position as guardian of the pool. Just because no motive had come to light for the murder of the girl, it didn't follow that there was none.

When I was a boy I was never keen to tangle with the forces of law and order, and I could therefore imagine what effect the idea of mixing it with a policeman would have on one of Ruby's age and environment. You notice that I don't say tender age. Still, it was nice to think that there might be some reason for what that kid had done to me, besides the mere gratification of a childish spite.

Now that I harked back, I had a vivid mental picture of the blood draining out of the policeman's face when I first reported to him my discovery of the crime. Was every cop so squeamish, however inexperienced?

But even if Ruby had made me a present of the killer, what good was it likely to do me? I shouldn't like to see the expression on the sergeant's face if I'd be so foolish as to trot to the police station with this new theory.

And suddenly I saw the whole thing from the point of view of the police, and knew myself that it was only a pack of lies, or rather, that mixture of truth and tarradiddle in which Ruby specialized.

Well, let bygones be bygones, I thought. Thanks to Ruby, I should always be a man with a past . . . no need to allow her to complicate my future.

I felt that I needed a drink to strengthen my resolution, even if it was only a strong black coffee, and as this feeling happened to coincide with my passing one of the local milk bars, I pushed the door and went in.

It was one of those narrow affairs like a tramcar, with tables in front and the works at the end. I was nearly up to the counter, when I saw something which pulled me up dead.

There, perched up on a stool, with her back three-quarters-wise to me, was that demon-child. She had her skinny elbows planted on the counter, and her monkey paws round a beakerful of something.

But she wasn't drinking. She seemed to be in a sort of ecstasy, gazing up with rapt adoration at the face of the Adonis presiding over the counter. The man was sleek and dark and as handsome as a rattlesnake. You know the type.

There was a loud sort of buzzing noise in my ears. I stood perfectly still, and deep down inside me I had that sudden

138

hideous conviction of truth without proof such as a chap gets sometimes.

I added my stare to Ruby's.

The man must have finished buttering some slices of cut bread ready for sandwiches, because he still held the knife loosely in his right hand, while with the index finger of the left he was absent-mindedly testing the sharpness of the blade.

He was not interested in either of us.

All his attention was centred on the pair of young girls who sat at the table next to the counter, chattering away together in the animated way girls have if within ten yards of any personable male. His eyes, half-narrowed, feasted on them as on some delectable prospect.

Then, as if drawn by a magnet, he released the knife, and came forward, brushing past the entranced Ruby, to collect their empty cups.

As he bent over them in his regulation short white jacket, murmuring who knows what sweet inducements, he revealed to me the back view of a pair of pants of peculiarly revolting shade. I decided not to stop for refreshment.

I did a rightabout turn, and was out of those surroundings in less time than it takes to say 'Blue Murder'.

Oh yes, I agree there are loose ends. There are several things I should like to know myself.

For instance, just when did Mistress Ruby catch up with him?

Did she track him down systematically by his choice in suiting? Had she known him before? Or was it one of those odd chances, beginner's luck, as you might say?

How long was he prepared to go on stuffing her up with free ice cream, hot chocolate and what have you, to keep her on his side?

And what was going to happen when he stopped?

Or when . . . well, never mind.

These questions, or any variants on same, are likely to go unanswered as far as I'm concerned.

When two tigers get together, that's no place for me.

NEW MURDERS FOR OLD

CARTER DICKSON

HARGREAVES did not speak until he had turned on two lamps. Even then he did not remove his overcoat. The room, though cold, was stuffy, and held a faintly sweet odour. Outside the Venetian blinds, which were not quite closed, you saw the restless, shifting presence of snow past street lights. For the first time, Hargreaves hesitated.

"The—the object," he explained, indicating the bed, "was there. *He* came in by this door, here. Perhaps you understand a little better now?"

Hargreaves' companion nodded.

"No," said Hargreaves, and smiled. "I'm not trying to invoke illusions. On the contrary, I am trying to dispel them. Shall we go downstairs?"

It was a tall, heavy house, where no clocks ticked. But the treads of the stairs creaked and cracked sharply, even under their padding of carpet. At the back, in a kind of small study, a gas-fire had been lighted. Its hissing could be heard from a distance; it roared up blue, like solid blue flames, into the white fretwork of the heater; but it did little to dispel the chill of the room. Hargreaves motioned his companion to a chair at the other side of the fire.

"I want to tell you about it," he went on. "Don't think I'm trying to be"—his wrist hesitated over a word, as though over a chesspiece—"highbrow. Don't think I'm trying to be highbrow if I tell it to you"—again his wrist hesitated —"objectively. As though you know nothing about it. As though you weren't concerned in it. It's the only way you will understand the problem he had to face."

Hargreaves was very intent when he said this. He was bending forward, looking up from under his eyebrows; his heavy overcoat flopped over the sides of his knees, and his gloved hands, seldom still, either made a slight gesture or pressed flat on his knees.

"Take Tony Marvell, to begin with," he argued. "A good fellow, whom everybody liked. Not a good business man, perhaps; too generous to be a good business man; but as conscientious as the very devil, and with so fine a mathematical brain that he got over the practical difficulties.

"Tony was Senior Wrangler at Cambridge, and intended to go on with his mathematics. But then his uncle died, so he had to take over the business. You know what the business was then: three luxury hotels, built, equipped and run by Old Jim, the uncle, in Old Jim's most flamboyant style: all going to rack and ruin.

"Everybody said it was madness for Tony to push his shoulder up against the business world. His brother—that's Stephen Marvell, the former surgeon—said Tony would only bring Old Jim's card-houses down on everybody and swamp them all with more debts. But you know what happened. At twenty-five, Tony took over the business. At twenty-seven, he had the hotels on a paying basis. At thirty, they were hotels to which everybody went as a matter of course: blazing their sky-signs, humming with efficiency, piling up profits which startled even Tony.

"And all because he sneered at the idea that there could be any such thing as overwork. He never let up. You can imagine that dogged expression of his: 'Well, I don't like this work, but let's clean it up satisfactorily so that we can get on to more important things'—like his studies. He did it partly because he had promised Old Jim he would, and partly *because* (you see?) he thought the business so unimportant that he wanted to show how easy it was. But it wasn't easy. No man could stand that pace. London, Brighton, Eastbourne; he knew everything there was to know about the Marvell Hotels, down to the price of a pillow-case and the cost of grease for the lifts. At the end of the fifth year he collapsed one morning in his office. His brother Stephen told him what he had to do.

" 'You're getting out of this,' Stephen said. 'You're going clear away. Round the world, anywhere; but for six or eight months at the shortest time. During that time, you're not even so much as to think of your work. Is that clear?'

"Tony told me the story himself last night. He says that the whole thing might never have happened if he had not been forbidden to write to anybody while he was away.

" 'Not even so much as a postcard,' snapped Stephen, 'to

anybody. If you do, it'll be more business; and then God help you.'

" 'But Judith——' Tony protested.

" 'Particularly to Judith,' said Stephen. 'If you insist on marrying your secretary, that's your affair. But you don't ruin your rest-cure by exchanging long letters about the hotels.'

"You can imagine Stephen's over-aristocratic, thin-nosed face towering over him, dull with anger. You can imagine Stephen in his black coat and striped trousers, standing up beside the polished desk of his office in Harley Street. Stephen Marvell (and, to a certain extent, Tony, too) had that overbred air which Old Jim Marvell had always wanted and never achieved.

"Tony did not argue. He was willing enough, because he was tired. Even if he were forbidden to write to Judith, he could always think about her. In the middle of September, more than eight months ago, he sailed by the *Queen Anne* from Southampton. And on that night the terrors began."

Hargreaves paused. The gas-fire still hissed in the little, dim study. You would have known that this was a house in which death had occurred, and occurred recently, by the look on the face of Hargreaves' companion. He went on:

"The *Queen Anne* sailed at midnight. Tony saw her soaring up above the docks, as high as the sky. He saw the long decks, white and shiny like shoe-boxes, gleaming under skeins of lights; he saw the black dots of passengers moving along them; he heard the click rattle-rush of winches as great cranes swung over the crowd on the docks; and he felt the queer, pleasurable, restless feeling which stirs the nerves at the beginning of an ocean voyage.

"At first he was as excited as a schoolboy. Stephen Marvell and Judith Gates, Tony's fiancée, went down to Southampton with him. Afterward he recalled talking to Judith; holding her arm, piloting her through the rubbery-smelling passages of the ship to show her how fine it was. They went to Tony's cabin, where his luggage had been piled together with a basket of fruit. Everybody agreed that it was a fine cabin.

"It was not until a few minutes before the 'all-ashore' gong that the first pang of loneliness struck him. Stephen and Judith had already gone ashore, for all of them disliked these awkward, last-minute leave-takings. They were standing on the docks, far below. By leaning over the rail of the ship he could just see them. Judith's face was tiny, remote and smiling; infinitely loved. She was waving to him. Round him surged the crowd; faces, hats, noise under naked lights, accentuating the break with home and the water that would widen between. Next he heard the gong begin to bang: hollow, quivering, pulsing to loudness over the cry: 'All ashore that's going ashore!'; and dying away into the ship. He did not want to go. There was still plenty of time. He could still gather up his luggage and get off.

"For a time he stood by the rail, with the breeze from Southampton Water in his face. Such a notion was foolish. He would stay. With a last wave to Judith and Stephen, he drew himself determinedly away. He would be sensible. He would go below and unpack his things. Feeling the unreality of that hollow night, he went down to his cabin on C Deck. And his luggage was not there! He stared round the stuffy cabin with its neat curtains at the portholes. There had been a trunk and two suitcases, gaudily labelled, to say nothing of the basket of fruit. Now the cabin was empty.

Tony ran upstairs again to the purser's office. The purser, a harassed man behind a kind of ticket-window desk, was just getting rid of a clamouring crowd. In the intervals of striking a hand-bell and calling orders, he caught Tony's eye.

" 'My luggage——' Tony said.

" 'That's all right, Mr Marvell,' said the harassed official. 'It's being taken ashore. But you'd better hurry yourself.'

"Tony had here only a feeling of extreme stupidity. 'Taken ashore?' he said. 'But why? Who told you to send it ashore?'

" 'Why, *you* did,' said the purser, looking up suddenly from a sheet of names and figures.

"Tony only looked at him.

" 'You came here,' the purser went on, with sharply narrowing eyes, 'not ten minutes ago. You said you had decided not to take the trip, and asked for your luggage to be taken off. I told you that at this date we could not, of course, refund the——'

" 'Get it back!' said Tony. His own voice sounded wrong. 'I couldn't have told you that. Get it back!'

" 'Just as you like, sir,' said the purser, smiting on the bell, '*if* there's time.'

"Overhead the hoarse blast of the whistle, the mournfullest of all sounds at sea, beat out against Southampton Water. B Deck, between open doors, was cold and gusty.

"Now Tony Marvell had not the slightest recollection of

143

having spoken to the purser before. That was what struck him between the eyes like a blow, and what, for the moment, almost drove him to run away from the *Queen Anne* before they should lift the gangplank. It was the nightmare again. One of the worst features of his nervous breakdown had been the conviction, coming in flashes at night, that he was not real any longer; that his body and his inner self had moved apart, the first walking or talking in everyday life like an articulate dummy, while the brain remained in another place. It was as though he were dead, and seeing his body move. Dead.

"To steady his wits, he tried to concentrate on familiar human things. Judith, for instance; he recalled Judith's hazel eyes, the soft line of her cheek as she turned her head, the paper cuffs she wore at the office. Judith, his fiancée, his secretary, who would take care of things while he was away; whom he loved, and who was so maddeningly close even now. But he must not think of Judith. Instead, he pictured his brother Stephen, and Johnny Cleaver, and any other friends who occurred to him. He even thought of Old Jim Marvell, who was dead. And—so strong is the power of imaginative visualization—at that moment, in the breezy lounge-room facing the purser's office, he thought he saw Old Jim looking at him round the corner of a potted palm.

"All this, you understand, went through Tony's mind in the brief second while he heard the ship's whistle hoot out over his head.

"He made some excuse to the purser, and went below. He was grateful for the chatter of noise, for the people passing up and down below decks. None of them paid any attention to him, but at least they were there. But, when he opened the door of his cabin, he stopped and stood very still in the doorway.

"The propellers had begun to churn. A throb, a heavy vibration, shook upwards through the ship; it made the tooth-glass tinkle in the rack, and sent a series of creaks through the bulkheads. The *Queen Anne* was moving. Tony Marvell took hold of the door as though that movement had been a lurch, and he stared at the bed across the cabin. On the white bed-spread, where it had not been before, lay an automatic pistol."

The gas-fire had heated its asbestos pillars to glowing red. Again there was a brief silence in the little study of the house in St John's Wood. Hargreaves—Sir Charles Hargreaves, Assistant Commissioner of Police for the Criminal Investigation Department—leaned down and lowered the flame of the heater. Even the tone of his voice seemed to change when the gas ceased its loud hissing.

"Wait!" he said, lifting his hand. "I don't want you to get the wrong impression. Don't think that the fear, the slow approach of what was going to happen, pursued Tony all through his trip round the world. It didn't. That's the most curious part of the whole affair.

"Tony has told me that it was a brief, bad bout, lasting perhaps fifteen minutes in all, just before and just after the *Queen Anne* sailed. It was not alone the uncanny feeling that things had ceased to be real. It was a sensation of active malignancy—of hatred, of danger, or what you like—surrounding him and pressing on him. He could feel it like a weak current from a battery.

"But five minutes after the ship had headed out to open sea, every such notion fell away from him. It was as though he had emerged out of an evil fog. That hardly seems reasonable. Even supposing that there are evil emanations, or evil spirits, it is difficult to think that they are confined to one country; that their tentacles are broken by half a mile's distance; that they cannot cross water. Yet there it was. One moment he was standing there with the automatic pistol in his hand, the noise of the engines beating in his ears and a horrible impulse joggling his elbow to put the muzzle of the pistol into his mouth and——

"Then—snap! Something broke: that is the only way he can describe it. He stood upright. He felt like a man coming out of a fever, shaken and sweating, but back from behind the curtain into the real world again. He gulped deep breaths. He went to the porthole and opened it. From that time on, he says, he began to get well.

"How the automatic had got into his cabin he did not know. He knew he must have brought it himself, in one of those blind flashes. But he could not remember. He stared at it with new eyes, and new feeling of the beauty and sweetness of life. He felt as though he had been reprieved from execution.

"You might have thought that he would have flung the pistol overboard in sheer fear of touching it. But he didn't. To him it was the part of a puzzle. He stared much at it: a Browning 38, of Belgian manufacture, fully loaded. After the first few days, when he did keep it locked away out of sight in his trunk, he pondered over it. It represented the one piece of evidence he could carry back home with him, the one tangible reality in a nightmare.

"At the New York Customs-shed it seemed to excite no surprise. He carried it overland with him—Cleveland, Chicago, Salt Lake City—to San Francisco, in a fog, and then down the kindled sea to Honolulu. At Yokohama they were going to take it away from him; only a huge bribe retrieved it. Afterward he carried it on his person, and was never searched. As the broken bones of his nerves knitted, as in the wash of the propellers, there was peace, it became a kind of mascot. It went with him through the blistering heat of the Indian Ocean, into the murky Red Sea, to the Mediterranean. To Port Said, to Cairo in early winter. To Naples and Marseilles and Gibraltar. It was tucked away in his hippocket on the bitter cold night, a little more than eight months after his departure, when Tony Marvell—a healed man again—landed back at Southampton in the ss *Chippenham Castle*.

"It was snowing that night, you remember? The boat-train roared through thickening snow. It was crowded, and the heat would not work.

"Tony knew that there could be nobody at Southampton to meet him. His itinerary had been laid out in advance, and he had stuck to the bitter letter of his instructions about not writing even so much as a postcard. But he had altered the itinerary, so as to take a ship that would get him home in time for Christmas; he would burst in on them a week early. For eight months he had lived in a void. In an hour or two he would be home. He would see Judith again.

"In the dimly lighted compartment of the train, his fellow-passengers were not talkative. The long voyage had squeezed their conversation dry; they almost hated each other. Even the snow roused only a flicker of enthusiasm.

" 'Real old-fashioned Christmas!' said one.

" 'Hah!' said another appreciatively, scratching with his fingernails at the frosted window.

" 'Damn cold, *I* call it,' snarled a third. 'Can't they ever make the heat work in these trains? I'm damn well going to make a complaint!'

"After that, with a sympathetic grunt or mutter, each retired behind his newspaper; a white, blank wall which rustled occasionally, and behind which they drank up news of home.

146

"In other words (Tony remembers that he thought then), he was in England again. He was home. For himself, he only pretended to read. He leaned back in his seat, listening vaguely to the clackety-roar of the wheels, and the long blast of the whistle that was torn behind as the train gathered speed.

"He knew exactly what he would do. It would be barely ten o'clock when they reached Waterloo. He would jump into a cab, and hurry home—to this house—for a wash and brush-up. Then he would pelt up to Judith's flat at Hampstead as hard as he could go. Yet this thought, which should have made him glow, left him curiously chilly round the heart. He fought the chill. He laughed at himself. Determinedly he opened the newspaper, distracting himself, turning from page to page, running his eye down each column. Then he stopped. Something familiar caught his eye, some familiar name. It was an obscure item on a middle page.

"He was reading in this paper the news of his own death. Just that.

"Mr Anthony Dean Marvell, of Upper Avenue Road, St John's Wood, and owner of Marvell Hotels, Ltd, was found shot dead last night in his bedroom at home. A bullet had penetrated up through the roof of the mouth into the brain, and a small-calibre automatic was in his hand. The body was found by Mrs Reach, Mr Marvell's housekeeper, who . . ."

"A suicide!"

"And once again, as suddenly as it had left him aboard ship, the grasp fell on him, shutting him off from the real world into the unreal. The compartment, as I told you, was very dimly lighted. So it was perhaps natural that he could only dimly see a blank wall of upheld newspapers facing him; as though there were no fellow-passengers there, as though they had deserted him in a body, leaving only the screen of papers that joggled a little with the rush of the train.

"Yes, he was alone.

"He got up blindly, dragging open the door of the compartment to get into the corridor. The confined space seemed to be choking him. Holding his own newspaper up high, so as to catch the light from the compartment, he read the item again.

"There could be no possibility of a mistake. The account

147

was too detailed. It told all about him, his past and present . . .

"'. . . His brother, Mr Stephen Marvell, the eminent Harley Street surgeon, was hurriedly summoned. . . . His fiancée, Miss Judith Gates . . . It is understood that in September Mr Marvell suffered a nervous breakdown, from which even a long rest had not effected a cure. . . .'

"Tony looked at the date of the newspaper, afraid of what he might see. But it was the date of that day: the twenty-third of December. From this account, it appeared that he had shot himself forty-eight hours before.

"And the gun was in his hip-pocket now.

"Tony folded up the newspaper. The train moved under his feet with a dancing sway, jerking above the click of the wheels; and another thin blast of the whistle went by. It reminded him of the whistle aboard the *Queen Anne*. He glanced along the dusky corridor. It was empty except for someone, whom he supposed to be another passenger, leaning elbows on the rail past the windows and staring out at the flying snow.

"He remembers nothing else until the train reached Waterloo. But something—an impression, a subconscious memory—registered in his mind about that passenger he had seen in the corridor. First it had to do with the shape of the person's shoulders. Then Tony realized that this was because the person was wearing a greatcoat with an old-fashioned brown fur collar. He was jumping wildly out of the train at Waterloo when he remembered that Old Jim Marvell always used to wear such a collar.

"After that he seemed to see it everywhere.

"When he hurried up to the guard's van to claim his trunk and suitcases, the luggage-ticket in his hand, he was in such a crowd that he could not move his arms. But he thought he felt brown fur press the back of his shoulders.

"A porter got him a taxi. It was a relief to see a London cab again, in a coughing London terminus, and hear the bump of the trunk as it went up under the strap, and friendly voices again. He gave the address to the driver, tipped the porter, and jumped inside. Even so, the porter seemed to be holding open the door of the taxi longer than was necessary.

"'Close it, man!' Tony found himself shouting. 'Close it, quick!'

148

" 'Yessir,' said the porter, jumping back. The door slammed. Afterward, the porter stood and stared after the taxi. Tony, glancing out through the little back window, saw him still standing there.

"It was dark in the cab, and as close as though a photographer's black hood had been drawn over him. Tony could see little. But he carefully felt with his hands all over the seat, all over the open space; and he found nothing."

At this point in the story, Hargreaves broke off for a moment or two. He had been speaking with difficulty; not as though he expected to be doubted, but as though the right words were hard to find. His gloved fingers opened and closed on his knee.

For the first time his companion—Miss Judith Gates—interrupted him. Judith spoke from the shadow on the other side of the gas-fire.

"Wait!" she said. "Please!"

"Yes?" said Hargreaves.

"This person who was following Tony. She spoke also with difficulty. "You aren't telling me that it was—well, was——?"

"Was what?"

"Dead," said Judith.

"I don't know who it was," answered Hargreaves, looking at her steadily. "Except that it seemed to be somebody with a fur collar on his coat. I'm telling you Tony's story, which I believe."

Judith's hand shaded her eyes. "All the same," she insisted, and her pleasant voice went high, "even supposing it was! I mean, even supposing it was the person you think. *He* of all people, living or dead, wouldn't have tried to put any evil influence round Tony. Old Jim loved Tony. He left Tony every penny he owned, and not a farthing to Stephen. He always told Tony he'd look after him."

"And so he did," said Hargreaves.

"But——"

"You see," Hargreaves told her slowly. "You still don't understand the source of the evil influence. Tony didn't, himself. All he knew was that he was bowling along in a dark taxi, through slippery, snowy streets; and whatever might be following him, good or bad, he couldn't endure it.

"Even so, everything might have ended well if the taxidriver had been careful. But he wasn't. That was the first snowfall of the year, and the driver miscalculated. When they were only two hundred yards from Upper Avenue Road, he tried to take a turn too fast. Tony felt the helpless swing of the skid; he saw the glass partition tilt, and a black tree-trunk rush up, huge at them until it exploded against the outer windscreen. They landed upright against the tree, with a buckled wheel.

" 'I *'ad* to swerve,' the driver was crying. 'I *'ad* to! An old gent with a fur collar walked smack out in front of——'

"And so, you see, Tony had to walk home alone.

"He knew something was following him before he had taken half a dozen steps. Two hundred yards don't sound like a great distance. First right, first left, and you're home. But here it seemed to stretch out interminably, as such things do in dreams. He did not want to leave the taxi-driver. The driver thought this was because Tony doubted his honesty about bringing the luggage on when the wheel was repaired. But it was not that.

"For the first part of the way, Tony walked rapidly. The other thing walked at an equal pace behind him. By the light of a street-lamp Tony could see the wet fur collar on the coat, but nothing else. Afterward he increased his pace to what was almost a run; and, though no difference could be seen in the gait of what was behind him, it was still there. Unlike you, Tony didn't wonder whether it might be good or evil. These nice differences don't occur to you when you're dealing with something that may be dead. All he knew was that he mustn't let it *identify* itself with him or he was done for.

"Then it began to gain on him, and he ran.

"The pavement was black, the snow dirty grey. He saw the familiar turning, where front gardens were built up above the low, stone walls; he saw the street sign fastened to one of those corners, white lettering on black; and, in a sudden blind panic, he plunged for the steps that led up to his home.

"The house was dark. He got the cold keys out of his pocket, but the key-ring slipped round in his fingers, like soap in bath-water, and fell on the tiled floor of the vestibule. He groped after it in the dark—just as the thing turned in at the gate. In fact, Tony heard the gate creak. He found the keys, found the lock by a miracle, and opened the door.

"But he was too late, because the other thing was already coming up the front steps. Tony says that at close range, against a street-lamp, the fur collar looked more wet and moth-eaten; that is all he can describe. He was in a dark hall with the door open. Even familiar things had fled his wits and he could not remember the position of the light-switch.

"The other person walked in.

"In his hip-pocket, Tony remembered, he still had the weapon he had carried round the world. He fumbled under his overcoat to get the gun out of his pocket; but even that weak gesture was no good to him, for he dropped the gun on the carpet. Since the visitor was now within six feet of him, he did not stop. He bolted up the stairs.

"At the top of the stairs he risked a short glance down. The other thing had stopped. In faint bluish patches of light which came through the open front door, Tony could see that it was stooping down to pick up the automatic pistol from the carpet.

"Tony thinks—now—that he began to switch on lights in the upper hall. Also, he shouted something. He was standing before the door of his bedroom. He threw open this door, blundered in, and began to turn on more lamps. He had got two lamps lighted before he turned to look at the bed, which was occupied.

"The man on the bed did not, however, sit up at the coming of noise or lights. A sheet covered him from head to feet; and even under the outline of the sheet you could trace the line of the wasted, sunken features. Tony Marvell then did what was perhaps the most courageous act of his life. He had to know. He walked across and turned down the upper edge of the sheet, and looked down at his own face; a dead face, turned sightlessly up from the bed.

"Shock? Yes. But more terror? No. For this dead man was real, he was flesh and blood—as Tony was flesh and blood. He looked exactly like Tony. But it was now no question of a real world and an unreal world; it was no question of going mad. This man was real; and that meant fraud and imposture.

"A voice from across the room said: '*So you're alive!*' And Tony turned round, to find his brother Stephen looking at him from the doorway.

"Stephen wore a red dressing-gown, hastily pulled round him, and his hair was tousled. His face was one of collapse.

"'I didn't mean to do it!' Stephen was crying out at him. Even though Tony did not understand, he felt that the words were a confession of guilt; they were babbling words, words which made you pity the man who said them.

" 'I never really meant to have you killed aboard that ship,' said Stephen. 'It was all a joke. You know I wouldn't have hurt you; you know that, don't you? Listen——'

"Now Stephen (as I said) was standing in the doorway, clutching his dressing-gown round him. What made him look round toward the hall behind, quickly, Tony did not know. Perhaps he heard a sound behind him. Perhaps he saw something out of the corner of his eyes. But Stephen did look round, and he began to scream.

"Tony saw no more, for the light in the hall went out. The fear was back on him again, and he could not move. For he saw a hand. It was only, so to speak, the flicker of a hand. This hand darted in from the darkness out in the hall; it caught hold of the knob on the bedroom door, and closed the door. It turned a key on the outside, locking Tony into the room. It kept Stephen outside in the dark hall—and Stephen was still screaming.

"A good thing, too, that Tony had been locked in the room. That saved trouble with the police afterward.

"The rest of the testimony comes from Mrs Reach, the housekeeper. Her room was next door to Stephen's bedroom, at the end of the upstairs hall. She was awakened by screams, by what seemed to be thrashing sounds, and the noise of hard breathing. These sounds passed her door toward Stephen's room.

"Just as she was getting out of her bed and putting on a dressing-gown, she heard Stephen's door close. Just as she went out into the hall, she heard, for the second time in forty-eight hours, the noise of a pistol-shot.

"Now, Mrs Reach will testify in a coroner's court that nobody left, or could have left Stephen's room after the shot. She was looking at the door, though it was several minutes before she could screw up enough courage to open the door. When she did open it, all sounds had ceased. He had been shot through the right temple at close range; presumably by himself, since the weapon was discovered in a tangle of stained bed-clothing. There was nobody else in the room, and all the windows were locked on the inside. The only other thing Mrs Reach noticed was an unpleasant, an intensely unpleasant smell of mildewed cloth and wet fur."

Again Hargreaves paused. It seemed that he had come to

the end of the story. An outsider might have thought, too, that he had emphasized these horrors too much, for the girl across from him kept her hands pressed against her eyes. But Hargreaves knew his business.

"Well?" he said gently. "You see the explanation, don't you?"

Judith took her hands away from her eyes. "Explanation?"

"The natural explanation," repeated Hargreaves, spacing his words. "Tony Marvell is not going mad. He never had any brainstorms or 'blind flashes'. He only thought he had. The whole thing was a cruel and murderous fake, engineered by Stephen, and it went wrong. But if it had succeeded, Stephen Marvell would have committed a very nearly perfect murder."

The relief he saw flash across Judith's face, the sudden dazed catching at hope, went to Hargreaves' heart. But he did not show this.

"Let's go back eight months," he went on, "and take it from the beginning. Now, Tony is a very wealthy young man. The distinguished Stephen, on the other hand, was swamped with debts and always on the thin edge of bankruptcy. If Tony were to die, Stephen, the next of kin, would inherit the whole estate. So Stephen decided that Tony had to die.

"But Stephen, a medical man, knew the risks of murder. No matter how cleverly you plan it, there is always *some* suspicion; and Stephen was bound to be suspected. He was unwilling to risk those prying detectives, those awkward questions, those damning post-mortem reports—until, more than eight months ago, he suddenly saw how he could destroy Tony without the smallest suspicion attaching to himself.

"In St Jude's Hospital, where he did some charity work, Stephen had found a broken-down ex-schoolmaster named Rupert Hayes. Every man in this world, they say, has his exact double. Hayes was Tony's double to the slightest feature. He was, in fact, so uncannily like Tony that the very sight of him made Stephen flinch. Now, Hayes was dying of tuberculosis. He had, at most, not more than a year to live. He would be eager to listen to any scheme which would allow him to spend the rest of his life in luxury, and die of natural causes in a soft bed. To him Stephen explained the trick.

"Tony should be ordered off—apparently—on a trip round the world. On the night he was to sail, Tony should be allowed to go aboard.

"Hayes should be waiting aboard that same ship, with a gun in his pocket. After Stephen or any other friends had left the ship conveniently early, Hayes should entice Tony up to the dark boat-deck. Then he was to shoot Tony through the head, and drop the body overboard.

"Haven't you ever realized that a giant ocean-liner, just before it leaves port, is the ideal place to commit a murder? Not a soul will remember you afterward. The passengers notice nothing; they are too excited. The crew notice nothing; they are kept too busy. The confusion of the crowd is intense. And what happens to your victim after he goes overboard? He will be sucked under and presently caught by the terrible propellers, to make him unrecognizable. When a body is found—if it is found at all—it will be presumed to be some dock-roysterer. Certainly it will never be connected with the ocean-liner, because there will be nobody missing from the liner's passenger list.

"Missing from the passenger-list? Of course not! Hayes, you see, was to go to the purser and order Tony's luggage to be sent ashore. He was to say he was cancelling the trip, and not going after all. After killing Tony he was then to walk ashore as——"

The girl uttered an exclamation.

Hargreaves nodded. "You see it now. He was to walk ashore *as Tony*. He was to say to his friends that he couldn't face the journey after all; and everybody would be happy. Why not? The real Tony was within an ace of doing just that.

"Then, Hayes, well coached, would simply settle down to play the part of Tony for the rest of his natural life. Mark that: his natural life; a year at most. He would be too ill to attend to the business, of course. He wouldn't even see you, his fiancée, too often. If ever he made any bad slips, that, of course, would be his bad nerves. He would be allowed to 'develop' lung trouble. At the end of a year, amid sorrowing friends . . .

"Stephen had planned brilliantly. 'Murder'? What do you mean, murder? Let the doctors examine as much as they like! Let the police ask what questions they like! Whatever steps are taken, Stephen Marvell is absolutely safe. For the poor devil in bed really has died a natural death.

"Only—well, it went wrong. Hayes wasn't cut out to be a murderer. I hadn't the favour of his acquaintance, but he must have been a decent sort. He promised to do this. But,

154

when it came to the actual fact, he couldn't force himself to kill Tony: literally, physically couldn't. He threw away his pistol and ran. On the other hand, once off the ship, he couldn't confess to Stephen that Tony was still alive. He couldn't give up that year of sweet luxury, with all Tony's money at his disposal to soothe his aching lungs. So he pretended to Stephen that he had done the job, and Stephen danced for joy. But Hayes, as the months went on, did not dance. He knew Tony wasn't dead. He knew there would be a reckoning soon. And he couldn't let it end like that. A week before he thought Tony was coming home, after writing a letter to the police to explain everything, Hayes shot himself rather than face exposure."

There was a silence. "That, I think," Hargreaves said quietly, "explains everything about Tony."

Judith Gates bit her lips. Her pretty face was working; and she could not control the twitching of her capable hands. For a moment she seemed to be praying.

"Thank God!" she murmured. "I was afraid——"

"Yes," said Hargreaves; "I know."

"But it still doesn't explain everything. It——"

Hargreaves stopped her.

"I said," he pointed out, "that it explains everything about Tony. That's all you need worry about. Tony is free. You are free. As for Stephen Marvell's death, it was suicide. That is the official record."

"But that's absurd!" cried Judith. "I didn't like Stephen; I always knew he hated Tony; but he wasn't one to kill himself, even if he were exposed. Don't you see, you haven't explained the one real horror? I must know. I mean, I must know if you think what I think about it. Who was the man with the brown fur collar? Who followed Tony home that night? Who stuck close by him, to keep the evil influences off him? Who was his guardian? Who shot Stephen in revenge?"

Sir Charles Hargreaves looked down at the sputtering gas-fire. His face, inscrutable, was wrinkled in sharp lines from mouth to nostril. His brain held many secrets. He was ready to lock away this one, once he knew that they understood each other.

"You tell me," he said.

TERRIFIED

C. B. GILFORD

PAUL SANTIN had had a good day. Small town doctors and drug stores were doing a thriving business, and, therefore, so was Paul Santin, pharmaceutical salesman. But it had been a long day, and now it was past eleven. Santin was driving fast on the country back road, trying to make it home before midnight.

He was tired, sleepy, fighting to stay awake for another half hour. But he was not dozing. He was in complete control of his car. He knew what he was doing.

He'd passed few other cars. Right now the road seemed deserted. He'd chosen this route just for that reason. Light traffic. And that's the way it was—an almost empty road—when he saw the other car.

He saw it first as a pair of headlights rounding the curve a quarter mile ahead. The lights were fantastically bright, and the driver failed to dim them. Santin cursed him, whoever he was. He dimmed his own lights, but received no answering courtesy. He cursed again, vindictively switched his own lights back to highway brightness. But he sensed no real danger in it.

He was vaguely aware that the other car was rocketing toward him at high speed. Too much speed for the kind of road they were on. Mechanically, he slacked off on the accelerator, concentrated on staying on his own side of the road, and on not looking directly at those oncoming lights.

But it was much too late when he realized the other car was hogging the centre of the road. And he had to make his decision too quickly. Whether to bore right in, perhaps leaning on his horn, hoping the other driver would pull aside. Or to hit the shoulder and take his chances with gravel and dirt.

He took the second choice, but not soon enough. He saw the other car wasn't going to concede an inch; so he swerved to the right. The blow was delivered against his left rear

156

fender and wheel. The rear of his car skidded ditchward ahead of the front. Then the whole car seemed to defy gravity. It rolled sideways, leaped into the air, throwing Santin clear of itself at the top of the leap.

He didn't see or hear the final crash of the machine. All his consciousness was in the impact of his body against the hill-side that met him like a solid wall; then he slid downwards in the midst of a miniature avalanche of small stones and dirt. Afterward he lay still, and so was all the world around him.

In that first moment, he felt no pain. The shock had numbed him. But he knew he was alive. He knew he was somehow conscious. He was also distantly, vaguely aware that his body was broken and beginning to bleed.

The blinding lights were gone. He was lying on his back in a patch of weeds. Above him were the stars and a bright full moon. They seemed closer to him than they had ever seemed before. Perhaps it was that optical illusion that first gave him the idea he was going to die.

At that moment, he felt no anger about it. He could remember his anger before the crash, but it was a distant, unreal thing to him. Again the thought of dying flitted across his mind. The dying feel nothing toward other creatures. They are completely concerned with themselves.

Then he heard the voices. A renewal of contact with the world. There'd been people in that other car. He wondered about them, calmly, without fury, without sympathy. But he gave all his attention to the listening.

"He isn't here." A masculine voice a bit young.

The other car had been hit too. It had been stopped. Or perhaps the driver had stopped the car without being forced to. Anyway, the people from that car, whoever they were, had walked back to his car and were looking for him.

To help him? His first instinct was to call out, guide them to where he lay. They'd been selfish in hogging the road, but now they were charitable, wanting to aid. But then another instinct rose to fight against the first. Would they really be friendly? Suddenly he felt terrified of them. Without knowing why. Surely everybody wants to help accident victims. Don't they?

"He must have been thown out." A girl's voice answering. Frightened.

"I guess so. What'll we do?" The same masculine voice. So there must be only two of them.

"Look for him," the girl said.

A hesitation. "Why?"

Another hesitation. "Don't you want to know what happened to him . . . or her?"

"I don't know." The masculine voice trembled. "I don't know . . ."

"I think we ought to look around and find him."

"Okay . . . It's dark though."

"You've got a flashlight, haven't you?"

"Sure. I'll get it."

Footsteps up on the road. The boy returning to his own car for the flashlight. And then silence again.

Santin waited, trembling in a sweat of new fear. He hadn't liked the sound of those voices. That boy and girl weren't people who would care. If he was dying, they weren't people who would be of much help.

If he was dying? He was certain of it. The pain was beginning now. He could identify it in several places. His face, his chest, both his legs. And somewhere deep inside him, where nobody could reach but a doctor. That was the area of pain that made him certain of death.

So it didn't matter, did it? Whether or not they found him with their flashlight?

"Okay, I've got it." The boy's voice. "Where do we look?"

"In the ditch, I guess."

Scuffling footsteps, disturbing gravel, crunching through grass and brush. Then a winking light, sweeping back and forth. Both the light and the footsteps getting nearer. Inevitably, they would find him. He could speed their search by calling to them. But he didn't. He waited.

"Hey!"

The light was in his face. Paralyzed, he couldn't seem to turn away from it. The footsteps hurried. And then they were there. Two forms standing over him, outlined against the sky. And the light shining in his eyes. He blinked, but they didn't seem to understand that the light bothered him.

"He's alive." The girl. "His eyes are open."

"Yeah. I see . . ."

"But he's hurt." The figure who was the girl knelt down beside him, mercifully shielding him from the flashlight. Because of the brightness of the moon, he could see her face.

She was young, terribly young, sixteen maybe. She was

158

pretty too, her hair dark, her skin pale, perhaps abnormally so, her made-up mouth lurid in contrast. But there was no emotion in her face. She was in shock possibly. But as her eyes roved over his injuries, no sympathy lighted in her eyes.

"You're pretty badly hurt, aren't you?" The question was right at him.

"Yes . . ." He discovered he could speak without great difficulty.

"Where? Do you know?"

"All over, I guess. Inside especially."

The girl was thoughtful over his reply. Her next question seemed cold, calculated. "Do you think you could pull through if we got help?"

He thought too, gave himself time to answer. But even so, he made a mistake. "I think I'm going to die," he said, and knew he had made a mistake as soon as he'd said it.

The girl's face changed somehow, imperceptibly. Santin couldn't fathom the change. He only knew it had happened. She pulled away from him, rose to her feet, rejoining the boy.

"He's going to die," she said. As if she knew it as certainly as Santin himself.

"There's no use trying to find a doctor then, is there?" The boy sounded relieved, as if his responsibility for this whole thing had ended now.

"I guess not."

"What'll we do then?"

"Nothing, I guess. Just wait here. A car's bound to come along sometime."

"We can ride back to town then, huh?" The boy seemed to depend completely on the girl for leadership.

"Sure. We can send a doctor or somebody back. But this guy will probably be dead by then. And we'll have to report to the police."

"The police?"

"We'll have to. You killed a man."

There was silence then. Santin lay at their feet, looking up at the two silhouetted figures. They were talking about him as already dead. But somehow it didn't anger him yet. Maybe because he considered himself dead too.

"Arlene . . . what'll they do to me?"

"Who, the police?"

"Yes . . . You said I killed a man."

159

"Well, you did, didn't you?"

The boy hesitated. "But it was an accident," he managed finally. "You know it was an accident, don't you, Arlene? I mean, it just happened . . ."

"Sure."

They were talking softly, but Santin could hear every word they said. And he felt compelled somehow to speak. "Every accident is somebody's fault," he told them.

They were startled. He could see them look at each other, then down at him again. "What do you mean by that, mister?" the boy asked after a moment.

"This accident was your fault. That's what I mean." He still wasn't angry. That wasn't why he argued. But he felt the blame should be established.

"How was it my fault?"

"First of all, you didn't dim your lights . . ."

"Well, neither did you."

"I did at first."

"But you switched back to highway lights again."

"Only after you refused to dim."

The boy was silent again for a moment. Then he said, "But when we hit, you had your lights on bright."

Santin had to admit it. "I got mad," he said. "But that's not the most important thing. You were driving over on my side of the road."

The boy's face went around to the girl. "Arlene, was I on his side of the road?"

It seemed she giggled. Or something like it. "How do I know? We were——"

She didn't finish the sentence, but Santin guessed the rest of it. They'd been necking, or petting, or whatever young people called it these days. That was why the boy hadn't dimmed his lights. And that was why he'd had poor control of his car. And now he, Santin had to pay the price of their good time.

It angered him, finally. With a curious sort of anger. Detached somehow, separate from himself. Because now in the long run it didn't really matter to him. Since he was going to die.

But also Santin felt a certain satisfaction. He could speak vindictively, and with assurance. "You see, you were on the wrong side of the road. So it was your fault."

The boy heard him, but he kept looking at the girl. "What

160

will they do to me?" he asked her. "The police, I mean. What will they do to me?"

"How do I know?" she snapped at him. She'd been so calm. Now maybe the initial shock was wearing off. Now maybe she was becoming frightened, nervous.

"Even if I was on the wrong side of the road," the boy said, "it was still an accident. I didn't try to run into this guy's car. I didn't try to kill him."

"That's right . . ."

"You read about these things in the paper. Nothing much happens to the driver. Maybe he gets fined. But my dad can pay that. And even if I had to go to gaol, it wouldn't be for long, would it, Arlene? What do you think it would be? Thirty days?"

"Or maybe sixty. That wouldn't be so bad."

Santin listened to them. And slowly the anger welled higher in him. Or maybe even ninety days, he could have added. Some insurance company would pay. But the killer himself wouldn't pay nearly enough. Ninety days for murder.

"There's just one thing," the boy said suddenly.

"What?"

"It'll be called an accident. And maybe it'll be called my fault. A little bit anyway. That is, if this guy here doesn't spout off to anybody."

"About what?"

"About who dimmed lights and who didn't. And who was on whose side of the road. But of course he can't spout off if he's dead."

"That's right." There was suddenly something strange in the girl's voice, an awareness.

"So he's got to be dead. Do you see what I mean, Arlene?"

"He said he was going to die . . ."

"Yeah, but he doesn't know. And neither do we. But he's got to die. We've got to make sure he dies." The boy's voice went up suddenly, toward the pitch of hysteria.

Santin saw the girl clutch the boy's arm and look up into his face. The whole posture of her body denoted fear.

"There's another thing too." The boy spoke swiftly, almost babbling. "My dad has told me about insurance. They have to pay more for a guy who's just crippled than for a guy who's dead. They pay big money to cripples. I don't know whether our insurance is that big. If this guy doesn't die, and is just

161

hurt real bad, it might cost us a lot more than the insurance we got. And, man, what my dad would do to me then."

The girl was terrified now. "But he's going to die," she whispered hoarsely.

"How do we know that, Arlene? How do we know?"

Santin felt no pain now. Only fury. They hadn't offered to help him. They wanted him dead. They were selfish, unbelievably selfish. And they were cruel enough to discuss all this right in front of him.

Suddenly, the boy was kneeling, and the flashlight was probing Santin's face again. Santin blinked in the glare, but despite it, he got his first look at the boy. Young. Young like the girl. But not calm like she'd been. Panic was in his eyes. And he was hurt too. An ugly scalp wound marred the left side of his head, and blood was matted in his hair.

"How do you feel, mister?" the boy asked.

Santin disdained to answer. He wouldn't give them the same satisfaction again. He wouldn't tell them of the hot flood of pain that washed over him in ever-growing waves. He wouldn't tell them he'd already heard death whispering in his ear, cajoling him to let go of life.

But he saw the desperation in the boy's face. The boy searched farther with the flashlight, playing it up and down Santin's body. Then he stood up.

"He doesn't look like he's hurt bad enough to die," he told the girl.

No, it doesn't look like that, Santin thought. The damage is inside. But it's just as fatal. Don't tell them though. Let them sweat. And you might stay alive till somebody comes.

A sudden eruption of pain blotted out his thoughts, leaving him barely conscious.

The girl screamed, and it was as though she was screaming for him. The boy had apparently struck him in some way. "What are you doing?" she demanded.

The boy's answer was almost a scream too. "He's got to die. I've got to make him die."

There was a strain of decency in the girl somewhere. Or a woman's compassion. "But you can't kill him," she told the boy fiercely.

"What difference does it make?" he argued back, with hysteria in his voice again. "I've already killed him, haven't I? He's just got to die quick, that's all. Don't you understand, Arlene?"

162

Obviously she didn't. She clung to him, holding him back.

"Nobody will ever know the difference," he told her. There was logic in his argument. "He's hurt already. They'll think it's from the accident."

They were silent for a litle while. By twisting his head as far as he could, Santin could see them. They were two dark shadows against the lighter background of the sky, so close together that they merged. Santin could sense the desperation in their embrace. The girl with her feminine instinct for mercy. The boy nothing more than a brute, mad with the desire for self-preservation. Yet somehow the girl could love him. And because she loved him, she was in this together with him.

"All right, Vince," he heard her say finally.

And still all Santin could do was to lie there. Probably he was going to be beaten and kicked to death. Murdered deliberately, logically, to protect a weak, vicious kid. Somehow he hadn't been so afraid of that other death. But he was afraid of this one. This death had a quality of horror about it.

"No!" he yelled at them with all his strength. "No!"

His cry broke up their embrace. The flashlight in the boy's hand probed his face again. Santin had been proud before, but he wasn't now. He didn't turn away from the light. He let them see his terror.

"Do you think you can do it, Vince?" the girl asked. Her voice was steady. Now that she'd been convinced, she'd be the stronger of the two.

"I don't know," he said. "But I've got to."

Santin saw him coming and closed his eyes.

"Wait a minute," he heard the girl say, as from the far end of a long tunnel. He existed in a red haze of agony now, and her voice seemed far away.

"What's the matter?"

"You're getting blood on yourself, aren't you?"

"I don't know."

"Look and see."

"Yes, I am. But what difference does it make?"

"Vince, Vince, are you crazy? They'll see the blood. And maybe somebody will get suspicious. They can analyze blood, and tell who it belonged to."

A spark of hope, and Santin dared to open his eyes again.

The boy was poised over him for another onslaught, but now he hesitated.

"I know what to do," he said finally.

He left suddenly, exited from Santin's view. But Santin could hear him thrashing around in the weeds. And then finally his shout.

"Arlene, come over and help me lift this."

More thrashing among the weeds. The girl joining the boy.

And the boy's excited voice. "The guy was thrown out of the car, wasn't he? Okay then, he just hit his head on this, that's all. We'll rearrange the body a little. Come on now, let's lift it together."

A slow returning of the footsteps. Wildly, Santin searched for them. Saw them. They were coming toward him together, their backs bent, straining. Between them they carried a wide flat object that seemed to be very heavy.

He didn't scream this time. He couldn't. Even his vocal cords were paralyzed. But he could watch them. They walked slowly, with great effort. They stopped, one on each side of him, and the huge, heavy, flat object they held blotted out the sky above his face.

Then, at the very last moment of his life, he became aware of something. A soothing calm flooded over him. I was going to die anyway, he thought. This is quicker, of course, maybe even merciful. But it's also murder.

He prayed. A strange prayer. He prayed for a smart cop.

Sergeant Vanneck of the State Highway Patrol was a smart cop. In the grey light of dawn, he studied tyre marks on the road. They were hard to see on the dark asphalt, and he couldn't be entirely sure.

He was a little surer how he felt about the pair who stood by his car and watched him as he went about his work. The boy called Vince and the girl called Arlene. They were like most other youngsters who got involved in fatal accidents, and they were also different. So, as the dawn grew brighter, he continued his search.

He found more than he'd expected to find. The body had been removed and the area was pretty well trampled. But he found the evidence nevertheless. It was clear, unquestionable.

He climbed back out of the ditch and walked over to the girl and the boy. There must have been something terrifying in his face, because it made the boy ask nervously, "What's the matter, Sergeant?"

"There are two sides to a rock," Sergeant Vanneck said. "The top side stays clean, washed by the rain. The bottom side is dirty from contact with the ground. Now you tell me, sonny, how Mr Santin was thrown from his car so that he hit his head on the bottom side of that rock?"

COMPOSITION FOR FOUR HANDS

HILDA LAWRENCE

PART ONE

THEY WHEELED her chair to the big bay window in her bedroom. She'd been fed and bathed. She'd had what they called her forty winks. They said it was a beautiful afternoon and wasn't she lucky to have such a nice window? Then they left her. It was Saturday. She knew it was Saturday, because school-children were playing in the little park across the way and the florist had come with her weekend roses. She'd bought the house because of that little park. Nice for a child. The park and the big rambling gardens. For swings and playhouses, later for tennis courts. . . . It was Saturday. Ralph, her husband, was home from the bank, and he'd helped with her lunch, spooning the broth so carefully, calling her his little baby. Not speaking to her, though; to the nurse. He'd said: "Miss Sills, she's all I've got now. She's my little baby girl, and she's all I've got."

Miss Sills had looked as if she had wanted to cry. Her hand had gone out as if she had wanted to touch his beautiful white hair. She had said: "You mustn't brood, Mr Manson. No matter how miserable you are, you must make yourself look happy for her sake. She's terribly sensitive, she feels things."

She could hear things, too. Sometimes they forgot that. When they spoke directly to her, they raised their voices and made gestures, as if she were deaf. But when they talked among themselves, they acted as if she weren't there. They seemed to think she couldn't hear unless they put their faces close to hers and waved their hands. That was all right; she wanted them to talk among themselves. The more they talked like that, the better. When they left the room, she wanted to know where they were going. She wanted to know where they were every hour of the day. And the night. The night.

They left her, and she heard their footsteps going down the

hall; Ralph's turned at the rose guest room. That was where he slept now. She'd heard the doctor tell him to sleep there, to be within call. Whose call? Not hers; she couldn't open her mouth. She could open it, but she couldn't make a sound. The nurse's call. Miss Sills'.

Miss Sills had a cot at the foot of her big bed. If Miss Sills called to him in the night, he could be there in less than a minute, down the hall or across the sleeping porch that ran along that side of the house. I suppose they talk among themselves, downstairs, and say that I may die in the night, she thought. I wonder if I can smile. I don't know, they never bring me a mirror. They never put my chair anywhere near a mirror. But if I can smile, then that's what I'm doing now inside. Careful. Be careful.

Miss Sills' footsteps went beyond the rose room to the head of the stairs, went down, and were lost in the thick rugs of the lower hall. Going for her afternoon exercise. Soon I'll hear the front door close, and then she'll wave to me from the garden. Then I'll see her across the street, in the little park, walking with long, easy steps, swinging her arms. Beautiful, beautiful motion. And pretty soon Emma will come in to sit, chirping and smiling and talking. Talking, talking, talking. But I'm used to Emma. She's been with me so long she's almost like a member of the family. She will tell me about the prices of things, pretending I still keep house. The butcher, the fruit man, the farmer with his wagon—robbers all, but what can a person do? And Emma will say: "My, but you look fine today. There's colour in your cheeks."

Rouge. Miss Sills had put it on. You couldn't stop her. Rouge and curling irons and manicures. She said it was good for morale. *Morale.*

Emma would sit in the low chair, neat as a pin in her afternoon uniform, and talk about tea and dinner. And she'd have her tatting. Emma did tatting now. She used to knit, but they made her stop—because of the needles. The needles were the right shape, as nearly the right shape and size as anything could be, anything you'd be lucky enough to get your hands on. Lucky enough if your hands, if only your hands——

Hands. Emma's old hands, worn and rough because she made her living with them, but strong. Emma's old hands that didn't need strength, gripping the lovely needles. Rolling them between her fingers, turning them over and over, beautiful motion, wasted on Emma.

Emma must have seen her watching the needles; she must have seen a look in her eyes, because she'd said, "No, no, Miss Nora, you mustn't think of such a terrible thing." Emma couldn't possibly know what she was really thinking, nobody could know. Nobody except—no, that wasn't possible. Or was it? She'd wondered and worried, driven herself half-crazy, until she overheard them talking when they thought she was asleep. Miss Sills said: "She wanted Emma's needles today. Emma saw the look. I don't like that, Mr Manson, I don't like it at all. She couldn't hold them even if we put them in her hands—she can't even hold a hankie, not yet, not now. But I don't like it. In these cases you sometimes get a sudden change—temporary, of course, like a muscular spasm. She could do herself a serious injury if she got hold of anything like that, anything with a point. So I told Emma to stop the knitting and work on something else. Like tatting. You can't hurt yourself with a little celluloid bobbin."

He said: "Hurt herself? How dreadful! But I'm afraid you're right. I saw her watching your pencil when you were writing the drugstore list. She wanted it, she craved it. A pencil! What could she do with a pencil?"

"I don't know. We can't get into her poor mind. But really, Mr Manson, we've got to be alert every minute. We've got to prepare ourselves for a physical change. You know she could put her—I hate to say this—she could put her—well, she could hurt her eyes. In the state she's in, I mean her emotional state, she may think of herself as useless, a burden to you. A self-inflicted injury—oh, it's too awful, the poor thing! Maybe she doesn't even want to *see*!"

His warm hands covered her then. He said: "Guard her, Miss Sills, don't let anything happen. She's all I have. Those lovely eyes, have you noticed how they—follow? They're the only thing about her that's alive."

That was why Emma gave up knitting for tatting, which she hated. That was why Miss Sills no longer wore pencil and pen clipped to her apron bib. A self-inflicted injury. . . . Don't think about it, she told herself. You're lucky, you're lucky, because they guessed wrong. Think of something else, make yourself think, hard, hard. Think of your hands, your fingers; think of a substitute for a pencil. Anything, anything that will turn and roll between useless fingers, turn and roll and give them strength. Secret strength that must be kept hidden. If you were a soldier in a hospital, they'd put something in your hands and help you turn and roll it. In a hospital they'd help you. That's why you're not in a hospital, that's why you're home. You heard them: "She'll be more comfortable in her own home with the people she loves." Self-inflicted injury; you heard that, too. You're lucky again because you can't laugh. You're lucky because if you once started, you couldn't stop. You'd give yourself away. Self-inflicted injury, when all you want to do is keep your life, not lose it. Keep it, such as it is, keep it until—— Why, I'm crying. Those are tears on my hands. I didn't know I could cry. Think of something else. Quick. . . . Bruce will be coming on the four-fifteen. Better not think of that, either. Every afternoon, bending down to look into your face, kissing your hands, telling you how well you look, teasing, pretending. . . . Stop that. Stop that.

Look at the fringe on your steamer rug. Old, happy rug; kind, thick fringe. Thick. Almost as thick as a pencil! Try it, try it while you're alone, hurry before—before Emma comes. Before anyone comes. Before they all come tramping back from their walks, their exercise, from the station. There, you almost did it that time. Almost. But don't worry because it seems impossible now; someday you'll make it. Try. Try again. There's a good thick strand, lying across your left wrist. See if you can touch it with your other hand. See if you can move your wrist, your arm, your arm, try. . . . No. No, but don't cry again, that's getting you nowhere. Keep trying, and thank God your mind is all right. That's what they aren't sure of, your mind. That's where you're ahead of them; that's how you'll win in the end. One of these days one of your hands will reach the fringe and close over it. One of these days you will take the fringe in your hand and open and close your fingers. Roll the soft, thick fringe between your fingers, endlessly, over and over, until they are strong enough to hold a pencil. Pencil. You'll never even see another pencil. You know that. But your fingers will be ready for whatever comes. It doesn't matter if you never walk again, if you never speak again. All you need is two fingers. Two? No, one. One will be enough, one finger can point. You can pretend to be writing with one finger, a pantomime. You can make it clear and unmistakable if you are ever alone with the right person. . . . But how will I know which person is right? I'm not sure even now. How will I know which one is both right and safe? Now, now, don't cry. It takes away the little strength you

169

have. Now, now, don't be a baby. "My little baby girl," he said. . . . There's Emma.

Milly Sills crossed the park and hurried to the Larchville station. The four-fifteen from New York was pulling in, and the platform was filled with families and dogs. She had time only to set her beret becomingly awry before George Perry and Mr Bruce Cory came shouldering through the crowd. Milly and George, who lived, with his father and mother, next door to the Mansons', had been friends for some time. She eyed Mr Cory rather hostilely, but had to admit he was a handsome devil for—what was it, fifty? Emma had told her that the other Mr Cory, Mrs Manson's first husband, had been about ten years older than Mrs Manson, and she was forty-two. And Bruce Cory was that Mr Cory's twin. Well, handsome devil for fifty-two or whatever it was. No fat, not an ounce. He made old George look like a puppy.

"Damn," Milly said under her breath, "it looks as if George and I can't be alone for even five minutes these days." She waved, and they waved over the other commuters' heads. She made rapid plans for the evening. Maybe a movie, maybe dancing, maybe both. "I'll work on him," she decided. "I don't care if he does look grim. He'll have to get over that. I, for one, won't have it. I, for one, am having too much as it is."

However, she noted, there was nothing grim about Bruce Cory, with the polo-field skin and the squash-court figure. She watched his approach with admiration and appropriate distrust. He walked as if he had oiled hinges.

"Mr Perry, I believe," she said to George when they came up to her. She hooked an affectionate arm through George's and gave him a pinch, but he didn't seem to feel it. To Bruce Cory she gave the smile she kept in reserve for patients' relatives.

"Hi," George said. "I ran into Mr Cory in the smoker."

Cory returned her smile with a look of approval that travelled from her white canvas shoes to her white beret. She felt herself liking it. George had given her one look, a quick one, with absolutely nothing in it. But nothing.

They moved across the platform. "Cab or walk?" George asked.

"Walk," she said. "This is my airing."

Cory was instantly solicitous, looking down with a worried air. "Are you having any fun?" he asked. "Or is it all perfectly deadly?"

Having any fun, she jeered silently. What a thing to say! I know you, my friend. To date you've given no trouble, but there's one of your kind on every case. . . . She gave him the smile she kept in reserve for that kind, the one that said: 'When I go downstairs at midnight in my bathrobe, I'm going for hot cocoa—get it? Cocoa.' Aloud, "Everything's fine, Mr Cory, thank you," she said.

"Anything happen after I left this morning? Any change?"

"No change. No change is considered fine in cases like this. We can't ask for more than that for a while. But she had a good lunch—good for her, I mean—and she seems to be making an effort in other ways, too."

"Splendid! What kind of effort?"

"Well, she seems to notice things. I haven't said much about it except to Mr Manson, but I do feel encouraged. I think she's trying to concentrate. You know, listen. She seems to realize that she's helpless, and her eyes——"

Cory spoke sharply. "What about her eyes?"

"Oh, nothing like that, Mr Cory!" He did love her, they all did. In her way she was lucky. Some people had no one, had to go to city hospitals and wear dark, shapeless robes all day long because they didn't show the dirt or the food that got spilled. Mrs Manson had real silk and fine wool, and there wasn't a single minute when somebody wasn't trying to anticipate her wants, read her thoughts. Read her thoughts—if she had any. That was something they weren't sure about.

"Oh, no, Mr Cory, there's nothing wrong with her vision. I only mean she notices more and tries to watch everything we do, although she can't turn her head, not yet. But I'm pretty sure she'll be able to do that soon. I even told Mr Manson so." Then, because Mr Cory still looked unhappy and unconvinced, she added: "Cheer up. It could be worse. Think how poor Mr Manson feels."

Cory nodded. "Good little Sills," he said. "We were lucky to get you."

They walked on in silence.

Tonight she would be free from eight to twelve. Once a week she had a night like that. Sometimes she went home, a fifteen-minute walk across town, lugging a suitcase of laundry for her mother to do. It wasn't necessary, but her mother liked to do it. Her mother always met her at the front door and took the suitcase before she kissed her. She dumped the

171

clothes into the washing machine as if she were fighting a plague. Then she sat in the rocker she kept in the kitchen and double-dared anybody to come within a yard of the machine. The washer was a Christmas present from Milly, and the capable, elderly maid was a present, too. But Mrs Sills chose to regard the washer as her own invention and the maid as an indigent relative, not right in the head. 'Maybe I ought to go home,' Milly thought. 'I missed last week.' Then she looked at George. Still grim. A face like granite. Jealous, she gloated. What do you know! Her heart suddenly warmed. "Movies tonight, George?"

"Not tonight."

"What's the matter with you?"

"Toothache."

"Of course you've seen the dentist?"

"No."

"Well, of course you will, won't you?"

"Maybe."

Fool, she thought. Why do I bother? Suit yourself, lie awake all night and suffer. See if I care. . . . Later, when she remembered that, she felt as if she'd been daring an axe to fall on her neck. Because George didn't go to the dentist, and he did lie awake. He got up at three in the morning to spit a poultice out the window, and she cared a great deal.

Now Cory was saying something and she turned with elaborate interest. "I beg your pardon, Mr Cory. I didn't get that."

"I asked you what you thought of Doctor Babcock," Cory said carelessly.

"I have every confidence in Doctor Babcock," she said primly. "So has Mr Manson."

"I know he has. Babcock's the only one who's lasted. I understand you've worked with him before?"

It was a question, not a statement. She was pleased. He doesn't know how green I am, she thought. I must be doing all right. Maybe none of them knows. . . . Her reply was short, but lofty. "Oh, my, yes." One tonsillectomy.

She remembered the night, a little less than two weeks before, when Doctor Babcock had routed her out of bed. He didn't tell her what the case was, and she turned it down, because she'd just wound up six weeks with a simple fracture, age twelve, who slept all day and demanded comics at night. She said she needed sleep. But he told her he was desperate, his patient was unhappy with her present nurse. He was perfectly frank; he admitted the woman was difficult and would probably be unhappy with Florence Nightingale. It was like Babcock to drag in Nightingale. Then he'd said the patient was Mrs Manson. At that, she'd gone with him, at once, at one o'clock in the morning.

She'd been glad of her decision ever since, and it had hing to do with the fact that good old George's house was tically in the Manson back yard. Mrs Manson liked her, could see that. And Babcock looked pleased. That meant . Her first really important case. If she made good, there wouldn't be any more spoiled kids and old women. If she made good, she could stay with Mrs Manson until the end. The end? Well, say until something happened one way or another. Or until Milly herself couldn't take it.

"What did Babcock say this morning?" Cory was pressing her arm.

"He didn't come, Mr Cory. He called up right after you left. He said he'd drop in this afternoon. I don't like to be away when he comes, even when Mr Manson and Emma are there, but if I don't go out at my regular hours, I get dopey. And that's not good for Mrs Manson."

"What about another nurse? I don't know why we haven't insisted on that."

"Not a chance. I suggested it myself, and if you'd seen the look in her eyes—— She's terrified of people, even old friends who come to inquire. We've had to stop all that. We have to be awfully careful, even with the people in the house. Like Hattie, the cook. The cook's all right when she keeps her mouth shut, but the other day she burst into tears and talked about Mrs Manson's son."

"About Robbie?" At her nod, Cory looked away. "Bad," he said.

"Bad? It was criminal. George was there; he saw the whole thing. But we didn't tell a soul. No use getting Hattie fired. We simply gave her—we laid her out. She won't do that again."

"You can tell me about it, can't you? Forget that I'm Robbie's uncle."

She answered eagerly, appealing to George, forcing him into the conversation. "Of course we can tell Mr Cory, can't we, George? You do it; you know the background better than I do. You see, I didn't know about Robbie's birthday, Mr

Cory. How could I? If I'd known, I'd have got Hattie out the minute she started. Tell it, George."

George complied, slowly and reluctantly. "It isn't much," he said. "But it was a nuisance. You know I'm in and out of the house a lot these days, at odd hours. And you know I practically lived in the place when I was a kid. Mrs Manson never let them fill in the hedge."

Cory said, "Yes, I know. He knew that the Perry Cottage backed on the Manson garden, and that the dividing hedge still showed gaps made by small boys in a hurry. He knew all about the childhood friendship and that George was a few years older than Robbie, and that after they outgrew the swings, the play-houses, and the gym apparatus, they didn't see much of each other.

"We went with different crowds when we grew up," George said. "Naturally. You know how that happens. This last year I hardly ever saw him. He was twenty-one and I was twenty-six—that makes a lot of difference. To say nothing of Robbie's unlimited money." In spite of himself he emphasized money.

"Forget that," Cory said. "Go on with your story."

According to George, his mother said it would be nice if he began to hang around the Mansons again—second-son stuff. And Mrs Manson seemed to like it. At least, he said, she didn't have a relapse. Not until the Hattie episode. He'd been dropping in for several weeks when that happened, having drinks in Mrs Manson's room, talking about anything that came into his head, never mentioning Robbie. Nothing ever upset her when he was there alone, even though he was pretty sure she didn't hear half he said. She just looked at him, accepted him, and that was all anybody hoped for. Then the cook business happened.

"Small thing in its way," George said, "but a fine example of the chances you take when you don't control the people who go to see her."

He said he'd been doing his usual routine that afternoon, rambling on about the weather, the pretty sky, and see how the leaves are turning, Mrs Manson. Thanksgiving on the way, Hallowe'en before you know it, and so on. Then Hattie came in with a lamb chop and a piece of chicken on a plate. Raw. A custom of the house, a scheme to coax Mrs Manson into thinking. Emma's idea. Here are two pieces of meat. You may have one for your dinner. Which? Emma swore it

174

worked; she said Hattie could tell which one Mrs Manson wanted by the way she looked.

George said he had reached Hallowe'en in his therapeutic travelogue, pumpkin faces, and so on, when Hattie burst into tears and started to babble.

"I was sunk," George said. "I'd forgotten that Robbie's birthday was all tied up with pumpkins. But Hattie hadn't. She carried on about the jack-o'-lanterns they used to put in his room on birthdays. They did that from the time he was three until he was eighteen. Then he made them stop it. Did you know that?"

"Yes," Cory said. "They all babied him."

"Exactly," George agreed. "Well, that's all, but it sent Mrs Manson right up to the taking off place and turned me into an old man. Hattie still comes in with her plate of raw meat, but she doesn't talk."

The little park was straight ahead, and across the park the big house stood in its bright fall garden. Milly thought of the motionless figure she had left by the window, and her steps dragged. She listened half-heartedly to the conversation. They were getting along all right without her; George was warming up, for him. Giving out information instead of hoarding it, treating Cory like an equal. Now he was saying something in a soft voice about a dreamy kid.

"Always was," George said. "Always lived in another world. Robbie had his mother's features, but he didn't have her—excitement. Of course, I never saw his father; but taking you as a model, I'd say Robbie wasn't like a Cory, either."

It was an obvious compliment, George's voice was deferential and admiring, and Cory flushed. Milly said to herself, "Good old George, he'll get a job out of Cory yet."

"When my brother died," Cory said quietly, "I rather hoped she'd remarry. I was glad when she did. No, Robbie wasn't like my brother. Robbie was—himself."

George said: "I don't like to think about it. I don't even like to talk about it."

But Milly thought about it as they entered the park and crossed under the yellow maples, between flaming beds of scarlet sage. The maple leaves were gold, and the gold of new coin. A boy with all the money in the world, with any-thing—— "Do you think they'll ever find out what he did with it?" she asked vaguely.

Cory didn't answer. He said, "Is she in her window?"

"She should be," she told him. "We put her there as usual, Mr Manson and I, just before I came out. She likes to watch the park—at least, I think she does. I told Emma not to touch her, to wait until I came back. It's sort of queer——" She stopped to challenge her own words and to wonder why they suddenly asked for challenge.

"What's queer?" Cory was smiling. "The window? Or Emma?"

She answered slowly. "Neither. I only mean she's funny about being touched. I don't think she likes it, and we're pretty sure it isn't a question of pain. But when I get back from my walks and go to her room, I always feel as if she's been waiting for me. For *me*. Almost—well, anxiously. And I've only been on the case a little while; it isn't as if I were an old friend. I guess it's the uniform. People seem to trust nurses." I've said something idiotic, she told herself instantly. Cory had given her a quick, sharp look, and George was rolling his eyes to heaven. As if I'd pulled a boner, she thought, as if I were feeble-minded. I'll show them.

"And the more fools, they," she said briskly. "I mean, for trusting nurses. I can count cases on all ten fingers that would curl your hair. Helpless patient plus renegade husband, son, brother, doctor, lawyer, friend. Take your choice. Willing female confederate, uniform from a theatrical place. Object, money. And believe me——" She stopped again, appalled. Why don't you pack up and get out before you're fired? she mourned to herself.

"Brilliant girl," George said to Cory. "And simply crazy about Milly Sills, RN."

They turned in at the gate.

Mrs Manson was still by the window. She'd seen them turn into the park and cross, talking.

Emma had seen them, too. "There, now," Emma said, "there's Mr Brucie and George Perry with Miss Sills. I'd say she went to the station to meet them, wouldn't you?" Emma smiled and nodded and waved. She looked as if she were glad to see someone who could smile and wave in return. And talk. Poor Emma. Talking, talking, talking, and never being quite sure that she was heard.

"You're lucky, that's what you are," Emma insisted. "And I want you to remember it, and appreciate it. A nice young girl like Miss Sills to look after you, a daughter couldn't do more. And Mr Bruce Cory, giving up his beautiful New York apartment to come out here and cheer you up, for old time's sake. Giving up his gay city life, when we all know he hates the country. He's popular, too, he is. In the gossip columns nearly every day, but in a nice way. No café society for Mr Brucie; he runs with the cream dee lah cream."

She stopped listening to Emma. There were other things to listen to.

The front door opened, and they walked across the strip of floor that was bare. Then they walked on the rugs. Then the sound of their voices. Ralph's voice, low, greeting them. Then another door, the library. They were going to have a drink before they all came up, trooping in full of smiles. "How wonderful you look! You keep this up, and you'll be out for Christmas!" Out? Out where? Out beside Robbie.

Doctor Babcock encouraged them to talk like that. He himself talked like that, rocking back and forth on his strong legs. They all did that, rocked; they thought it made them look as if they had nothing on their minds. But she'd seen the look Babcock had given Ralph the day before. She'd been keeping her eyes almost closed, as children do when they pretend to be asleep, looking between her lashes. Babcock had looked at Ralph and shaken his head. Hopeless, the look had said. And he'd shrugged and raised his eyebrows in answer to an unspoken question of Ralph's. The shrug and brows said, "Hopeless, except for a miracle."

They were all watching for a miracle, for a sign of change. She saw it in their faces, heard it in their voices. They knew what to watch for; they discussed its improbability as if she were already dead. And one of them knew how much that kind of talk meant to her. One of the people who came to her room was quietly alert, lying in wait for a sign that showed she understood. She had read the speculation in one pair of eyes. She was much cleverer than that; she was careful to let her own eyes show nothing. If the miracle came, she knew she must hide it. The first sign of a twitch, the first small movement, one finger, one muscle in her body, and the news would go all over the house, over the town. And that would be the end of her. "Have you heard about Mrs Manson? Too bad, just when she was beginning to show improvement." Maybe it would happen before that. In a panic, in a sudden panic——

She looked at the rug, at the fringe lying across her knees. She looked at it until her eyes burned. "Emma," she implored silently, "Emma——"

"Now, what's wrong with your nice rug?" Emma scolded. "I declare you're looking as if you wanted to eat it up! Could that mean you're cold? No, your face is nice and warm. Let Emma feel your hands. So that's it, hands freezing. Well, we'll tuck them in a little wool nest. There you are. Oh, my Poor Miss Nora. Oh, my poor lady."

The hands were covered, that was luck again. Or was it something else? Was she projecting her thoughts, making Emma think what she wanted her to think? Good, simple, childish Emma and her good, simple mind. Could her own mind possibly direct Emma's? Concentrate! If you can do that, who knows what may happen? If you can will Emma to come and go, you may have a minute alone. A minute alone when you need it. A minute alone when the time comes. . . . Don't think about that now, she's watching you. Close your eyes. Somebody said the eyes are windows of the soul. If that's true, close them.

The thick fringe, the good thick fringe, was in the palm of one hidden hand. She closed her eyes and dreamed about it lying there, afraid to try anything stronger than a dream.

They came in, all four of them, through the door that was beyond the half-circle of her vision, all four and a fifth. Ralph, Brucie, George Perry, Miss Sills, and another one. A strange one. She closed a door in her mind; she'd been away on a journey of her own, crawling inch by inch, even walking, in her dream world. When they filed across the room and stood in a line before her chair, she saw who the fifth one was. Doctor Babcock. She made herself look down at his feet, she could just manage it, turning her eyes down until they hurt. He was wearing overshoes. That was why she hadn't known his muffled tread. It was raining, then. Yes, it was growing dark outside, there was rain on the windows.

Miss Sills said brightly: "We're going to have a little party. As soon as George builds up the fire. See, here's George! He says he wants a drink, but we're going to make him work for it. And here's another man—picked me up at the station, he did, claiming he lives here now. Shall we give him a drink, too?"

Miss Sills was flushed and happy. *She's in love with one of them. Which?*

Ralph had a tray, and he put it on the tea cart that held the medicine and rubbing oils, the strong glass feeding tube, the lipstick, the firm cylindrical lipstick. A tray of drinks.

One for her? There was a rattle of coal in the grate, then a sound of smothered laughter. Miss Sills and George. It was George she loved.

Brucie bent to kiss her cheek. "How's our baby?" He drew her hands from beneath the rug and massaged them gently, smiling down into her face. "We started to have drinks downstairs, and then Ralph got this idea. Babcock came in and said it was okay. See the glass of milk? Look. Funny colour." He took it from the tray and held it before her. "Milk plus. The plus is rum. Good for girls."

The fringe was lying across her knees, wasting its beautiful potentialities.

Doctor Babcock didn't wait for the others. He took his drink, raised it in a toast to the rest, and gulped half of it. "Good for boys," he said.

They laughed. Even Emma. Emma said, "Doctor, you never give me any medicine like that!" They laughed again, and Emma's shrill cackle rose above the rich, masculine rumbles and the light, applauding ripple that nurses always save for doctors.

Ralph handed the drinks around, Scotch and soda in the hunting-scene glasses. The glasses she'd bought at Tiffany's six weeks before. Only six weeks? Only that? The day she had lunch with Robbie at the Plaza. The day——

Ralph's strong brown hand held the milk close to her mouth. His other hand held the feeding tube. He said: "No dreaming, darling, this is a party. For you. Now take a nice long swallow for the old man."

She closed her lips, made them tight.

He coaxed. "Come, darling, it's good. Bruce made it himself. See? I'll take a swallow first."

Brucie's face, full of mock chagrin. His laughing voice. "What's the idea—testing for poison?"

Awful, awful, awful to say a thing like that. To say it out loud, to make a joke of it. To say it, to say it.

Miss Sills, crossing the room rapidly, coming to her chair. "Hey!" Miss Sills, rattling off a long sentence, addressing them all, meaningless words ending with the same letters. Pig Latin. Robbie used to——Pig Latin.

Miss Sills was telling them not to say things like that. Miss Sills was all right. Watch Miss Sills closely, make sure. If Miss Sills is all right, then——

They both took her hands, Ralph and Brucie.

179

"Baby," Ralph said, "forgive us. We're clumsy fools. You've always been such a good sport, we sometimes forget we must be careful now. You understand?"

Brucie kissed the hand he held and placed it on top of the rug. On top. He took the milk from Ralph. "Let me," he said. He slipped the feeding tube between her lips.

The drink was all right. It tasted good. Rum and milk. Nothing else, simply rum and milk, with a little grated nutmeg. She should have known there would be nothing else. Poison would be ridiculous, unintelligent.

Emma fussed with her sewing basket and said she was going. "Going to see that the table's set properly. Doctor Babcock's having dinner with us. He invited himself when they told him it was steak. You're going to have steak, too, a special treat. I'll cut it up myself, nice and fine. Nice and rare, to build you up. What do you want, Miss Nora? Oh, dear, tell Emma what it is you want? I can feel you asking."

Concentrate. Hard, hard. The rug, the rug over your hands, both hands. The fringe.

They all watched, they crowded her chair, looking at her, at Emma, at one another.

Doctor Babcock said, "Emma, I'm afraid you'll have to go unless you——"

Emma crowed. "I know! Don't tell me what I'm to do and what not to do! It's her hands! See how she looks at them! She likes them covered up, wrapped up in that old rug. I found that out this afternoon, and I'm no doctor. They get cold, no activity, you might say. It stands to reason—you don't need college to know that. There you are, my pretty girl, my smart, pretty girl!"

She closed her eyes because the relief was almost unbearable. It works, I can make her do what I want her to do. The fringe was thick and firm between her hidden fingers. Look as if you were sleeping, look as if you were sleeping, and concentrate.

"Wheel her chair to the fire, and leave her alone for a bit." Emma, firm and arrogant with success. "She'll be happy by the fire and knowing you're all with her. No loud talk and laughing, mind you, none of your wicked jokes. Surrounded by her loved ones, all cosy and warm, that's what she needs."

Miss Sills: "Who's the nurse around here? Let me see your credentials, madam."

Soft laughter. Her chair moving forward, the warmth in-

180

creasing, the door closing on Emma, the hushed regrouping of other chairs, the crack of coal in the grate, the ring of ice cubes against glass. Low voices talking about football. She didn't have to listen to that. She could travel back and pick up the threads. The threads would make a tapestry, and the tapestry would show the figures.

The day she bought the glasses with the hunting scenes, Fifth Avenue was all the world's great streets in one; the day was all September days together. She remembered to put a bag of cracked corn in her purse for St Patrick's pigeons, and she sent her car to a garage, because she wanted to walk. Once she saw her reflection in a window and preened like a girl. "I look thirty," she said to herself, "and why not? All the other women have only painted faces and lovers, but I have Ralph and Robbie."

It was too early for lunch. Robbie couldn't make it until one. That was ridiculous, and she'd told Ralph so; when a bank is practically a family business, it ought to make concessions to the young squire. But Robbie wouldn't have it that way. She'd asked him once why he worked so hard, and he'd said it was because he hated it. "You have a frightful conscience," she'd said. "You got it from me, you poor thing, but I'll make it up to you."

Walking up Fifth Avenue, she planned a surprise. She'd tell him he needn't stay at the bank after the first of the year. By that time Ralph and Brucie would know he wasn't lazy. She'd tell him he could go abroad and write. These youngsters who wanted to write! It was the Left Bank or sterility. No good telling them they were wrong, no good telling them that a kitchen table in Brooklyn and a stack of paper are all a writer needs.

McCutcheon's. Dinner napkins. Big, heavy, luscious dinner napkins with fat, rich monograms. She didn't need them, she had too many, and hardly anyone used them any more. But square, solid piles of damask carefully wrapped in muslin and reaching to the top of the closet shelf, that was a beautiful sight. And practical in case you felt like giving a buffet supper for a couple of hundred people. You might feel like that. For instance, you might have a wedding. She ordered two dozen.

Tiffany's. Just to look around, that's all. Everybody did that. Look around like a tourist, ogle the diamonds. Beautiful diamonds, solitaires, very practical in case you had an——

She hurried to the floor where the glassware was, struggling to keep her face straight, and ordered three dozen highball glasses with hunting scenes. Practical if you felt like giving a hunt breakfast. No, that's champagne. Or doesn't it matter? It does. She ordered the champagne glasses, too.

The Plaza. The hacks, the coachmen, one old fellow with a wilted orchid pinned to his coat. Some girl last night, some pretty young thing with her best beau, jogging through Central Park. Maybe the girl got engaged; maybe she gave it to him and told him to wear it for luck.

The waiter captain. Robbie had phoned that he'd be a little late and she wasn't to wait. The captain gave her the message. "Mrs Manson, Mr Cory said you were to go ahead. He suggested a nice old-fashioned."

She ordered the drink. One-fifteen, one-twenty. Then she knew he was there even before he bent over the back of her chair and kissed her neck. Demonstrative, for Robbie.

"Toper," he said.

"Robbie!" He looked dreadful. "Robbie, what have you been doing to yourself?"

"Working for your living. Why?" He rubbed a hand over his face. "Maybe I forgot to shave."

"You did not! Robbie, if I positively didn't know you were in your own bed at ten, I'd say you'd spent the night in sin. Tell me what's wrong. Don't lie to me, tell me!"

He said he was tired, that was all. Tired, so help him. "Do you want me to cross my heart in a joint like this?" He wouldn't look at her. He ordered his lunch without the menu; shirred eggs, black coffee. Drink? No, no drink.

She talked, talked her head off, told him about the new napkins, the new glasses; but he wasn't listening. He was sick, he must be dreadfully sick. "Robbie, where does it hurt? Now, don't be childish. You've got a pain somewhere, and I want to know. It can't be your appendix, that's out. What *have* you got left? I always forget which of yours came out and which of mine. No tonsils, no appendix, no—no—Robbie, your heart!"

"I still have that," he assured her. And he laughed; too loud, too sharp. He parried every personal allusion and kept the conversation on her weakness for linen and crystal, her transportation of cracked corn from Larchville in a Bergdorf bag, when she could buy a paper sack of it from a little man who hung around the cathedral for that very purpose.

She gave up. She'd get him alone that night; she'd go to his room whether he liked it or not; she'd make him tell her what was wrong. "Home for dinner, Robbie?"

"You bet."

That was all. He phoned for her car and waited until it came. He handed her in and strode off, across the street, into Central Park.

"Nora, we're going down to dinner, darling. Miss Sills will stay until Emma comes." Ralph.

"No roller-skating in the halls, baby. It's bad for the carpet." Brucie.

"Lucky Mrs Manson, to be able to sleep so gracefully. You're better, my dear lady, I know it, I can see it. I've been waiting for it. I think I'll speak to the masseur. Perhaps we can lengthen the treatments. If I had your fine spirit and this charming room, I wouldn't mind a touch of invalidism myself!" Dr Babcock.

"Thanks for the drinks, Mrs Manson. Goodnight." George Perry.

"Thanks for getting out of here, all of you, and quick." Miss Sills.

"That's right, slam the door. Deliver me from men in a sickroom!" Miss Sills again, patting her shoulder. "I thought they'd cheer you up, but you don't look too cheery. Hear me tell Babcock to get out with the others? I don't know the meaning of fear. I'll say anything. If he fires me off this case, I'll come straight back. I'll climb the ivy and crawl through the window. Baby this and baby that. Don't you make any mistake about whose baby you are. You're mine."

Miss Sills was all right, she must be, she had to be. When the time came, Miss Sills would stand fast. She was young—how young? Twenty-four or -five? But she was physically strong, and she'd been trained to think and act fast. Stand fast. Stand. At bay? No, not at bay. It wouldn't come like that. It would come in the dark, on silent feet, as it had come before. Come when she was alone. But if there were no time to lose, if minutes, even seconds, were precious, it would strike without waiting, without warning.

If it came like that, Miss Sills would have to die, too. Not Miss Sills, not a young girl who'd done nothing!

"Isn't that rug too hot now? Mrs Manson, I think the rug's too hot with the fire going full blast. Here, let me take it. You're roasting. You look like a little red beet."

Take the rug? Take the fringe away? No! No!

"Now what have I said that's wrong? Don't you like being called a little red beet? Golly, honey—I mean, Mrs Manson, I wish I knew what you wanted. You do want something, don't you? I wish I—say, has it something to do with your rug? Emma said you'd taken a sudden fancy to it. Did I guess right? Right! Well, then, it's yours. You keep it. I'll just move your chair back from the fire. That's better, isn't it? You know something, Mrs Manson? One of these days you're going to smile at me, and that's the day I'm waiting for."

Dear Miss Sills. Be careful, Miss Sills. Don't be too good to me. . . .

At nine o'clock that evening Alice Perry walked into her son's room. George was reading in bed, and he looked up at her without speaking when she entered.

"Sulking, George?" Alice Perry's hair was like cotton batting, and her round face was fresh and firm. Her voice was firm also.

"No. Toothache."

"You've seen a dentist?"

"No. It'll go away."

"Sometimes you act like a child, dear. You'll find a package of those small poultices in the medicine cabinet. Use one tonight, and see a dentist in the morning. I shouldn't have to tell you that." She walked about the small room, rearranging chairs, replacing books on shelves, frowning at a bowl of yellow chrysanthemums. "Who brought these in here? You?"

"Yes, I like the colour. Nothing wrong with that, is there?"

"No, of course not. But you're clumsy with flowers. These are much too stiff, and the bowl's all wrong. Never mind that now, I'll do them over tomorrow. George?"

"Yes, Mother." He put his book aside.

"You stopped there on the way home, didn't you?"

He didn't need her half-look at the windows that faced the Perry back yard, the gaping hedge, and the Manson garden. "Yes, for a little while."

"How is she?"

"Tut, tut. I can remember when you gave me the devil for say 'she'. Like this: 'If you mean Mrs Manson, say so.' Sure I stopped. I had a couple of drinks." He was entirely good-humoured and smiling. "Mrs Manson is the same."

"Still helpless? I mean, still dependent?" She added, "Poor creature."

"Still all of that. No speech, no movement."

"Ralph Manson tells me nothing. Bruce Cory is just as bad. I ask every day, by telephone or in person. I knew Nora Manson when she was Nora Cory. I took you to call when she moved here and Robbie was a toddler and you weren't much more. Ralph and Bruce know that as well as they know their own names. Yet sometimes I think they don't want me in the house."

"No." He answered carefully. "You mustn't make it a personal issue. I think they feel it's better for her to see no one outside the immediate family. If she's beginning to be aware of her condition—and they think she is— why——"

"Why what, George?" She laughed. "Talked yourself into a corner that time, didn't you? *You* see her, don't you?"

"Yes. But luckily for me, my connection with the family is on a different plane. I represent bicycles in the hall, peanut butter on the piano keys, stuff like that. All very wholesome and nostalgic in the right way."

"And exactly what do I represent, you silly?" She ruffled his hair.

"Now, Mother, use your pretty little head. You're another woman, and you're healthy, and you haven't had any trouble. Also, and very important, you were there that day; if she sees you, it's bound to—upset her. They don't want that. They want her to live as she does, from hour to hour, in a sort of merciful stupor, segregated from the past. Because if she ever does get well, she'll have plenty of time to mull things over. She'll have a whole lifetime to look back on, and she won't see a pretty picture. Let her have this, whatever you call it, hiatus. If she gets well and looks back on *this,* it'll seem like heaven."

"George, you get more like your father every day. You treat me as if I didn't have good sense. . . . I don't think she's going to get well."

"Why not?"

"Those specialists from town. They came and went. If they'd been hopeful, we'd have heard about it. But there hasn't been a word, at least not what *I* call a word. And now there's only Babcock. She's lost her mind, hasn't she? Frankly, she never had much of one to lose."

He picked up his book and flipped over a page. If he meant it for a signal to dismissal, it wasn't heeded.

"Cat got your tongue, Georgie?" She was amused, standing by the bed, looking down and smiling.

"Toothache. No, she hasn't lost her mind."

"Then what do they call this—this state?"

"Shock and paralysis, one bound up with the other. Some cases have been cured."

"Have they? Well, I'm glad to hear it."

She walked to the windows, examined the chintz curtains and admired the design. "This was a good buy," she said. "I'm a good shopper." The rain fell lightly against the glass. She tapped the pane with immaculate little fingers. "Your father went to the movies. On a night like this, he must be crazy. Or bored. I asked him which, and he looked as if he couldn't decide what to answer. Funny man."

"He likes the rain," George said. "He likes to walk in it."

"The ground is soaking." She hummed and tapped a pane, peering out into the dark, dripping gardens. Then: "George, the lights are on in her room. Why, at this hour?"

"Masseur. This is the time he comes. She sleeps afterward."

"Sedatives, of course?"

"Yep." He looked up from his book, startled by the sudden sound of curtain rings travelling across the rods. "What's the idea?" he asked agreeably. "I like them the way they were. I like to look out."

"There's nothing to see."

"Sure there is. The rain. I like it, same as the old man."

"It's depressing. And there's a draught. These windows never did fit properly. Shoddy building in the first place, but what can I do? Your father's satisfied as long as the roof doesn't leak on his bed. . . . That girl went out a while ago, George. I saw her from the kitchen window. I think she saw me, too. She came around the side of the house and looked over here. Then she went away in a hurry."

"Name of Sills, Mother. Miss or Milly, take your choice."

"Now, George, there's absolutely no need for that frozen stare. You know how I feel. She's not—she's not your type. You've had every advantage, I've seen to that, and you can thank me for it. I honestly think it would kill me if you threw yourself away on an ordinary——"

"Easy, Mater. How do you like the Mater touch? That's my fine education." He looked contrite at once. "Listen, Ma, I've got a toothache, I don't feel like talking. Run along now, like a good egg."

"Don't think you can get around me with that 'egg'. Are you going to slip out and meet her later?"

"I hadn't thought of it, but since you've given me the idea——"

"George! I can't imagine where a girl like that goes at night. It was nearly half-past eight when she left. I must say it looks very odd."

"This happens to be her night off. She usually goes home to see her mother. She's nuts about her mother. And her father, unfortunately dead and unable to speak for himself, was an honest-Injun college man. Now you know it all. So how about me bringing Miss Sills over here some afternoon? She has time off in the afternoon too."

"Really, George!"

"Well, why not? I'll tip her off to wear the Sophie original, and you won't be able to tell her from a lady."

He was pleased when the door slammed on his last words. For a while he stayed where he was, stretching his long legs and staring at the ceiling, prodding his tender jaw with a pessimistic finger. Then he got up and went down the hall to the medicine cabinet in the bathroom.

The poultices were there—everything was always where she said it would be. He tucked one of them over his aching tooth, laughed to himself in the mirror, and returned to his room. There he drew back the curtains, raised a window, and stood looking out into the dark, wet night. Far across the stretch of Gardens the lamps on the Mansons' street were a chain of dim yellow haloes. There was almost no traffic; an occasional car crept warily over the shining asphalt and was lost in the blur of rain and trees and lights that marked the shopping centre across the park. The rain hung like a veil a few inches before his face; he felt as if he could part it with his hand and look through to something that was now obscured.

Mrs Manson's sleeping porch filled the centre of a landscaped vista. He remembered when she'd had that vista made. She'd said she wanted to watch them while they played. Watch him and Robbie. Two men had put ladders against the trees and swung in the branches like monkeys while she directed them from the ground. A great day for him and Robbie, with branches falling from the air and the servants running around in circles.

Now her room was bright with lights; but as he watched, they went out, one by one, until a single lamp burned. He knew that room so well that he knew where each lamp was and what it looked like. The one that was left stood on a small table by the glass door that opened onto the porch. The bulb was purposely weak. It was meant to give comfort to sleepless eyes, nothing more.

Two figures came to the glass door and stood there, a slight woman in black and a stocky man in white. He knew their silhouettes and their unvarying ritual; he didn't need their black and white for identification. Emma and the masseur; a last-minute chat, whispered amenities, compliments given and taken by two people in the pay of the same household. The masseur moved like a chimpanzee disguised as a man or a man disguised as a chimpanzee. But Milly said he was good. The best in the business, she said.

George watched the man take his leave. He could count every invisible step, every foot of the upper hall, stairway, and lower hall, and give to each its allotted time. So much for the hat-and-coat routine, so much for the walk to the front gate, so much for crossing the street to the park, for the left turn toward the station, which would bring him into view again.

His bare elbows were on the dripping window-sill and the wet wind was making his tooth jump, but he was too intent to notice. It was the final, hissing exhalation of his breath that startled him out of his absorption. What am I doing this for? He asked himself. What am I breathing heavily about?

The man, whose name was Breitman, had come into view on schedule and was moving in the right direction for the station, head lowered, trunk forward, long arms hanging wide. What am I doing this for? George asked himself again. What's the big idea of keeping tabs? The guy could have stopped for a drink with Manson and Cory—he sometimes does. So what? . . . His eyes returned to the glass door. The single lamp had been moved back. Its light was as faint as the glow of a distant city reflected in the sky, but it was enough to show the passing to and fro of Emma's slight, black figure. She raised and lowered the linen shades that covered the glass panes of the door, then raised them again and opened half of the door. She disappeared and returned with a painted screen, which she dragged into place before the open section. He smiled, because he knew she was making faces and talking to herself. When Emma took charge of things she always told herself she was the only person in the house who saw that

Miss Nora got what was good for her. The screen wasn't Emma's job, it was Manson's or Cory's, even Milly's; but Emma beat them to it when she could. Once or twice he had been in the house at bedtime and tried to lend a hand; but Emma had brushed him aside and tossed him out with a few choice words. Well, he thought, tonight she's having it her way, and tomorrow the family will pay and pay. And so will I, he decided, touching his cheek and preparing to wince. But the tooth wasn't too bad; in fact, it was much better. He returned to his bed and book and settled against the pillows.

The wet wind blew in at the open window, spattering the curtains that were such a good buy. He told himself they could take it. It was good to be under the covers, in an empty room, with thoughts instead of people for company. The upstairs telephone extension rang faintly. It was at the end of the hall, outside his mother's room. He didn't notice how many times it rang; his mind was far away, across the dark, wet gardens, across the little park with its dripping trees, as far away as the Sills' cottage. When he thought of the phone again, it had stopped ringing. The whole house was silent.

Emma wedged a hassock and a low chair against the screen, settled the backs of her hands on her hips, and quietly dared the result to fall down. The screen stood firm. She examined the remainder of the room, properly darkened for a restful night; the fire banked with ashes, her work; the roses on the window sill, her work; chairs in place, tables cleaned, also hers. Hot milk in a vacuum jug on the bed table and the bottle of sleeping pills beside it. The milk was Hattie's work. But everything to hand in case it was needed. The milk and the pills weren't needed, not now. Sleeping like an angel, breathing nice and regular. When she was like that, Miss Sills didn't want her to have a pill. Miss Sills said she was the one to decide whether or not a pill was necessary and nobody but herself was to touch the bottle, either. She had said accidents could happen and sometimes did. "Not when I'm around," Emma had said coldly.

The mantel clock said nine-thirty. A good long wait before Miss Sills came back, Emma reflected, unless the rain drove her home early, which wasn't likely. Young people made out like they could walk between the drops.

She rubbed her eyes furtively. She was sleepy, and she longed for her own bed with its overabundance of thick quilts and the paper sack of hard white peppermints under the pillow. But she put them out of her mind, and her heart warmed with a martyr's glow. I'll wash my face with cold water, she told herself. That'll keep me awake. I'll just run down the hall to the lavatory—take me a couple of minutes, no more.

There was a bath adjoining the bedroom, but she obstinately chose to accept Miss Sills' instruction about that. Miss Sills said it was a private, not a public bath. Emma turned up her nose at the gleaming tile and spotless basins. Like a hospital. You could do an operation in it.

She gave a last, quick look at the figure on the bed. So flat, so thin, so still. Dark lashes smudged the pale cheeks; dark hair lay across the pillow. The old rug was spread over the eiderdown—she'd want it that way, you could tell. It was too hot, but Miss Sills could take it away later. And that massage, it was a punishing treatment. Those poor thin arms and legs, you'd think they'd break in two.

Emma went quietly down the hall, stopping once to peer over the stair railing. The lower hall was dim. Her sharp old ears identified and placed the faint sound of music under the hardier sound of rain and vines blowing against the landing window. They were playing the radio down there, in Mr Ralph's little study at the far end of the hall. Turned down low and the door shut. The masseur's report must have been good; otherwise, they wouldn't be playing the radio. If the report had been bad, they'd be glooming in and out of her room, keeping her awake with their talk about how well she looked and how she'd be horseback riding in another month. Not fooling a cat, either. Laughing and smiling all over. That's how they acted when the report was bad. A child would catch on. . . . And I'm no child, she added, even though they think so. I can read them like a book. That goes for Breitman, too, and I'll tell him the same next time I see him.

She sent an indulgent smile down the dim stairs and pattered softly to the lavatory at the end of the hall. The afternoon towels hadn't been changed. Her job, and she'd forgotten it. Well, considering the company and all the extra work, you'd think Miss Sills would be kind enough to—— Someone had left a tube of toothpaste on the washbasin. Miss Sills! Her brand and the top not screwed on.

She studied the tube for almost a minute, then squeezed it in the middle and twisted it awry. That'll show her what co-operation is, she gloated. But when she admired her work, she felt uneasy. The result was so clearly a piece of thoughtful

190

malice that she tried to straighten out the tube. But it broke and covered her hands with paste. She hid it in the towel hamper. The wastebasket was too public.

After that she was wide awake and decided she didn't need cold water on her face. She started back.

Across from the lavatory a closed door stood in a deep recess. Every day she looked at that door and said a prayer under her breath. Now she looked at it again, and her eyes filled. The hall light lay softly on the smooth, waxed panels; but no amount of waxing and rubbing had been able to erase the deep dents at the bottom or the new scars that bit into the area around the lock. That lock was new, too. It was so new that it glittered like gold.

The deep dents were made long ago by small, stout shoes kicking for admittance to an attic that was always locked a week before Christmas and kept that way until late on Christmas Eve. But no matter how careful they were, little Robbie managed to be around when the bulky packages were carried up the back stairs and smuggled through the attic door. No matter how quiet they tried to be, he always heard them and came on the run. As far back as the first rocking-horse time, when he couldn't run without falling down. The rocking-horse time was the first; then the scooter, then the tricycle, then the bicycle and the sled, not to mention all the other things like railroads and trucks that cost too much and were big enough to ride in. Well, maybe they did spoil him. What happened later must have been their fault. A child grew up to be what you let him be. Yet——

She raised her eyes to the lock. The scars were deep. Once again she saw frenzied hands working against time with whatever tools they'd been able to find in the cellar chest. Once again she heard the heavy breathing of men doing something they never had done before, heard the hopeless clatter of a screwdriver as it slipped through sweating fingers, heard the loud, insistent ringing of the front door-bell. Above it all, the ringing of the bell. . . . How long ago? Six weeks ago. Yes, six weeks.

Emma turned from the door and went back to the room, walking slowly, with bent head. She was more than sleepy now; she was old and beaten, and she knew it. If she woke up dead in the morning, she wouldn't care. As she found her way to a chair by the banked fire she told herself she wouldn't care at all. The light from the single lamp found and lingered on the rose-coloured jug and the bottle of pills that stood on the bed table. Before she closed her eyes, she sent a long compassionate look across the room to the figure lying under the blankets and rug. It was still. Of course it was still. But something that could have been a shadow rippled over the rug at the fold where the hidden hands lay. It could have been the shadow of the ivy that swayed in the wind outside the glass door. She told herself it was the ivy and the lamplight, and that satisfied her.

Emma went to sleep with her hands folded under her neat black apron, sitting upright in her chair. Sometimes she stirred in her sleep, because she was running away from horror. She was running up the attic stairs, followed by bells and voices. And all the while she knew she was running in the wrong direction, but she couldn't turn back.

She heard Emma moan in her sleep like a tired and labouring animal, and the sound dragged her up from the depths of a beautiful dream. She was dreaming that her fingers had wrapped themselves around the fringe at last, had turned and twisted and grown strong. She fought to keep the dream, clinging in her sleep to the heavy strands, because they made a chain that bound her to life. No dream had ever held the ecstasy of this one. She could almost feel pain. She could almost persuade herself that her hands——

It was no use. She was awake. That was wishful thinking, she told herself despairingly; that was childish. She couldn't afford to be childish.

She opened her eyes and looked at Emma. Emma sat in shadow, the fireplace was dark, the corners of the room were darker. She couldn't see the clock, but Emma's presence and the screen, the jug, and the sleeping medicine told her it was still too early for Miss Sills. The screen, with its flanking chair and hassock, was Emma's work. Miss Sills could make it stand without support.

And there were four pills left in the bottle. It was easy to count them, four pills neatly covering the bottom. That was correct. She knew how many there ought to be; every night she counted them. The dose was one, and it was placed in her mouth and followed by a drink of the hot milk. When she couldn't see the bottle, or when the number of visible pills was uncertain, she refused the milk. There were too many opportunities for slipping extra pills into the jug. Sometimes the jug was brought by one person, sometimes by another, all the way from the kitchen, with stops en route to talk or answer the telephone. And sometimes there were as many as six people in her room at one time, all talking and moving about. And too often she was in her chair by the window, turned away from the table.

Four pills; that was right for tonight. Unless a new prescription had come and—— Stop that. Stop. Don't waste emotion on imagination. Save the emotion for things you know. Let the things you know feed you and make you strong. Listen to the rain on the roof, on the porch. Faint and clear and clean and measured. Like fingers on the keys of a typewriter in a distant room with a closed door. See how everything falls into place when you make your mind behave? Always make your mind remember the things it must. Try again. Begin again with the rain.

The rain has nothing to do with us, but it seems to belong. Perhaps because it sounds the way the typewriter keys used to sound. Night after night, before that day.

It didn't rain that day. That was the day of sun and St Patrick's, and McCutcheon's, and Tiffany's and the Plaza. . . .

She didn't go home when she left the Plaza; she shopped for another hour and then drove to the bank. Maybe Robbie would drive home with her, maybe Ralph, maybe even Bruce. There was no earthly reason Bruce couldn't drive out for dinner at least, and she'd tell him so. It was about time he paid them a little attention. A good dinner and a good talk. She'd ask his advice about Robbie. And she'd tell him he could leave early for whatever it was that kept him so close to town. Probably a girl, and a young one at that. He always looked foolish when she asked him what he did in the evenings. A very, very young girl, with plucked eyebrows. Men like Brucie are invariably trapped in the end by girls young enough to be their daughters.

When the car stopped at the bank, she had her own trap set for Bruce. She'd tell him how much she missed the long walks and rides they used to take together. She'd tell him he was almost as dear to her as his own brother had been. No. No, that wouldn't do. That might sound as if—— She felt the colour surge to her cheeks. Hussy, she said to herself, what a mind you've got.

She entered the bank and walked briskly to the offices in the rear. I'll simply tell Bruce that I'm worried about Robbie, she decided, that Robbie looks like the devil. Maybe he's noticed it himself. I'll remind him that he's Robbie's only relative and that, while Ralph does his best, it still isn't quite enough. And we'll have something very special for dinner, just the four of us, me and my three men. I'll make it a gala. I'll wear my new dress and that crazy rouge I haven't dared try yet.

She was beaming when she went into Ralph's office. Ralph wasn't there.

Miss Harper, his secretary, was doing her nails and looked embarrassed. "Mr Manson left about an hour ago," Miss Harper said. "Can I do anything for you, Mrs Manson?"

"No." She hesitated. "Do you know where he went? Home or the club or what?"

"He didn't say, Mrs Manson, but I think he went home. He filled his brief-case, and when he does that——"

"Yes, I know." Ralph and his homework. Ridiculous, but he got a big kick out of being an executive, even after hours. Nice old Ralph, doing his best to act like a Cory and a banker and doing it too hard. "What about my son? Do you think the bank will bust if I take him home with me? I've got the car."

"Mr Robbie didn't come back after lunch," Miss Harper said. "I believe he—I heard Mr Manson and Mr Cory mention it." Miss Harper's embarrassment had turned into something stronger. She didn't seem to know where to look.

"Mention it in what way? You mean they needed Mr Robbie and couldn't locate him? They knew he was with me."

"Oh, I don't know anything about it, Mrs Manson! Nobody said—— I mean, I simply heard Mr Cory ask where Mr Robbie was, and Mr Manson seemed to think he—— I really don't know anything about it, Mrs Manson."

She told herself Miss Harper was an idiot, a maladjusted, fluttering, stammering little fool. "It's all right, Miss Harper, thank you." She wanted to say that Robbie could come and go as he liked in his own father's and grandfather's bank. "I'll go in and see Mr Cory. Perhaps he'll ride home with me."

Miss Harper started to say something about Bruce, discarded the sentence before it was fairly launched, and substituted a noisy and frantic hunt through her desk. "My bag and gloves," she explained, waving them as if they were a last-minute reprieve. "I know you'll excuse me, Mrs Manson, but I've got to rush, I really have. Heavy date, you know, heavy date." She smiled falsely and scurried out of the office.

She followed Miss Harper slowly, aware of a sudden and unaccountable depression. Perhaps the gloves and bag *were* a reprieve. Miss Harper's pale eyes had shown an absurd relief when she held them up.

Bruce's office door was closed, and when she got no answer to her knock, she went in. Empty. All at once she was too tired to question even herself. She nodded to a clerk, who stopped at the open door with a startled look, and then she went back to the car.

All the way home she told herself she had been too happy in the morning. When that happened, you always ate dust in the afternoon. For no good reason, for no reason at all. Of course there was no reason. She planned dinner all over again, confident that all three would be home when she got there. All three, even Brucie. Brucie, coming out with the others for a surprise. But why, after all these months, why a surprise? Was it a silly anniversary or something? Had she forgotten one of her big-little days? No, she hadn't forgotten.

On the station side of the little park she saw Alice Perry walking with her head down. Alice looked dejected, not brisk and trim as usual. Poor Alice. Always too ambitious, always expecting too much of her two Georges, husband and son, never satisfied with the small, pleasant comforts of her life.

She raised her hand to beckon, then remembered something Ralph had said. She hadn't agreed with him then, but she dropped her hand now. He'd said: "Go easy on the indiscriminate lifts, darling. In bad weather it's all right, but you stop for anybody and everybody, and it looks patronizing. Especially to people like Alice Perry. She's apt to think you're rubbing her nose in your fine car."

She'd been indignant. "I've known Alice Perry since George and Robbie were children. I like her, and you're crazy, darling."

"All right, I'm crazy. But Alice doesn't like you. She wants what you have."

She'd laughed. Maybe Alice did want what she had, but that was only because Alice was born discontented. It wasn't a personal thing. They'd always been friends of a sort, as two women are when their children play together. Now she turned from the plodding figure and pretended not to see it. I don't feel like talking to her anyway, she told herself. I don't feel like talking to anybody. I want to get home in a hurry.

Emma let her in. Emma was wearing her hat, she'd been

to the stores, and just got back. No, she didn't know if Mr Ralph or Mr Robbie had come home. She didn't know anything about Mr Brucie. She'd look in the coat closet and find out in a minute.

"Don't bother," she told Emma. "I've got something for you to do. I'm going to call Mr Bruce in town and ask him out for dinner. A very special dinner, because I feel that way. I want you to huddle with Hattie. Open all the stuff you've been hoarding, stuff like caviar, use all the eggs and cream and butter in the house, and get more. See if that man has pheasants. And don't tell me anything about it. I want to be surprised."

She went to her room and, still wearing her outdoor clothing and dialling with gloved fingers, called Bruce's apartment on her own phone. Why am I acting as if this were a life-and-death performance? she wondered. But Bruce's apartment didn't answer. She tried his club. He was expected for bridge, and she left word that he was to call her as soon as he came in.

The upper hall was quiet; the doors were all closed. They weren't home. When they were home, you could hear them through walls and doors. She drew her bath and laid out the new dress. Diamonds? No. Plain gold? Chic. Or sapphires? Yes, sapphires because her eyes—— Hussy.

She was in the bath when she heard someone come into her room. "Ralph?" she called.

"It's Bruce, dear. I'll wait here until you come out."

"How perfectly wonderful! You're a mind reader! I've been trying to get you. You've got to stay for dinner."

"That's what I came for. Take your time, Nora."

"What's the matter with your voice? Got a cold?"

"No. I don't know. Yes, I guess I have."

"I'll fix that. I know the very thing. Is Ralph with you, or Robbie?"

"No. I came alone."

"Brucie, I went to the bank today. Am I screaming too loud? Anyway, I went to the bank after lunch with Robbie. I'm worried about Robbie, he looks awful. But you'd all gone. That crazy Miss Harper—I don't see how Ralph stands her. . . . See Robbie anywhere around?"

"I haven't looked. How are you anyway, Nora? It's been so long——"

"Your fault." She left the tub and got into her dressing

196

gown. "Be with you in a minute. If you want a drink, ring for Emma. This is going to be a party."

She went into the room and saw him bending over the laid fire. He was putting a match to the paper, and when he turned to greet her, his face was stiff and white.

"You really are sick!" She ran across the room and touched his cheek. "You are, and I love it. We'll keep you here tonight and take care of you. Brucie, if you want to marry a little fool, go right ahead. She'll be better for you than that creeping, crawling gentleman's gentleman. That man doesn't know the first thing about——"

Bruce was looking over her shoulder, and she turned. Ralph was coming in. Ralph didn't speak; he didn't have to.

They can't both be sick, she told herself. Not both of them, not all of them. Something's happened. They've got bad news, and they're here to tell me. The bank—— No, Robbie! I knew it. I've known it all day. . . . She wrapped the dressing gown close; she was bitterly cold with a sweeping, numbing cold that rushed from all sides. She found a chair by the crackling fire and sat erect. "All right," she said. "Don't waste time. Let me have it. He's run away, hasn't he? He can't be dead."

"Dead?" Ralph's voice was startled, his face accusing. "Whatever makes you think—— Bruce, will you?"

"Yes," Bruce said. "Nora, you haven't seen Robbie since you two had lunch?"

"You know I haven't!"

"Did he say anything to you—about us, about the bank?"

"No, no. But he looked dreadful. Go on, Bruce!"

Then he told her. Ralph stood by the window with his back to the room. As Bruce spoke, she knew it was right that he should be the one to tell her. Bruce and Robbie had the same blood.

He told her that almost two hundred thousand dollars had been stolen from the bank over a period of two years, a job so carefully contrived that no one had known about it until yesterday. There was no doubt about Robbie. She barely heard the damaging phrases, words like 'estate' and 'trustee'; she heard only that there was no doubt about Robbie. The Board was convinced.

Bruce and Ralph had asked the Board for a few days' grace. They were going to talk to Robbie—that was why they were both there. But Robbie hadn't come back from lunch, and that had forced their hands and frightened them a little. They had both looked for him.

"He wasn't at any of his old hangouts," Bruce said. "So I came here, because I was pretty sure he'd turn up, if only to see you. I don't think he's made a bolt."

"I don't believe it," she said.

"I find it hard to believe myself. But it looks—— Apparently it began when he first came to the bank. We're going to give him every chance."

"He didn't do it."

"I want to believe that, too. We'll soon know, Nora. He'll tell us; he's no liar."

"He didn't do it. He wouldn't know how. Find him—both of you go and find him. How long have you been in the house, and what have you done?"

Bruce said he had come alone on the three o'clock train, let himself in with the key he always had had, and seen no one. Then he'd gone for a walk and just returned.

Ralph said he had come on the following train, found Robbie's room empty and no one about, and locked himself in his own room to think. Ralph's hands, on the back of a chair, were white around the knuckles.

"Ring for Emma," she said.

Emma came. She had a menu in her hand and began to read it aloud the minute she crossed the threshold. "Turtle soup," she said. "I don't care whether you want to be surprised or not, you've got to listen. A good turtle soup with sherry, not too heavy for what comes after and nice for a coolish evening. Then a small fresh salmon——" She stopped. "What are they saying to you, Miss Nora? What's happening here?"

"Have you seen Robbie?"

"I told you before, I haven't seen a soul until now. I was out from lunch on. But if you want to know if he's home, I guess he is. Or was. Hattie says she heard the typewriter going a while back. Up in the attic."

Bruce said quickly, "Attic?"

"Where else? That's where he keeps his machine, that's where he does his writing, the young monkey. Sometimes, when he comes home early, he justs slips in and goes up there."

Ralph said: "I'll check. I'll go right away. That'll be all, Emma."

198

Emma stood where she was. "It will not be all," she said. "It's my right to know what's happening here."

They stood in a tight little group before the attic door and watched Ralph put his hand on the knob. The door was locked.

"He's taken the key," he said over his shoulder. He sounded as if he were swallowing a scream.

"Scream," she cried, "scream, get help. Scream, scream, or I will. Get that door open!"

Bruce ran downstairs. He was gone for a lifetime, in which Robbie was conceived, born, bathed and fed, sung to in the evening dusk, played with in the morning sun. She leaned against the wall and bore him again with pain.

Bruce returned with the cellar tool chest. The front doorbell rang and rang through the house.

"I'll pay, I'll pay," she heard herself say. "Restitution, recompense, I don't know the word. He didn't do it, but I'll pay."

"Stop that," Bruce said. "Somebody go down and send that woman away. Mrs Perry. She's at the door. Somebody send her away."

Something heavy and metallic slipped through his fingers and clattered to the floor. She went down on her knees before the locked door. They were all on their knees, even Emma, pounding with tools, boring, prying, calling his name.

She knew her lips were shaping his name now. She tried to tighten them. Useless. She tried again. Better. Now she had her lower lip between her teeth, holding it fast. The muscles in her face were rigid, under control.

Could I do that yesterday? she wondered. Could I have done that a few days ago? Am I getting stronger or am I dreaming again? Don't dream; don't. You'll know when the time comes. Concentrate on facts, on things that have body and substance. If you don't, you'll lose your mind. Concentrate on anything. The bed, the lamp, the jug, the glass bottle. Never take the medicine unless you are able to count the pills. Remember that. Never take it unless you can count, and take it only from Miss Sills. If you could talk, what would you say first. If you could walk, which way would you go? No, no, think of something that is real.

This room is real; it has body and substance. The jug of milk, the bottle, the painted screen, all real. There are grey clouds and black birds and green rushes on the screen. That's right, that's right. And there's one small bird deep in the rushes at the bottom, sitting on a nest. Find the small bird on the nest. Low on the left, near the floor—you know where it is. Find it. . . .

There was a gloved hand lying on the floor under the screen.

It moved along the floor, in the space beneath the frame, a bright-yellow hand with thick, spread fingers. Another hand crept out and moved beside it. They minced to the right and then to the left, feeling their way, like two blind, glutted things.

Her lips curled back from her teeth.

The two hands travelled to the end of the screen and stopped. A few inches above them another hand crept around the frame and curled and slipped and clung. Then another. Four thick, yellow hands close together, beckoning. . . .

"I don't know why you want to leave before your time's up," Mrs Sills said to her daughter. "It's not half past ten yet. What do you think I cut that cake for? Not for myself, I can assure you. Stale bakery cake is good enough for me. I made that cake for my only child, who brings me a bundle of messy old uniforms and says it's such a bad night that she'd better be going out in it. Going where?"

Milly was unimpressed. "Don't give me that cake routine again. You're fifteen pounds overweight from four-layer chocolate fresh out of the oven. And I'll take my laundry to the Steam Hand, if you don't like it. I hate rain, and you know it, and George has a toothache."

"I begin to see the light," Mrs Sills said. "George has a toothache, and Mrs Perry won't let him out. So you haven't any place to go except to see your old mother. When I was your age, I had four or five on the string and glad enough to come running when I called the tune. . . . Are you going to marry him, or am I being personal?"

Milly said nothing.

"Don't do it," her mother said, "unless you can afford a place of your own. Don't do it unless he can support you. None of this career-after-marriage business, because when the babies begin to come and you have to stop work, they always get mad—because they miss the extra money and won't admit it. And don't economize on cheap furniture; it doesn't pay in the end. No veneers—good solid walnut or cherry. I'll give you half of my silver. . . . Was that George you called up a while ago?"

200

"Yes."

"I couldn't hear, because you lowered your voice. I don't know what you have to tell a man that your own mother can't know about."

"You couldn't hear because I didn't say anything. He wasn't home—or wouldn't answer the phone."

"Toothache!"

"Goodnight, Mother." Milly started for the door.

"Have I said something wrong?" Mrs Sills wondered wistfully.

"Not a word." Milly gave her mother a kiss and a hug. "I'm going to stop at Marge's to return a library book. Then I'm going straight back to my nice, sick baby, and I don't want any other kind for a long while. Now you know, and I'll drop in tomorrow afternoon on my exercise. If I can. Be good." She closed the front door and went down the short path to the sidewalk.

The rain fell steadily, evenly, meeting the pavement with a hiss but sinking into the sodden grass without a sound. . . . You'd think it had a home under the grass, she thought. You'd think it had a special place to go. Worms. Nothing under grass but worms. But under this particular grass, under this very super Mrs Nathaniel-Sills-and-daughter grass, there are also bones. Cat, dog, canary, and goldfish bones, in shoeboxes and matchboxes, all rotted and gone. I have the soul of a poet. . . . After that it was too easy to think of another kind of grass, trim and park-like, where the same rain was sinking into the earth and finding——

She ran past the lighted drugstore on the corner, turned and ran the length of a block to Marge Foster's shop. "Hi," she said in a breathless voice that she tried to make casual.

Marge, sorting rental cards at her worktable, looked up. "Put that umbrella in the stand before I drown. What brings you out in all weathers?"

Milly slid her book across the table. "I make it twenty-four cents due. Here's a quarter, and I want change."

"You kill me," Marge said. "I can remember the day when you patronized Carnegie's Free. Why don't you go back there? Sit down. How are you, honey?"

"So-so." Milly pulled up a chair. Miss Foster's Lending Library and Gift Bazaar was empty except for the proprietress and Milly "Terrible night. George is sick. He says.

Mother's going to give me half her silver. She says. What do you know, Marge?"

"What do *I* know? You're the one who lives the life."

"I'm gaining weight—they feed me swell. On some cases you share a bowl with the dog."

"You're lucky. You look wonderful." Marge gave the rain-blurred windows a rapid survey. "I don't feel like business, I feel like talking to an old school tie. Put your feet up and relax." She crossed to the door, locked it, and returned. "And they call me money-mad."

Milly settled her feet on the edge of a bookshelf. "I ought not to stay, honestly. I'm not due back till twelve, but she's acting kind of funny tonight. Got a cigarette?"

"Here." Marge pushed the box across the table. "Milly, you know I'm as safe as houses. I wouldn't open my mouth about anything you told me."

"I haven't got anything to tell. Match? Thanks. What's the matter with you. You look as if you didn't believe me."

"Sure I believe you. George Perry's mother was in this afternoon looking for 'a little love story, nothing modern.' The whole time she was here she was talking at the top of her lungs about how her son is the light of Mrs Manson's life. Is he?"

"Of course not. Half the time he's there she doesn't even look at him. If I know you, Mrs P. said something else and you're working up to it. What?"

"Well, she did want to know how well I knew you. Casual-like. Quote: 'Are you friendly with that little nurse of Mrs Manson's? I believe Mrs Manson has become quite attached to her.' I don't think she loves you."

"She doesn't even know me. I'm taking my time about that. What else?"

"She thinks Bruce Cory is too good-looking. She sort of hinted that he liked Mrs Manson too well before she up and married his brother. To say nothing of marrying Manson, too. And now that he's hanging around again, using her illness as an excuse—— Her and her little love stories! Milly, is Mrs Manson going to die?"

"Not if I can help it." Milly turned and looked at the dripping windows. They showed a strange, new world. But the single, wavering blur of light was only a street lamp that stood on the kerb; the twisted shape that rapped on the pane and sprung away and rapped again was nothing but a branch. "Not if I can help it," she repeated. "I'm a good nurse. I know that. And Babcock must think so, too, or he wouldn't have wanted me. Not for a patient like Mrs Manson." Milly's voice grew soft. "She's a darling, she's a pet, and I worry about her all the time. I want her to get well. I want her to get even half-well. The minute she shows a definite improvement, they want to take her away somewhere, a change of scene. Any kind of change ought to help. But I don't know. The other day I dressed her up in her jewellery, rings, bracelets, clips—stuff to knock your eyes out. But she no like, I could tell. Had to take it all off and lock it away. Emma says it was on her dressing table, ready to put on, the day Robbie died. Maybe that's why she doesn't like it."

"I like the way you say 'died'. All right, but you don't have to look at me like that. Is Emma nice to you? In books, the servants are terrible to nurses."

"She's okay. She isn't like a servant; she sort of runs things. She's been there for years and years. Emma was the one who found her."

"I know." Marge removed her glasses and polished them thoroughly. "Change of subject coming up. Somebody was in here yesterday asking about you."

"Who?"

"I don't know. A woman. She looked sort of familiar, but I couldn't place her. This shop is like a railway station. Strangers drop in maybe once or twice a year, motorists and so on, people from New York buying a book for a weekend present. Maybe she was somebody like that, just a face I'd seen once before. Anyway, she didn't know you, didn't know your name. She wanted to know if I was acquainted with the nurse at Mr Manson's."

"Maybe somebody who used to know them. Didn't like to inquire at the house. You know, tragedy and all that."

"Maybe. They came from New York themselves years ago. But I got the idea it was you she was interested in."

"Me? No. You know everybody I know. Funny. What did she say?"

"Nothing much. She just ambled around, bought a couple of Hallowe'en cards, and acted friendly in a pushing way. You know, the great big smile that goes with spending ten cents. First she asked how Mrs Manson was getting along—lots of people ask me that, because they know I know you or they've seen you in here. Then she wanted to know where you lived."

"For heaven's sake! I'm getting a reputation."

"Think so? Wait. She said, 'Does the young lady live in Larchville, or did they get her from New York?' I said Larchville. And I also said what do you want to know for, but in a nice way, of course. And she said she thought maybe she knew you and was just making sure. She did a lot of smiling and hemming and hawing and said she thought maybe you'd trained at the hospital with her cousin or somebody. She said she was interested in young nurses starting out who'd trained where her cousin had."

"Crazy. No sense to it. Who's her cousin?"

"She very carefully didn't say, even when I asked." Marge lighted a cigarette. "Know what I think? I think she was a snooper, a busy-body, one of those women who try to get the dope on other people's troubles so they can brag to the bridge club. She had a face like bridge-every-afternoon; sharp. Also heavy around the hips, too many of those bridge desserts. So when she said your name had slipped her mind and wasn't it Johnson or something like that, I closed up like a clam."

"Right. Thanks."

Marge was thoughtful. "You know, there could be something behind it, Milly. Something like family trouble, for instance. She might be a relative of the Cory family, still sore about Manson's marrying the money Cory left. Or she might be an old girl friend of Cory's—I mean the first husband."

"Did she look like the kind of girl friend a Cory would have? They say Bruce is the living image of his brother. Was she the kind of woman a man like Bruce Cory would—look at?"

"From what I've seen of him I'd say no, but fast. Her clothes weren't any better than mine. She was all right, you understand, but she didn't have the kind of manner you expect in a woman connected with a Cory or a Manson. But you can't always tell about boys like Cory and Manson."

"What a brain," Milly admired. "Sensational!" She dragged her feet from the shelf. "After eleven. I ought to start back."

"Aw, wait. I've got coffee. It's on the hotplate."

With the coffee they had bakery doughnuts, which tasted

204

better than four-layer chocolate because they came out of a paper bag.

It was ten minutes to twelve when Marge locked the shop door behind them. They walked to the corner before they separated. Marge stood on the kerbstone and watched Milly cross the deserted street and strike out in the direction of the park. The slight, rain-coated figure and the big umbrella were swallowed in mist and fog. The rain had turned into an aimless drizzle.

Marge went home and tried to remember where she'd seen the woman who was interested in young nurses. The woman was beginning to fill her mind. . . . Not a one-shot customer, Marge decided. I'm sure of that. Maybe somebody who just moved to Larchville, one of those people you stand next to at the grocery store. Maybe. Green coat and hat. Drop a brick out any window this year, and you'll hit that same green coat and hat.

Milly let herself in. One light was burning in the hall, the one they always left burning when she was out. It was a signal for her to put the chain on the door. It meant everyone else was in. She fixed the chain, turned out the light, and crept upstairs.

The doors along the upper hall were closed. All except Mrs Manson's at the front. Light came from that doorway, a dim, straight shaft on the dark hall carpet, like a path cut through the shadows. She stopped in the lavatory and brushed her teeth with just water, because she couldn't find her toothpaste. Her hooded coat and umbrella were dripping, so she hung them on the lavatory door.

Emma was asleep in a chair before the dead fire, but she'd done her usual job on the glass door and screen. Milly grinned at the screen, anchored with chair and hassock. One of these nights Emma would use the bureau, too.

She walked to the bed. Mrs Manson was awake, wide awake. Her face was white, and her eyes were glittering. "Hey," Milly said softly, "what's the idea?" She remembered then that the door to the hall was open and went back to close it. We're about to have a little one-sided argument, she told herself, but we needn't let the whole house in on it. "Hey," she said again, "you're bad tonight. What makes you so bad, honey—I mean, Mrs Manson?"

Mrs Manson's eyes met hers.

"Now, wait," Milly said. "One thing at a time. You don't

like something. I can see that. Well, we'll take care of it, we'll toss it right out, whatever it is. But the pulse comes first." She drew the cold hands from under the rug and held one limp wrist.

The eyes clouded; then the glitter returned. They gleamed like the eyes of an animal caught in a trap that was imperfectly sprung. Milly had seen a squirrel once——

The pulse was too rapid. She held the cold hands in hers. "You're frightened," she said. "I know. But it's all over now. Milly's here. Still, I don't know why your hands should be freezing, you've got plenty of blankets and the room's exactly right. Nervous about something? Now, now, you mustn't be." She sat on the edge of the bed and talked softly and persuasively. "I bet I know what happened," she said. "You had a bad dream. And because you're sick and sort of helpless, you couldn't throw it off. Now me, when I have a bad dream, I practically kick myself out of bed and wake up screaming. They're terrible, aren't they? But everybody has them once in a while, pal—I mean, Mrs Manson. I mean, you're not the only one."

No, that wasn't it. According to Mrs Manson's eyes, it wasn't a dream. They said so, as plain as words. They said they had seen something.

Milly felt a prickle along her spine. Got me doing it now, she thought. Not that I haven't been getting ready for it. Bones in boxes. . . . For two cents I wouldn't look over my shoulder, even at Emma.

She rubbed the hands gently. They were like ice, but Mrs Manson's forehead was beaded with perspiration. Get busy, Milly told herself. Get to the bottom of this, but don't let her see that you're worried. She couldn't possibly have seen anything. There's nothing to see. Maybe she heard——

"Listen, honey, I'm going to wake Emma up and send her to bed. And maybe Emma can tell me what—what you want." She went to Emma and touched the old woman's shoulder. Emma was a heavy sleeper. Milly had to shake her awake.

"Well," Emma said. "Is it time for you already? I must have dozed off."

"You must have taken one of Mrs Manson's pills. What happened in here while I was out?"

"Nothing." Emma was indignant. "You don't have to glare at me like that, Miss Sills. Everything was as quiet as you

206

please. We slept like a baby, same as if you'd been here." Emma looked at the bed. "She's all right. Even I can see that."

"You're as blind as a bat," Milly whispered. "She's anything but all right. No, Emma, don't go over there now. I want to talk to you."

Emma struggled to her feet, blustering and protesting. "I'm sure I don't know what you're getting at, Miss Sills! I can see as well as you can, and I say she's all right."

Milly said: "Please keep your voice down, Emma. Who was in this room tonight?"

"Nobody. What do you think I am? I wouldn't let anybody in. Mr Manson and Mr Cory stopped for a minute or two before the masseur came, but you know that as well as I do. And that's all."

Milly observed to herself that the whole town of Larchville could have trooped in and out while Emma was having her doze. Aloud she said: "Did Breitman say anything while he was here? Did he say anything about her condition?"

"Not a word. He never does. He's very close-mouthed. He and I talked the same as we always do, nothing more. Miss Sills, I——" Emma began to break. Milly's stern young face was full of foreboding. "Miss Sills," she wavered, "if anything's gone wrong, while I—Miss Sills what's gone wrong?"

Mrs Manson is frightened, and I want to know why. At first I thought she'd had a nightmare, but now I'm not so sure. I think she may have overheard something. Or she may have been—remembering things again. That's always a bad business when you're alone at night, to say nothing of being sick. . . . Exactly what did Breitman say?"

"Nothing. Nothing about her. He never spoke her name once. We talked about the weather. He said the country was nice after New York, and he liked to come out here. That's all."

"Didn't say anything that she could misunderstand? Mention any names, any names at all?"

"No, Miss Sills. Just the ordinary talk, like we always have. She was frightened then, Miss Sills, I know it. Because after he left, I washed her face and hands and covered her up good, and she was nice and drowsy. I was thinking maybe she wouldn't need her pill tonight and how that was a good sign." Emma's hands were limp against the folds of her black apron, but her voice said she was wringing them mentally. "I'd like to stay here tonight," she beseeched. "I could sleep in a chair. If she's going to have trouble, then this is where I belong."

Milly softened. "No. You get your regular sleep. But I promise to call you if I need anything."

"Mr Manson?"

"I'll call him, too, but not now. The fewer people in here the better. Run along, Emma. Say goodnight to her, but make it snappy and happy."

Emma hesitated. "You know that second bell on the wall over there rings in my room, don't you? My own room, not the kitchen. It rings right over my bed, nice and loud. If you should——"

"I will." She eased Emma to the bed and watched the old hands gather up the younger ones and fold them under the rug.

When Emma looked down at the face on the pillow, she obviously didn't trust her voice. But she covered the staring eyes with one of her hands, gently, as if she were telling a wakeful child it was time to sleep.

Milly closed the door behind Emma and went back to the bed. The room seemed darker with Emma gone, darker and quieter. Even larger. I'm crazy, Milly told herself. A fine state of mind I'm getting into. Missing Emma, thinking of Emma like the Marines, This is what they told us in training. This is what they said would happen sometime, and I thought they were bats. They said there'd come a time in the night, in the wards and in homes, when you were on duty alone and felt as if you were being watched. Not by a patient, by something else. They said it was a natural thing and not to be frightened. That's what they said. But some of the older nurses, the old war horses who'd seen everything, they said it was death watching you. Waiting for you to turn your back. . . . She turned around slowly, looking into every corner of the room and listening. What she saw was luxury and security, what she heard was silence. She bent over the bed. "Never let the patient know you're nervous," they said. That's what they said.

She smiled. "Time for the nightcap," she said, "and maybe I'll join you." She took the bottle of pills and reached for the jug of hot milk. "I'll get the bathroom glass for myself. I can use some of this milk. I'm worn thin; we had too much company today." She smiled steadily. "You probably feel worse than I do—you can't tell people to shut up, and I can."

She knew Mrs Manson was watching her hands as they uncorked the jug and filled the cup. She replaced the jug and shook a single pill into the palm of her hand, talking all the while. "If the sun comes out tomorrow, I'm going to park you on the sleeping porch. Tomorrow's Sunday, you remember that, and old George will be home all day. Maybe he'll hang out his window with his face all tied up like the Robber Kitten. He says he has a toothache. Well, we'll make fun of him and he won't know it. . . . Here you are. Open wide."

Mrs Manson refused. It was more than mutiny; she tightened her lips in a straight, hard line, and her eyes blazed. The muscles in her throat were like cords.

Milly stared, holding the milk in a hand that shook. Her eyes widened with delight. Mrs Manson's throat muscles were the most beautiful things she had ever seen. They were strong, pulsing, and controlled. For the first time.

She exulted. "Well, what do you know about that! You ought to see yourself! You're still a bad girl, and don't think I'm not mad at you, because I am, but I do believe you've turned the corner! You hear that? You're better! You couldn't make those mean, ugly faces a week ago. You couldn't even make them this morning. Well, am I tickled!"

But there was no responsive smile, and that was what she wanted most of all. Response. Anything that would prove cooperation and receptiveness and settle the question of a clouded mind.

"Mrs Manson, smile. Smile just once, and we'll forget about the nightcap."

The agony in the eyes that returned her look was almost more that she could bear. Mrs Manson was trying to smile, but she might as well have tried to run.

Milly said: "Never mind, never mind, baby. Forget it."

She rolled the pill about in the palm of her hand; it was a capsule, and it rolled lightly and evenly. What am I going to do now? I can't force her—not when she looks like that. But I've got to make her understand that I'm on her side, that the things I ask her to do are the right things. I've got to find out why she's terrified. She can't go through the night this way. Neither can I. If I try the milk again, if I try selling myself with the milk——

Aloud, she said: "Mrs Manson, please take the milk. I

won't bother you about the pill. I know you hate it even though it's good for you. But please take the milk. This is my job, Mrs Manson, I need it. Doctor Babcock might send me away if he found out that I couldn't——couldn't persuade you. And I don't want to go away. Please, Mrs Manson, just a little milk for my sake."

Mrs Manson's eyes filled with tears. They gathered slowly and clung to her lashes. Only when there were too many did they begin to fall.

Milly put the milk back on the table and dropped the pill into the bottle. "I want to help you," she said miserably, "but I'm hopeless myself. I can't think of anything to do. Can't you give me a sign of some sort? Can't you look at something in the room that will give me a clue?"

Mrs Manson's eyes blazed with hope. It was a look that even a child could have read.

"There, now," Milly rejoiced. "You see? We're all right, we're fine. We're getting this thing licked, aren't we? Is it something in the room that frightens you, something I don't know about?"

The eyes met hers and held, like a hand reaching out to take another hand. They directed her to the bed table. There was nothing on the table but the milk jug, the cup of cooling milk, and the small glass bottle. And two linen handkerchiefs, neatly folded. The same things that were there every night.

It couldn't be the handkerchiefs. They were her own, marked with her initials, N.M., in a little circle of flowers. There was nothing frightening about a handkerchief. She shook them out. They were clean, empty, fragrant. She touched one of the wet cheeks and studied the table again, following the direction of the eyes, pinning the look to a definite place. The pills?

"Now, you're not afraid of those pills, Mrs Manson. You've had them every single night. They're the same as always; we haven't changed them." She turned the bottle between her fingers. "See? Same druggist and everything. Same old stuff. Four little pills for four more nights. . . . Well, I'll be! I've hit it, haven't I?"

The look had changed; it was eager, urgent, full of horror. It was almost like speech. It warned and pleaded and prayed. Mrs Manson had been in the depths, but she was emerging.

Afraid of the medicine all of a sudden, Milly marvelled. I'll fix that right now. She got her handbag and put the

210

bottle in it, holding the bag so Mrs Manson could see every move. "See?" she said. "Just as good as thrown out. And tomorrow I'll tell Babcock you like it the same as you like poison." Poison. That crack about poison when they were all having drinks in the afternoon; that might have started it. Lying alone, half-asleep, half-awake, listening to the rain, thinking back. When she returned to the bed, she said: "Those pills are okay, silly. I'm just humouring you because I think you're nice. All right now?"

No, Mrs Manson wasn't all right. She still looked at the table; her eyes still talked. Her lips, stiff and dry, struggled with the shape of a word. Mrs Manson was seeing something that only she could see, and she was trying to tell about it. It was hopeless, and she knew it, but she was trying.

Suddenly Milly was engulfed and defeated. This was hysteria, this was something she couldn't fight alone. Manson? Cory? She looked at the bedroom door, at the glass door. George? Beyond the glass door and the porch, across the garden, George was safe in his own house. She went to the screen and walked around it, unconscious of the horrified eyes that followed her. It was cold on the porch, and the wind was wet and mournful. It sighed in the trees and the ivy, and touched her face with damp fingers.

George's room was dark, the whole cottage was dark. She looked to her left, along the length of sleeping porch. The porch ran to the end of the house, wide and shadowed, overhung with trees and vines. Mr Manson's room opened on to it, so did Bruce Cory's. But their rooms were dark, too. There were no lights in any of the rooms that she could see.

Mrs Manson must have been all right when they went to bed, she thought, or they wouldn't have gone. They'd have waited for her or called Babcock. Then she knew what she wanted to do. Call Babcock. It was only a quarter of one. He wouldn't mind, he was used to late calls. And it was later than this the night he came to her house and asked her to take the case. He was crazy about Mrs Manson.

She went back to the room, smiling easily. "I'm going downstairs to get you a drink of water. Ice water. You won't mind if I leave you for such a little while." She didn't wait for an answering look in Mrs Manson's eyes. She wanted to get away, to hear Doctor Babcock's reassuring voice, to hear his booming laugh. He'd tell her that hallucinations were common in cases like Mrs Manson's; he'd say he'd be right over.

She closed the door quietly and went down to the first floor, hugging the stair rail, not turning on lights. She didn't want to wake the others. Not unless it was necessary. At the rear of the hall she fumbled for the kitchen door. There was no sound anywhere. And I used to have ideas about Bruce Cory, she scoffed. I had the repartee all ready. He doesn't even know I'm alive.

When she was safe inside, she closed the door behind her and found the light switch. The kitchen phone looked beautiful in the clear, strong light.

Doctor Babcock's housekeeper answered after a long wait. Milly knew the woman slightly, but she didn't identify herself. "Doctor Babcock, please."

"He's not here."

Her heart sank. "Do you know where he is? It's fairly important."

"No, I don't know. He got a call around ten, and he hasn't come back. You want to leave a message?"

"No. No, thanks. I—— Did he say how long he'd be?"

"He said he didn't know. He said he might be a long time, and I was to lock up. I wouldn't be surprised if it was a confinement."

"Oh, well, I guess—well, if he comes in during the next hour or so——" She thought of Babcock ringing the bell, rousing the house, Emma, Hattie, Mr Manson, Bruce Cory. She saw Emma and Hattie peering from behind doors, Mr Manson and Bruce Cory, bathrobed and tousled, stumbling down the stairs. She began to have doubts. They might think she'd been forward, calling the doctor without consulting them. And suppose, after all that, they went to Mrs Manson's room and found her asleep. Asleep in spite of herself, exhausted by her own imagination. That happened sometimes. They'd think *she* was the crazy one.

"Well?" The woman's voice was impatient. "Are you still there, and if you are, what do you want me to do?"

"Oh, I'm sorry. No, there's nothing, thank you. I'll see Doctor Babcock in the morning." She hung up. She could call again. In another hour, if Mrs Manson was still awake. She filled a glass with water from the refrigerator bottle and went back the way she had come.

She watched the door, waiting for Miss Sills to return. Miss Sills was taking more time than she needed for a glass of water, and that was good. It was good if it meant that Miss

212

Sills had stopped in the kitchen to make cocoa for herself. Sometimes she did that. If she did that tonight, if she drank cocoa that she herself had made, then she wouldn't be thirsty, then she wouldn't drink the milk in the jug. Sometimes she drank what was left out of the milk in the jug. Everybody knew that. Miss Sills told everybody about it and laughed. If she drank the milk tonight——

When the hands had come, she had tried to scream. She screamed silently in her heart and soul while Emma slept by the fire. She watched the dark, shapeless mass that crept from behind the screen and cavorted on the floor, dragging its thick, yellow hands. Hands where feet should be. It was big enough to stand alone, strong enough, but it didn't. It rose and fell like a strong black jelly and made a sound like laughing. Then it went away.

The clock on the mantel ticked on. Minutes passed, uncounted. She watched the screen.

Then the door to her room opened quietly, and she turned her eyes in an agony of hope. *Emma, Emma. Try to hear me, Emma.*

She watched the silent approach over the soft rugs, the deft opening of two capsules, the addition of their contents to the jug of milk. The refilling of the capsules with her talcum powder, the refitting of the halves, the return to the bottle. She was ignored as if she didn't exist. She might not have been there. She was the same as dead then. . . .

"Here you are," Milly said. "Did you think I'd run away?" She held the glass of water to Mrs Manson's lips. "Right out of the icebox. Now, you and I are going to sleep whether we feel like it or not. I'll leave the light on. And I won't go to bed. I'll do my sleeping in a chair, right where I can see you and you can see me. Now, don't look at me like that. It's all right. I've done it lots of times before, and you never knew it."

She moved Emma's chair to the bed; any chair that Emma selected for herself would be comfortable. Mrs Manson watched. The eiderdown from the cot, an extra blanket for her shoulders.

The chair faced the bed; it was nearer the foot than the head. It's back was to the screen.

Before Milly settled down to what she told herself was a sleepless night, she opened both sides of the porch door. George's room was still dark. She sent him a wan smile across the garden and returned to the chair. It wasn't too bad; it was almost as good as a bed.

Then she got up again.

She knew there was another cupful of milk in the jug, and she was thirsty. She filled the empty water glass with the milk and saluted Mrs Manson before she drank.

Miss Sills was nodding. Soon Miss Sills would be asleep. A deep sleep. In the morning Miss Sills would have a headache.

In the morning I will be dead. . . .

How will it happen? It couldn't have been planned for tonight—no one could have known she'd drink the rest of the milk. It was a lucky break. The way had been prepared for a lucky break, and it had come. And it wasn't needed, it wasn't necessary at all. It was simply an extra precaution, a weapon in reserve, devious, typical.

How long will I have to wait now?

Not long. This is too good to miss. It would have been better if there'd been more time for frightening me. It must have been a wrench to give that up. I see the whole thing now, I know the plan. I was to be frightened out of my wits until that grew tiresome and wasn't exciting any more. Then, when the time was right, when I was alone or with Emma only, I was to be killed. How? Perhaps smothered. Smothering will be easy.

Emma left me alone tonight. There was plenty of time then. Emma was asleep tonight, over by the fire out of sight of the screen. There was time then, too. But I had to be frightened first, because that was exciting. That would have gone on night after night until it got to be a bore. Or until a foolproof opportunity came. An opportunity too good to miss. Like tonight.

Were Miss Sills and I being watched? Yes, of course we were. But what difference does that make now?

Soon the hands will come back and move along the edge of the screen. The black shape will rise from the floor and stand up, and one of the hands will uncover the face, and I will see it.

The face is being saved for the end, like a big scene. Like a scene at the end of a melodrama, when the audience is supposed to be surprised. It won't be played for my benefit; the face knows that I know now. It will be played for the excitement the actor gets.

I know even about the hands. I know what they are.

214

Moving along the floor, under the screen, close together as if they belonged to an animal.

That is too vile.

Miss Sills is asleep. Her head is bowed. She sleeps like a little girl.

When they find me in the morning, will they say I turned in my sleep and smothered myself? "She turned in her sleep—the pillow. It's the miracle we've been waiting for, but we didn't know, we didn't think——"

Will the police believe that?

Miss Sills sleeps like a little girl.

Can they do anything to her? Can they accuse her of negligence? Or will someone suggest that she was in love with——

Waiting is dreadful. Why is it taking so long? . . .

At last. . . . Miss Sills. Miss Sills. *Miss Sills!*

PART TWO

IT was Hattie who screamed. The sound ripped through the quiet house, rose and fell, and left in its wake a deeper silence than before. It dragged Emma from the refuge of sleep.

Emma's room was separated from Hattie's by the bath they shared. She knew where the scream came from, but the hush that followed it was endless and shocking. She told herself that everybody was dead. There was no breath in the house; when people are sleeping and breathing in a house, you always know it. She sat up in bed and turned on the light. She wanted to see the clock although she was convinced she had no more need of time.

It was three o'clock. She covered her mouth with a thin, gnarled hand, to keep herself from screaming, too. Then she heard other sounds, doors opening and closing, feet on the floors above and on the stairs. Feet on the kitchen floor, a chair overturned. Voices. Someone knocked on the door to the kitchen. "Emma?" It was Mr Cory.

She managed to say, "Yes, sir?"

"We want you out here."

She opened the door. "Mrs Manson, Miss Nora——"

"We want you in the library," he said.

215

She put on her robe and slippers and pinned up her scant braids, taking her time because the next few minutes would tell her something she didn't want to hear. When she reached the library, Hattie was already there, alive, and wrapped in a blanket. She looked for the others—Mr Cory, Mr Manson, Miss Sills. Mr Cory was standing by the fireplace, Mr Manson was telephoning, Miss Sills was absent.

"Miss Nora?" Emma faltered. "Miss Sills?"

"Miss Sills is all right. Everybody's all right except Mrs Manson."

"Not——"

"We're trying to get Doctor Babcock. Mrs Manson is unconscious, and Miss Sills quite rightly refuses to accept the responsibility. We don't know what—Emma, can you do anything with Hattie? Nothing she says makes sense."

Emma turned on Hattie. Hattie's shrill, wailing voice rose above the telephone conversation, but they heard enough of the latter to know that Doctor Babcock wasn't home.

She hadn't slept well, Hattie said; the ivy had kept her awake. All night long it had been making noises at her window, scratching against the wooden shutters, and she'd listened to it for hours before she'd made up her mind that she couldn't stand it another minute. She'd got out of bed then, not turning on a light, and found the scissors in her workbasket.

"I was going to cut it off," she said. "The ivy. I could see it moving back and forth, a long, black, ugly-looking thing out there in the dark. Like a snake. So I was going to cut it off. And then——" She stopped short when Manson left the phone.

"I got hold of Pleydell," Manson said. "He's younger than I like, but he's the best I could do. Get on with it, Hattie."

"Yes, sir. So I was going to cut it off. I was half out the window and had it in my hands when the arm came down."

Cory looked at Manson. Their faces were white, but they smiled and shrugged. "There's no reason you should listen to this again," Cory said to Manson. "Why don't you wait at the door for Pleydell? He hasn't far to come. Emma and I——"

Manson left gratefully.

Emma said: "I don't want to hear the rest of it. She's crazy. I want to go upstairs. I want to see Miss Nora."

"No," Cory said. "We've got to kill this thing right now.

Your window is only a few feet from Hattie's. You may be able to persuade Hattie that she——"

"Nobody's going to persuade me, now or ever!" Hattie wailed. "And not Emma Vinup either! I tell you I saw an arm, a long arm, six feet long if it was an inch. It could've choked me to death and would've done it, too, only I frightened it away!"

"Away where?" Cory's voice was soft.

"Don't ask me. Away, that's all. I think up."

"Up where?"

"How do I know?" Hattie thought it over. "If it went down, it would've gone to join its body. And I'd've seen a body if there was one, because it would've been standing on the ground right in front of me. There wasn't a body. There was only this arm, hanging down like the ivy, right in front of my face. Six feet long if it was an inch, with a yellow glove on."

"Yellow! Hattie, listen. It was dark, it was——"

"A yellow glove, Mr. Cory. There's some light out there, you get a little light from the street lamp. I saw that glove like I see you. It swung sideways, like it was looking for something to hold onto, and it hit me in the face." Hattie touched her cheek with a fat finger, and her eyes rolled. "Not hard, but I felt it. Like it didn't know I was there."

Cory turned to Emma. "Doesn't that sound like some kid warming up for Hallowe'en?"

"Not," said Emma, "at three in the morning. This is a nice residential district. It was something she ate. Go back to bed, Hattie. I'll come in and see you later." The look she gave Cory said that she was in control and he was less than nothing.

When Hattie had gone, trailing her blanket and sniffling, Emma made sure the door was closed. Then she said: "Mr Brucie, what happened upstairs? What happened to Miss Nora? Was it Hattie screaming like that?"

"It must have been."

"But could she hear it? Her door's always closed at night. I've heard Hattie many times before. She did break her record tonight, but that's a long way off. I don't know, I——"

"The porch door was open," he reminded her. "And Hattie's window is on that side of the house. I think we can assume it was Hattie's work."

"Unconscious." Emma was thoughtful. "I never knew her

217

even to faint. Never. Even when Robbie—you know that as well as I do! She never was the kind to faint and carry on."

"But she's sick now, Emma."

"Are you telling me? And there's something else, too." Emma frowned. "She was upset tonight, what you might call wild-eyed. Miss Sills thought she'd had a nightmare." She told him about Miss Sills' return at midnight. "Miss Sills was sharp with me, too, as if I'd done something. Me! I'd lay down my life, and you know it. Miss Sills said Miss Nora was terrified, that's what she said."

Cory walked to one of the long windows. "Lights on over at Perry's. . . . How terrified? When a woman can't speak, can't move——"

"It was the way she looked. She looked awful." Emma faltered. "It could have been a bad dream—but it wouldn't go away when she woke up. She couldn't shake it off. Miss Sills sent me down to my room. She said she could handle it better alone. I don't know what she did, though."

"That was midnight?"

"Yes. Twelve or a little after. Mr Brucie, what does Miss Sills say?"

"Miss Sills seems to know less than anyone else. She didn't hear Hattie. She didn't know anything was wrong until I woke her up. She wasn't easy to wake, either. And Nora——" He prowled about the room.

Emma fought for patience. "If it's a cigarette you're looking for, then for mercy's sake, sit down and let me get it." She found matches and cigarettes in a table drawer. "Here. You heard Hattie yourself, didn't you?"

"Of course. My door was open and the back stairs—I went to Mrs Manson's room at once."

"I'd have thought you'd have gone to the place where the scream came from."

"You'd have thought nothing of the sort. You'd have done as I did. . . . What are you listening to?"

"Somebody came in the front door without ringing the bell. Can that be the doctor so soon?" She opened the library door. Voices came down the hall. "George Perry, wouldn't you know it, and the new doctor, too. He looks too young. I'm going upstairs. I can be useful." She was gone before he could stop her.

George wore a raincoat over his pyjamas and galoshes on

what he said were bare feet. He breathed as if he had been running. "I saw your lights go on," he said to Cory. "I was looking out my window. If you're going to search the grounds, I can help. That's what I came for."

"Do you know what you're talking about?" Cory asked mildly.

George said: "I think I'd better sit down. I'm winded. Sure I know. If you're trying to keep this thing a secret, you're out of luck. I met Pleydell on the porch, and he told me, but I didn't need that. I got an eyeful myself, and I'm not surprised that Mrs Manson passed out."

Cory studied George closely. "Exactly what do you think you saw?"

George coloured. "I don't know," he admitted. "Listen. I'm far from being the kind of guy who hangs out windows spying on the neighbours, but——"

He told Cory he'd gone to his window to spit out a dental poultice, and he looked ridiculously young when he said it. "I looked across the grounds to this house because—well, there it was and there I was, and I saw something moving. Back and forth, under the porch. I thought it was a dog, a big dog, maybe a collie. But there aren't any big dogs around here. So I kept on looking." He said the dog prowled close to the house, as if it were stalking something, and that was all right, because the place was full of moles and so on. Then it disappeared. By that time he was wide-awake and he went to get a cigarette. When he returned to the window, the dog was on the sleeping porch. "No wonder Mrs Manson fainted, big brute like that, strolling around the porch, walking in her room, place half-dark."

"Do you have a theory about how a dog could climb that porch?"

"The tone of voice is all right with me," George said agreeably. "I didn't see him go up, but I saw him come down. He came down like a monkey. Maybe he was a monkey. I saw him swing over the railing and hang on the vines. Come to think of it, I didn't actually see him hit the ground. By that time I was falling around my own room, looking for my shoes. Maybe he was a monkey or maybe he was the Hound of the Baskervilles. I don't know or care much, except that he ought to be found and shot. He gave me the creeps. . . . How's Miss Sills?"

"There's nothing wrong with Miss Sills."

"I'm glad to hear that." George's voice was faintly chiding, and he looked as if he had more to say, all of it censorable. But when he continued, he was mild enough. "And how come Pleydell instead of Babcock? Not that I don't think Pleydell is good. I do. My mother had him once, and he saw through her like a window. But I thought Babcock had this house staked."

"Babcock's out on a case."

"Pleydell says Hattie woke the dead."

"Yes. Now see here, George, don't talk about this to anyone but me. You'll have us in the papers, and there's been enough of that. To say nothing of demoralizing the neighbourhood. You know our Hattie."

"I sure do. I used to help Hattie to set traps for the nonexistent mice. This time, according to Pleydell, she saw an arm six feet long."

"Pleydell talks too much. So, apparently, does Manson."

"So, and I'm not kidding, will my mother. Wait till she hears this one! I slid a note under her door, telling her where I'd gone. In case you wanted me to stick around for a while and help search. You know, in case we decide to take it seriously."

"Now, George——"

"In case we found something that looked like paw marks. The ground is soaking, so they show. Or something like torn leaves, broken twigs, and so on. Or footprints. It could have been a cat burglar, you know. Man instead of dog; object, Mrs Manson's jewellery."

"All insured."

"But not enough to pay for being frightened out of your wits. I'd feel better if you and I slipped outside and took a look around. We could take a quick look and satisfy ourselves."

Cory was indulgent. "Stop romancing, George. I'm satisfied now."

"I'm not," George complained. "Some of the porch ivy is hanging loose, and it wasn't like that this afternoon. I saw it just now by Hattie's window."

"It's too dark to see anything like that, and you know it."

George put his hand in his pocket. "Not with this," he said. He played his flashlight around the room. "I used it when I came across the garden. I saw what I saw, all right."

"Put it away, George, and grow up."

"That's what my mother always says," George agreed. "Grow up. Oh, well."

They sat on without talking. The doorbell rang once, and Cory answered it. When he came back, he said it was Babcock. Babcock had finally returned to his house and found the message Manson had left.

George ambled about the room. He showed a mild interest when Pleydell, young, red in the face, and clearly unrecovered from a snub, came to the door and asked to be taken to Hattie. Cory led him away. After that, George's wanderings took him to the garden windows. He whistled softly. His father and mother, armed with flashlights, were picking their way across the wet grass, turning into the path that led to the front door. His father was only half-dressed, but his mother was gloved, hatted, and veiled. He went back to his chair and waited for the bell to ring.

Milly said she didn't need anything. Mr Manson said: "Yes, you do. Come downstairs for a drink when you're through in here." Then he left to answer the doorbell.

Milly stood by the bed with Emma and Doctor Babcock, touching the smooth covers to reassure herself, talking softly, although there was no need for that now. Mrs Manson was mercifully asleep.

Babcock listened, one plump hand embracing his chin. When she finished her story, he said: "Absurd. And dreadful."

"I didn't hear a thing," Milly said. "It wouldn't have frightened me if I had. I've heard Hattie give out before— she does it when she thinks she sees a bug. But poor Mrs Manson——"

"There, there," Babcock said. "It's all over now."

Milly looked at Mrs Manson's closed eyes. Pleydell had been wonderful. He brought her out of the faint, or whatever it was, and talked as if he gave her credit for being adult and sensible. He described what he called Hattie's nightmare as if he'd dreamed it himself, and he made Emma laugh with him. Mrs Manson listened, her eyes never leaving his young face. Then he gave her a sedative, but not from the bottle on the table. His hand went toward the bottle, but her look stopped it in mid-air. So he took a bottle from his very new bag and held it for her to see. Even then she refused; she looked at Emma as if she were talking to her. And Emma said: "I'll sleep here, I'll sleep in the same bed. And it won't

221

be the first time, either." After that it was all right; now Mrs Manson was asleep, and Emma was sitting on the bed and yawning and all but telling them to get out.

Babcock touched Milly's arm. "Come, Miss Sills, there's nothing more for you to do here. You heard what Mr Manson said. A small refresher—you've earned it, and I need it. A long, trying day, a miserable night." He led her from the room and guided her along the hall as if she were ill.

She was relieved, she'd been afraid he'd blame her for sleeping. He was being fair and understanding. Two wonderful men, Pleydell and Babcock. She was lucky.

All the doors along the hall except two were open; there were lights in the rooms. On the right, the rose guest-room adjoining Mrs Manson's bath—the room Mr Manson used now. Rose blankets thrown back, rose sheets dragging on the floor, the porch door open and the curtains not drawn. Mr Manson had left that room in a hurry. A funny-looking room for Mr Manson to be sleeping in.

Robbie's room on the left. That one was locked. It was always locked. It would be dark and dusty if you could see inside. Were the sheets still on Robbie's bed? Plain white sheets, wrinkled where his body had lain; soft white pillows showing the print of his head? No. No, that bed would be smooth, because he hadn't slept in it.

Beyond Robbie's, the room Bruce Cory used. A brown room, an English-looking room, like those you saw in English movies. Plain dark furniture, heavy and handsome; brushes and jars on the big chest, tortoise, ebony, and crystal. Expensive. Mr Bruce Cory got out of bed like a Boy Scout, no matter who screamed. No matter what. Sheets folded back, dark brown blankets neat and tidy. The lavatory next door. Then the stairs that went down to the kitchen.

Across the hall from Bruce Cory's, Mr Manson's suite that he wasn't using. But someone had been in there. Lights in the bath and in the dressing-room. Drawers pulled out of the dressing-room chest. As if somebody wanted something in a hurry. Handkerchiefs on the floor, a dark-blue scarf trailing from an open drawer. Everything dark blue and cream. . . . Wanted what in a hurry? A revolver in the handkerchief drawer? That could be. A scream in the night. . . .

The second closed door was next to Mr Manson's suite. The attic door. Doctor Babcock's hand pressed her arm. "My arm must be shaking," she decided. "My knees are. And my head aches." She smiled at Doctor Babcock, to let him know she was grateful. The wide stairs to the first floor were straight ahead.

"Take things easy tomorrow," Babcock said. "Don't worry about your patient, she's in good shape. Take long walks, think of pleasant things. We can't have *you* cracking up!" They went down.

She had seen George's father before, putting in his flower beds, a greying, gangling replica of George. His old tweed topcoat, worn over pyjamas, was wet and wrinkled. He looked cold and unhappy as he huddled by the fire. Alice Perry was a familiar figure, too, and also from a distance. Alice Perry was complete, from pearls to corset. No one introduced them.

Milly went to a chair by a window, out of the circle of light. Cory brought her a drink. When she had time to look around, she saw Pleydell in the far corner, making himself small in a huge chair, looking like a choirboy waiting for words from a bishop.

It was after four o'clock; it could have been four in the afternoon except for the dark windows, the lamps, and the assorted clothing. George looked like a perfect fool. She'd tell him so when she got the chance. And he was grinning. There was nothing to grin about.

Alice Perry was laughing, a brisk, efficient, party laugh. "Ordinarily I sleep like a baby," she declared, "but tonight I was restless. Of course, I heard George prowling, but I thought it was his poor tooth. Then I heard my big George, also prowling. Such men! That was when I got up and found little George's amazing note. Of course we came at once— the neighbourly thing to do. Dear Mrs Manson. I'd cut Hattie's wages if she were mine."

Everyone laughed.

"The villain was the wind," Cory said. "George says the ivy's down. Of course that's what she saw."

"Oh, naturally, the wind," Alice Perry agreed. "Our poor chrysanthemums, absolutely beaten to the ground. I showed you, dear, as we came over. George dear, *big* Georgie, didn't I show you?"

Mr Perry nodded.

"The wind was pretty stiff," Manson said. "Frightful racket in those old trees, almost human. So human that for a minute I thought Hattie was a particularly big blow."

Everyone laughed again. Hattie is a very comic character, Milly thought. All you have to do is mention Hattie's name, and everybody howls.

Babcock took it up. "The wind was bad in town, too. I didn't like it at all."

"The wind, the wind," George chanted. They all looked at him. He was playing with his flashlight, turning it on and off.

"Put that thing away," Alice Perry said. "It looks silly, and your hands aren't clean."

"The wind, the wind," George said again. "I am forcibly reminded of a little blue-and-gold copy of *A Child's Garden of Verses*. Robbie and I each had one; we learned some of the stuff by heart; we were very, very cute. I quote. Title: *The Wind*. Line: 'And all around I heard you pass—like ladies' skirts across the grass.' Did it sound like that to any of you, or am I just being sentimental?"

They laughed at George almost as much as they laughed at Hattie. Even little Pleydell made a co-operative sound, but he kept it up too long.

Milly looked at him with sudden anger, and he coloured. Why do I always get interested in fools? she asked herself. Why am I down here, anyway? Why doesn't George introduce me to his parents? Why do I stay, like a dope? Because I am a dope. She got up. "Excuse me, everyone," she said. "I belong upstairs."

They began to talk again before she left the room. She heard Babcock say something about the masseur. His report had been a good one. Babcock had called him in town. They were going to try the treatment every night. Mrs Manson was responding. George said something about Hattie and the masseur.

Milly closed the door on a fresh burst of laughter. George had started them off again. He had an IQ of six.

She was half way up the stairs when George came after her. He didn't say anything, but he put his arms around her and held her close. It was better than putting a ring on her finger. It was the first time he'd ever done that. His IQ rose to the height of heaven; exactly heaven.

"Be over in the morning," he whispered.

That light is the sun. The Sunday-morning sun. That is Emma over there. Emma, coming out of the bathroom with the vacuum jug, the cup, the glass. All clean, dry, sparkling; everything washed away. No traces left. Nothing.

Watch Emma through your lashes. The old trick.

Emma is rubbing the damp places on the carpet, blotting out the prints of four hands. She is brushing dried leaves from the floor and talking about the wind. Soon nothing will be left of the night. She is destroying me.

There is a crack in the bowl of the lamp. Will she see that? A new crack in my fine lamp. She won't like it, she'll be angry, she'll talk about it. Emma or Miss Sills, either will do. Emma or Miss Sills, bending over the bed, saying: "What a shame. Something happened to her lamp, and she liked it so much. Does anybody know what happened to her lamp?"

My lamp was knocked to the floor by two thick yellow hands in a hurry. After that there was not enough light. Not enough to see in, not enough safely to kill in. No sound, except the thud of the lamp and the breathing of two people. Not my breathing. I held my breath in the dark, and it was the same as hiding. Two people breathing, Miss Sills in the chair and the other at the head of the bed. Slow, drugged breathing for Miss Sills; rapid, frightened breathing for the other.

She waited for Miss Sills to wake. Miss Sills hadn't heard the lamp go over, but she'd heard something. Or felt something. She'd stirred in her sleep and moaned. Poor Miss Sills. No, rich Miss Sills. Rich, powerful Miss Sills, who had given her the gift of another day.

The four hands had scrabbled over the floor to the screen and safety. Frightened off, but playing the part to the end. If Miss Sills had waked, she'd have seen a shapeless mass on all fours. She would have screamed as Hattie screamed. Then: "My dear Miss Sills, you are not yourself. It's been too much for you. A few weeks' rest——" Then there would be no more Miss Sills. Then there would be no more.

Will the lamp be taken away before someone sees the crack, someone who is all right? And if so, what excuse will be given? . . . Never mind that, you know the lamp will go. Forget the lamp, try to remember the rest of it. There may be something, some small thing.

Hattie. How much later was that? One minute, two minutes? Who thinks of time in that kind of dark? The new doctor that Ralph called in was too young, too inexperienced, but kind and instinctively wise. He'd known at once that it was useless to offer the pills from her own bottle, but he didn't try to find out why. His bottle was a new one, and he'd let

her see him open it. A safe, new bottle, and with Emma in
the room all night as well as Miss Sills. . . . That's enough,
that's enough, go back to Hattie. Maybe Hattie——

The new doctor said Hattie screamed because she had a
nightmare. But Miss Sills said Hattie had been frightened by
the ivy outside her window. They believed what they said; it
was what they'd been told. But Hattie knew every leaf on that
vine, every loop and tendril. What Hattie had seen was a
black shape with four hands, but she would be talked out of
it. If only Hattie would talk first, talk everywhere, to everybody. Even to tradesmen. Tradesmen gossip and pass things
along. Had there been light enough for Hattie to see the
hands? If Hattie talked about the hands, and it reached the
right person—Who is the right person this time? Who knows
about the hands?

Who knows? You do. You saw him making them. It was
a secret, a joke. He told you he was making them for a present. He said, "Who's always asking for two pair of hands?"
He laughed when he said it.

Think, think. There was someone else who knew, someone
who came into the room and saw. Who? Who came in? . . .
Now, now, you're doing it the wrong way again. You're letting your mind wander, you're seeing his face. That's bad for
you. You're hearing his voice again. Stop for a minute and
think of something else. Call yourself nice names Miss Sills
calls you. It isn't a foolish thing to do. Go on. Call yourself a
good girl, a honey, a baby. . . . I'm a good girl, a honey, a
baby.

Now go back to last night. Maybe you've overlooked
something, something that will talk for you, point a finger
for you. Soon. *Soon.*

The lamp that rolled on the floor. The darkness. The waiting. The scream. Then nothing. Nothing, nothing, nothing.
Give up.

"You're awake," Emma said. "That's fine. And Miss Sills
has brought your breakfast. You slept like an angel, and that's
because you knew I was beside you."

Emma fed her, using a spoon and the glass tube, chirping
and fluttering, full of importance. "Telephone ringing like
mad—everybody heard about your fright and wants to say
they were sorry. Only ten o'clock and people come to call
already. Doctor Babcock, the Perrys, and that nice little new
doctor. But he went away again. Mrs Perry brought a lovely

226

jelly for your lunch and a bottle of sherry. Now eat this egg, and I'll let them all come in to see you."

Miss Sills arranged her chair. "Too cold for the porch," Miss Sills said. "I think we'll sit in the window. All cosy in the sunny window, and you can doze like a little cat. You need more sleep, you know. . . . Look, Emma, she wants that old rug. All right, you can have it when we get you settled. You're spoiled, that's what you are. Next week I'm going to use discipline."

Emma put the breakfast tray in the hall, and they wheeled her to the window. She heard the others coming, walking softly as befitted people who knew she had weathered a bad night.

"Let me see your feet, the lot of you," Emma said. "I saw you out in the garden, and I'll have no more things tracked in on my clean floor."

"Things?" George Perry.

"Leaves and grit all over. Tramping in and out of here last night, and I had to clean it upon my knees."

They surrounded her chair, smiling, paying their compliments. She was brave, she'd behaved like a soldier. She was a fine woman, getting better every day, no doubt about it. She was good-morning Mrs Manson; she was dear Mrs Manson, who frightened them so. She was okay, Mrs Manson, okay. . . . She closed her eyes, because she didn't want to see their faces. The voices told her where they stood and sat.

Miss Sills, on the window seat, spoke to someone. "No, don't take the rug away. I know it's hot, but she wants it."

"Is she asleep, Miss Sills?"

"Only relaxed. It's a good sign. She's always like this when you come in. Don't stop talking, go right ahead. She likes to hear voices around her, doesn't she, Doctor Babcock?"

"Oh, quite, quite. And what, may I ask, is the immediate future of the good neighbour's sherry?"

Ralph, doubtful, hesitating. "Well, I suppose we might——"

"It's eleven o'clock," Doctor Babcock said. "We had a hard night."

"You men! That's a *special bottle* for Mrs Manson!"

"Emma, do you think——"

Emma, full of pleased complaints at the social turn of affairs, brought the house sherry from the dining room. The voices murmured on. Emma rattled glasses, rustled back and forth, and finally subsided. "I'm thankful to sit down. My legs ache. I'm an old woman, but nobody thinks of that. A person needs two pairs of hands around here."

Listen! Listen! All of you listen! Emma's quoting someone, Emma's teasing—can't you hear? Watch Emma's eyes, watch where Emma's looking. Say it again, Emma. Emma, say it again!

"Thank you," Emma said. "I don't care if I do. I'll get as giddy as all get out, but I like a nip now and then."

"You may have anything your heart desires, Emma. The house is yours."

"I'm glad to know that," Emma said, "because I want something this minute."

Then it came.

Emma said, "I want your permission to get rid of that lamp by the bed."

"What's wrong with it?"

"It's awkward, that's what. The shade's too big. It gets in the way."

Emma. Look at the lamp. Look at it.

Is Emma—no, wait, don't open your eyes. They're moving about; someone has come to stand behind your chair. Careful. Someone is waiting to see if you—— *Take your hand away from my neck. Can't you wait for the dark?*

"Hey!" Miss Sills was beside her. "Hey, what goes on here? What have you got to shiver about? You're as warm as toast. Easy, honey, easy. All right now?"

"Lamp," George said. "That reminds me. Say, is it all right to talk about last night?"

"Why not?" Doctor Babcock. "Last night is already forgotten. Lamp, did you say?"

"Yeah. At what I figure was a crucial moment, somebody turned it out."

"What are you talking about?"

"The lamp Emma doesn't like. I was hanging out my window, and suddenly this room went dark. For about two or three minutes. The little one by the screen was already out. But the big one by the bed went out, stayed out, and came on again."

"You're crazy," Miss Sills said. "It was on when I went to sleep, and it was on when Mr Cory woke me up. Wasn't it, Mr Cory—or am I the crazy one?"

"Nobody's crazy, and George is right. The lamp was on the

228

floor when I came in. I fell over it." His voice was rueful. "But I got it back on the table, and it worked, thank God. That was a bad minute."

"Floor?" George was puzzled.

"Floor?" Miss Sills repeated. "Well, I didn't hear it fall. I didn't hear a thing. I ought to be fired. All I know is that Mr Cory nearly shook my teeth out trying to wake me up and Mr Manson was running around in circles. Excuse me, Mr Manson."

"My dear Miss Sills, that's libellous. I ran in a very straight line, in the wrong direction. Straight down the back stairs, because I'd recognized Hattie's clarion call. Then, halfway down, I heard Cory begging you to show signs of life at the top of his lungs."

Doctor Babcock was torn between grief and laughter, sighs and chuckles. "Dreadful, dreadful, but not without an amusing side."

"I didn't hear a thing," Miss Sills repeated. "I ought to be fired, but please don't."

"You ought to have more sherry." Bruce, walking to Miss Sills. "Here, all's well that ends well. And speaking of Hattie, have any of you good people ever heard a moose?"

They seized Hattie's name, hugged it and tossed it about. Hattie was a moose. She looked like a moose. The left profile? No, silly, the right! And isn't there a wart, too? On the nose? Stop, stop, I haven't laughed so much in years. Dear Mrs Manson would love this, we must tell when she's better. Hattie is a moose with a wart. Hattie——

Emma called from across the room. She sounded happy. "Look! Look here! This lamp's got a crack in it. It's not fit to use; it's not safe. This lamp's going to the White Elephant Sale at All Saints'." The cord and plug struck the carpet softly.

"Emma, how perfectly wonderful!" Mrs Perry said. "Mr Manson, do let us have it. I'm chairman this year, and it's simply dreadful the way people won't give us things."

"I don't know, but I don't see why not."

"I can't tell you how grateful—— George dear, will you carry—— George, stop whistling. Not nice, when poor Mrs Manson—— George!"

George said: "All right. But how do you suppose a heavy lamp like that managed to fall over? Could that be the wind again?"

"Wind? Oh, undoubtedly. She couldn't do it herself, poor lamb."

"Blowing leaves and little sticks, not to mention grit and mud. My nice clean floor. We'll have to keep that porch door shut," Emma said.

"By all means keep it shut," George said.

"George, what are you mumbling about?" Alice Perry asked.

"I'm quoting poetry to myself. My little blue-and-gold book."

"Well, stop it. No one's interested."

"I am. Listen. Still the pretty one about the wind that rips the ivy off the porch and blows a fifteen-pound lamp around. 'I saw the different things you did, but always you yourself you hid.' . . . I think we ought to go home."

Chairs moved at once, quickly; glasses were set down on tables and mantel; voices mingled; sentences overlapped. Mr Perry, you haven't said a word. George darling, no more sherry. The lamp, Mrs Perry, don't run off without your white elephant! Lovely, lovely, and all for foreign missions, it means so much. George, I said no more sherry, it gives your eyes a funny look. Thank you for calling, thank you. Yes, we're on our way, Miss Sills. Don't look so pleased, we're all going. These little sherry parties are good for all of us. George? George, I'm not going to speak to you again.

Gone. Everything gone.

Emma collecting the glasses. Emma washes everything, the fingermarks, the muddy prints. Emma gave the lamp away. Nothing left, nothing, and the prints on the floor were clear, even I could see what they were. . . . Emma saw the cracks in the lamp, and they said it was the wind.

All but George! There was something in his voice, wasn't there, wasn't there? He knows there was no wind, not enough for that, doesn't he? George, remember the wind; you made a joke of it, but you know it isn't a joke, don't you? Keep remembering the wind, remember the little book with the poems in it. I gave you that book, George. I gave one to you and one to Robbie. Robbie and George, George and Robbie. They were always together. . . . George!

George is the one who knows about the hands, George saw them when I did, George is the one I was trying to think of! George is the right person, the safe person!

Emma knows the phrase about the hands, but that's all.

230

Stop, go slowly, make a list like a shopping list. What do you need?

You need Hattie to have seen the hands; you need Hattie to talk. You need George to hear. You need Emma to use the phrase again. You need George to hear. You need—you need George to remember. . . . But if Hattie——

That hand on my neck. I thought my heart would stop then. Listen. Emma.

"You can carry these glasses down to the kichen on your way out," Emma said to Miss Sills, "but don't you go waking her up to say goodbye. I'll sit right beside her all the time. She won't lack for anything if she wakes, and if she looks hungry, I'll see to her lunch. No need for you to hurry yourself. The doctor says you're to take it easy. And don't stop in the kitchen gossiping with Hattie. If you want the truth, that woman hasn't got all her buttons. That's a pretty coat. I always favoured red. Get along now."

"Yes, Matron," Miss Sills said. . . .

Miss Sills is going for a walk, wearing her red coat. Watch for Miss Sills. Open your eyes and watch for Miss Sills. No matter which way she goes, you can see the red coat. Look at the children in their Sunday clothes. Dark blue and brown for the big ones, pale blue and pink for the little ones. Nurses, parents. Young parents, full of pride. Who is that woman in the green coat and hat?

Emma, don't talk. Emma, be quiet. Emma, that woman in the green coat and hat!

"So you've decided to wake up and take notice, have you? I'll set my chair right here beside you. I know you—you were playing possum for the others, but the minute you knew you were alone with old Emma, you decided to wake up. That Miss Sills, there she goes, over to see her mother, I expect. Well, bless my soul, look at that rug! What happened to that, I want to know! I tucked it in myself, as tight as tight. You can't have—bless my soul, you're all tied up with fringe. A person'd almost think—but no, you can't do that. . . . There, that's better. That won't hurt my girl again. Such an ugly, big red mark. . . . Miss Nora, you aren't even listening to me. What are you looking at? What's out there? Some old thing that's there every day, unless it's Miss Sills. Of course, if you can't even listen to your old Emma. . . . Well, I hope you're satisfied. There she is traipsing along like she didn't work for a living same as the rest of us!"

It is! It is! Miss Byrd. The nurse I had before Miss Sills. She wore that green coat when she went away! She came back! She came back, she had to come back. She knew something was wrong, she couldn't hide it, I could see her trying to hide it. She knew, or saw, or guessed; she watched everybody; she was uneasy. She showed it in the way she watched and listened. So she was sent away. . . . The patient is unhappy, Miss Byrd; we'll have to make a change. You understand that this is no reflection on your work. There's no criticism of you, Miss Byrd, none at all, but the patient isn't happy, and we can't have that. Mr Manson thinks perhaps an extra cheque—we're very grateful. . . . She hadn't looked surprised; she'd almost smiled. She'd looked as if she'd expected it.

Miss Byrd. Everybody laughed at the Byrd because she looked like a hawk.

Miss Byrd, Miss Byrd, I'm up here in my window. Listen. That girl in the bright-red coat is my new nurse. Stop her, Miss Byrd, say something, anything. Make friends with her. Her name is Sills, Milly Sills. She's a nice child, she'll be courteous and kind. Talk to her—you'll know how to do it. Tell her what you know. What do you know, Miss Byrd? What did you see or hear? She's almost there, Miss Byrd, the girl in the bright-red coat and no hat. She's there, see, she's there! In front of you, in front! Say good-morning, say it's a lovely day, ask her the name of the park, ask anything. Stop her, Miss Byrd. *Miss Byrd!*

Now, now, close your eyes again. Don't cry. . . . You're a good girl, you're a honey, you're a baby. You're my good, good girl.

The lamp is gone; the tracks on the floor are gone. Miss Byrd—forget Miss Byrd. You have another day, this day. How much of this day do you have? Six hours? Six hours until dark. Spend them to the last minute, not on hope, not on fear. Spend them in preparation for tonight. Tonight you will be going——

This is the time to climb the attic stairs again. Climb the attic stairs the way you did before, and raise your head when you get to the top. The way you did before. That is a preparation of a kind. . . . Climb.

Alice Perry circled her living room with the lamp in her hands, measuring the table tops with speculative eyes. "Nobody but Nora Manson would have cupids and a ruffled shade. At her age! For a young girl's room, yes; rather sweet for a young girl, but Nora Manson! Cupids!'"

"That thing's Dresden," George said mildly. "Bruce Cory gave it to her last Christmas, and she bawled him out. It cost like the devil." He went to a window and looked across the hedge. "Emma's too openhanded with other people's property when other people can't talk. . . . Did you happen to see Cory's face while that was going on?"

She said: "I wasn't watching him then. George, this crack won't show when the lamp is properly placed. It might look rather fine against the right kind of wall. A soft, grey wall. You know, if I thought people wouldn't—— George, don't you think it will be perfectly fair if I——"

"Sure," George said. "Give the White Elephant Sale a buck and tell the All Saints' ladies you took a piece of junk off their hands."

Alice sat down with the lamp in her lap and gave her son a bright smile. "Where's your father, dear?"

"Upstairs, lying down until lunch. I think I'll do the same."

Alice smiled again. "What's wrong with you, dear? Toothache, too much sherry, plain meanness, or are you in love with Nora Manson, too?"

"God help me," George said, "and I'm not swearing." He took the chair opposite his mother. "Say some more. Don't stop."

"Well, Bruce Cory's in love with her. I've always thought so, and I made up my mind to watch him this morning. Ralph Manson must be blind. Love, hate, sometimes you can't tell, but the way Bruce Cory looked at her! If Ralph Manson would come off his high horse and pay a little attention to his wife and her brother-in-law, he might see what I did."

"What did you see?"

"Well—oh, nothing. I simply mean—oh, you wouldn't understand."

"I might."

"No. You've always made a heroine of Nora Manson. I've often thought you cared more for her than you did for me. But I never interfered. I've always wanted you to have the best."

"This," George said, "gets crazier and crazier. I haven't been in that house a dozen times in the past year. At least, not until Robbie——"

"Now what have I said that's wrong?" Alice sighed. "Such a long face. Don't you like to talk to your own mother?"

"Robbie, I was thinking about Robbie. Sure I like to talk to you, but when Robbie's name popped up——"

"Morbid, dear."

"No. I have a conscience about Robbie. I didn't know he——? Listen, there's something I've always wanted to ask you. Did you see Robbie that last day?"

"I? Certainly not."

"But you went there to call that afternoon for the first time in months. You got as far as the front door, and they stopped you. I've always wondered how you happened to choose that particular day and hour."

"I have an idiot child," Alice mourned. "I did *not* choose that particular day and hour, and I was *not* stopped: I simply had a feeling that I wanted to see Nora Manson, so I went over. But when I was told it was inconvenient, naturally I went away."

"Not far, though."

"Not——"

"I was coming down the street from the station when you left their porch. You walked around to the side of the house and looked up at the attic window."

Alice flicked the ruffled shade with a careless finger. "Very well then, so I did. And the explanation is childish, so you ought to understand it. When they opened the door, I heard Nora Manson crying, and it worried me. Although we'd grown away from each other, I never once let myself forget that we both were mothers of sons."

"You didn't have a hunch about what was going on? You didn't see anything? That little trek to the attic window was unadulterated mother-for-mother instinct?"

"George dear, I don't expect you to understand my feelings. Wait until you have a child of your own. I hardly knew what I was doing. I didn't even remember now."

"I can help you out there. You looked up at the attic window and then you got down on your knees and hunted in the grass. I was practically enchanted. Four-leaf clovers?"

She said, "Why haven't you mentioned this before?"

"It never came up before. That day, Robbie's day, is shrouded in a black cloud that seems to cover everybody. The way people act, you'd think the world stopped then and everybody stood still."

234

"All right, but don't look like that." Her eyes shifted from George to the garden window. "I did see him. Robbie. I was sitting in that window, and I saw him run up the path to the house. 'He's home early,' I thought. 'What a pity Nora isn't there.' I'd seen her drive off in the morning, all dressed up for town. Then after a while I went to my room to change for my little walk, and quite by accident I noticed that their attic window was open. Robbie, I thought, working at his writing when he ought to be out in the sun. And then the most extraordinary thing happened. I saw something fly out the attic window and fall in the grass. Something shiny. I was really agog. But I didn't do anything about it. I took my little walk, and then I felt like seeing Nora Manson. And I call this a silly conversation!"

"It was the key."

"What?"

"The key to the attic. Robbie locked himself in and tossed it out."

She didn't speak at once. Then: "You didn't see me pick it up."

"No. I saw you get up and go home. You're right about this conversation. Why are we having it? It's ancient history, dead and buried. Like Robbie. Who started it anyway?"

She said, "You started it."

"Maybe I did. Well, nobody ever found that key. Manson had a new lock put on."

"I saw it this morning. . . . Here we sit as if I didn't have a thing to do. I ought to be getting lunch, and I don't feel like it. Look at my hands—disgusting! Dishwater! I don't know why other women can afford maids and I can't. There's no better manager in Larchville than I am, yet I never have a cent left over. Money! It makes me sick."

"Maybe you think too much about money."

"Well, if I do, it's because I'm the only one around here who thinks at all. Look at you and your father. Look at Ralph Manson. Look at this house and look at theirs. I knew Ralph Manson when he was nothing but a clerk in that bank, and now he practically owns it. All a man needs in this world is a little ambition to get ahead, a little common sense about the future, like——"

"Like what?"

"Like not falling in love with a penniless nobody, and you know what I mean. . . . If she dies, he'll be rich."

"No," he said easily, "if she dies, Cory will be richer. It's Cory money. And with Robbie gone, too——"

She fretted. "I really must do something about lunch. George, how rich is Bruce Cory?"

"Rolling."

"More than Ralph Manson?"

"Manson has a damn' big salary, and he's in with the money-making crowd. It all helps."

"That's what I thought. . . . George, what's out there, what are you looking at?"

He was at the garden window. "That's Milly's red coat. She's going for a walk. She doesn't usually go at this hour."

"You heard them pampering her, didn't you? Rest, drink this, eat that, take care of yourself, you're precious. Manson, Cory, and Babcock. Men!"

"What do you think of Milly, Mother?"

"I'll do my thinking about that when the time comes. George, are you sure you really——"

"I'm sure."

Milly picked up the gold-and-scarlet ball that rolled between her feet and tossed it gently to the fat blue reefer with brass buttons. It came back at once, this time to her stomach. She returned it again. "You're an apple dumpling," she said, "but that'll be all today."

She had reached the far end of the park; there were no more benches, but across the street, where the buses stopped, the Larchville Women's Civic League had built a circular seat around the trunk of a spreading maple. Home was a few minutes away, with possible roast chicken and certain chocolate cake. And talk. But she wasn't hungry, and she didn't want talk. Not the kind she'd have to give, and take.

I won't be able to hide a thing, she told herself. I never can. Her mother would worry and say it wasn't safe. She'd try to make her leave the case. I won't go home, she decided.

Hattie was bats, pure bats. Washing the sherry glasses and rolling her eyes toward her bedroom. "You can go in and see for yourself, Miss Sills. The ivy's still hanging there, a fresh break in the vine. A long, thin piece like a snake, not like an arm. The arm was an arm, not ivy."

She'd listened to Hattie with amazement and disbelief. She said, "What's all this about an arm?"

Hattie had described, explained, and relived the night. The arm had a hand on the end of it, a six-foot arm and a yellow-

236

looking hand. Or light-looking. A big hand, all spread out. A starfish-looking hand, like in the aquarium. "It came down and swung in front of my face, and then it went up."

"Up?"

"Up where it came from. I don't know where that was, but that's where it went. I wasn't asleep, Miss Sills, I wasn't dreaming. And what's more, I heard feet over my head. But nobody listens to me, not even the doctors. 'Don't let Mrs Manson hear you talking like that, or we'll have to give you a bad-tasting tonic.' If I hadn't waked up when I did, we'd've been robbed."

"By a starfish hand, yellow-looking?"

"I hope you never have to laugh out of the other side of your mouth," Hattie had said.

Now Milly walked to the seat under the tree and sat down. When she thought of what her mother could do with Hattie's hand, she quailed. No, she couldn't face that. She'd rest a while and then go back. Nobody knew what Emma would do next. She might let the Perrys in again. That had been too much. Mrs Manson had looked dreadful. . . . Mrs Perry, saying, "So you're Miss Sills?" And turning away. Mr Perry, patting her shoulder and saying nothing. George——

A voice beside her said, "You have a good heart."

A woman in a green coat and hat was smiling at her. "I hope you don't mind if I sit here, too. I was watching you in the park. You're nice with children—that's what I meant by a good heart."

Milly flushed. "Thank you."

The woman was familiar in an indeterminate way. Sharp, thin face, thickly powdered, and a spotted veil. The rouge and powder were like a mask.

"You're Mrs Manson's nurse, aren't you?"

"Yes, I am." She looked at the woman again. Nervous hands, roving eyes. Hypochondriac, following nurses around? She'd change her clothes the next time she came out. The uniform showed under the coat, the white shoes.

"I saw you leave the house. I was sitting in the park. . . . I used to know Mrs Manson slightly. How is she?"

Hypochondriac with curiosity bump. "She's much better, thank you," Milly said. "Now run along," she added silently. "You make me feel as if I were under a microscope."

"I'm glad of that," the woman said quietly. "I heard somewhere that she'd had a bad relapse. I'm glad it isn't true."

"Oh, no. She's much, much better."

"I know them all," the woman went on. "Not intimately, but I know them. The Mansons, Bruce Cory, and those people next door, the Perry's. And Doctor Babcock."

Milly shifted uneasily. There was too much emotion under the quiet voice. Is she trying to tell me something? she wondered. Or does she want me to tell her? Suddenly she remembered the anonymous customer in her friend Marge's book store, the woman who'd tried to buy information about Milly with a ten-cent greeting card. Finish this as soon as you decently can, she told herself, and move on.

"I'm sorry I don't know your name." The woman's smile was stiff and strained. "It seems rude to be talking to you without knowing. But mine is Byrd. B-y-r-d. I live in New York, but I often come out here because it's so pretty." As she talked, she watched Milly's face. "Byrd," she repeated. "Miss Byrd."

Milly smiled and said nothing.

"Is Emma well? I know Emma, too."

"Emma's fine."

A bus lumbered to the stop, and Milly looked at her watch. "Glendale bus, that means it's—golly, I've got to run." She got up.

Miss Byrd took her arm. "I'd appreciate it if you'd—what I want to say is—Miss—Miss—if you'd give me just a minute of your time!"

"I'm awfully sorry, Miss Byrd, but I'm due at my mother's. See you again sometime." She ducked into the crowd that surged toward the bus, crossed the street, and walked rapidly in the wrong direction for home. Miss Byrd looked like the kind of woman who'd compromise on a nurse's mother.

Marge's apartment was a few blocks farther on. She rang the bell, but there was no answer. After that she walked on small, empty side streets and bought herself a chocolate bar and a tube of toothpaste in a shabby store that smelled of kerosene. . . . If Miss Byrd washed her face, she might look human. But then, she might not, either. She might look——

She told herself to stop thinking about Miss Byrd. She walked on, eating the chocolate, killing time, putting off her return. What am I stalling about? she wondered. Why don't I go back where I belong?

Climb. You'll have to climb.

The attic door was open, the last tool clattered to the floor.

Her hands were aching, they were all she could feel. Emma was behind her. Ralph and Bruce were crowding ahead of her.

"My hands hurt," she said. "Give me your hand to hold, Ralph. Brucie, give me yours. Don't leave me."

Ralph said, "Here, darling, but I wish you wouldn't——"

Bruce said, "She can't stop now."

There was a draught on the attic stairs, coming down to meet them, blowing her robe, lifting the hair from her forehead. She thought: We're wrong about this, we'll have champagne tonight in celebration of being wrong. He's writing up there, he locked the door because he hates to be interrupted, and he's dead to the world in some silly plot and can't hear us. She called his name, laughing, but no sound came out of her mouth.

Ralph said, "There must be a window open."

Bruce said: "There is. I saw it from the street."

She answered them in her mind: "You fools, of course there's a window open. The boy has to have air. It's always suffocating in that place."

The climb was endless, there had never been so many steps before. It was years before they came to the turn halfway up. Emma panted behind them. It was hard on Emma. What was? Only the stairs, that's all, the stairs. Emma was old.

Ten to one he went to sleep, she wagered silently. They give him too much to do down there at the bank, he hates figures, they wear him out. He was exhausted, and he came home early and went to sleep on that old sofa he won't let me throw away. Ten to one—— Why are you saying ten to one, even to yourself? You never talk like that. . . . You're talking like that because you don't want to think. Well, you'd better think. Think hard, and be ashamed of yourself for even listening to their monstrous story. Monstrous? Criminal! You could sue, you could easily sue the whole lot of them for saying the things they did. Ten to one.

"Bruce," she said, "you're going too fast."

"We're crawling, Nora. You're holding us back."

"No, no! Ralph, Bruce, keep my hands!"

The attic floor was level with her eyes now. It was washed with gold from the western windows. She raised her eyes.

"What's the boy doing?" Emma's head appeared beside hers. "Robbie, you stop whatever you're doing and come straight down here!"

Robbie's shoes, above the sunny floor, were swinging in space. His brown shoes, his—he——

She went the rest of the way alone and stood before him. When she wanted to see his face, she had to raise her head, because he was hanging from the rafters.

Emma looked up when she heard the clatter of the lunch tray. "You didn't have to bring that," she said. "I was going to ring for one of the others. You're back too soon."

"I got bored." Milly put the tray on the table.

"It looks good," Emma said. "That jelly looks good. She's a fine cook, Mrs Perry. Maybe she'll teach you one of these days." Emma's eyes had the mating look.

"Move your work-basket, Emma. No tatting in the soup, please. Thanks. Why don't you ask me to save you a piece of wedding cake? You're slipping."

"What are you so high and mighty about?"

"I'm not." Milly slid out of her coat. "Yes, I am, and I don't know why. I hate everything. Maybe I need sleep." She walked around to the front of the chair. "Hello, there. Haven't I seen you somewhere before?"

"Bless my soul, is she awake? Must have just happened." Emma joined Milly at the chair, and they smiled steadily.

"We look nice and rested after our little nap," Emma said. "And we're going to eat every crumb and spoonful of our lunch, because if we do, then maybe we can have our lovely sherry before dinner. Can't we, Miss Sills?"

"I wouldn't know about that. I'm only the night nurse. I don't come on until seven."

Emma chortled. "Isn't she a one, Miss Nora? Aren't you a lucky girl to have Miss Sills around? I never thought I'd laugh again, not in this house. I never——" Emma caught her guilty tongue between her teeth. "Miss Nora, I—I'm going to get another lamp, and I'm the only one who knows how to do it." She hesitated at the door.. "What about you? Did you have lunch at your mother's?"

"I'm not hungry. And hurry up. It'll be dark in about five hours."

Milly unfolded the heavy napkin, spread it carefully, and admired the lavish monogram. She patted the thin, still hands under the steamer rug. "Don't get wrong ideas about Emma and me," she said. "We're crazy about each other. And now let's eat whatever Hattie felt like sending up. This is beef broth, as if you couldn't see for yourself. And this is a sweetbread, as if you couldn't see that, too. And here we have the madame's jelly, shaking in its shoes. Want to start with the dessert and work back, just for the—for the fun of it?"

Mrs Manson's eyes looked steadily into hers.

She returned the dessert spoon to the tray and dropped the prattle and the professional smile. What she saw in Mrs Manson's eyes filled her own with dismay. Mrs Manson was looking at her from the bottom of a pit.

"Mrs Manson?" she said quietly. "Mrs Manson, I haven't given you what you need. I've tried, but everything I've done is only what anybody else could do. You need more than that, every day you seem to need more. It isn't only that you're sick and unhappy. I'm not very old, Mrs Manson, but I've seen a lot of sick people, working in wards with the kind of people you never even passed on the street, never even dreamed of. And now, in the last few days, I'm beginning to see a resemblance between them and you. That's awful, Mrs Manson, but I have to say it. You and I are friends, we both know that, and friends tell each other the truth. You're more than sick and unhappy. All day and night you live with your eyes on death, watching, waiting for—the nod. That's not right. You don't have to die. There's no medical reason for it. No reason at all unless you want to, and if that's the case, then I can't stop you. If you want to get well, you can. You're better than you were—they're not kidding when they tell you that. And you know me, I wouldn't kid you ever, not if they paid me for it. Not you, I wouldn't. You're my friend. Mrs Manson, I want you to stop looking like that. I won't let you die if you'll help me."

Mrs Manson's eyes closed for an instant, and her breast rose and fell as if she were climbing.

"That's better," Milly said. "And it's all right to cry. You'd been crying when I came in, but I didn't want to say anything before Emma. Golly, Mrs Manson, I wish I knew someone who was an old friend of yours, like someone you went to school with. Someone who's your own kind. A person like that might be able to help me. A person like that could tell me what your mind is like and how you used to act when things went wrong. I've got a feeling you always act the right way, no matter what. And that scares me. It means that whatever is wrong is terribly wrong, and acting right and thinking straight can't change it."

Miss Sills, Miss Sills, don't let anyone hear you say that.

Not today, not tonight. Tomorrow you'll be safe, but not today or tonight. Don't talk to anyone until tomorrow. Tomorrow you'll be interviewed, that's when you must talk. Tomorrow, tomorrow morning. . . . Miss Sills, Miss Sills, there was a woman in the park. I know she could help us both, I know it in my heart. But she didn't speak, I watched and she didn't speak, and you walked by.

"I told you it was all right to cry," Milly said. "Take a look at me, it's getting to be like the common cold. There now. I'm getting fresh again and that's all right, too. No more sad talk until tomorrow. What do you want first, jelly or soup? Soup? Oke."

Emma came in with a lamp, looking like a child who has made a beautiful thing out of something nobody wanted.

Milly crowed. "Bring that thing around here, Emma. I want Mrs Manson to see it. Glory be, and they sent the other one to the White Elephant Sale! If ever I saw a white elephant in the beaded flesh——"

"It's my own property," Emma said indignantly. "I've had it for years, and I take good care of it. I like beads."

"Where did you get it?"

"At the White—never you mind. It gives me a nice, soft light, easy on the eyes. How are we coming on?"

"Fine."

"You going out again this evening? Doctor Babcock said you could. He said you should take things easy."

"What's behind the unselfish build-up?"

"Well, I thought if you were going to be in, I might slip out for a while myself. My sister's daughter just had her first —only five pounds for all her trouble. Still and all, I thought I'd like to hear my sister brag."

"Go ahead. I don't want to go out again. And five pounds is okay, so let her brag."

"You, and not even married yet. You never did tell me where you went this morning and what you did."

"I didn't do anything, just walked. Bounced a ball with a cute kid. Oh, sure, and I got picked up, too."

"If you did, then you invited it."

"Not me, not this one. This was a woman, and she said she knew—now, now, Mrs Manson, please."

"Maybe that spoon's too full. It looks too full to me."

"Don't rile me, Emma. She picked me up at the bus stop. She said she knew you, Emma. She asked how you were."

242

Miss Sills! Emma! Emma, listen. This is what I prayed for. Listen, Emma, it's Miss Byrd, I know it's Miss Byrd. Emma, ask questions, ask——

Emma said, "I know everybody in this town, and everybody knows me and how I am." She smoothed her apron and looked at the clock. "I promised Hattie—— What was the woman like?"

"Ordinary, except for her face. Too much make-up."

"Don't know her."

"Green coat and hat."

"I know seven, eight women with green coats and hats. All my friends know how I am. You might as well give up that jelly, Miss Sills. Can't you see she don't want it. I'll give it to Hattie. Well, I promised Hattie I'd take the front door and the phone while she has a rest. If you want me, ring. I'll come back later, anyway." Emma took the lunch tray when she left.

Milly tucked in the edges of the steamer rug and moved her chair beside Mrs Manson's. Mrs Manson closed her eyes again; it was the same as closing a door. There was nothing to do about that.

Behind Milly, the door to the hall was open and the house was as quiet as the room. The roses on the table were dropping their petals; they weren't lasting. Not the way they should. Only one day old, and they were dying.

The chair was low. From where she sat she could see the yellow trees against the sky. Now and then a leaf fell, drifting slowly as if it knew the first, lone journey downward from the sun led to the end.

It was silly to shiver in a warm room. The fire was ready for lighting if she wanted it. All she had to do was walk across the room. But it was too much trouble, too much effort. I'm tired, she thought, and why shouldn't I be? Maybe I can sleep. At least I can try. Her head dropped forward, and she sighed.

They sat side by side with closed eyes, but only one of them slept. The clock ticked on, the minutes passed, but only one of them counted.

It was after four when Doctor Babcock came in. Milly woke and saw him standing before her. She got to her feet, stumbling, only half-awake. "Doctor Babcock, I'm sorry! But Mrs Manson seemed to be resting, and I——"

He waved her apologies aside. "A charming picture, Miss

Sills, charming; and no harm done, no harm at all." His hand took one of Mrs Manson's. "Any change? I'm afraid we're in a state of depression."

She stood behind Mrs Manson's chair and nodded. He was a fool to talk like that where she could hear.

He went on. "But that's to be expected—yes, we expected that. And Emma says there's an aversion to food."

"I wouldn't call it that. I think she does very well, considering. Doctor Babcock, if it's warm tomorrow, can I wheel her out on the porch?"

He thought it over. "Not yet, Miss Sills. This lovely room, the sanctuary of four walls—I think we'll be happier here. The outdoors is sometimes—frightening."

Since when? Milly answered silently. Put them out in the sun and air as soon as they can sit up, that's the way I heard it. "Yes, Doctor Babcock," she said.

Doctor Babcock left Mrs Manson and made a slow tour of the room, examining everything small enough to handle. Even Emma's workbasket was looked into. Milly adjusted the rug again and whispered to Mrs Manson. "The way he's looking at things, you'd think he was going to put us up at auction."

Doctor Babcock made another turn around the room and came to a stop behind Mrs Manson's chair. "Miss Sills," he said, "I'm distressed. About you. I'm not happy about you, not at all happy. You're beginning to show the strain. Now, I want you to understand that this is no reflection on your capabilities, but I truly believe you need assistance, or even better than that, a little rest."

"No, I don't," Milly said. "I mean, thank you, but I'm not tired and we don't want another nurse. Mrs Manson and I get along fine, we're used to each other, we can practically talk. You don't want anybody else, do you, Mrs Manson? See, she says no. That look means no. She says you're very kind, Doctor Babcock, but Miss Sills is my one and only dream girl and she's all I need." A fine line to give the boss, she mourned; every word a step home to mother, and sitting by the phone all day waiting for a call to take care of more tonsils. "But whatever you say, Doctor Babcock. I only mean——"

He smiled broadly. "No explanations, my dear. I understand. We'll wait and see how things develop. Now, about Emma, I've suggested to Emma that she sleep in her own bed

244

tonight. I don't want Mrs Manson relying too much on Emma. Someone unconnected with the past, a stranger like yourself, a—dream girl, did you say? Ah, yes, a dream girl is what we need!" His laughter filled the room.

No tonsils today, she decided. "Any instructions, Doctor Babcock?"

"No. Everything as usual."

When he left, she returned to her chair beside Mrs Manson. She studied the pale face and closed her eyes until Emma came. It was four-thirty then.

Emma lighted the fire, and they both sat before it. Mrs Manson had shown no interest in the fire; she'd looked at it once and closed her eyes again.

"We'll leave her where she is," Milly said softly to Emma. "It's the only privacy she has, sitting off by herself like that. It's all right for a little while."

Emma held her hands to the blaze. "I've got the blues," she whispered. "I can't get Robbie out of my mind. He's been walking behind me all day."

"Is today anything special?" Her own voice was low.

"No, just a Sunday. He was always around all day Sunday, running up- and downstairs, slamming doors. Hattie says she heard him last night."

"Hattie's crazy. You said so yourself."

"I know I did. And so she is. But——"

Milly looked over at the chair. "Are you awake, Mrs Manson?" She turned back to Emma. "No, this time she's really asleep. She never tries to fool me, she knows she can't. We can talk if we're careful, you know. . . . Robbie. I don't know much about Robbie. George keeps changing the subject, and the papers were careful not to say more than they had to."

"They always do that when it's money and banks and prominent people. But she paid up, every cent. There's no reason you shouldn't know about it. Nobody lost a penny through us. We paid."

She could hardly bring herself to believe it even now, Emma said. "Robbie was spoiled, we know that. But why would he steal a lot of money that he didn't need or even spend? Nobody could ever prove that he spent a penny more than his regular income. Why would he steal money, then, and where did it go? Not so much as a nickel ever showed up."

What's more, she said, they'd never been able to find a

single person who'd ever seen him in the wrong kind of company. No gambling, no horse racing, no bad women. There was no sense to it, none at all, and as for what he did afterward——

Emma described what she knew of Robbie's last day. "He came home while I was at the stores," she said. "I'd have spotted something wrong if I'd been home and seen him. But I was at the stores, and Hattie had the kitchen door shut and didn't hear him come in. And when I came back, I started to work right away. I was busy phoning for the extra things Miss Nora wanted for a special dinner. She was counting on Mr Brucie to come. I was planning a wonderful dinner, like she wanted, and then they told me."

Her tremulous whisper led Milly step by step. They stared into the fire as Emma filled the hall with running feet, crouched before the attic door, and emptied the dusty tool chest on the floor. They heard the doorbell ring above the sound of tools.

"Mrs Perry was calling," Emma said, "and the man with the pheasant, because Hattie was afraid to open the back door. That pheasant was in the icebox for over a week—we had to give it away. . . . He'd written her a little note. It was in his typewriter. He said, 'I never was any good, but you wouldn't believe it.' No love or nothing. She saw it before we did—we couldn't help that. We were trying to—you know, you—you have to cut the rope. . . . I gave that boy the first bath he ever had."

Milly's hands went out to Emma. "Don't talk any more," she whispered. "That's enough. I know how you feel."

"You know? In a million years you wouldn't know. And it wasn't enough that I saw him as I did. I had to be the one to find her, too. Lying at my feet, the same as dead, and Mr Ralph and Mr Brucie out of their minds. She'd be dead this minute if it hadn't been that Doctor Babcock had come to call. . . . I don't know what we've done, it's like a punishment."

"Hush."

The coal crackled, the firelight was on their faces. They drew together, the bent black figure and the straight white one. On the other side of the room a shaft of setting sun came in at the window and found the chair.

Hattie came in at five-fifteen with her plate of meat, an uncooked lamb chop and a slice of turkey breast. Her mouth

246

was set in an obstinate line. She had clearly been told to keep it shut, and just as clearly she was going to make somebody suffer.

"That's a poor-looking chop," Emma said. She took the plate and crossed to the chair. "Open your eyes, Miss Nora, time to wake up. Hattie's here with your dinner meat, and if you want my advice, you'll take the turkey. The lamb that gave that chop could ill afford to spare it."

Mrs Manson looked at the plate. For the first time, she seemed unwilling to play their little game.

"Serve them both, Hattie," Milly said. "Two dinner trays, one for me, too. We'll decide which we want then. It's all right, isn't it, if I eat up here tonight?"

"No reason why you can't," Emma said. She bustled to the door. "Come along, chatterbox. I'll bring up that sherry, too, Miss Sills. A nip of sherry, a nice fire——Hattie!"

The sun was low in the sky; long shadows came into the room. Milly moved aimlessly from window to porch door, from door to bed to fireplace. Once she returned to the bed, for no reason that she knew. She smoothed the covers as if she were removing the outline of a body, not preparing to receive one.

The room slowly filled with dusk, but she ignored the lamps. She sat by the fire, wondering if the radio would bother Mrs Manson if she played it softly. There was a radio within reach of her hand; she stretched out her hand, but let it fall almost at once. Nothing she could think of was worth doing. . . . I used to like the autumn, she thought, but this year it's different. It used to be full of—I don't know, promise or something—but this time I feel old, and I'm not old. Tonight I'm so old that I can't look forward. I can't think of anything I want, and I've always wanted something. Now that I don't want anything, what's the use?

She looked at the still figure, shrouded in dusk. Sleep, she said to herself, sleep, Mrs Manson. You think too much when you're awake, I know. Those attic stairs—Emma says they're dreadful. How could she do it? . . .

Miss Sills, Miss Sills, go home, Miss Sills. It's growing dark. Your mother has a house; go there. All day I've seen the night getting ready. The things that could have held it back—Hattie, the lamp, Miss Byrd—are gone. Go home, Miss Sills. Miss Sills, so young and so wise, leaning forward to look into my face, telling me how frightful life can be.

Little Miss Sills, my friend, go home. You don't know what comes and goes in this house. . . .

One by one the others drifted in, Mr Manson, Bruce Cory, George. There were no highballs this time; they seemed to know that talk and laughter were out of place this time. This time.

Milly offered chairs, but they were declined. Someone turned the radio on, and the soft, invoking voices of a Negro choir filled the dusky room. *Abide with me: fast falls the eventide.* The voices and the dark together were unsupportable.

"Turn that off," Milly heard herself say. "I don't like it." She was startled by the sound of her voice. It cracked like a whip. "It's gloomy," she said defensively. Some tactless fool, she thought. If I knew which one, I'd give him what for.

The music stopped. George walked around the room, turning on lights. Bruce Cory said, "I'm sorry, Miss Sills."

Why did I do that? she wondered. *Miss Sills, this is no reflection on your capabilities, but you're beginning to show the strain.*

Mr Manson said: "I'm afraid we came at a bad time. Is anything wrong?"

"No, Mr Manson. I guess we're tired, that's all. It's been a tiring day."

"We'll go. Babcock was here, wasn't he?"

"Yes, he was. But he didn't say anything in particular. He stayed only a little while."

"Cory and I went into town for an hour or so. I wish I'd —well, we'll get along and let you rest. Anything you want, Miss Sills? You don't make many demands. I wish you did."

"No, sir, I don't want anything."

They left, Manson and Cory, but George stayed.

"Come out on the porch," George whispered. "You can, can't you? I want to talk."

The garden was dark; across the autumn grass, patched with fallen leaves, the Perrys' lights gleamed through the trees. Mr Perry was working on his side of the hedge, a stooped, black figure in the stream of yellow lamplight, curiously alone. "His flowers," George said vaguely. "Come along this way." He led her to the far end of the porch. She knew Hattie's room was directly beneath them.

"I've got the wind up," George said.

248

"Same old wind you're always talking about? I didn't come out here for that."

"Milly, listen. I'm not kidding. There wasn't any wind last night. That lamp didn't blow over; it couldn't. It was knocked over, by you or Emma or somebody else. And I don't mean Mrs Manson, either. Do you think Emma did it?"

"No. She'd tell everybody right away and start paying off, week by week. And it wasn't me. You make me feel funny, and I was bad enough before."

"Listen. I prowled around here at the crack of dawn, also before I came in just now. I was looking for prints. I wasn't sure that what I saw last night was a dog. It ran on all fours, but it was too big. If it was a cat burglar making a fancy get-away, then we ought to tell the cops. And if it was a dog, we ought to tell them just the same. A dog that walks into second-floor bedrooms and knocks over fifteen-pound lamps ought to be tied up—or shot."

Milly rested her arm on the railing and looked down into the dark tangle of ivy. There was a light in Hattie's window. The ivy was broken; she could see the loose, limp rope of leaves and stem.

"I know that poem, too," she said slowly. "I can even quote a different line."

"You're catching on," he said. "But let me. I do it prettier. 'Are you a beast of field and tree, or just a stronger child than me?' "

They drew together; his hand was on her shoulder, her face was close to his.

"George," she whispered, "where were you at ten-thirty last night?"

"Bed. Why?"

"I called you up from home, but nobody answered."

"I heard the phone, but I didn't do anything about it. . . . I've got you close, Milly. Don't shiver."

"Who's shivering? You haven't said anything about finding prints."

"I found some, all right. Of shoes, men's shoes. Manson and Cory were out there this morning with Babcock. Their prints are all over the place now."

"But you didn't see anything the first time—I mean, at the crack of dawn? You didn't, George, did you?"

He was a long time answering. His hand left her shoulder and pressed her cheek. "I'm going down to the barracks and

249

talk to Ferd Pross. There was something funny going on around here last night. Ferdie will know what to do."

"George, you did see something! What was it?"

"Something stood in the flower bed under Hattie's window, either before or after climbing the ivy. The same thing that got into Mrs Manson's room. It was frightened off—my guess is that it knocked over the lamp—and I don't know where it went. But at one time during the night it stood in soft, wet earth, ran along the porch, swung over the railing, and tore the ivy. That's one of the things I'm going to tell Pross."

"What—what's the other?"

"It left the wrong kind of tracks. Wrong for an animal, wrong for a man. They were spaced as an animal's would be, four nice clear prints, front and back. And big. Maybe I ought to laugh, but I don't feel like it. Because they weren't feet, and they weren't paws. They were hands."

She heard herself say, "Hands?"

"Yeah." He went on, softly. "So: 'Are you beast of field and tree, or just a stronger child than me?' If that's some guy's idea of a practical joke, Ferdie and I can act funny, too. Of course they aren't there now; they got stepped on this morning. Ferdie may try to tell me I'm crazy, but I'm not."

"George, what did they look like? Were they—like a starfish?"

He said, "How did you know that?"

She quoted Hattie, "But she said only *one*."

"That can be all right, that can still make sense. It could have been reaching down to get a grip or a foothold. When she yelled, it swung back to the porch, out of sight. Then when she left, it dropped to the flower bed and vanished. Don't ask me where or how. One set of prints was all I could find. Maybe it floated."

"I'm not afraid," she said.

"No reason to be. A dirty trick by some heel whose mind didn't grow as fast as his body. Just keep the door locked. I'm pretty sure that was a one-night stand." He kissed her briefly. "This is no time for prolonging pleasure. I've got to get down to see Ferdie. Maybe somebody else saw the thing and reported it. Maybe Ferdie will hang around here to-night." He kissed her again. "Maybe I'll drop in myself."

He had reached his side of the hedge when a sudden recollection made him stop and look back at the house he had just left. *You need two pairs of hands around here.* Who said that? When? Hattie? No, Emma. This morning, Emma. That was right, but it wasn't enough. It was older than that, it went farther back. Two pairs of hands. Now, what does that——

His mother was in the living room, knitting. "Well?" she asked.

"No dinner for me," he said. "I've got to see a man about a dog."

"Knowing you, dear," she said thoughtfully, "I suspect that's vulgar."

It was six-thirty when Emma brought two dinners on a large tray. Emma and Hattie had surpassed themselves, but Mrs Manson wouldn't eat. Milly cajoled, begged, and threatened, but Mrs Manson refused to open her mouth. Even the sherry, which she ordinarily liked, brought no response. When they saw it was useless, they put her to bed. She fought that, too, if it could be called fighting. The mutiny was in her eyes. It was the same look Milly had seen the night before when she'd refused the hot milk and the sleeping pills.

"You run along, Emma," Milly said. "Maybe she'll change her mind when she sees me eating."

After several half-hearted offers to stay, Emma agreed to go. "If you want anything, ring for Hattie; but don't expect any conversation—she's still not talking. And she know's my sister's telephone number, in case, which I hope not."

Milly ate her dinner with elaborate and false enjoyment, and drank a glass of sherry. Mrs Manson watched without expression. When the tray had been placed in the hall and the fire built up, there was nothing else to do. Emma's lamp shed a dim light on the bed and the inevitable steamer rug. The porch door was closed, and so was the door to the hall. The room was too hot, but Mrs Manson liked it that way; at least, they thought she did. They thought, they thought, they thought. Would there ever come a time when anyone knew what she wanted?

Milly went to the window seat and huddled on the cushions like a child, with her arms around her knees. The lights across the park looked far away.

Emma has gone, and Miss Sills is asleep. Curled like a kitten, her head in her arms. How long will it be before she wakes? How long before Emma comes home? One hour? Two?

251

Emma. Does it mean anything that Emma is out? Each time, Emma was out. Each time the house was empty except for Hattie, in the kitchen with the door closed. Except for Hattie and me and——

Why does my body ache? Perhaps because it is fighting or because I'm thinking of the last time it was alive.

Why did I go up there the last time? If I hadn't gone, I'd be living tomorrow. I'd be walking tomorrow, riding, driving, going to the theatre. My heart would be empty, but I'd be living, and perhaps in time someone else would have learned what I learned. In time to do something. Someone else, even a curious stranger; it couldn't have stayed hidden forever.

Why did I go up there? You know why. You went because you always turned the knob; every time you passed, you turned the knob slowly and quietly, knowing the door would be locked, but turning the knob because you had to. And that time the door opened.

And you told yourself you were alone in the house!

It's all right, it's all right. This is preparation of a kind, too.

Climb again. . . .

The knob turned soundlessly, and the door swung open. She stood at the foot of the winding stairs, looking up, listening to the soft footfalls above. Someone else had found the unlocked door.

Hattie? No, Hattie was in the kitchen or in her own room. Emma? Emma had gone to market; she'd seen her less than ten minutes ago, haggling over fish. Ralph? Brucie? Brucie had promised to come out. No, too early for them. They were in town, at the bank.

Someone who knew their daily plans and schedules had broken in. She was supposed to be at the Civic League meeting, but the pity in the other women's faces had driven her home.

She started up the stairs, shaking with fury, not fear. Robbie's attic, his own place, his last place on earth. She moved without sound, hugging the wall hesitating only once, asking herself what she would do or say when she reached the top. She told herself she ought to call the police. I ought to call the police but I don't want—I don't want the story in the papers. They'll reprint the pictures, they'll——

Why don't I go to my room first and see if he's taken anything? If he has, I'll tell him he can keep it. I won't prosecute.

I'll reason with him. I'll tell him to go, go quickly. I'll explain how we feel about the attic.

But if he has my jewellery, why did he go to the attic?

Hattie. It must be Hattie, looking for extra blankets. It has to be Hattie.

Then she heard the laughter, low, almost bubbling, happy victorious, and familiar. She covered her mouth with her hand and crept forward.

At the top of the stairs she crouched behind the partition. There was sun on the floor again. Robbie's old toy trunk, filled with broken treasures, had been brought from its corner, and it was open. Herself unseen, she watched the hands as they lifted the packages one after the other, lovingly. There was no look of surprised discovery on the face. It was the face of one who had returned to gloat.

She stood erect. "Thief," she said quietly.

The answering voice was as quiet as hers. "This is unfortunate."

Neither moved. They looked at each other over the open trunk. A golden bar of sunlight slanted through the western window and fell between them, a metaphoric pale that placed the other one beyond the limit of civilized mercy and protection.

When she could force herself to look down again, she saw that the money in the trunk was incredibly green. The building blocks were drab and dull beside it, the once-bright trains and trucks, the painted wagons, and the battered wooden animals were ghosts. The money was real.

She said: "I misjudged you. I didn't know you had the mind for a thing like this. I thought you were reliable and capable. I even thought you lacked imagination. I didn't know you could plan and execute a thing like this. Did you do it alone, or did someone help you? I can't understand how you did it alone."

"No imagination? Yes, everyone thinks that. Dull and pompous. Yes, I did it alone. I've always been underestimated."

"Why did you do it?"

"Because I like money, and I don't like rich women who inherit theirs. Because my own efforts never got me quite enough of my own. I thought a secret nest egg would be very pleasant, doubly pleasant when I found I could arrange it with complete safety to myself. I still think so."

She told herself to wake up. She spoke aloud, but didn't know it. "Why don't you wake up?" she said. "Why doesn't somebody wake me up?" She looked from the face to the trunk again. There were splashes of brilliant yellow among the clean green and faded blues and reds.

She said, "He made those—for Christmas, I think. He made them for a joke, like a stocking toy. They were supposed to be funny. You think they're funny now, don't you? I don't. I——" She put her hands to her head. "I'm the dull one," she said, "but then, I never had to be anything else. I never had to worry about anything, or work to live. There was always someone to take care of me and do my thinking for me. But now I want to think for myself."

"Don't."

"But I want to know how you did it. I used to hear people talk about the way we managed the bank. They used to laugh and say it looked wide open, that the Board of Directors and even the watchmen thought they could go anywhere and carry off anything—until they tried."

"It wasn't difficult. I'm capable and reliable. You said so yourself."

"You are also—— You killed him."

"I did."

"Why? Wasn't there anyone else you could use?"

"There may have been. I didn't look very far. He was there; he was made to order. That's how it started. Then he had the effrontery to spot me, *me,* the last person in the world they'd have thought of! So I had no choice. He had Cory blood—the inquisitive, shrewd, banker blood. He'd taken me completely, I didn't know he could even add. Fortunately, he couldn't hide his feelings, and I saw the end in time. So I did a little talking in the right places."

"That's what was wrong with him at lunch. He wouldn't tell me then." She could have been standing before a counter of merchandise, accepting and rejecting. One finger lay along her cheek. I will not scream, she thought, I will not scream, not yet, not for days and days. I will not scream now.

"That's why he came home early," she went on. "To tell me the truth. He had been openly accused, and he knew——"

"Don't burden yourself with details. They don't matter."

She thought that over. They don't matter. The details don't matter. Why don't they? I know, I know why. Because

I won't have any use for them. I'm to kill myself like Robbie; disgrace and shame will make me follow my son. Mrs Ralph Manson, of Larchville, whose son——"You don't know me," she said.

"No?" The low laugh bubbled up again.

She pretended not to hear it. She took a step backward—a small, unnoticeable step. "Tell me one thing more," she said. "Didn't he—defend himself?"

"Oh, yes. That surprised me. I'd always thought of him as a spoiled brat, without stamina. But he was no coward."

"Thank you. You see, some of the details do matter, after all. And the open window? I wonder now why you didn't close it. Wasn't that—dangerous for you. He might have cried out."

"You're underestimating me again. I opened the window afterward. You know, you're taking this almost too well, so I'll give you the rest of it. Bodies stay warm. In a place like this, he would have been warm for an uncomfortable length of time—for me. So I opened the window to—you understand?"

"Yes, I understand. Haven't we all been stupid? You came in the front door?"

"Certainly. You've also been stupid about that, leaving it unlocked to save your servants. I made sure, of course, that there was no one in sight."

"It's only unlocked in the afternoons," she explained carefully. "I always thought that afternoons in a place like this—— I'm glad it was you who typed that note."

"I thought it was a good note, under the circumstances. I'm not much of a writer. He could have done a better job himself, but we didn't have time for that. And speaking of time, there isn't much of it left now."

"No," she agreed. "Emma will be coming soon. I saw her in the market, and she knows I'm home."

There was tolerant curiosity behind the soft voice. It was more human than the fresh peal of bubbling laughter. "I'm glad she knows you're in the house alone. But how, exactly, do you think that can help you?"

"Help me? Emma? I don't need Emma for what I'm going to do. I'd rather she didn't come. This is all mine."

"Wait. What do you think you're going to do?"

"I'm going to the police. I'm going to hang you higher than that rafter."

The air churned. Between her and the sun a human, black

projectile rose and catapulted forward. She closed her eyes when it struck.

When her body rolled against the wall at the turn in the stairs, like a log jammed in midstream, she knew she hadn't long to wait. Strong hands turned her over and sent her the rest of the way. A thin scream came from nowhere.

She opened her eyes to nothing. After an endless search she saw a lighted lamp in another world. Soon it became familiar; it was her lamp, her room. Her bed.

Living, she told herself. Why?

Voices drifted through the gloom, like recorded voices on an old record. Thin, without bodies. But when she tried, she could see bodies standing in a row at the foot of the bed.

"At my feet, on the floor, at my feet. I came in, and I heard a sound, and I ran. I knew where it came from. Unconscious, I said to myself, or dead."

"Lucky for us that we happened to be——"

"She should be dead. She should be dead. I don't understand it."

"I've been afraid——"

She was lying at the foot of the attic stairs again, hearing Emma scream in the lower hall, looking up at the figure bending above her, reading the eyes that looked down into hers, watching the quick retreat to the top of the stairs so that whoever came—— Forget that now, she told herself. Listen to the voices, listen to every word. One of them will tell you what you must do.

"Shock and paralysis. I beg your pardon, you were saying?"

"She telephoned, she told me to come as soon as I could. I thought she was ill. When I came, she asked me to wait while she went upstairs. After a while I followed. I was uneasy, disturbed——"

Who said that? Who? Listen.

"And the attic door was open. Obviously she'd found the key. She was preparing to take her life in the same way. I struggled with her, she was demoralizing, raving. She fell. When I heard Emma and the rest of you, I——"

Liar, her mind said. Thief, murderer, liar. You flung me like a sack of meal, but the others came and you couldn't finish. Wait until I tell them that.

"At my feet. Lying there on the floor. Oh, Mr Ralph, Mr Brucie!"

"Quiet, please. Miss Byrd?"

"Yes, Doctor Babcock?"

"A close watch for the next five hours. At the slightest change, call me."

"All of us will watch. Babcock, it was Providence that you were——"

"Providence? Not at all. The dear lady had been on my mind, I felt that a little call—— But I must warn you, this will be a hopeless vigil. She will live from hour to hour—perhaps."

"Will she talk to us before she——"

"There will be no speech, no movement."

"No speech?"

"We'll get another opinion, we must. You understand how we——"

"Naturally another opinion. I was about to suggest it myself. Mr Cory, not too close, please. When and if consciousness returns, she must see no one—strange."

"Strange? I? But she'll expect to see me, she knows I'm here, she asked me——"

The voices faded, the figures melted away.

So that's the story! . . . She could feel the bitter laughter in her throat. Wait until I tell mine. Not now, in a little while. When I'm alone with someone who will believe me.

Why aren't my bones broken? Perhaps because I didn't fight. Why don't I feel pain? They said I should be dead. Yes, I should be. I would be if the others hadn't come when they did. I will be, unless I tell. They said no speech, no movement. That's not true, either. I can talk and I can move. I——

It's true.

The light from Emma's lamp was a dim pool on the bed table. In it were the bottle with its four pills, the vacuum jug, a clean, folded handkerchief, the jar of talcum powder. Undisturbed, still in the same positions. . . . No one has come while I've been away, she thought. It's too early. Is the door locked?

Miss Sills' cap is white against the dark window. Her stiff white skirt, her square-toed white shoes. Small, square white shoes like a summer Sunday morning. Sunday School. Clean them with the shoe white; you can do that yourself. Now wipe the edges of the soles—no, no, not with the sponge, there's too much whitener on the sponge. Use the cloth, that's what it's for. Stand them on the window sill, one behind the other; they'll dry in no time at all. . . . I never spoiled a child in my life.

The door to the hall is closed, the door to the porch is closed. Miss Sills and I are closed in. The doors may be locked from the outside, we may be locked in. The door to the hall——

The door to the hall opened.

She watched the white figure emerge from the shadows on silent feet. It had no face. It was covered with white. Two arms reached down to her.

Miss Sills.

Miss Sills said: "Hey! Sorry. But what's the big idea? Why the pussyfoot, why the disguise?"

He said something through the mask.

"Sure," Miss Sills said. "That's sensible. I didn't mean to yell at you, but I was only half-awake. I don't mind admitting you scared the—you scared me for a minute. I thought we had Martians." Miss Sills went to the bed and turned back the covers. She bent down. "He frightened you, too, didn't he? That's a shame. I should have stayed over here. But it's all right, it's all right now. You really did frighten her. Take that thing off, and come out in the open for a second. See, Mrs Manson? It's only Breitman."

Only Breitman.

"He has a cold, Mrs Manson. He caught it last night when he left here. He's only taking precautions for your sake. He'd just as soon scare you to death, but he draws the line at a sneeze."

Only Breitman.

He talked to Miss Sills while he worked; she couldn't hear all he said. Miss Sills stood at the foot of the bed, her cap awry, her stiff skirt wrinkled where her arms had hugged her knees. She watched him and laughed with him. He wore a wrist watch. It said eight-thirty.

When he was through, he went to the fire, and Miss Sills gave him a glass of sherry from the bottle that was still on the mantel. He slipped the mask under his chin when he drank. Miss Sills laughed again. She knew Breitman; they had worked together before. Breitman was the best masseur in the business, she said.

When Breitman left, Miss Sills followed him to the

door. She sounded as if she were sorry to see him go. Miss Sills was lonely, she liked people, she liked life around her.

After Breitman left, Milly went to the end of the hall and looked down the main stairs. The lower hall was dim. She crossed to the head of the kitchen stairs. No light or sound there, either. Hattie had gone to bed. Or slipped out. Usually on Sunday nights Hattie moaned hymns with the door open.

They're getting mighty casual around here, she complained to herself. You'd think they'd tell me when they go out; you'd think they'd ask me if I wanted anything. She returned to the room, rinsed Breitman's glass, and looked for something to do.

There was nothing in Emma's work-basket, no mending or darning, only the tatting, which looked so effortless in Emma's hands and turned into a cat's cradle in her own. Even Mrs Manson was all right. Mrs Manson was taking one of her little jaunts into another world; she was seeing something far away, far away and high up. Maybe a mountain top; she'd travelled a lot in Europe. Well, whatever it was, there was peace in her eyes. Peace, or something just as good. There was no fright.

She went to the porch door and rested her forehead on the cool glass. No lights over at the Perrys'. Half past nine. They couldn't be in bed. Gone to the movies. Mr Perry liked movies. George said he liked the tough ones. George said that sometimes when the old man thought he was alone in his flower beds, he flattened his back against the hedge and made like standing against a warehouse wall. Fist in pocket, making like a gun. A lookout. The old man was cute, poor thing. Acting tough all by himself and saying, "Yes, dear," the rest of the time.

Maybe George was with Ferd Pross, the State Trooper. He and Ferdie had gone to Boys' High together. He could tell Ferdie anything and know he wouldn't be laughed at. George was up in the air, all right; he couldn't fool her. And so am I, she admitted, and I'm not fooling myself either. . . . Why doesn't George talk to Manson and Cory? Maybe he has; maybe they're doing something about it this minute.

She was suddenly relieved. That's why they're out, she decided. That's why they didn't say anything to me. They didn't want me to know they were worried.

She went to the fire. It was burning itself out. Nearly

ten o'clock. It would last until bedtime, until Emma came back.

She sat in Emma's chair, and planned a spring offensive against George's mother, the whole thing to take place in the Sills' back garden, which was big enough and had two dogwood trees. Let's say the first of May, and no veil—I'd feel like a fool in a veil after this cap. No bouquet; let the dogwood handle that. A white prayer-book and high heels, even if I do fall flat on my face. And Mrs Manson in her chair, under the trees. With me. Beside me. Mrs Manson will give me away. Oh, oh, trouble ahead. Now listen, Mother, I've been everything a daughter should be. I hate to talk like this, but you force me. And I do think that, on this day of all days, you might at least try to understand and have a little consideration. Who am I fighting with? What's all the rush? . . . Maybe I'd better tell George.

She was almost sorry when Emma came in at eleven. By that time everything had been settled but the chicken salad; veal or no veal.

"Hello," she said. "Have a nice time?"

Emma said: "It's blowing up outside, a nasty, damp fog all over. I hate it. But you're cosy enough in here. You sound real happy, too."

"That's the voice that breathed o'er Eden."

"Whatever that may be. Well, I just looked in for a minute. I'm going down to my bed. I'm beginning to feel my neuralgia. That fog. Will you be going down yourself, for hot milk?"

"I don't know." They looked at the bed. Mrs Manson's eyes were closed. "If she stays like that, I won't. Better not start anything."

"Well, if you do, don't lock up. They're still out. No trouble?"

"Breitman got himself up in a mask, because he's playing with the idea of influenza. Frightened her at first, the big gorilla. But aside from that, everything's fine."

"George come over?"

"No. Haven't seen a soul."

"Well——" Emma opened her handbag. "Your mother sent you a note." She drew out an envelope and gave it to Milly.

"My mother? But how did she know——"

"Sent it to my sister's. My sister's boy took it. Don't be so fussy. You've got it, haven't you? Well, I'm for bed. Be sure you ring if you want me." Emma was still talking when she closed the door.

Milly stared at the envelope in her hand. The address was lettered in pencil: "THE NURSE. KINDNESS OF EMMA. PERSONAL." She took it to the lamp by the bed. Mrs Manson was watching her.

"So you're curious, too?" Milly said. "You don't miss much, do you?" She held the envelope before Mrs Manson's eyes. "That's not from my mother, and you know it as well as I do. Emma's out of her mind. Well, there's only one way to find out. May I sit on the edge of your bed, madam, if I promise not to bounce? . . . Well, what do you know, there's something in it. Feels like money, like a quarter or something." She opened the envelope and took out a key. "Look!" she marvelled. She held the key to the light before she put it on the bed table. "Wait till I read it, then I'll tell you."

The note was also in pencil. Across the top of the first page a sentence in capital letters said: "DO NOT READ THIS UNLESS YOU ARE ALONE." She winked at Mrs Manson. "This is going to be good. Wait."

She read to herself, frowning, engrossed; she forgot Mrs Manson. She was alone with the crackling paper in her hand.

"I won't sign my name to this, but you will know who I am. I said you had a good heart. There is something wrong in that house. I know it. It isn't a thing I can take to the police, because I haven't proof of anything, only what you might call my convictions. Too many things have happened in that house, and those people are not the kind that have such things happen to them. Also, I cannot go to the police because they would have to take my name, and then if they investigated and found nothing, my name would leak out, and that would be the end of me. Even now I think somebody watches my apartment at night.

"Once I knew a lady who feared for her life, I don't mean myself, and people thought she was imagining things, even the police thought she was. But it was proved that she wasn't. Your patient has the same look this other lady had. That's what I mean.

"It is not my wish to get you into trouble or danger, but I've no one else to tell this to. I couldn't find out your name, because I was afraid my interest would become known to the wrong person. I'm not sure who the wrong person is.

"This key fits the attic door. It was made from an impression. Never mind how I came by it. Now, this is why I'm sending it to you. Every time there is no one in the house but the patient and her nurse, and maybe the cook in the kitchen, somebody walks in the attic. I've heard them, because my hearing is very acute, even when they walked softly. Sometimes in daylight, sometimes at night. The patient has heard it, too. She knows what it is, but she can't tell you. That's when she has the same look as the other lady I told you about."

Milly turned the page with a shaking hand. It was ridiculous, it was crazy. It could be true. She read on.

"I couldn't use the key myself. I never had a chance. Never mind why I never had a chance—just let us say I came into possession too late. But if you know someone you are sure of, give the key to them. And tell them to be careful. Tell them to watch everybody, to trust nobody. But go to the attic.

"Maybe someday I will see you again. You didn't think much of me, I could see that; but I don't blame you. I've been half out of my mind and very nervous and not myself. But you'll understand that later.

"I remain, Your Friend."

She folded the letter and put it in her pocket. "Mrs Manson," she said, turning slowly, "do you mind if I—*Mrs Manson*!"

Mrs Manson didn't hear.

One of Mrs Manson's arms was uncovered. One hand was inching forward through space, the fingers opening and closing, taking handfuls of air, curling around the air, holding it, letting it go. The hand crept on until it reached the bed table and dropped. It struck the lid of the powder jar; the lid spun on the rim of the table and fell soundlessly on the carpet. The jar overturned.

"*Mrs Manson.*" Milly's voice was a whisper.

Mrs Manson's hand covered the key. Her mouth twisted and stiffened and relaxed. Her eyes met Milly's. I can't talk, her eyes said, but this is the smile you've been waiting for. Her eyes blazed and talked.

"Don't," Milly said. "Don't try. Let me. Mrs Manson, do you know who sent that key? It's the other nurse, isn't it?"

It was.

"Do you know what she means— She says it's a key to the attic. I know it is—you've proved that. But do you know

262

what she wants? She wants someone to go up there, she says you——"

There was no need for more. Mrs Manson's eyes blazed their verification.

"Shall I go? Shall I go now? There's no one home."

Mrs Manson tried to say yes, but fear and pity struggled with frenzied hope; the fear and pity and hope were as clear as printed words, clearer than speech.

"There's no one at home," Milly whispered. "This is a safe time. It's better for me to go myself, now. If we wait until I call George—Mrs Manson, we'll never sleep if I don't go now. If we wait, we might not have another chance. . . . But I don't know what I'm supposed to find, or see. I don't know what's there. I——"

Mrs Manson's eyes led her to the hand covering the key. Covering the key, lying in the spilled powder.

"Mrs Manson! Can you move one finger, can you write in that powder? Can you write even one word?"

Their breathing was like a thunder in their ears. One finger. One. It moved, slowly. One word, one. The word grew, letter by letter. It was 'trunk'.

Milly took the key. There was a flashlight in the table drawer. She took that, too. She went to the hall door and looked at the outside lock.

"There's no key here. I can't lock you in, but I promise to hurry." She returned to the table and blotted out the word with her palm. She was smiling. "I'm going to put that hand back where it used to be, too," she said. "Just for fun. And here's my watch, right here, under the light. So you can see how quick I am, so you won't stew."

She didn't look back.

The house was still silent. The attic key was stiff in the lock, like all new keys, but the door opened without sound. She closed it behind her and climbed the stairs, following the flashlight beam.

Trunk. Trunk. What trunk? Attics are full of trunks. How will I know which one? What will I find? How will I know it's what I want, even when I see it?

She came to the top and turned her light around the room. There was a table holding a covered typewriter. There was a leather sofa with broken springs. There were cardboard boxes, hampers, discarded luggage, a dusty rocking-horse, three bicycles that told how fast a boy grows. There was a round-topped trunk with something painted on the side in large, red, crooked letters. Robbie. . . .

The hand crept from under the rug and found its laborious way to the table again. . . . Don't let anything happen, she prayed. I am on my knees. Heaven, I am on my knees. Don't make her pay for me. . . . The fingers curled once more. Her face was dark with pain. It would be a longer word this time.

She looked down into the trunk. The flashlight beam dug into the corners, picked out the colours and shapes. She saw bundles of paper money, play money for keeping store. Building blocks, trucks and trains, battered little wagons. When she took one of the bundles in her hand, she saw the money was real. She knew what it was then.

She looked from the money to the four gloves. Big cotton gloves, covered with thick bright-yellow paint, with bleeding hearts and arrows on the cuffs. She made herself take one of them in her hand. The paint was soiled and cracking, but it had been fresh and new not too long ago. At one time they had been what her mother called furnace gloves. You bought them at the five-and-ten and wore them when you did things like carrying out ashes. They were padded on the inside; two of them had room enough for hands. They were stiff and firm; the fingers were spread, but you could wear them on your hands. The other two were fastened to shoes, pulled over a pair of old shoes, filled out as if they held hands, but fastened to a pair of shoes. Like starfish.

She crept down the stairs in the dark. When she reached the hall, she heard the front door open and close softly.

Mrs Manson watched her as she closed the room door behind her and moved a chair against the knob. Her hands left wet prints on the chair, but she didn't know that.

When she went to the bed, she said: "Don't worry about that chair. It's just a—well, it's a precaution."

Mrs Manson's eyes questioned her steadily.

"Yes," she answered, "I saw it. Mrs Manson, I can't use the phone. The one in here is disconnected—you know that, don't you? It was done before I came. And the others aren't safe. I won't kid you, Mrs Manson, but don't be frightened. I'll think of something. I saw everything you wanted me to see. You saw it, too, didn't you? You went up there and saw it, too, and that was when you fell. I know you didn't fall, not like they say. But don't be frightened. It'll be all right. I'll think of something."

She left the bed and went to the porch door. She didn't open it. She dropped the latch into its slot, a flimsy latch that wouldn't keep a child out. A latch that a hairpin——

The Perry cottage was still dark. They could have come home while I was up there. It doesn't mean they're still out, just because it's dark. They could be home, in bed.

The street lamp shed a faint light along the edge of the garden, contesting the fog. There were no figures out there; no one moved along the hedges or under the trees. If Ferd Pross had agreed to watch, he hadn't come. But it wasn't much after twelve. He might think it was too early. Too early for a prowler, that's what Ferd might think.

She went back to the bed and sat down. "I have an idea," she whispered. "I'm going to turn out the lamp. You won't mind the dark, will you, if I hold your hand? This is what I mean about the dark. Last night George saw the lamp go out. Maybe he'll see it now, maybe he's watching. If he is, then maybe——"

She reached for the lamp and saw the new word cut into the film of powder. It gleamed up from the polished wood. *Murderer*.

"I know," she said. "Mrs Manson, *can you write the name?*" His father and mother had gone to bed; their doors were closed. George closed his own quietly and went to the window without turning on the light. Mrs Manson's lamp was still on. So far, okay. He went to his desk and groped for a cigarette. He smoked it, sitting on the edge of his bed.

Ferd Pross hadn't laughed. He'd looked as if he'd wanted to, but not for long. They'd gone for coffee at the dog wagon, and Ferdie had listened and asked questions. He'd promised to watch the house. He'd said, "I'll do it myself, part of the time anyway, and I'll put a man on when I leave." He'd added, "If anybody but you gave me a line like this, he'd get the alcohol routine."

George had answered, "Not me, Ferd, not this time."

"What do you think it is, George?"

"I don't think. Not now. Not yet."

He went to the window again, raised it and leaned out. There was no one in sight. The fog was low on the ground; the lights along the distant street were dim; but he knew he would see Ferdie when he came.

"Give me half an hour or so," Ferdie had said. "I'll be around, front or back."

Maybe I'm sticking my neck out, George told himself. Maybe they gave all his things away. Maybe she wanted all his stuff out of the house, and they gave it to some playground outfit. Maybe some kid just happened to get hold of——

No. Not a kid, not a trick like that. An overgrown lout? . . . Stop thinking with your mind closed, walk right into forbidden territory and see if you can find a way out. Now, then, suppose Robbie——

No, no, no. Wait a minute. Don't say no so quick; you've been saying no all day. To yourself. Who are you fooling? Say yes for a change, and see what you get. Suppose Robbie——

He shivered and went back for another cigarette. The first one had burned down to his fingers. When he returned to the window, the street was still empty. The garden was empty. Mrs Manson's light——

Mrs Manson's light went out while he watched. Out and on, out and on. Out.

By that time he almost knew the answer was yes.

He dialled the barracks on the hall phone. Pross? Pross, a calm voice said, had left. Had he said where he was going? No, he hadn't said anything, but he'd made a couple of phone calls and sounded excited.

He thought of the phone calls he would like to make, but he was afraid to use the time. But when he saw his mother standing in her doorway, he gambled with a handful of minutes.

"Listen," he said, "this is more important than it sounds. That afternoon when Robbie came home early, did you see anyone else? Anyone, *anyone*."

"Did you wake me up for that? Is that all you can say, after staying out all night and leaving me alone with your father?"

"Please, Mother," he begged. "Quick, did you? Anyone, anyone at all."

She told him, divided between curiosity and anger. "And what's wrong with that? George, you're hurting my shoulder!"

"Sorry, sorry. Was it before or after Robbie came home?"

"A few minutes after. But why I should be half-killed because—*George!*"

"Stay where you are," he said. "I mean it."

The fire was nearly dead. It was the only light; it was

266

almost no light at all. Milly reached for Mrs Manson's hand in the dark. "That business with the lamp was a signal," she lied softly. "I told George that if I ever wanted him, for anything, I'd do that. I wish I could see your face, Mrs Manson. I'd like to look you straight in the eye and tell you what I think of you. I'll tell you tomorrow."

She knew they both were listening. If the porch door opens, I'll hear it, she thought. She'll hear it, too. If the hall door opens, there'll be a light along the edge, from the hall. Unless the light——

"Do you want to hear about my wedding?" she whispered. "It's going to be in the spring, and you're in it. If you want to be. I've got it all planned in my head. We'll be the talk of the town. We'll——"

She heard the latch on the porch door. Something was pressing against the glass, a dark shape.

"Mrs Manson?" She put her lips to Mrs Manson's ear. "I'm going to carry you. I'm going to carry you to the window seat. You'll be all right there. George will be here in a minute. No, Mrs Manson, don't cry now. No, Mrs Manson, not now."

The porch door opened. She stood with her back to the window seat, making a wall of her body and outstretched arms.

It swayed across the floor on all fours; she knew how it would look if the lights were on. She could hear the soft padding of the four starfish hands as they moved over the thick carpet to the bed.

She tried to kill it with her mind. She willed it to die. Beast, beast, I'm killing you.

She heard the bed shake as the body lunged.

Light burst. From the ceiling, from the hall, from the porch, it flooded the room. She was blind with light. Sound crashed and reverberated. George's voice rose above a hideous clamour. George shouted, "Ferd!" from somewhere, Ferd answered.

She began to see, then. The grappling, rolling figures on the floor began to take shape. She reached behind her and covered Mrs Manson's eyes with her hand.

George, Ferd Pross, battered and bleeding. Babcock? Babcock and young Doctor Pleydell. How did Pleydell——

They rose and fell in a heaving mass, separating, coming together, a swollen sea of speechless men, young and old, with one objective.

Cory. Cory had a gun. George flung himself at Cory's arm. Milly gathered her strength and screamed. "No, George, no!"

The end of time had been reached when they dragged the black shape from the floor. They took away its masquerading cape. They made it stand alone and let its face be seen.

She turned and hid her own face on Mrs Manson's breast.

She knew it was George who came to stand beside them. She knew his hand with the high-school class ring that he wore because she always made fun of it. There was no powder on his hand; he saw it when she did, and he rubbed it off on his coat. She knew then that Ralph Manson's name and story were no longer written on the table.

Someone said her name softly. A new voice. "Miss Sills." She raised her head, afraid to believe. Then she cried as she had never cried before. . . .

She was in her chair, in the window, waiting for morning. Morning was almost there. They had left her again, but not all of them. The ones she loved had stayed.

They said it was all right to think now. They said she could think all she wanted to. They said she could sit up all day and night, forever, if she wanted to. And think herself black in the face because she was a good, good—— Stop that, she told herself. You don't have to do that any more.

That young man, the State Trooper. He was the one who'd called Babcock and Pleydell. He'd told them what he thought and asked them if his theory were possible. Medically possible, emotionally. And Babcock said he had been thinking the same way, had almost come to the same conclusion. . . . The Trooper said he didn't want a car for Christmas. Would a big red bow look too silly on a windshield? Ask Bruce. No, not now, later.

Bruce. Bruce had thought like Babcock. The first night had been too full of individual anachronisms. Miss Sills had been too hard to wake; not compatible with Miss Sills. The other one—she still couldn't say his name, even to herself—the other one had given too much attention to the porch door, the lamp, the litter of twigs and leaves on the floor. Bruce, trying desperately to prove himself wrong, had mapped out and timed a possible route, using the porch door as entrance and exit, starting from the rose room, allowing for the flight to the garden, the return. Then, at dinner, he'd told them all he was going into town. But he'd gone to Robbie's room and aited in the dark. . . . Robbie's room was the right place. Thank you, Bruce.

"Want anything?" Bruce asked now.

She shook her head. Her eyes told him she had everything. It was still hard to talk.

George Perry came in from the porch with Milly Sills. His look of confusion was not improved by his temporarily vertical hair. He bent over her chair. "What does a woman mean," he asked, "when she says 'no veal'?"

THESE ARE PAN BOOKS

Herbert van Thal

THE PAN BOOK OF HORROR STORIES

A Pan Original. A terrifying selection of twenty-two stories fiendish and fantastic. A real spine-chiller by masters of the macabre.   (3/6)

Herbert van Thal

THE SECOND PAN BOOK OF HORROR STORIES

A Pan Original. Clammy hands, irregular heart beats, tingling of the scalp—readers' reactions to the first Book of Horror Stories. This superb new collection is even more varied in its terrifying aspects of horror.   (3/6)

Herbert van Thal

THE THIRD PAN BOOK OF HORROR STORIES

A Pan Original. Twenty-one stories by Algernon Blackwood, William Faulkner, Edgar Allan Poe, H. G. Wells and other masters of the macabre. As hair-raising as the first and second books in this now famous series.   (3/6)

ALFRED HITCHCOCK PRESENTS

A sinister collection of 25 spine-chilling stories, which 'they wouldn't let me do on TV'. Here are stories, by famous authors, so grotesque and terrifying that they 'would not only send the viewers screaming up the walls but would probably qualify the cast for a strait-jacket' —BBC.   (3/6)

John Ross Macdonald
THE GALTON CASE

'On the evidence of *The Galton Case* Ross Macdonald must now be saluted as the best writer of private-detective stories in the United States'—*Birmingham Post*. 'Every new book of his proves that he is just about the best thriller-writer in America' — *London Mystery Magazine*. (2/6)

John Burke
THE BOYS

A Pan Original. Were they young toughs whose night of violence ended in robbery and murder? Or innocent victims of prejudice? A biting and sensational drama of today's youth. Now filmed for Gala release, starring Richard Todd. (2/6)

Malcolm Gair
A LONG HARD LOOK

Somewhere among the men and women she had used, abused, discarded, was her killer. Which one? Exciting, ingenious Mark Raeburn thriller. 'Distinctly grippish' — *Observer*. (2/6)

Anthony Gilbert
DEATH AGAINST THE CLOCK

That rumbustious lawyer-sleuth Arthur Crook is at the top of his exuberant form when the murder of an elderly spinster puts an innocent man in jeopardy. (2/6)